W9-BZZ-548

DON'T MISS THIS NEW THRILLING EPISODE IN THE HOLT SAGA, AS A GREAT AMERICAN DYNASTY BRINGS OUR COUNTRY'S PAST TO LIFE WITH THEIR ADVENTURES. NOW THE MOST IMPORTANT EVENTS OF A DECADE LEAD THIS YOUNG, COURAGEOUS GENERATION INTO LIFE-AND-DEATH STRUGGLES AS THEY FIGHT WITH THEIR FISTS—AND THEIR HEARTS— TO BUILD AN OIL EMPIRE, TO BATTLE FOR FREEDOM, AND TO BE ALL THAT THEIR HERITAGE OF STRONG AMER- ICAN VALUES CAN MAKE THEM . . . THE WONDERFUL, INSPIRING MEN AND WOMEN WHO FORGED THE FOUNDATIONS OF THE MODERN WORLD!

FROM THE VAST UNKNOWN OF LIFE ON THE ROAD, TO THE CAMPAIGN TRAIL OF SUFFRAG- ISTS INTO IDAHO—A STATE CHALLENGED TO LET WOMEN VOTE—THE HOLTS JOURNEY DOWN THE PATHS OF AMERICAN HISTORY WITH PASSIONS AT WHITE HEAT . . . DETER- MINED TO REACH FOR TOMORROW FEAR- LESSLY AND WITH INDOMITABLE PRIDE!

TIM HOLT

Don't Tread on Me is the sign this brawny, brainy California newsman figures he'd better hang on his heart as he seeks to forget Rosebay Ware, his best friend's wife. Instead, Tim finds himself squared against an infuriating woman who makes him mad enough to fight for her and never let her go.

ELIZABETH EMORY

Men are the enemy—and no one makes her angrier than that pigheaded, outspoken, very handsome Tim Holt. Her rabble-rousing high spirits may put her in a deadly line of fire when she becomes embroiled in Idaho's landmark political event . . . but the greatest danger may be from her own heart.

ROSEBAY WARE

Unbearably lovely to look at, the kind of woman a man wants to kiss, she is torn between her passion for Tim Holt and her marriage vows to Hugo . . . and yet she flirts with a fire that can only burn them all.

HOBO BILL

This mysterious man has seen more of life than most and done things that are spoken about in fearful whispers in the hobo jungles of America. Now he offers the innocent Frank Blake his friendship . . . with smiles that hide a sinister plan.

FRANK BLAKE

Cindy and Henry's son, he has the Holt clan's stubborn individualism and lust for excitement coursing through his veins. He leaves behind a stunned family when he runs off and joins the kings of the road . . . on a cross-country quest that will test his manhood with treachery and peril.

HENRY BLAKE

A powerful mover and shaker in bustling Washington, D.C., he has pinned his hopes and pride on his young son, Frank—until a foolish father-son argument opens a rift that destroys a family . . . and may crack a father's heart into shards of broken dreams.

PETER BLAKE

This brilliant older son of Henry Blake has an uncanny knack for touching the future—investing first in automobiles and now in that black gold, oil! But he also has the bad luck to be seducing the same girl as his own brother . . . in a deadly triangle of desire, greed, and death.

PEGGY DELANEY

Sweet Peg o' My Heart is an earthy Irish lass determined to escape her alcoholic father and dreary work in a laundry any way she can . . . even by using her irresistible body to tempt two brothers into her bed.

EULALIA HOLT

This matriarch of the Holt clan doesn't like to interfere in her children's lives, but the years have taught her wisdom and given her secrets that she needs to reveal . . . to spare those she loves from throwing away their chance for happiness.

SANFORD RUTLEDGE

Oil is his business, and he rules California's Sierra Oil Company with a fist of steel and a heart of stone. Now his company's newest investor, a meddling rich Easterner named Peter Blake, may be a problem he'll have to erase . . . with murder.

Wagons West
INDEPENDENCE!—Volume I
NEBRASKA!—Volume II
WYOMING!—Volume III
OREGON!—Volume IV
TEXAS!—Volume V
CALIFORNIA!—Volume VI
COLORADO!—Volume VII
NEVADA!—Volume VIII
WASHINGTON!—Volume IX
MONTANA!—Volume X
DAKOTA!—Volume XI
UTAH!—Volume XII
IDAHO!—Volume XIII
MISSOURI!—Volume XIV
MISSISSIPPI!—Volume XV
LOUISIANA!—Volume XVI
TENNESSEE!—Volume XVII
ILLINOIS!—Volume XVIII
WISCONSIN!—Volume XIX
KENTUCKY!—Volume XX
ARIZONA!—Volume XXI
NEW MEXICO!—Volume XXII
OKLAHOMA!—Volume XXIII

The Holts: An American Dynasty
OREGON LEGACY—Volume One
OKLAHOMA PRIDE—Volume Two
CAROLINA COURAGE—Volume Three
CALIFORNIA GLORY—Volume Four
HAWAII HERITAGE—Volume Five

THE HOLTS: AN AMERICAN DYNASTY
VOLUME SIX

SIERRA
TRIUMPH

DANA FULLER ROSS

 Producers of **The White Indian,**
The First Americans, and **Cody's Law.**

Book Creations Inc., Canaan, NY • Lyle Kenyon Engel, Founder

BANTAM BOOKS
NEW YORK • TORONTO • LONDON • SYDNEY • AUCKLAND

SIERRA TRIUMPH

A Bantam Domain Book / published by arrangement with
Book Creations, Inc.

Bantam edition / May 1992

Produced by Book Creations, Inc.
Lyle Kenyon Engel, Founder

ISBN 0-553-29750-3

Published simultaneously in the United States and Canada

PRINTED IN THE UNITED STATES OF AMERICA

RAD   0 9 8 7 6 5 4 3 2 1

This book is for Tony Neuron,
who knows all the reasons why.

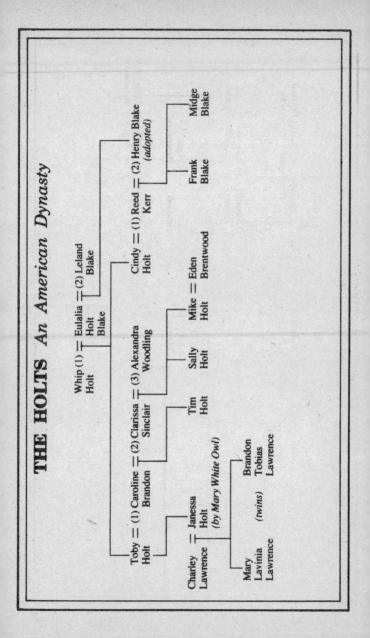

THE HOLTS *An American Dynasty*

THE BLAKES, THE MARTINS, AND THE BRENTWOODS

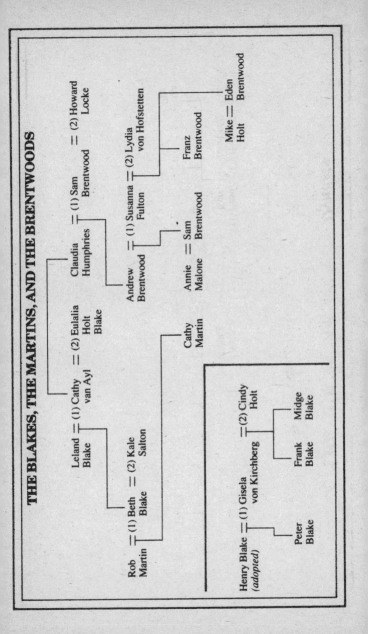

I

San Francisco, December 1895

"What do you mean you won't come to my Christmas dinner?" Rosebay Ware fixed a piercing blue gaze on her employer. "I've had it all planned for a month now." Her lower lip quivered. "It was goin' to be so nice." A trace of her Appalachian accent, a remnant of her girlhood, could be detected under the more refined San Francisco overlay.

Tim Holt cast around for some explanation. "I have to take my grandmother to Washington for the holidays. She's much too old to travel alone."

"Stuff." Rosebay pulled off her eyeshade and slapped it down on her desk, whapping it solidly on a stack of ledgers. "Peter's going east, and she's his granny, too. There's not one reason why you have to go."

"Well, my family's all there."

"And you should've thought of that a month ago when you told me you'd come. Hugo's been counting on it."

Tim cast an apprehensive glance down the *Clarion's* hallway toward the newsroom. Rosebay's husband, Hugo, was supposedly out on assignment, but you never knew. "Rosebay, I just couldn't face it," he said desperately.

"Well, you just got to," Rosebay said. "We made our bed, Tim, and we're going to have to lie in it."

Tim winced. It was *too* appropriate an expression, but Rosebay would not appreciate his pointing that out.

1

She was a literal-minded soul; puns left her puzzled. She had used the expression in its usual sense. Any reference to the bed that the two of them had once made—or unmade—together would not be a good idea.

Tim looked at her despairingly. Rosebay was a little thing, pale and graceful with a lily-stalk slenderness that he knew covered an interior as tough as gristle. Her hair was so blond it was nearly white, and it framed her beautiful face in a pale aureole that not even a green eyeshade could make ugly. Rosebay Ware was self-taught, and she had a natural gift for mathematics. In a fit of inspiration, Tim's cousin Peter Blake had installed her as the *Clarion*'s business manager. She had the *Clarion* in the black now, and Tim was fiercely proud of her, particularly in the face of predictions of disaster from the rival *Chronicle*'s accounting office. If the unconventionality of a female accountant was all that troubled him about Rosebay Ware, he would be a happy man. Tim hunched his muscular shoulders and dug his fists into the pockets of his frock coat.

"Don't do that," Rosebay said. "It makes you look like a tough. And it'll spoil your coat."

Tim took his fists out of his pockets and ran his fingers through his thick sandy hair, then over his face. In accordance with prevailing fashion, he had recently shaved off his handlebar mustache and couldn't rid himself of feeling that he had lost some privacy. He stuck his hands back in his pockets, but he didn't ball them into fists.

"It's my coat," he said mildly. "Rosebay, I can't come to dinner. I can't stand it. We agreed we'd have to go on as if nothing had happened between us, but seeing you across Hugo's table, carving up Hugo's turkey, is more than I can take."

When Hugo had proposed to Rosebay, Tim, totally unaware that she was in love with *him*, had cheered her on to marry Hugo. Only after it was too late to do either of them any good had Tim managed to fall in love with her.

"You're going to spoil my table," Rosebay said. "Now I'm going to be one man short."

"Then you'll have to find her another dinner partner," Tim said. "I can't take any more of that, either."

"Tim Holt, I've never done anything but introduce you to nice girls when one happens to be staying with me." Tears filled her eyes. "I was just trying to help."

Rosebay took in boarders in the big old house she and Hugo owned at the foot of Telegraph Hill. Altruistically, she introduced Tim to the pretty ones.

"That isn't going to help," Tim said. "Just take my word for it. I'm sorry to bow out so late, but I've got to. Gran's expecting me." *Thank God for Gran*, he thought.

"What about Peter?"

"Peter's going direct from here. He's got two big buyers for his motorcars lined up within a week of each other—one here and one in Washington. He hasn't got time to detour through Oregon and pick up Gran."

Rosebay snorted. It was a ladylike snort, but it indicated derision and disbelief.

"I can handle being your boss in the office," Tim said with finality, "but don't expect me to socialize or try to be pals."

"I thought we *were* pals," Rosebay said sadly.

"It hurts too much to be pals!" Tim discovered he was yelling and lowered his voice. He came closer to the desk and leaned over her. "Being friends works fine for you. You've got Hugo, who worships you, and you've got me on a string, too, to see whenever you feel like it. But it doesn't work out so well for me. I haven't even got what you might call half a loaf."

"What about Hugo?" Rosebay demanded. "You going to disappoint him, too?"

"He's just going to have to stand up to it," Tim said sarcastically. He snatched up his hat—he had deliberately chosen to confront Rosebay on his way *out* of the *Clarion* building. That way he knew he could cut and run as soon as it was over. "Rosebay, I am not going to be your tame beau forever, and I am *not* coming to Christmas dinner!"

He jammed the tall hat down on his head and marched out, avoiding both the newsroom and his own office, where some unfortunate soul might have his head bitten off for the crime of needing to talk with the boss.

Outside the weather was cold and dank—one of those gray, miserable San Francisco days when the cold saltwater seemed to come out of the bay and wrap itself around buildings and citizens until everyone felt chilled to the bone and pickled in brine. Even the gargoyle above the *Clarion*'s main door on Kearny Street looked cold and disgruntled. A pigeon landed on the pencil behind the gargoyle's ear and, after fluffing its feathers for warmth, turned itself into a ball. Tim wound his muffler around his throat. There were days when he hated to leave San Francisco. This wasn't one of them.

Maryland

"Sir!" Tim's cousin Frank Blake, aged seventeen, saluted General Wallace (Retired), commanding officer of Hargreaves Academy. Frank's polished bootheels were aligned precisely in the center of the general's carpet, his spine was ramrod straight, and his right arm was cocked at precisely the proper angle. His blue uniform jacket, without a bulge or a crease, was buttoned to the chin.

"At ease, Blake." The general's gruff expression would have struck terror into a stranger, but Frank recognized it as the general's smile. "So you're going home to Alexandria for the holidays."

"Yes, sir. My bags are waiting outside for the station hack."

"Be certain to give my regards to your father. A fine man. You do him credit. I've seen your midyear marks."

"Thank you, sir." Frank was immensely proud of those midyear marks.

"You might be pleased to know, Blake, that they are not only the highest of any cadet's this year, they are the highest in the past twenty-six years of the school's history. I have a letter, which I wish you to deliver to Colonel Blake, apprising him of that fact."

"Thank you, sir."

The general's gray marble eyes were steely and unblinking beneath a hedgerow of bushy eyebrows. "Have you made any decision about your future, Blake?"

"Yes, sir, I'm hoping to go to West Point if they'll have me."

"They'll have you," the general said. "An excellent choice. Your father will be pleased. Did I ever tell you, I knew your grandfather?"

"I believe you mentioned it, sir."

Frank's grandfather, General Leland Blake, had been a soldier of distinction all his life. Frank's father, Henry, was acquiring much the same reputation. The general viewed Frank with relief. It was gratifying to be able to present to Colonel Henry Blake a son who was so obviously qualified to wear the family mantle— particularly since Frank's elder half brother, Peter, had been asked politely to withdraw from Hargreaves.

The general managed to smile. Francis Leland Blake was the perfect cadet. Even at his young age he had his father's height and bulk—tall, dashing, muscular, and handsome. He cut an imposing figure, from his thick sandy hair, close-cropped now in a proper military cut, to the size-twelve boots, which this year had looked more in proportion with the rest of his frame. In the past he had looked like a huge-footed puppy.

The general presented him with the letter, and Frank snapped a salute.

"Go along now, Blake. Rest and enjoy yourself. Dance with all the girls. We've work to do in January."

"Yes, sir!" Frank saluted again, pivoted in the prescribed pattern, then marched through the general's oiled mahogany door. Outside in the corridor he let out a whoop and threw his cap in the air.

Alexandria, Virginia

Tim found himself lulled by the warmth of the room into a kind of somnolent watchfulness as he observed the workings of his clan's interlocking family machinery. It seemed to him that the farther away the children moved and the older they got, the more their parents yearned to collect them all in one place on holidays. His aunt, Cindy Blake, looked with vast contentment down the length of her dining table and with a kind of happy wriggle settled deeper in her chair. The servants had put all three extension leaves in the table, so that it stretched the length of the dining room and into the entrance foyer.

Tim looked through the window. Outside it was snowing, which it so rarely did at Christmas in Alexandria that everyone considered it a present. The old cobbled streets were covered with snow, and it muted the sound of harness bells and the shrieking of children turned loose from Christmas dinner.

The Blakes and the Holts were still feasting, halfway into a pair of roasted geese and a Virginia ham. Between Cindy and her husband, Henry, at opposite ends of the table, were Tim's parents, Toby and Alexandra, who had driven across the river from their house in the District; Toby and Cindy's mother, Eulalia, dutifully delivered from Oregon by Tim; and all the children. Tim's brother, Mike, and his new wife, Eden, and Tim's sister Janessa, and her husband, Charley Lawrence, had all come from New York, the Lawrences with twins to show off.

Peter had arrived from San Francisco, as had Frank, looking proud and grown-up in his dress uniform. The table was rounded out by Cindy's Midge and Toby's Sally, trying to look grown-up, too, but, being ten and twelve years old respectively, lapsing into Christmas silliness and the giggles.

When was the last time they had all been together?

Tim wondered. Probably Grandpa Lee Blake's funeral—
not a happy occasion. Eulalia, twice widowed, seemed
increasingly frail to Tim, although she had withstood the
railway trip well, all the way from the Madrona, the Holt
home ranch in Oregon. Cindy and Toby, and then Toby's
children, had all grown up on that ranch but were firmly
rooted elsewhere now. Selling it was unthinkable, and
the family joke that Sally had to grow up and marry an
Oregon boy wasn't very far from the truth. Toby or
Cindy might go back to the Madrona one day, but not so
long as Henry was with the army and Toby was in the
State Department.

Tim eyed his father, aware that that appointment
could change with the next presidential election, only a
year away. Grover Cleveland wouldn't run again, Tim
mused. What would the new man do? Toby seemed
unconcerned about his job security just now, as he
happily ate goose and new potatoes and interrogated
Mike on his finances. Mike was making motion pictures,
and his father considered that to be as potentially
profitable as trying to filter gold out of seawater. Mike
was dodging the questions; but Eden was wearing a new
dress that Sally, who knew about these things, had
informed Tim could only be from the best shop in New
York, so Tim couldn't decide whether or not Mike was
doing well.

Tim wondered if his aunt Cindy's blissful expression
might be a result of the fact that none of the Blake
offspring was doing anything so risky. Peter was building
motorcars, but despite Henry's dire predictions, that
venture had proved to be profitable. And Frank had
arrived home for the holidays with such glowing marks
for the first semester that Henry was practically floating
on a cloud of pride.

"Did I tell you that the general himself wrote to
me?" Henry inquired of Toby. "To tell me that Frank had
the highest midterm ranking of any senior at the academy?"

"You mentioned it," Toby replied. "Once or twice."

"Well, I'm proud," Henry said.

"We all are." Mike Holt looked relieved to have his father's attention diverted.

Peter Blake grinned. Peter, considered a threat to military order, had been asked to leave the same academy, and he seemed relieved that the family tradition was being assumed by his half brother. "Frank looks the part, doesn't he?" he murmured, one eyebrow raised in good humor. "Dashing. I'm sure he's destined for fame."

Although Peter sounded jovial, Tim imagined that the young man might find it aggravating that Frank, four years his junior, was already half a head taller. Peter took after his mother, Gisela, who had been small. Frank came from big-boned stock on both sides and promised to be as formidable as Henry or any of the Holts.

"A dead certainty," Tim said. "Four stars at least."

Frank knew they were proud of him and bound to tease him. He was sitting straight but was beginning to look embarrassed. "First I have to get into West Point," he pointed out.

"Listen," Peter teased. "He's modest."

A much-tried Frank glared at him.

"I doubt that West Point will prove a problem," Toby said. "Your marks alone ought to get you in, with Henry's reputation preceding you. And you'll certainly have my recommendation."

"He'll be so swell we won't know him," Peter predicted.

Frank squirmed, blushed, then applied himself to his plate. He looked up at his mother and smiled.

Cindy smiled back. Tim thought she looked smug. As well she might, of course, but Tim decided they should be giving more attention to Peter, who had come all the way from San Francisco just to spend Christmas with them. Well, that and to baby-sit for a motorcar, too. The ambassador from Japan had actually purchased a Blake. The diplomat, Peter reported, had driven it down Massachusetts Avenue and sent a horse into hysterics. The horse was being ridden at the time by the third assistant secretary to the deputy to the ambassador from Turkey, and furious complaints were working their way up the Washington embassy hierarchy. All the same, it was a triumph for Peter. Several other ambassadors and attachés had made inquiries about purchasing Blakes— probably hoping to scare one another's horses, Tim thought. His experience both as a newspaper editor and as a politician's son had taught him something about the diplomatic version of counting coup.

Henry ought to be prouder of Peter than he was, Tim thought, and he felt the urge to poke a little at the family machinery and set more wheels to turning before his own parents, who were eyeing him thoughtfully, decided to question him next.

In a lull in the conversation, Tim caught Peter's eye. "Have you decided whether or not to expand the Blake Company?" he inquired.

The rest of the family pricked up their ears. Peter had come into his inheritance—a sizable fortune from his German mother—earlier in the year, on his twenty-first birthday. Everyone naturally had an opinion as to what he ought to do with the money. So far Peter had thanked everyone politely for the advice and sat tight.

"I'm still trying to make a decision," Peter said seriously now. "I'm tempted, but it's also possible to expand too fast with a new product. Demand has to match production." Despite his youth, with his slicked-down brown hair and high, serious collar he looked very much the businessman.

"I've heard several demands for the things to be kept off the streets," Henry said. He grinned. He had predicted that motorcars would never catch on, but he had predicted wrong. They were not commonplace, but it was beginning to be clear that they would be. "What are you contemplating, if not more motorcars?" he asked. "Flying machines?"

Everyone at the table chuckled.

"I haven't lost my mind," Peter responded. "I really don't know. I need advice—from someone with economic expertise," he added hastily, since most of his relatives looked prepared to offer theirs.

"What would *you* recommend, Henry?" Cindy

looked at her husband with wifely expectation, but Henry coughed and shook his head.

"Don't ask me," he said, helping himself to more of the Christmas goose. "I'm not an economist. Edward Blackstone, Son. That's who you want to talk to."

"Edward Blackstone?" Peter knitted his brows.

"You met him when we were in Oklahoma visiting the Martins, dear," Cindy said.

"Edward and his wife have the next spread over," Henry said. "He's been playing gentleman farmer on that ranch for years, but the man's got a Midas touch like I never saw. Anything Edward Blackstone invests in turns into solid gold." Henry stabbed a bite of goose and pointed his fork at Peter. "Edward Blackstone, that's who you want."

"He does have a knack," Toby agreed. "And he'd be glad to see you. He's an old friend."

"I remember him now," Peter said. "His wife's Indian. From India, I mean."

"Half Indian," Toby corrected. "I believe her father was British. Ramedha. A charming woman. Very exotic. A corker, in fact."

"Yes, I remember you thought so." Alexandra gave Toby a look from under half-lidded eyes.

"Sure did," Toby said, unrepentant. He grinned at his wife across the table. "You're safe, though. I only get steamed up over redheads."

Alexandra patted her auburn pompadour. "We will not," she murmured, "*count* the redheads."

"Can't remember 'em all," Toby said happily.

The old man, Tim thought, was enjoying himself, with all the family clustered around. Just like his aunt Cindy. Toby liked being a patriarch. His thick sandy hair had a dignified sweep of gray through it, and his waistline was ten pounds heavier than it had been in his youth—just enough to display a watch chain to good effect. Gold-rimmed spectacles, adopted several years before, gave him a more bookish air than he had had before but didn't hide the light that shone in his blue eyes when he was amused—or suspicious. Unfortunately for Tim, the subject of romance brought Toby's antennae forward, and he focused on Tim, the only one of his three elder children to remain single.

"And what have you been doing, Son? Your mother complains you never write."

"I write all the time," Tim protested, wishing he had dodged quicker. "I assume you've been reading my letters." What Alexandra meant, he realized, was that the letters contained no personal details—no engagement announcements, for instance. Tim was twenty-eight. In a couple more years he would be solidified in the family mind as the bachelor uncle, bouncing Janessa's and presumably Eden's babies on his avuncular knee. Maybe then his parents would give up on him, Tim thought. He couldn't very well stand up and announce at Christmas dinner, *I'm not married because I'm in love with my best friend's wife*. It would answer their questions, of course. *I spent three days in a railway car to avoid having Christmas dinner with her and her husband*. That ought to put a damper on the current frivolities. *Oh, hell*. Tim turned his thoughts away from this increasingly morose introspection.

Across the table, Eulalia was cooing at her greatgrandchildren, Janessa's twins, who had woken and were drooling happily in their bassinets in the corner. Alexandra reached for a baby and soon was bouncing Mary Lavinia, familiarly known as Lally, in her lap. Tim could tell the twins apart because Lally had enough hair to put a ribbon in. Brandon Tobias was still bald. "You got a medical school picked out for them yet?" he asked Janessa.

"We're planning to send them to our alma mater in Los Angeles," Charley said solemnly. Charley and Janessa had graduated together from the University of Southern California Medical College. "Assuming they don't decide on a less strenuous profession."

"Why can't Lally just get married?" Midge asked. She made kissy faces at the baby in Alexandra's lap.

"Well, she can, of course, dear." Cindy smiled at her daughter. "But these days many women choose to have a profession as well." She glanced at Janessa. "Of course it can be difficult to balance it with one's domestic duties."

Janessa chuckled ruefully. "So we're learning."

"We *are* getting tired of the Immigration Service, though," Charley said. He peered suspiciously at Brandon Tobias, whom Eulalia had just picked up. Charley patted his son's bottom. "Just as I thought. Come with me, young man." He scooped the baby up and departed with him under one arm.

"Well, don't stare at me like that," Janessa said defensively as the rest of the family gaped at her. "Charley has very advanced ideas on child rearing."

"He certainly does," murmured Toby, who had never changed a diaper in his life and wouldn't have dreamed of it.

Alexandra and Cindy looked just as startled. "Doesn't it bother you, dear?" Cindy asked. "Are you sure he knows what he's doing?"

"Of course he does," Janessa said crossly. "He knows as well as I do." She looked as if she was a little tired of having to defend their nursery arrangements. "I can't continue to practice medicine *and* have full charge of the babies, even with a nursemaid, and Charley knows it."

"Must you continue to practice, dear?" Eulalia asked her. "I thought perhaps Charley would go back in the field?" The Lawrences were commissioned Hospital Service doctors and had done epidemic work until the twins were born.

"He won't go without me," Janessa said. "He doesn't think we should be separated."

Toby and Henry, both of whom had spent much of their married lives elsewhere than at home, raised their eyebrows a trifle higher.

"Maybe when the twins are older, we'll both go back to it," Janessa said. "Right now Charley says it's important that the babies spend as much time with him as they do with me."

"Charley certainly *does* have advanced ideas," Cindy said.

"Well, if I were you," Alexandra said practically, "I'd be very grateful for them." She gave Toby a look as if calculating how much time he had spent with *his* children.

"I *am* grateful," Janessa said. "I'm just tired of trying to explain it to people. Everyone thinks he's hen-pecked."

Tim gave a hoot of laughter, and Janessa narrowed her eyes at him. "*I* don't think so," Tim said hastily. "Charley's one of those very quietly tenacious people. He's simply doing what he wants to do. The hen that tries to peck him would probably wear down her beak."

"A model for us all then," Henry said dryly, and Toby chuckled. Both were possessed of strong-minded wives.

Charley returned and deposited Brandon Tobias in Eulalia's lap. He wore the bland expression of a man who knows he has been talked about. "I have many peculiarities," he admitted mildly, "but I'm considered to be harmless. Freethinking is my worst vice."

"Nothing of the sort, old man," Henry said hastily, heartily. "Entitled to change a diaper if you want to." Henry's expression, however, conveyed that no one but an eccentric would want to.

Cindy's kitchen maid came in to clear the table for dessert, and Henry seized the opportunity to change the subject. "I've probably jawed everyone to death with how proud I am of Frank," he said, beaming. "But I have to say it one more time because I have an announcement to make. Frank, you can thank your cousins for this as well, because they've offered you their hospitality if your mother and I give you a trip to New York as a reward for your hard work and good grades."

Frank gave his father a startled smile.

"You'll have two weeks to see all the shows and the sights, and pocket money to amuse yourself. A week with Janessa and Charley and a week with Michael and Eden. To show you how proud we are."

There was a spatter of applause from the rest of the family. They were all proud, and it was not unlike them to cooperate in an expression of that pride, just as they pulled together in times of crisis. Of course the Holts and the Blakes were close-knit despite the geographic distances between them. Being close-knit had the disadvantage of everybody's wanting to mind everyone else's business. Tim and Janessa glanced at each other now, satisfied to have the family attention diverted to Frank, away from their own domestic arrangements or lack of them.

"Honestly," Janessa whispered to Tim later, "I felt like the bearded lady in a dime show. Charley's either completely oblivious to people thinking we're odd, or else he doesn't care. But I hate giving everyone more to be interested in than they've got already." She poked moodily with one finger at a green glass ball ornament on the Christmas tree.

"It's just the family," Tim said. "Nobody was criticizing you."

"But they wanted to. And if it's just the family, why were *you* wriggling out from under the microscope?" Janessa demanded.

"Umm . . ."

"I know they mean well," she said. "But ever since I had the twins, everyone has known how I ought to raise them—except me, presumably. Alexandra thinks I dress them too warmly and they'll get prickly heat. Aunt Cindy thinks they need heavier sweaters so they don't get quinsy."

"Their maternal instinct overpowers their knowing when they ought to stay out of something," Tim said. "You'll be a terror yourself as a grandmother, with a medical degree to back you up."

"I suppose," Janessa allowed. "The worst of it is, *I'm* not sure I'm doing it right. I watched Alex raise Mike and Sally, of course, and Aunt Cindy and Alex raise you, too, to some extent. But I don't recall my own mother ever treating me with such care. I always felt more like a little adult." Janessa's mother had been Cherokee, and Janessa hadn't come to live with her father until she was nearly ten. Janessa had loved her mother, but they had lived through hard times. Now, at thirty-four, Janessa seemed to feel she might be lacking something she needed to raise her own babies. "They *seem* all right," she said, fidgeting with the cherubs in the tree.

"Fat and sassy," Tim agreed.

"And Charley has definite ideas. . . ."

"Is Charley treading a little heavily on your territory?"

Janessa bit her lip. "I don't know. In theory, it's a matter of equality, and I believe in that. Do you remember Laura Gillette? She had a great deal to say about that, and I thought she was right."

Tim shook his head.

"Laura boarded with me at Mrs. Burnside's while I was in school. She was a member of the Woman's Suffrage Association and very dedicated."

"Am I supposed to see a connection?" Tim asked.

"It's tenuous," Janessa admitted, "at least the way I'm describing it. But what I'm getting at is a matter of equality—men and women being permitted to function in what has always been the other's sphere, and the other being willing to *let* them."

"Men's being willing to let you vote and your being willing to let Charley change diapers? At the risk of injecting a note of reality here, most men don't regard that as a goal to be striven for."

Janessa gnawed the edge of her thumbnail. "I know. Charley gets a lot of criticism for it. Even Steve Jurgen thinks it's odd." Jurgen was an old friend who had gone through medical school with them.

"So which are you worried about? Charley usurping your position or Charley getting laughed at?"

"Both, I suppose," Janessa confessed. "I'm sort of ashamed of myself. I used to be so brave. If Charley has the courage of his convictions, I ought to, too."

"You should, if they're your convictions," Tim pointed out. "Are they?"

"I don't know!" Janessa said honestly. "I just wanted to

be a doctor. I never really got into the rest of it. Oh, I think women ought to have the vote, of course. But I just want to be a doctor and raise my babies, and—and—"

"And there aren't any guidebooks, are there?" Tim put an arm around his sister's shoulders. "Poor old Janessa. You didn't really mean to be a pioneer, did you?"

"I'm not sure. I just followed my own mind without paying much attention to who was in front or behind."

"I've always found pioneers to be particularly single-minded," Tim observed. "Lord knows the world needs them, but it makes them an awful trial to their families and friends. No reason you should take on that identity if you don't want to. Personally, I think you're much more pleasant without it."

Janessa slid an arm around Tim's waist and hugged him back. They looked at their reflection in the green glass ball, heads together, faces strangely pear-shaped in the sphere. They had different mothers, but the Holt strain was dominant in both of them, as it was in Alexandra's children, Mike and Sally. The Holts were like goldenrod, Alexandra once said. Their physical features flourished anywhere and took over the landscape.

"And tell me, Tim dear, now that we've pinpointed the source of *my* difficulties, what have *you* been doing? You looked particularly evasive at dinner."

"Shifty eyed," Tim said. "It's my profession. It's in the Journalists' Creed."

"Something's wrong," Janessa said. "Come on, Tim, spill it."

"No. Thank you."

Cindy had sat down at the parlor piano on the other side of the Christmas tree, and she began to play. The rest of them gathered around, and Tim dragged Janessa out from behind the tree. Mike had his arm around Eden's waist, and they stood so close together that it was a wonder they could still sing. They had only been married since the summer, and anyone could tell just by looking at them how each completed the other. Mike's lips rested against Eden's golden hair, the red sweep of his mustache barely moving, and Tim thought he was singing only to her.

Tim began to sing, too; but his voice was ragged, and Janessa looked up in distress at his profile. Tim was watching his brother and his brother's bride, but his face might have been carved of stone.

Frank Blake, oblivious to the undercurrents running among his elders, sang joyfully. "Joy to the World" was the song his mother was playing, and Frank felt that it was perfect. Life was perfect. The world was joyful. After they had sung "Hark! The Herald Angels Sing," "Adeste, Fideles," and "The Holly and the Ivy," and had one final round of champagne and hot cider and chocolates from the huge gold box that Henry had presented to Cindy, Toby and Alexandra collected their offspring and bundled them into the two waiting carriages.

"Good-bye!" Janessa called as she hurried out into the light snowfall, a bundled baby in her arms. "We'll pick you up tomorrow on the way to the station, Frank."

Frank waved. "I'll be ready!"

His sister, Midge, beside him in the doorway, sighed. "Why does Christmas always have to be over?"

"So you don't get too spoiled," Frank answered.

"I wish I had a dress like Sally's." Midge tugged fretfully at one braid.

"She's spoiled," Frank said. "And she's too young to be wearing that dress. I heard Mother say so to Dad."

"I still wish I had one."

The dress was a talisman, Frank realized with sudden perception. A talisman to confer beauty. Midge was acutely conscious of the fact that Sally was prettier than she was.

"You looked awfully pretty tonight," he told her.

"You don't need to worry," Midge said, appraising her brother's handsome face. "You got all the looks in the family. I don't see why Peter and I had to be plain."

"Here," Frank said. He produced a foil-wrapped bonbon from his pocket. "You can have my chocolate. I'm too full to eat it." He ruffled her hair, and she gave him a smile.

He went on upstairs, feeling cloaked in a cloud of

benevolence. Peter remained in the parlor, reading by the fire, but Frank felt too good to sit still. He felt grown-up and responsible, capable of comforting his little sister, old enough to go by himself to New York.

In his bedroom Frank got out his suitcase and began packing it, not with his Hargreaves uniforms but with his Washington clothes: two good suits, stacks of carefully laundered shirts, extra collars and cuffs, his best neckties. He took off his evening clothes—his first tailcoat and stiff-bosomed shirt—and folded them carefully. He laughed scornfully at the outgrown knee pants that hung in the back of his closet and brought out gray flannel slacks and a blue blazer.

He put on a clean nightshirt and added two others to the suitcase. It felt good to be trusted the way his parents were trusting him, good to be grown-up, good to have a tradition of service to follow. He had always known he would go to West Point, the way his father and grandfather had done; it was understood that he would serve his country the way they had. Lee Blake had fought with Andrew Jackson and served the Union with distinction in the Civil War. Henry Blake had followed his stepfather into the army and was now a colonel involved in exploits that even his children didn't comprehend in detail. He spent more time out of uniform than in, and Frank had gradually come to realize that what his father did for the army was more dangerous than his grandfather's better-publicized career. Henry Blake's name was not a household word to the public, but it was well-known to the heavy old men in uniform who came to the house in Alexandria or stopped to clap him on the shoulder in a restaurant or the theater. God willing, Frank thought, he would have a career as distinguished. He would serve his country with honor and protect it the way his father and grandfather had done.

Frank closed the suitcase and buckled the strap. Then he knelt by the bed to say the same prayers he had said every night since he had been old enough to talk.

II

The whole family turned out to put the New York-bound party on the train at the Baltimore & Ohio station on New Jersey Avenue below the Capitol.

"Look at Frank," Mike whispered to Peter, pointing at the wooden window frame. The fringed shade was raised. "He looks like a kid on a Sunday-school outing."

Frank was on board already, determined not to miss a moment of the journey. Excited, he sat bolt upright. Charley and Janessa, also on board, were waving out their window.

"Take care of him, will you?" Peter asked.

"Aw, hell, Frank'll have a fine time." Mike swung aboard behind Eden as the engine shrieked and let off steam. A cloud boiled up around them. The conductor brought up the steps. The train began to move, chuffing slowly, its huge drive wheels gathering momentum. Frank was leaning halfway out the window now, waving, his face alight with anticipation. The train picked up speed, lumbered past the platform, and was gone, leaving drifting steam behind it and hot clinkers on the tracks.

"What are you worried about?" Tim asked Peter. "At his age you were a printer's devil in a boomtown, learning to chase women and sneak into saloons."

"I didn't do much of either," Peter said. He sounded dissatisfied about that now. "Frank's pretty young and starry-eyed. New York's not exactly a tame town. I just don't want him to get into trouble."

"Your father thinks he can handle himself. Besides,

he'll be staying with my brother and sister, who *live* in New York and aren't going to let him wander down on the Bowery with all his money in his pocket."

"Yeah, yeah. Come on, *I've* got a train to catch now." Peter dutifully hugged his father and stepmother and went with Tim to see his luggage loaded into a hack for Union Station, whence he would catch a connection with the Santa Fe line to Oklahoma. He had decided to take his father's advice about consulting with Edward Blackstone. A telegram of inquiry sent that morning had elicited the immediate reply that the welcome mat was out for any Blake, and a fatted calf would be killed forthwith.

Peter wasn't sure what it was about Frank that troubled him. He decided, making a conscientious examination of his motives, that he didn't begrudge Frank his trip or their father's praise. But it was somehow annoying that Frank had won it by following so perfectly the same sort of program that Peter hadn't been able to live with—and Frank *liked* it. He lived and breathed the Hargreaves Academy and his military future. That was fine, just fine, Peter admitted as he climbed into the hack. But why, he wondered, had that life been so easy for Frank to love but so impossible for him? *Why couldn't I be earnest and starry-eyed, too? It would have made my life so simple.*

"He's very malleable," Peter said grumpily to Tim. "I don't mean that in any bad sense. Frank has a strong sense of duty. But our dad proposed a plan for his life from the cradle to the grave, and Frank has been perfectly content to swallow it whole."

"Maybe it was what he wanted to do in the first place?" Tim suggested.

"Oh, it was," Peter confirmed. "He never thought about anything else."

"Then why do you sound so disgruntled?"

"I'm damned if I know," Peter said.

"I do," Tim said. "What *you* wanted didn't happen to be what your father had planned. You're going to make a whopping success of the Blake, and, Lord help us, you're going to feel guilty because you didn't join the army instead."

"Um, here we are." Peter handed his bag to a porter. Tim was probably right, he decided. But it wasn't that he himself hadn't done what his father wanted, it was just that Frank had done it so *easily*. He wondered if his rebelliousness was inherited from his mother, Gisela. Had she always fought against what was expected of her? She must have, or she wouldn't have told all her trustees and relatives to push off and married an American with no fortune. Peter had no memory of her, but he didn't ask about her at home. Henry had married Gisela while he was stationed in Germany and ostensibly engaged to Cindy Holt. There had been a lot of hard feelings at the time. After Gisela had died, though, Henry and Cindy found their way back to each other. Peter, only a tiny boy at the time, had stolen Cindy's heart and helped in the reconciliation. There were still sore spots, he knew. They were long scabbed over, but not entirely healed.

Maybe Edward Blackstone knew why it was he didn't quite fit into the family mold. Blackstone had met Gisela once and would have no reason to hold back on the subject. He would ask Blackstone, Peter decided.

"Welcome! Welcome to Oklahoma!" Edward Blackstone boomed at Peter, pumping his hand, clapping him on the shoulder. "I've a rug in the carriage. You'll freeze to death in that lightweight overcoat." It was snowing— not the picturesque snow of Christmas Day in Washington but a serious-minded storm, cold and wet, coming out of a leaden sky that obliterated the horizon in all directions. Edward whipped up the team jovially, and Peter supposed the man knew how to find his way home.

Edward Blackstone was a handsome bear of a man, urbane, sophisticated, well into his fifties, with dark grizzled hair and a booming British voice. He was a transplanted Englishman who had made a fortune in America with Brahman crossbred cattle and a spot of adventuring that had resulted in smuggling rubber-tree seeds out of the Amazon and setting up a tropical rubber plantation in India.

"You warm enough?" he shouted at Peter over the whistle of a departing train in the depot behind them.

Peter nodded, muffled to the eyeballs in a plaid carriage rug. "I'm fine. Thank you."

"They're all waiting to welcome you." The snow muffled the horses' hooves and ordinary street traffic, and Blackstone lowered his voice a notch. "You remember my wife, Ramedha, and India and Winslow? India's fifteen now, and Winslow's twelve. And Rob and Kale Martin are coming to dinner if we don't all get snowed in."

Peter remembered winters in Guthrie, not far from the depot at Folsom where Edward had met him. "How far is it out to the M Bar B?" He hoped he did not sound too much like a city slicker when he asked that question. But he knew from experience what a prairie blizzard could do.

"We'll just make it," Edward said. He didn't sound worried, but he seemed to recognize the source of Peter's anxiety. "You were in Guthrie when they opened it, weren't you? Those were some times."

"Wild times," Peter confirmed.

"I hear the same of San Francisco." Edward chuckled.

At some distance the air seemed almost tangible, a white cottony substance like the spun sugar at a fair. It dissolved into individual flakes, as fat as June bugs whirling around the carriage. In an hour the faint yellow lights of M Bar B could be seen glowing out of the storm. Peter let out a little breath of relief.

The Martins, unwilling to be done out of a chance for company, were waiting at the Blackstones' house. If they got snowed in, they would just stay, Kale Martin explained to Peter as she greeted him with a kiss. Then, standing back, she said, "Lord, you've grown."

"You haven't seen me in a while," Peter reminded her.

Kale sighed wistfully. "You all grow up too fast."

"You do." Ramedha Blackstone kissed him, then drew him into the house. She sighed, too, apparently at the size of her own children. Ramedha was nearly forty now, still the "corker" of Toby's description. She pulled Winslow and India forward to be introduced. Winslow, wearing a pair of trousers in which he had been riding bareback, was sent upstairs to change.

He gave his mother an expression of aggrieved innocence. "They look fine from the front."

"We are not looking only at your front," she said, indignant. "Peter, this is my daughter, India."

India looked up shyly at Peter. Her triangular little smile held infinite charm. Her hair cascaded down her back in dark ringlets. She was wearing a dress of heavy teal-colored satin and black kid boots. She was slender in the waist, and the cut of the dress, similar to her mother's, displayed the beginnings of a fashionable hourglass figure. She was not as obviously exotic as her mother, but she was very definitely going to be a corker, too.

"How do you do?" Peter bowed gravely to her.

Someone reached out to take his overcoat, and someone else pressed a cup of hot spiced wine into his hand.

"New Year's grog," Edward explained. "Cheers."

They towed him into the parlor and settled him in the best chair, his feet by the brass fender.

"Peter, you dog. You've gotten grown-up and handsome." A feminine face bent over the back of his chair and kissed him on the forehead. Peter blinked and craned his head up and around. Cathy Martin, Rob and Kale's daughter—well, her stepdaughter, really, Peter knew—came around the chair. She was towing a young man Peter didn't recognize.

"I thought you were on tour," Peter said. "Wowing them in Peoria." Cathy was an actress, a fact to which her parents seemed finally to have resigned themselves.

"We're between shows, so I brought Doug down for Christmas."

Doug was dark and handsome and presumably an

actor. Peter wondered if Rob and Kale had resigned themselves to Doug. His manners were polished, but there was a trace of the dramatic in his gestures—the alert, expressive turn of a hand and the cock of his head. He shook Peter's hand, then settled in a chair. He had the attitude of a man prepared to listen attentively to family small talk.

"Tell us everything," Kale urged. "How is your mother? Does your uncle Toby think we're going to have a war with Spain? Have you seen Janessa's twins?"

"Mother's fine, Uncle Toby doesn't know, and yes." Peter grinned at her.

"Peter Blake—"

"Yes, ma'am." Peter took another sip of his wine, luxuriating in the warmth, and launched into the complete statistics on everyone in the family. "Mother has a gallery. . . ."

He had nearly run through all their questions by the time Ramedha's cook announced dinner. They took him off to the table for the promised fatted calf, in the form of an M Bar B steer. The Martins were the *M* in the M Bar B, and the Blackstones were the *B*. The roast was accompanied by jade-colored beans and scarlet beets, put up in the summer, a spiced shrimp soup made with the tins that Ramedha hoarded for visitors, saffron rice with curry, and hot apple pie and tipsy parson for dessert. Having had two days to get hungry again since the excesses of Christmas dinner, Peter ate with the ravenous appetite of the young male while Ramedha and Kale watched him approvingly. When they thought he was probably not starving any longer, they resumed their questions.

"And how is Tim?" Kale asked with a quick sidelong glance at Cathy. "Is that newspaper of his doing well? I've always felt that informing the public was a worthwhile occupation."

Better than capering around on a stage for people's amusement? Peter wondered. He had been under the impression for several years that Kale considered Tim a perfect match for Cathy. That neither Tim nor Cathy had seemed so inclined apparently hadn't changed Kale's mind—maybe particularly now that she was sitting across the table from Doug.

"The *Clarion*'s in the black," Peter said, laughing. "That is a definite improvement over the state it was in when Tim bought it. And it's very up-to-the-moment. We have Linotype," he said proudly. "Well, they do. The *Clarion* and I parted company a bit over a year ago when I found Tim someone who could keep his books straight for him. She—" Peter swerved. "She's a good paper, the *Clarion*. Beginning to be a voice in this country, not just in California."

"What does he think about this situation in Cuba?" Rob Martin asked.

"And he's not married?" Kale asked.

Peter decided to go with Rob's question. "The *Clarion* has maintained a more balanced editorial stand than most papers, I think. Public opinion in favor of the Cuban rebels has been growing; but whether or not we as a country have the right to interfere is another matter."

Edward Blackstone snorted. "With Spain sitting on our doorstep?"

"The press has printed very bad things about Spain's General Weyler," Ramedha said. "Don't we have a duty to help the Cubans?"

"Possibly. The question, I suppose, is whether or not we can police the world—particularly since we ourselves are in the midst of an economic depression. Our own people are starving. Do we have the resources to save the Cubans, too?"

"That's exactly the point that troubles me," Rob Martin said.

"We'd better have the resources," Edward commented. "Cuba is one of our most important national markets, and Spain has no place in this hemisphere. Dictators are a danger to the United States."

"Nonsense, Edward," Rob grumbled. "You sound as if we have a divine mission to impose democracy on the world."

"In my opinion, we do."

"In the meantime making a substantial profit."

"Stop it, you two," Kale said. "You do this every time we get together."

Ramedha rose. "I think," she said tactfully, "that it is time the ladies adjourned to the drawing room and left the gentlemen to their port and politics." She smiled at her husband with a look that said not to carry it too far. "We trust you will join us shortly. Winslow, you may be excused as well."

"In case we use bad language," Blackstone said solemnly.

"Come now, Peter," Rob Martin said after the women had departed and Edward had served port from a decanter on the sideboard. "You told us what Tim's editorial stance is, but what does he *think*? Are we going to have a war? And what does Toby say?"

Peter noticed that Doug was staying out of it, either from lack of opinion or from a natural disinclination to debate politics with a prospective father-in-law. "What Uncle Toby said at Christmas was that Secretary of State Olney certainly seems to be trying to start one. But Uncle Toby doesn't think Cleveland will go that far. Tim doesn't think so, either, as far as I can tell, although he did say he thinks Cleveland could win another term in office if he went to war."

"He could indeed," Blackstone said. "I'd vote for the man if he'd just take a stand, and I'm a Republican."

"That's what's wrong with you," Rob said, grinning.

"Most of your own party favors war," Blackstone pointed out.

Peter contemplated his port, turning the bloodred wine in its glass. "If it's any comfort to you, both Tim and Uncle Toby think we're going to get a war anyway, probably in the next administration."

"There!" Blackstone said.

"That doesn't comfort *me*," Rob Martin said.

The Martins and Doug spent the night, Edward Blackstone having decreed that it wasn't fit for the devil himself out there. When they all appeared at the table the next morning, Ramedha and Kale both declared politics a forbidden subject.

"If I'm not allowed to vote for the men who set the policies, then I don't wish to be subjected to discussion of them over breakfast," Ramedha said firmly.

"You don't need to vote, my dear," Edward said. "You can trust me to cast the ballot for you."

"Certainly," Ramedha said. "But it *is* possible that not every woman is married to a man as astute as you." She kissed him on the forehead and took her place at the head of the table. Peter thought he saw a gleam of affectionate sarcasm in her eye. Edward appeared not to have noticed it.

"Very true," he said, "but not all women are as astute as you, so it all evens out." He helped himself to a plate of steak and eggs.

"What do *you* think?" India whispered to Peter.

"About women voting? I never really thought about it much," Peter said, startled. Now that he considered it, he really didn't see any reason why they shouldn't . . . provided they were carefully educated in politics, of course. But that didn't seem a good notion to put into India Blackstone's head, given her father's point of view.

After everyone had eaten, the Martins and their guest departed, and Ramedha and India settled in the parlor with the mending basket. Edward took Peter off into his private study.

"Now we'll talk business," he said cheerfully, lighting the oil lamp that sat on his massive desk, then replacing the shade. The M Bar B was too far out in the country for either gas lines or electricity. The oil lamp gave the room a warm yellow glow that reminded Peter of his childhood.

"So you're sitting on a fortune, are you, young man?"

"Well, yes, sir."

"And what state is your Blake Company in, eh?"

Peter produced a set of figures from his jacket

pocket. He knew Edward wasn't asking for generalities.

"Hmmm." Blackstone stroked his beard as he studied the numbers. "Very promising. And you're considering expansion?"

"I don't know, sir," Peter replied. "A motorcar is an expensive purchase. I'm not sure that enough of the public can afford one in this economy to make expansion advisable."

"You're astute," Blackstone commented. "Money sense, my boy. Not everyone has it. It's a knack. Needs training, of course. But in my opinion men who have it are born with it. You can thank your mother for that." He looked a trifle embarrassed at his own words and tapped the stack of *Wall Street Journals* on his desk with two fingers. "Your father is an admirable man, of course. I never met a braver chap. But—"

"Tell me about my mother," Peter said abruptly.

Blackstone chuckled. "Oh, she was most extraordinary for a woman. I didn't know her well, of course. Met her when I was passing through Germany, so to speak. She and your father offered me their hospitality at Grevenhof."

"What was she like?"

"Well, beautiful. Imperious. You've seen her portrait. But the living woman was—a force to be reckoned with, my boy, that's what she was. She always called your father Heinrich, you know. Pronounced his name to suit her."

"I know," Peter said. "It's my middle name, or part of it. Peter Heinrich von Kirchberg Blake. It was a trial for a child to memorize."

Blackstone chuckled. "I don't doubt it. Your mother was the sort who would have expected you to rise above having such a formidable name to tote around. Went her own way, if you know what I mean. You know about the, er, marriage."

"I know I was born somewhat before it," Peter said. "We don't spread it around, but Dad's never made a secret of it, either."

"Neither did your mother. I was always under the

impression that she agreed to get married only because of you. She did love you."

"It must have been a difficult situation for her."

"Not as much as you might expect, given her circumstance. I don't need to tell *you* that she was very wealthy and that her first husband had a title—a very old title. So, as far as most of the citizens in Grevenhof were concerned, they expected the baroness to do whatever she pleased. An amazing story, really." Blackstone fixed Peter with a firm stare. "Be proud of that side of your family. Don't get pious and try to sanitize it. You'll take life out of her. She's still around, you know—in you, in your business acumen. Don't deny her, or you'll lose your touch."

Peter nodded, startled.

Blackstone spread Peter's figures across the desktop and motioned Peter to draw his chair closer. "You're quite right about the economy, young man. You can't lower your price without raising your volume of sales. And vice versa. Both will happen as the automobile gains acceptance, but you must exercise caution. You need to diversify and still prepare for the future. Why do your machines run on gasoline?"

"It's the best design," Peter answered. He was becoming accustomed to the abrupt jumps that Blackstone's conversation took. "Believe me, we studied it thoroughly. Electricity is never going to have the range, and steam is hopelessly cumbersome."

"You're certain of that?"

"I'm positive."

"Excellent," Blackstone said, grinning. "That was my opinion as well."

"So you don't think I should diversify into models using alternate fuels?" Peter asked, trying to figure out where this was going.

"Certainly not. I think you should invest in petroleum."

Peter blinked. "Petroleum! Oil wells?"

"Where do you think gasoline comes from?" Blackstone demanded.

"It's refined from petroleum. I know that. I just don't know anything about the process. Isn't oil drilling extremely risky?"

Blackstone chuckled. "If you want a perfectly safe investment, then buy government bonds and let them plod along. If you want to put your money in something that will be mutually beneficial to your other investments, put it in an up-and-coming petroleum company."

Peter, turning this notion over in his mind, stared out the window. A lot of swampland got sold to suckers, Peter thought, and he knew as much about oil geology as he knew about knitting. Did Blackstone know any more?

Apparently he did—or thought he did. He tapped Peter on the shoulder for his attention. "Stay away from Standard Oil. Rockefeller hasn't any intention of letting anyone but himself run that. And stay out of Standard's territory. Rockefeller eats little companies. If I were you, I'd invest in California."

"Why?"

"Because it appears to be floating on a damned sea of oil," Blackstone answered. "Fellow named Doheny dug a wildcat hole with a pick and shovel out there in Los Angeles. Now every Tom, Dick, and Harry's punched a well in his backyard. Place looks like a saltshaker. That's no use to you, of course, but there's serious drilling going on farther north. Company called Sierra Oil. Got in ahead of the Standard octopus and seems to be holding its own. Board of directors squabbles like a bunch of nursery brats. Just the thing for you."

Peter smiled. "Divide and conquer?"

"Hah! I knew you had the touch. A man with a good sum to invest could get himself elected to the board."

"I'd have to learn the ropes for a while," Peter murmured. He was beginning to be intrigued. The Blake Company was headquartered in San Francisco, and on occasion he had bought gasoline from Sierra. Sometimes with long delays, as he recalled. But he liked the interlocking quality of an investment there.

"My boy, there are vast untapped reservoirs of oil,"

Blackstone said. "It's a miraculous substance. Unsurpassed in the diversity of its use: fuel oil, kerosene, naphtha, benzene, asphalt, lubricating oil, and now gasoline. It's the modern energy source. It can be converted to heat, steam, and electricity. And there's enough of it to last virtually forever. That's my advice to you, Son, since you've asked."

"Do you have any money in petroleum?" Peter inquired.

Blackstone grinned, and his eyes crinkled half-shut. "I do." He shoulders shook once. "Mine's in Standard Oil. I only deplore their tactics in theory, you see. They pay excellent dividends."

California

"Most of our current operation is the upper valley." Sanford Rutledge, driving his carriage, spoke from behind woolly steel-gray whiskers that gave him an impressively biblical air.

Peter decided that the whiskers probably served as a useful screen for road dust if Rutledge made the trip often from San Buenaventura into the Ojai Valley. The railroad only went as far as the old Spanish mission on the coast. The settlement was recently rechristened Ventura by the Southern Pacific because the name, in its former grandeur, wouldn't fit in a printed timetable. Beyond the end of the tracks, a dirt road wound between foothills into the lower Ojai.

"We're upgrading our operation with a new refinery in your part of the state, Mr. Blake. A model facility." Rutledge fixed Peter with a bright stare. "We'll be glad to have you aboard for the transfer." Rutledge chuckled, hiding some secret satisfaction deep behind his whiskers.

Edward Blackstone had been right, Peter thought. The president and past president of Sierra Oil seemed locked in battle. With a sufficient investment, Peter could acquire enough clout to sway the outcome. And had better, as Blackstone had pointed out, before Rutledge and his adversary ran the company into the ground because they were snapping at each other's throats instead of taking care of business. But if Peter could put the company back on the track, he stood to reap far more for his investment than a safe purchase of established oil stock—Standard, for instance—would net him.

"It's a gamble, Son," Blackstone had said. "But not all luck, you understand. Financial poker."

Peter inspected the countryside. This was his first venture into southern California. Stepping off the train in Los Angeles to change cars for the run to Ventura, he had been struck by a wave of sunlight that washed over him like warm bathwater. It was January, and in Los Angeles the temperature was at least seventy degrees. The porters were working in shirtsleeves. He knew that such mildness wouldn't last, but neither would the mercury drop much. San Francisco didn't freeze in the winter, either, of course; but neither did it offer any inducement to be out-of-doors.

The land seemed almost devoid of water except where irrigated. The countryside between Los Angeles and Ventura—and the hills they were passing through now—were covered with toast-colored grasses and the spreading, twisted limbs of live oaks, dusty green in the sunlight.

A few farmhouses were visible, and now and then the carriage clattered by a tiny post office or general store that passed for a town. It was a good sixteen miles from Ventura into the lower Ojai Valley, and when they arrived, Rutledge proudly pointed out a settlement that looked to Peter much as Guthrie had looked in its earliest days. Wooden sidewalks bordered a business district, which included a drugstore, feed store, grocery, two laundries, three barbers, and a harness maker. A Chinese man drove a produce wagon, a portable store, down the street. Unlike Guthrie, the settlement didn't appear to be in any hurry to change.

Beyond the town the road passed through cattle-dotted fields alternating with citrus groves behind waist-high drystone walls. Masses of green leaves with the fiery globes of oranges resembled Christmas trees with orange ornaments. Here and there through the trees Peter could see a frame house or one constructed of the stone that littered the countryside. Rutledge sent the carriage rattling across a narrow bridge and past a butcher's wagon turning out of the road that led to one of the ranch houses. Peter peered out of the carriage and down into the muddy creek bed.

"Is the water always this low?"

"Except when it rains. Then it flows like a demon," Rutledge said. "Don't trust these dry washes in a rain." A rancher seated on a bay horse with a silver-mounted saddle trotted by, and Rutledge raised his whip in greeting. "Don't have much business in this valley," he said to Peter. "Sierra's head office is in the town of Santa Paula, over the mountain. I brought you around the long way so you could see the drilling operation. But it pays to keep in good with the locals. There's more money in this valley than you'd suspect."

The upper valley was reached after a series of switchback turns that took them high above the lower floor. When they pulled up on the edge of Sierra Oil's Yellow Mountain field, Peter began to discover how cold it could get at night after a warm afternoon. The sun was dropping quickly behind the crest and sending long fingers of shadow between the derricks. The hillsides were covered with scrub and manzanita, cut through with rutted wagon tracks. A light glowed in the field office.

"Step down, Mr. Blake," Rutledge said. "I'll have one of the men show you around, if you're still set on it."

"Oh, I'm set on it," Peter responded. He climbed out and stretched, peering curiously through the dusk.

The oil field was like a city from someone's nightmare: Wooden derricks rhythmically dipped into squat skeletal spires against the sky; well houses huddled at their feet under the rumble of the pumps. Everywhere was the sharp, acrid odor of oil mixed with a strong smell of sulfur. Peter would not have been surprised to see the devil himself lumber from one of the well houses—and almost thought he had when a dark-visaged form appeared at his shoulder.

The intruder proved instead to be a man in a cloth cap. His face was blackened with grease but friendly enough in its smile, and his hobnailed boots offered no glimpse of cloven hooves.

"Good evening, Harkness," Rutledge said. "I want you to show us around the field this evening." He sounded as if he were conferring great privilege upon the fortunate Harkness. He did not trouble to introduce Peter to him.

Harkness, however, appeared to take no offense. "Sure thing." He tipped his cap at Rutledge and Peter. "I reckon you ought to step in the office and put a duster on, though."

"Indeed." Rutledge led the way. "You'll spoil your suit without some cover," he explained to Peter. "I keep gloves on, too."

Inside the office, a one-room frame building, Harkness presented a pair of gloves to Peter, along with a linen duster from a hook on the wall. A half-dozen men, as oil-grimed as Harkness, trudged in and signed their names in a book on the desk, glancing without much curiosity at Rutledge and Peter.

"Day shift's just going off," Harkness explained.

Outside, Peter saw a buckboard wagon draw up, and men climbed wearily into it.

"Most of our roustabouts come from Sierra," Rutledge told him. "Sierra Oil has pretty well built the economy of that town in the past few years. We're appreciated by the local citizenry, I can tell you."

"They appreciate the refinery, too," Harkness said quietly, opening the door into the main well house.

Rutledge didn't respond to that. Peter couldn't even be certain that he had heard Harkness correctly. Harkness held the door open to let them pass in and held the lantern high while they watched the weighty beam of the pump head above them rising and falling, monstrous, methodical, heavy.

Peter wondered if, like the complicated mechanics of the pump, Sierra Oil held ominous workings within it.

III

New York

"Say, this is something!" Ecstatic, Frank looked out the streetcar window as he sat squeezed between Janessa and Charley. He tried to peer past Janessa's hat at the dirty, snow-crusted streets.

"Not exactly the most uptown scenery," Charley said, chuckling, clearly amused at Frank's boundless appreciation for anything and everything he had seen in New York. "We're pretty countrified out here."

"It's swell," Frank said.

It was all swell. Janessa and Charley's house on Staten Island, not far from the Hospital Service headquarters, was warm and welcoming and filled with the comfortable bustle generated by babies. And today he was going to Ellis Island with his cousins. They would ride the Staten Island ferry across to the Battery and then change boats for the Immigration Service offices on the island. That night they had plans to see a play in Manhattan and have a late dinner at Madison Square Garden; but to Frank the day's activities were just as exciting.

"He's easy to entertain, isn't he?" Charley remarked as the streetcar stopped at the ferry building and they climbed out. Charley and Janessa wore dark blue woolen uniforms, gold-braided with jackets buttoned in brass and the gold insignia of the Hospital Service on their collars and caps. They each carried a leather medical bag. Frank took Janessa's and happily carried it for her.

"He's a dear," Janessa said. "I wish I'd been that nice when I was his age."

Frank, coached by Charley, took a crust of bread saved from breakfast from his pocket and held it up to the seagulls squawking and circling overhead, scouting for garbage in the harbor. One swooped down and snatched it, fleeing from the others ready to rob him of it. Two of them caught up with him, and the three tumbled in midair. Frank laughed, and sucked his fingertips. "You've got to be careful with those guys! They've got beaks like pincers." Leaning on the railing as the ferry put out, he watched the foam curl under its bow.

In the upper bay the Statue of Liberty loomed ahead, lifting her lamp over the harbor and the snow-covered pedestal that supported her. The sky was thick with clouds as gray as the water, and the verdigris of her copper sheathing faded into them so that she seemed almost to be lifting herself out of the mist.

"Oh, there she is!" Frank breathed in awe.

"You saw her on the way in yesterday," Charley said.

"I don't care. I don't get tired of her."

Frank stared alternately at Liberty, at the skyline of Manhattan, and at the flotilla of ferries, tugs, barges, and ocean liners that crowded the harbor while the ferry chugged its four-mile course to the southern tip of Manhattan.

"Here we are," Janessa announced as they stepped onto the wooden pier in front of the ferry building. "Don't roam." She caught him as he drifted in the opposite direction, fascinated by the line of immigrants disembarking from a Cunard liner. "It's a madhouse from here on. Stay right with us."

"Yes, ma'am." Frank let her lead him toward the Ellis Island ferry. He walked half backward, still staring at the immigrants. A swarthy couple balanced a huge feather mattress on their heads, and a Cossack in boots and a karakul hat strode just behind them. They all appeared bound for the same ferry, but Janessa and Charley led Frank into a separate queue of immigration officials heading for their day's work. The officers had a cabin to themselves. The immigrants waited patiently to board. They came off the Cunard liner in a seemingly endless stream, all their possessions bound up in cardboard suitcases, straw satchels, and string bags. Papers were clenched in their teeth or pinned to lapels.

"First- and second-class passengers disembark here," Janessa explained to Frank. "Any foreigners among them receive their medical inspections in their cabins. Then the steerage passengers are taken to Ellis Island."

"Why do you separate them? The steerage passengers, I mean."

"Count them," Charley said. He motioned out the window of their cabin at the masses of people who packed the pier. "And they're from just one ship."

"There are so many," Janessa explained. "They're unmanageable unless we have some central point to funnel them through. The few immigrants who travel first and second class aren't so unwieldy."

"And they've paid for the privilege," another Marine Hospital Service doctor said, chuckling. He was sitting across the aisle, smoking a cigar and reading the morning newspaper. "And it saves us from making dreadful mistakes."

"One unfortunate doctor, whose name has since passed into legend, detained Pierpont Morgan for a skin condition," Charley told Frank. "Under the impression that Morgan was an immigrant, one assumes. No one ever saw such a mad old man. Can you imagine what would have happened if the doctor had hustled him off to Ellis Island instead of just making a fool of himself in Morgan's cabin?"

The ferry tooted, and the voice that had been shouting outside grew louder.

"What is it that he's yelling?" Frank asked. "I can't make it out."

"'This way. Hurry up,'" Charley translated. "In fourteen languages."

"No wonder it sounded queer. Do they have interpreters for all these people at the island?"

"Not enough," Charley said. "And there's always some poor devil who speaks a language no one's ever heard of. Obscure Balkan dialects, for example. We do a lot with sign language."

"And body English and picture books," Janessa added. "And we do pick a bit up. I, for instance, can say 'Please take off your shirtwaist' in Yiddish, German, Russian, Swedish, Italian, and, as of last week, Turkish." She showed Frank a little notebook tucked in a pocket of her bag. "I write them all down."

"'I have the pen of the gardener's aunt,'" Charley said solemnly, pretending to read over Frank's shoulder. "'Please drop your pants.'"

The ferry tooted again and pulled away from the pier, leaving it looking oddly empty. Inside, the passengers huddled together and looked anxiously across the mile of water to the Immigration Service building, a turreted castle with a blue slate roof, perched on a three-and-a-half-acre sand spit in the bay. Frank could see the newcomers' faces through the window that separated the doctors' cabin from theirs, his own face reflected over them. What were they thinking, he wondered, having come so far? What were they like under the odd fur hats and the black head scarves, behind the long beards and the foreign speech?

He stared at them as the ferry docked at Ellis Island and they began to straggle up the pier. Frank had never known any foreigners except for the diplomatic families in Washington—all urbane representatives of their ruling classes. These desperate, determined peasants clutching their luggage were different.

Frank crossed the gangplank, enthralled, and Janessa grabbed him by the arm. "Come on. You'll get lost and end up somewhere with an X on your coat." X was the doctors' code for suspected mental deficiency, chalked among other signs and symbols on the immigrants' clothing as they passed through their first battery of tests. Those so marked were singled out for further examination in the private cubicles inhabited by Janessa and Charley and other senior doctors.

Frank let Janessa shepherd him up the front steps to the first floor and then, bypassing the main staircase, through a side door that led to the second floor. He looked regretfully over his shoulder at the people trudging up those steps. They had put on their Sunday best—heavy dark suits, black velvet skirts, quilted petticoats—to greet America. The children were scrubbed and combed and wide-eyed, the parents tense because something might yet go wrong. Janessa said that about twenty percent were culled by the first examination, and of them two percent were eventually turned back, deported.

At the top of the steps, in the second-floor corridor outside Janessa's office, a cluster of men, coats chalked with various symbols, were already waiting. Around a bend in the hallway, Frank could hear the Babel hubbub of the main registry room. Every so often another immigrant would appear, coat marked with a *K* or an *H* or an *E* to join those waiting to be examined. A uniformed guard stood quietly nearby to make sure they stayed put, and a nurse appeared periodically, to pluck one from the group.

Charley disappeared into one of the doctors' offices. Beckoning Frank to follow, Janessa went into another. "You can stay with me if you're fairly unobtrusive," she said, giving him a chair in the corner. "If I have a female patient, you'll have to scram."

"Swell." Curious, Frank looked around the office. It was tiny, but the light from two big windows flooded it in a friendly fashion. Moving water below made the light shimmer and bounce on the white walls. Janessa had a desk with a leather swivel chair, two armchairs, and a backless stool. One wall was lined with bookcases. Old medical reference texts, children's picture books, a wooden cigar box full of tops and marbles, and a bowl of wrapped peppermints inhabited it. Janessa's slowly growing collection of foreign dictionaries occupied the lowest shelf. Opposite the bookcase was an eye chart. Frank squinted a little to see if he could read the bottom line.

"You aren't supposed to be that far away," Janessa said.

"I can read it, though."

"Eagle eye," Janessa said, impressed. "Here we go." She turned to give a reassuring smile to the first arrival, a middle-aged Serb whose face bore an expression of terror and pleading. He wore a heavy quilted coat that reached his knees and an astrakhan hat. He pointed to his eyes and vehemently said something over and over. A harried nurse with her hair coming unpinned under her cap said, "They marked him for his eyes out there. The interpreter told us that he says he can see perfectly; but he kept reading the chart wrong."

"Don't Serbs use the Cyrillic alphabet?" Janessa asked her. "Why not just give him something in Serbian to read? If he's blind he's not going to be able to read fine print."

"They tried that," the nurse said. "He couldn't make head nor tail of it."

The man began another speech, long, explosive, impassioned. The nurse rolled her eyes at Janessa.

"But he was giving answers on the eye chart?"

"Wrong ones."

"Is it possible that he knows his letters but not how to read?" Janessa asked. "Miss Morrison, why isn't an interpreter here with this man?"

"Can't spare one," the nurse replied. "It's bedlam out there. Everyone's in a hurry, more so than usual," she added distractedly. "Twenty-five ships cleared quarantine this morning, and they're all waiting to dock. Their captains are raising Cain because we can't take people off fast enough to please them. We can't spare our only Serbian interpreter because one fellow makes trouble." She jerked her thumb at the man.

He began to expostulate again, half-pleading, half-angry, smacking his fist solidly against his palm. He snatched off his hat, with some idea apparently of making an American gesture of deference, and tucked it under his arm. He began to talk rapidly again, this time solely to Janessa. Her gold braid and military cap made it obvious that she was a higher authority than the nurse.

"All right!" Janessa threw up her hands for silence. "Here. Sit." She pointed at the stool and the eye chart on the wall.

The man sat down facing the chart and groaned in despair. The realization that he was caught in the same tangle again made his nostrils flare. His eyes widened in frustration.

Janessa picked up a pointer and tapped it on the chart. She poked at the capital *P* and cocked her head at the man.

"Rrrrr!" he said stubbornly, with the look of someone prepared to argue about it.

"Yes."

"Yes?" The Serb looked startled. He seemed to know that word.

"Yes, indeedy," Janessa muttered. "Now what else?" She scanned the chart trying to summon up anything she could remember about Cyrillic letters. "This, please." She tapped the pointer on a middle-sized *C*.

"Sssss." The Serb looked at her defiantly.

"Yes. This please!" A smallish *M*.

"Mmmm."

Janessa nodded again.

Some letters of the two alphabets, Frank noted, were the same, others were different. What chaos languages were, after all. He had never studied anything but French and German, and German had been bad enough.

Janessa pointed at an *F*. The man shook his head, miserable, but Janessa smiled at him and nodded again. There was no *F* in the Cyrillic alphabet, Frank surmised. A test to make sure he wasn't just guessing.

Janessa got a pad of paper and pencil out of her desk and handed them to the man. She ran the pointer along the bottom line of the chart and then pointed to the pad. He stared at her blankly.

"Copy it for me. Just as you see it."

Incomprehension. He stared at the little letters, turned his head sideways like a bird, then back the other way. They remained mysterious except for the one or two that looked like Cyrillic. Janessa took the pencil back, knelt beside him, and copied the first two from the line onto the pad in his lap. She gave him back the pencil.

Squinting, he carefully reproduced a *J*, starting with the tail, then carefully adding the serif at the top.

"Yes." Janessa beamed at him, and he smiled back

suddenly, revealing two missing teeth and one capped with gold. He began to draw, not to write, the letters, but when he was finished, they were all correct.

Janessa took the pad, called for the nurse, and handed him back to her. "There's nothing wrong with his eyesight." She looked ruefully over her shoulder at Frank. "Although the phrase 'the blind leading the blind' does occur to me. Lord. There's no map for this work. We just stumble on."

The nurse brought in another patient and conferred quietly with Janessa. Janessa turned back to Frank.

"You'll have to wait in the hall for a while, dear."

Frank obeyed, standing back to let a young woman through the door first. She stared at Frank as she passed by. Not much older than he, the patient looked to him like one of the Greek dolls a friend had brought back from his grand tour. She wore layers and layers of skirts and petticoats, vests and blouses and aprons, fancifully embroidered and appliqued, so many that he couldn't be quite sure there was really a girl under there. She wore a fringed scarf on her head and hugged a paisley shawl tightly around her.

In the hall, more immigrants had gathered according to their nationalities, waiting, talking uneasily to one another in little groups. One with an *H* on his coat kept staring at the chalked letter, puzzling over it, brushing at it. He looked to be in his twenties, with broad shoulders and heavy boots and wide, callused hands. A nurse said something to him in German, and he shook his head vigorously. "Nein!"

Frank sidled over. Since he knew a little German, he decided to try it out. "Welcome to America," he said hesitantly.

The German's face lit up. "You are a doctor? You will tell them I have no rupture. No, never."

"I am just a visitor," Frank said hastily. "I just wanted . . . can I ask you a question?"

"They all ask me questions," he told Frank. "So why not you, too?" The German sighed theatrically, but he didn't seem annoyed. "Do I look like I have a rupture?" he demanded before Frank could ask a question of his own.

"No," Frank answered. "But I am not a doctor." He knew from Janessa and Charley that the doctors on the stairs would mark a suspected hernia because of certain oddnesses in a person's gait. The German appeared to know it, too.

"My brother warned me they watch you on the stairs." He looked earnestly at Frank. "But I had a stone in my boot. I am a hod carrier. How would I work if I had this rupture?"

Frank knew that if the man did have a hernia, his inability to work would account for his being sent back to Europe. He couldn't tell whether or not the German was lying. In either case the poor man had gone to great lengths and probably spent all the money he had ever saved to come here. "Why did you come to America?" Frank asked abruptly.

"Opportunity." The young man took off his woolen cap as if in respect to some unseen flag. "For freedom here. My brother has lived here a year. He paid my passage. I will pay for the next one. There are many, many of us at home. We come here, where there is room for everyone." He put the cap back on his thick pale hair. "America," he breathed. "I came because it is America."

Frank smiled, proud to belong to a country that the rest of the world looked toward for hope.

When he learned later that the girl in Janessa's office had been deported, he felt saddened that she had lost her opportunity to create a better life. Unfortunately, she had been unmarried and pregnant—her relatives had sent her to America to escape the disgrace. But, Charley explained, she couldn't be allowed to become a public burden.

It was all a shame, Frank thought, because she looked quite young, and probably some fellow had taken advantage of her; as Janessa pointed out, however, it wasn't likely that anyone would marry her now under the circumstances, and of course she would need someone to support her and the baby. When he told Janessa how sad it made him to think of the girl going back to Greece, she gave him a kiss on the forehead.

"He's so sweet," Janessa said later to Charley. "And so innocent. If he wasn't six feet tall and as strong as an ox, someone would take advantage of *him*."

"Probably," Charley allowed, "but he is, so I wouldn't worry about him."

Frank went with them to the island every day that week. He soaked up everything, escaping Janessa's clutches—at first illicitly and finally with permission—to roam through the immigration building and peek into every room unless some official chased him away. He asked endless questions and interviewed anyone with whom he could manage to communicate. Because of his ingenuousness, no one seemed to take offense at his probing. A motherly Polish lady, hauled into Janessa's office on suspicion of trachoma, mistook him for Janessa's son, told the doctor that she had a fine boy, and gave him a cookie from her suitcase. To Janessa's great relief, the woman's eyes were passable.

In the evenings Janessa and Charley took Frank to the theater, a magic lantern show, a music hall, or to Mike's moving pictures. Frank, with a wide-eyed stare of pleasure and a permanent grin, enjoyed them all indiscriminately. He couldn't wait to stay with Mike and Eden and meet all their friends, too.

"That ought to be a revelation to him," Charley murmured.

In the meantime, Frank was a model guest. He filled the coal scuttle and took out the garbage without being asked and was thoroughly spoiled by Janessa's Irish nursemaid, Kathleen, who baked him cakes and pies. Frank had a powerful effect on women, Janessa noted. They wanted to feed him—possibly because he was so huge and handsome and so perpetually ravenous. Janessa suspected Kathleen of having a secret yen for Frank, unsuitable to her religious beliefs and station; but so long as Kathleen satisfied it by providing him with sugary treats, Janessa saw no harm in the yearning and said nothing to Frank.

Kathleen was eighteen, devoutly religious (her room was plastered with holy cards), and looking for a man who didn't drink. Her father worked on the elevated railway and was a martyr to the whiskey, Kathleen confided to Frank while she kneaded biscuit dough.

"Sure and I'm sorry for Pa with the devil having such a hold on him," Kathleen said, punching the dough with her fist, "but I'd not be putting meself in the same boat. Me mother's life's been a burden to her from the day he touched the bottle."

"That's a shame," Frank said with ready sympathy. "And he won't stop?"

"Can't stop is more like it," Kathleen said morosely. "But maybe he wouldn't at that, if he could. He said to me when I first joined the Temperance Union and took him the pledge and all, he'd sooner sign away his health than his only bit of amusement in this life. He went to drinking that night and didn't stop till he was passed out cold on the floor. Me mother was all for picking him up, the same as she always did, but I wouldn't help her."

"Well, I call that a shame. A man ought to have more care for his own family than to spend his money on liquor." Frank was indignant.

Kathleen began cutting biscuits with a water glass. "The awfulness of it is, I can see why he does it," she said quietly. "All the same, I'll have a man that doesn't, or no man at all."

The next morning Mike and Eden came to collect Frank for their share of his visit. They were bundled against the cold—it was snowing again—and very red in the face. Mike's mustache was starred with flakes of white, and Eden peered out from between the nearly overlapping folds of a muffler and a stocking cap. She was still adjusting to New York's climate, having lived in Hawaii for some years.

The ferry to Manhattan was muggy with the body heat and moist breath of its crowded passengers, and when the cousins had settled in, Eden pulled off the muffler and pushed back the cap on her blond hair. She snuggled against Mike's shoulder.

"How did you like Ellis Island?" she asked Frank.

"Mike's thinking about making a motion picture there—the whole picture, not just a few shots—if he can get permission."

"It was something!" Frank enthused. "I never saw so many people. And all coming here. Think of it—five thousand people a day. Not just when I was there to see them, you know, but every single day. That's so many people, it's hard to think about. And they look so . . . so—"

"Foreign?" Mike chuckled.

"Yes! So different." Frank waved his arms, trying to convey some impression of the vastness of their difference. He knocked a black felt bonnet askew and had to apologize to the woman wearing it. "It was like the theater, or . . . a fairy tale. I felt as if I was watching Hansel and Gretel or Ali Baba, but they were real people. I wanted to know all about them."

"I think Mike and I will know how to entertain you." Eden smiled. "If you want to meet foreigners, we can oblige. Second generation, first generation, and just off the boat. Sometimes I think we don't employ anyone else."

"I can't afford to pay anyone else," Mike muttered.

That evening Frank wondered if *all* the people filling the parlor on the ninth floor of the Chelsea Apartments worked for Mike, in which case it was no wonder if he couldn't keep them paid. There were at least twenty people jammed into the room. They overflowed into the minuscule kitchen, where Eden was making potted-meat sandwiches. Mike, meanwhile, was packing cracked ice around a washtub full of long-necked beer bottles and arguing with a square, balding man with a pince-nez that clung like a dragonfly to the bridge of his nose.

The eyeglasses bounced as he gesticulated furiously. "So didn't I tell you? Art's for museums. Money it doesn't make—not until you been dead ten, twelve years, more maybe."

Frank squeezed past the guests in the kitchen.

"You'll see, Ira," Mike disagreed. "Have a beer and shut up."

"I'm your partner," Ira said. "I tell you when you're walking off a cliff. Particularly if you got me under your arm."

"Ira, this is Mike's cousin Frank," Eden said. "Frank, this is Ira Hirsch. Don't pay any attention to them; they argue like this all the time. There's lemonade in the icebox."

Frank found a glass and poured it full. The crowd in the parlor hailed him as he wandered back in there. The air was thick with smoke, and people were sitting on the settee and ottomans and cross-legged on the floor. Pyotr, the Russian artist who lived in the apartment next door, had brought a huge brass samovar and was brewing tea in it that looked like molasses. He had a heavy Slavic face, all flat planes and thick, solid angles, capped by a thatch of brown hair brushed down on his forehead. Near him, a thin, wistful-eyed young woman with a cloud of thick, dark hair had curled herself into the cushions at one end of the settee, her fingers laced around a glass. Frank recognized her from the moving picture he had seen with Charley and Janessa—she was Rochelle Blossom, the star of all Mike's pictures. On the screen she was fascinating, as exotic as an art-nouveau sprite. He had learned tonight, however, that her real name was Rachel Poliakov, and seeing her up close he realized that she wasn't any older than he was.

He sat down beside her. "Who are you, really?"

When she spoke it was with an accent he had heard over and over again on Ellis Island. "I'm Rachel. Here we all use first names. That is all right with you?"

"Sure. How did you come to work for my cousin?"

"I need the job," she said. "Already I am here six months, and I work for a baker who is brother-in-law to my second cousin Itzel." She made a sour face. "It is worse than Polotzk where I come from, except no Cossacks. So when Michael asks if I want to try this, I think anything is better than Blum's bakery, even if the rabbi doesn't like."

"'The rabbi,'" Pyotr said scornfully. "Who is keeping workers from making things better for themselves? Is priests and rabbis and all the rest."

Rachel glared at him. "A worker you're not."

"I make art," Pyotr said, defending himself. "Who is making art if artists don't? Who is feeding the soul? Ask Michael."

"Do all these people work for Mike?" Frank gestured at the crowded room.

"Many," Rachel answered. "You would be surprised how many it takes. All the time they are not working, though."

"Still," Frank said, "I expect it's better than where they came from, isn't it? To be in America, I mean."

A man in a red, flowing shirt spun around. He had been sitting with his back to Frank. "What do you mean?" he snapped. He had dark, curly hair, close cropped over his ears, and steel-rimmed spectacles.

"Why, why, that's the reason they've come here, isn't it?" Frank stammered, surprised. "Why you've all come here to America. For a better life, and hope and opportunity. Freedom."

The man looked Frank up and down, taking in his good tweed suit and his expensive tie. "What do you know about it? What do you know about anything?"

"Leave him alone, Niko," Rachel said.

Niko smacked his fist on the low table, sloshing the tea out of his glass. "They come here for freedom. For opportunity. For gold in the streets if they listen to the steamship companies. Pah! And what does America give them? A crust in the gutter and a kick from someone's boots."

"Now see here!" Frank was indignant. "If you're talking about my cousin—"

"Michael." Niko shrugged. "Michael is a capitalist."

"And so when would you have any work at all if he was not?" Rachel wanted to know. "From the railway you got fired."

"Because I do not knuckle under. Because I do not kowtow to pigs of bosses." As Niko spoke he stared at Frank.

"Was also because you were shouting bad words at foreman," Pyotr commented. He held up his hand. "But also you are right, you and union. Don't spit at me, wildcat. You have temper of fiend."

"I don't understand." Frank was hesitant, afraid of setting Niko off again. "I've been at Ellis Island with my other cousin all this week, and I've seen plenty of people. And talked to them, too. They all say America is better. Really a promised land. Honestly, the poor souls had no hope in their own country."

"Hope they haven't so much of here, either," Rachel said, forestalling Niko, who had opened his mouth angrily. "Not like they think when they come here. Better yes, good no."

"Better but not—?" Frank wrestled with that. It had not occurred to him that the promised land might be only an improvement, not a paradise.

"You never noticed the slums?" Niko asked sarcastically, raising his eyebrows. "Not even when your mama took time out from her bridge game to take the mission a charity basket?"

"My mother runs an art gallery," Frank said defensively.

"Exploiting men who create the art," Niko commented, as if he had expected as much.

"Niko, be *quiet!*" Rachel scolded.

"Niko, you treat guest this way, I take you outside." Pyotr flexed his wrists and fingers to indicate he could do it.

Niko stood up and stumbled against the table. Frank thought that the tea wasn't all he had been drinking. "I am going." He looked at Pyotr with disgust. "Stay and be cozy. You haven't the stomach for the cause."

He settled a hard gaze on Rachel. "You're a dilettante taking crumbs from a capitalist." He stalked past them.

"For Niko, cause demands constant discomfort," Pyotr commented as the door closed. "He thinks is great betrayal not to be cold and hungry—more cold and more hungry than anyone else."

"He was rude," Rachel said. "I am sorry."

"I don't really understand," Frank said. "What did I say wrong?" He genuinely wanted to know. His education had contained sharply delineated blacks and whites. The middling shades of gray were mysterious and murky whenever they rose unexpectedly before him. "Did I do something wrong?" It seemed appalling that he had started a quarrel with another guest in Mike and Eden's house.

"You're ignorant," Pyotr offered.

Frank contemplated that as Pyotr and Rachel watched him. He didn't think they meant his marks in school. "What is this cause you talk about?" he asked.

"Workers' cause," Pyotr explained. "Socialism. Don't mind Niko. If I am not worker, who is?"

Rachel snorted.

Pyotr took her glass, drained more tea into it from the samovar, then passed her a bowl of sugar cubes. "And you are? Miss Rochelle Blossom with fancy hat? Face on posters?"

Rachel accepted the tea, clenched a sugar cube between her teeth, and sipped the tea around it. "I am lucky. Others not so much." She looked speculatively at Frank. "We could show you."

"Yes, please." Frank felt lost. He wasn't sure what socialism was, wasn't sure why these people were so angry. He had never met anyone like Rachel and Pyotr or Niko. With their foreign accents and odd clothes they seemed as exotic to him as the people on Ellis Island— and yet they told him *he* was ignorant. *But I've lived here all my life*, he thought.

Pyotr took away Frank's lemonade glass and gave him a small glass of hot, sweet, sticky tea. "Tomorrow," he said. "Tomorrow I don't paint. We go out. I take sketchbook maybe." He stood up, looming above them. "I tell Michael we take you out. Promise him nobody eats you."

The first sensation that struck Frank was the smell. He stepped behind Rachel and Pyotr through the front door of the Cherry Street tenement that Pyotr had chosen for Frank's education. Even in winter the stench

was overpowering—of urine and feces, of cooking cabbage, of unwashed bodies. It was so dark he could barely
see, but the inescapable, almost tangible smell washed
over him, gagging him. A trio of dirty children, ghosts in
the gloom, were pitching pennies by the stairs. Frank,
trying to catch his breath, stumbled past them. A woman
filling a pail at a sink in the hallway stared at them
without curiosity. From the squeaking pump trickled a
thin stream of rusty water.

Frank coughed. "Why is it so close in here?"

"Do you see any windows?" Pyotr asked.

"No air," Rachel said. "Never any air."

They went up another flight, past closed doors
behind which Frank could hear voices, shouting and
quarreling, and the hacking cough of a child.

"It's very dirty."

"Could you keep clean in this?" Rachel prodded the
rotting edge of a stair tread with her toe. She pulled a
piece of flaking paint from the wall and dropped it in a
dank puddle that seeped across the hallway.

Frank's eyes were growing accustomed to the
gloom, and he saw that the water came from the cracked
bowl of a toilet in the hallway's bathroom. The cubicle
was filthy, and the door that stood half-open was nearly
off its hinges.

"About these people the landlords don't care,"
Rachel said angrily. "This is the only bathroom."

A little boy walked by them, and Frank noticed he
carried a tin can with extraordinary care.

"Boy! Where have you been?" Pyotr called after him.

"Working the growler for my pap." He backed away
from them. "I ain't done nothing."

"Take your dad his beer," Pyotr said. "We aren't
truant officers."

The child pulled a door open and disappeared
inside.

"Is always saloon next door," Pyotr said. "A man
needs to be numb to live in the tenement house."

They went up more flights of stairs, and Rachel
stopped finally on the seventh floor and tapped at a door.

"Who is it?" The voice inside sounded both weary and suspicious.

"Rachel Poliakov, Mrs. Horvath."

The door opened an inch, and a woman peered out at them. According to Rachel, Mrs. Horvath was younger than Janessa, but she might have been aeons older. Her face was marked by years of bad food and bad air, and too much work and too little hope. She was ravaged by the disease of despair. She wore a cardigan sweater and a shawl over a patched woolen dress, and her thinning hair was pulled back under a knitted scarf.

"Come in," she said. She seemed to know Pyotr, too.

"This is my friend Frank. It is all right that he comes with me?"

"All right." The woman nodded and stood aside.

"Mrs. Horvath's son came to our meetings," Rachel told Frank. "He was killed last month in an accident at work."

"At the slaughterhouse," Mrs. Horvath said. "My Erno." She stared at the floor for a moment and then looked up at the visitors as if to inquire why they had come.

"We brought you this." Rachel took an envelope out of her bag. "From all of us."

Mrs. Horvath clutched the envelope. She peered into it, then shook her head. "I can't take this."

"You can take," Rachel urged. "I told you, from all of us, at the meetings. You can take for Irene."

The shape that Frank had taken for a lump of rags was a child sprawled on a cot against the wall. One bare foot protruded from underneath a thin blanket. Her skin was pale, nearly translucent, and her eyelids were shadowed with dark smudges. She slept the shallow, restless sleep of the sick or starving. Beside her on the floor a paper box of artificial petals and luminous emerald leaves made a glow of color at odds with the torn and faded wallpaper and the bare, grimy boards of the tenement's floor. Another box, with finished flowers, sat on a stool by the cot. The rest of the room held a cast-iron stove and a sagging bed; there was nothing else. No more than two feet from the stove the room was cold.

"Irene is eight," Rachel said. "Fourteen hours a day they work to make flowers for rich women's hats. Four years they have been here since Ellis Island."

Frank swallowed hard. The pale child tossed an arm under her dirty blanket, cuddling something to her. Only a scrap of cloth, Frank saw. Not a doll, just a make-believe toy.

"Come." Pyotr tugged at his sleeve. "You have seen. Is no need to stare."

Frank stared anyway, feeling a sudden, uncontrollable surge of despair. The only window opened out to a central air shaft into which no light came—only gray, still air thick with soot, which settled on the lines of laundry hung with ropes and pulleys from the windows. They crisscrossed the air shaft like windless sails, disembodied, taking no ship anywhere.

When the three had gone outside again into the air, Frank took deep breaths. He turned in mute horror to look at the grim brick face of the building, not more than two feet from the tenements on either side. A pair of sharp-featured street Arabs bumped into him but scampered off when Pyotr raised his fist to cuff them.

"Stand gawking, and you will get your pocket picked," Pyotr warned.

Frank turned around, looked up and down the street, his hand on the wallet in his coat pocket. On the corner he saw three saloons and a tobacconist's.

"Always there is plenty to drink," Rachel said, "if you drink beer or whiskey. Water there is less of, especially in summer. Many children die here."

"But the landlords—? Can't they be made to see to these people?" Frank tried to grasp at some saving humanity.

"Landlords collect rent. Should they care about broken pumps that cost money to mend?"

"So much for land of opportunity," Pyotr said. "Come. I show you something else."

Rachel and he led Frank down the street, through thick gray slush. At the far corner, sandwiched between a saloon and the tobacconist's shop, was a chophouse.

The odor of hot grease spilled into the street. Behind the flyspecked window someone had propped a sign: "Waiters Wanted. No Jews."

Rachel glared at it.

"Is not just Jews," Pyotr said.

"Mostly it is Jews," she retorted.

The door of the tobacconist's shop swung open, and a newsboy came out. He was lighting a cigarette. Pyotr grabbed a paper out of the canvas bag slung over the boy's shoulder and tossed him a nickel. He made a swipe at the cigarette with the other hand.

"You'll stunt your growth."

"Bugger off, Russki. You ain't a copper." The boy flipped up his middle finger and swaggered off.

Pyotr shrugged. He opened the paper and stabbed his finger at classified advertisements as he read: "Irish need not apply . . . no Jews, no Italians . . . Americans only, no foreigners." He looked at Frank. "Who lives in these tenements? Foreigners. Immigrants. 'I lift my lamp beside the golden door.'" He snorted. "Just don't ask me for job."

"But everybody in America is an immigrant," Frank finally said. "Or their grandparents were. Unless you're an Indian."

"Old immigrants don't like new immigrants so much," Rachel said. "Unless they come from the same place. Sometimes they have reasons." She gave Pyotr a dark look.

"I never hurt Jews," Pyotr said. "I have enough troubles of my own in Russia."

"In Russia Jews have nothing *but* trouble," Rachel countered.

Pyotr pointed his finger at the chophouse window with its sign. "He is from Italy."

"So I should be happy because not just Russians are making my life miserable?"

"Is poverty making these people's lives miserable," Pyotr said. "Then they make misery for each other because they need some people to be better than."

"There should be—should be—some public outcry." In his bewilderment Frank stumbled for words. "People can't all be heartless. I can't believe that."

Pyotr scanned the newspaper pages and came to the society section. "Here." He handed the paper to Frank and poked the columns with a forefinger. "Think about Irene and her mama while you read this."

GLITTERING GATHERING OF
THE YOUNGER SET

Mr. Edward Gamble hosted an entertainment for the young and lively set at Sherry's Restaurant. Mr. Gamble, a well-known man-about-town, received an inheritance of twenty thousand dollars and, declaring it to be too small to be of any use, resolved to spend it on a single evening's entertainment for his friends. Two hundred of New York's most elegant and fashionable young people arrived through snow and ice to find a Mediterranean spring blooming inside Sherry's dining room. Bowers of flowering rosebushes perfumed the air, and immense clusters of hothouse grapes adorned the trellised walls.

The guests themselves were resplendent in costumes of the Italian Renaissance. Jeweled matchboxes for the gentlemen and jeweled perfume bottles for the ladies reposed upon every napkin.

The ten-course dinner began with elaborate hors d'oeuvres followed by oyster cocktails.

Outraged, Frank stared at the newspaper.

Pyotr jerked his thumb at the brownstone buildings, some of them dating to Colonial days. They loomed on all sides, menacing in their decay. "Poverty is living death in New York. Do you want to see worse? I could take you to Ragpickers' Lane."

"I—no, I believe you." Frank looked up, trying to catch some glimpse of sun past the sagging eaves and tangle of overhead wires that laced the air above Cherry Street. "Doesn't *anyone* want to help these people?"

IV

Second Avenue was crowded with cigar factory workers making their way home in the lamplit dusk or stopping for beer in the brightly lighted cafés of Little Hungary. A Gypsy musician in a ragged coat stood on the street corner, his open violin case at his feet. A pushcart peddler shouting his wares eased his way through the press in the street.

"Pots and pans! Good cheap pots and pans, a bargain! Kitchen knives! Gloves and hats! Best at the price. Balls, whistles, Teddy's teeth! Blow a whistle on the coppers!" He put a whistle shaped like a squirrel's two front teeth to his mouth and blew.

Frank laughed. He had heard from Mike and Eden about the antics of new Police Commissioner Theodore Roosevelt, who was given to skulking about the city at night, teeth and glasses gleaming in the streetlight, pouncing upon derelict policemen. His nocturnal adventures were beloved by the press. They nicknamed him Haroun-al-Roosevelt.

"There's something, by George," Frank said to Pyotr, who was striding along beside him, with Rachel on Pyotr's other side. "Teddy's cleaned up the police department. They can't prey on the shopkeepers and take bribes from the criminals anymore."

"Who can't?" Rachel looked at Frank in surprise. "The ones he's got busy closing soda fountains or keeping flower sellers so they don't make a few cents? It's not enough he shuts saloons on Sunday; now the workers

56

have to pay double to buy their beer. And he has to shut down pushcarts?"

"These people barely stay alive," Pyotr explained. "Seven days a week is enough time to make money to starve on. Six days? Is not enough. If God says is better to starve than to work on Sunday, I don't believe in God."

Frank looked shocked, and Rachel frowned at him. "Be quiet. We are not atheists." She stepped around Pyotr to Frank. "In this movement we have godly men. But—" She took Frank by the arm and looked earnestly up into his face. "Reform is not enough. The police are better, yes. And Mr. Roosevelt hires some Jews. But there *aren't* laws that landlords cannot charge six dollars a month for a filthy pit . . . that factory owners have to pay a living wage . . . that anyone has to care for these people!"

The crowd had grown thicker, and many of the pedestrians were heading in the same direction as Pyotr, Rachel, and Frank. They came to a meeting hall, which might have been an opera house or a theater when Second Avenue was fashionable. Now it was grimy in the gaslight, its outer coat of paint, of a particularly disgusting orange, peeling and marred with slogans scribbled in charcoal. But the extrawide set of shallow steps leading to the double doors had been swept, and the posters pasted to either side of the doors were printed on heavy cardboard and hand colored for added effect. A black-and-red border of clasped hands surrounded the type.

Daniel De Leon
Leader of the Socialist Labor Party
Editor of The People
One Night Only,
Thursday, January 4, 7:30

After Pyotr and Rachel drew Frank through the doors, they stopped to put twenty-five cents each in a basket on a table just inside. They looked pointedly at Frank until he did likewise. A girl with her hair pulled back into a bun handed him a piece of paper offering subscriptions to *The People* and advertising a fish dinner to raise funds for the cause.

Rachel and Pyotr led him to a seat, and Frank looked around at the audience. There were more men than women—workingmen in dark caps and hobnailed boots, their vests and trousers shiny from wear; Dutchmen with clay pipes, dark-haired Italians, Jews wearing side curls and yarmulkes. The women among them were mostly young, their expressions angry and earnest, their hands red and callused from scrubbing or sewing or rolling cigars for pennies. A few carried babies bundled in shawls in their arms.

People talked among themselves in myriad languages, each nationality keeping to its own kind. They didn't mix with one another even here, but they all came to hear Daniel De Leon, who began his speech by saying he could remake the world for them, give them hope for the fight, and maybe offer something for them to fight with.

The man enunciated slowly, carefully, as if conscious that he was speaking to an audience whose grasp of English was limited. But they nodded, apparently moved, seeming to comprehend. Frank forgot them, forgot Pyotr and Rachel, forgot even what the man in front of him looked like. He just heard the words:

"We socialists are not reformers; we are revolutionists. We do not propose merely to change forms. We want a change of the inside of the mechanism of society.

"Private ownership of the tools of production has reduced more than fifty-two percent of our population to the state of being utterly unable to feed themselves. Common laborers are forced to sell themselves into wage slavery. At the same time another thirty-nine percent of our people, the middle class, is made desperate. The private owners—a mere eight percent of the nation's inhabitants—are thereby enabled to live without toil and to compel the majority, the class of the proletariat, to toil without living!"

"All our elected officials and police departments care about is protecting property and not protecting life!" Frank rested his earnest blue gaze on his father, across a heavily laden dinner table. "Don't you see? The poor fend for themselves! The means of production *must* be given back to the people!"

Henry Blake laid down his fork, swallowed carefully, then unclenched his hands from the arms of the chair. "Let me see if I grasp this."

"It's simple really, sir. I knew you'd see. The socialists are trying to bring about a real change, a new form of justice for the poor. And all based on scientific thought, not on a mishmash of charity and religion."

"And what is wrong with religion?" Henry managed to inquire. Cindy had stopped chewing in midbite some time before.

"Oh, nothing, sir, nothing at all. As a form of comfort and a moral imperative it is invaluable. But in the hands of the upper and middle classes, it becomes a tool to keep the poor subservient."

"You are aware, I suppose," Henry said dryly, picking up his fork, "that you are a member of the upper end of the middle class."

"Absolutely. That's why I feel my obligation so strongly. This is the next logical step for America. As a patriot I feel it my duty to work toward that end."

"What's a socialist?" Midge asked, fascinated.

"A misguided reformer who is convinced that everyone should own everything equally so that nobody will be poor," Henry said around a mouthful of peas.

"And what's wrong with that?" Frank demanded.

"Well, it does leave out advancement through personal initiative, dear," Cindy ventured.

"It also leaves out your education, this house, your mother's and sister's comfort, and everything else I've worked hard all my life to ensure!" Henry snapped. "I have been poor, incidentally, and I did not find it necessary to begrudge anybody else their success in order to make my own way in the world!"

"You were adopted by Grandpa Lee," Frank said stubbornly. "That's when you quit being poor."

"Frank!" Cindy looked shocked. "That is rude and disrespectful."

"It's true, isn't it?"

Henry was furious. His jaw jutted out in a mirror image of Frank's. "I was sixteen when I was adopted, and what your grandfather gave me was the understanding that hard work and attention to my studies would make the difference in my life. You will apologize immediately."

"No, sir," Frank said. "I didn't mean to be disrespectful, but no, sir. Those slum children don't even have a chance to study. And they already work sixteen hours a day."

"The ones who aren't thieves," Henry said. "I'm waiting for your apology."

"You'd steal, too, if you were hungry."

Cindy looked from one to the other of them, horrified at the sudden anger that burned in both their faces. Midge had gone silent.

Henry dropped his fork onto his plate with a clatter, scattering peas on the tablecloth. "I have never in my life taken what was not mine. Nor has anyone in this family. *Apologize!*"

Clearly Frank wasn't going to. Midge's eyes were wide with fear. Frank's expression was almost as bewildered as it was stubborn. "I thought you'd understand," he said quietly.

"I understand that you're young and ignorant and not too old for a whipping," Henry said.

Cindy held both hands out over the table in a gesture of conciliation, but Henry and Frank ignored her.

"After your real father was killed and until Grandpa Lee found you, how did you eat?" Frank asked Henry. The boy's cheeks were flushed. He was ready to shove family history in his father's face.

"I went hunting." Henry's voice was loud, as ominous as gunfire over the silence of the table. "I am not required to justify myself to a child!"

"What should they hunt in New York?" Frank asked grimly. "Rats?"

"I've had enough of this!" Henry exploded, throwing down his napkin.

"Henry, wait!" Cindy leaned forward. "Frank, if you want to help the poor, the way to do it is to go to school, prepare to be a leader of this country, like your uncle Toby and your father. I know you've seen terrible things—"

"He's seen a bunch of anarchists preying on the poor, telling them the world owes them a living!" Henry shouted. "Michael Holt is a disgrace to this family!"

"Mike had nothing to do with it. And they aren't anarchists!"

"Socialists." Henry spat the word out as if it were a disease. "They *are* anarchists. They want to destroy everything this country stands for, everything it was built on. You are forbidden to have any further contact with these people *or* with Michael Holt."

"I told you it wasn't Mike. And this country was built on revolution. When a situation is intolerable, revolution is the only answer. That's in the Declaration of Independence."

"Don't you dare compare patriots like Thomas Jefferson and George Washington to sneaking, sniveling rioters!" Henry yelled. "You need a good dose of reality!"

"I got one!" Frank shouted back. "I saw what *you* never let me see before—starving, oppressed people whose only function is to be slaves to the rich. They're worse off than the Negroes were before the war. And we bring them over here by the boatload just like the Negroes, to work for us for nothing."

"These people are *free*! They came here of their own free will!"

"Because we promise them a better life! And then what do they get?"

"They get a better life than they had in Europe, I can tell you that! And that's something else I know and you don't!"

Midge, terrified by their bitter anger, burst into tears.

Neither Frank nor Henry noticed. Frank leaned across the table, knocked over the salt cellar, and shouted at his father. "So they're supposed to be grateful because we starve them and oppress them but just not quite as badly as their old government did? *That's* the opportunity this country stands for? Well, I don't want any part of it!"

"Be quiet this instant! I won't have you spouting the theories of treasonous rabble." Underneath his anger, Henry seemed honestly bewildered. "Your mother and I have given you everything. You have the highest marks ever earned at your school. You have an honorable future. You have a family tradition. Why you are taken in by the whining of this riffraff—"

"Who's riffraff?" Frank demanded, furious. "Anyone who doesn't wear blinders to what's going on in this country? Anyone who doesn't shut up and do what he's told?"

"You *will* do what you're told!" Henry warned. "If I hear one word from you about this when you get back to school—"

"I'm not going back."

"*What?*"

"Frank!" Cindy smacked her fist down on the table. Midge, who had been leaning against her mother for comfort, recoiled. "Frank, how can you even say such a thing?"

"I'm not going back," Frank repeated. "I'm not going to march around a parade ground all day while people are suffering."

"You don't know anything about suffering." Henry stood up. "You don't know anything about *life*! You will do what your parents tell you! You will do your *duty*!"

"If I don't know anything about life," Frank shouted, "whose fault is that? You planned everything for me. You picked my school, and you picked my friends. *You* decided I was going to West Point! *You* decided it was my duty to turn into some kind of imitation of you and Uncle Toby! When did I ever have a choice in the matter?"

"Frank, how can you say that?" Cindy asked, wounded. "You know you love that school. All you asked for for Christmas was your senior-class ring from Hargreaves."

Frank glanced at the gold signet on his hand, but he didn't answer.

"Maybe we made a mistake to give you this trip," Cindy soothed. "You're so young. Maybe it was too soon."

"You mean you should have waited until I had the same narrow-mindedness you have," Frank retorted. "Until I could look at suffering and not care!"

"You only have six months until graduation," Cindy pleaded.

"And then four years at West Point, and then a career like Dad's. At what point do you think I'll know anything? Ever? Not if you have your way. If I don't know anything about life, maybe it's time I found out! *You* aren't ever going to let me."

"How dare you speak to your mother that way?" Henry's anger went over the edge. His hands, clenched on the edge of the table, shook so hard that his wine spilled, staining the damask.

"You ungrateful puppy! If you want to see life, go see it. But don't expect any help from your mother and me. And don't come back until you can do your duty!"

"Henry, no!" Cindy turned to him, horrified. Midge shrank into her chair.

Frank stood, too, facing his father across the cold, congealed remains of dinner. "All right," he said icily. "That will be fine. Just don't expect me back." He kicked his chair out of his way, sending it skidding into the wall. "I don't want your help!" he yelled.

Father and son stood staring at each other, each feeling bitter and betrayed, until Frank turned on his heel. He snatched his Hargreaves greatcoat from the foyer hall tree, and then the front door banged behind him.

"Henry, stop him!" Cindy cried out.

Midge burst into sobs and ran from the room. Her footsteps pounded up the stairs. And then Henry and Cindy were left alone.

It was snowing. Frank turned up the collar of his greatcoat as he strode furiously up the street. His eyes stung with tears of indignation and humiliation as he

passed the comfortable houses that lined the block
beyond his parents' home—houses of the well-to-do,
with warmly lighted windows and smoke rising fatly
from their chimneys. The doors, still hung with holiday
wreaths, represented safety and security and were
closed to all outcasts. He had been so sure of his
newfound convictions, so certain that his father would
understand. He had been wrong, he thought grimly. His
father was like all the rest of them, as fat and certain of
his privilege as the New York socialites who squandered
their money on parties while the workers starved.

Frank turned the corner, not quite sure where he
was going, only certain that he wouldn't go back.

The front door slammed behind Frank with such
finality that his mother was rocked down to the bones of
her feet. "Henry!" She stared at her husband, terrified.
"Henry, call him back!"

"He'll come back when he's cold and hungry," he
snarled. "How could he do this to me?"

"He didn't do it," Cindy said, shaking. "You did."

"Don't you start on me now, too!" Henry shouted. "I
gave him everything. The best school. Values and
tradition and morals—everything he needs for an illus-
trious career."

"Call him back," Cindy pleaded.

"He needs a whipping," Henry said. "Let him get
one." His face was red, and the muscles in his neck were
taut.

"He left without anything." Cindy went toward the
door.

"You stay here! He needs to learn a lesson."

Cindy spun around and faced her husband. "So do
you!" She snatched a heavy driving wrap from the coat
tree and fumbled in the pocket for her gloves. "Annabelle!"

A frightened maid put her head over the banister
upstairs.

"Tell Jerome I want the carriage. Right now!"

"No!" Henry went to put his back to the front door.

Annabelle came down the stairs and looked uncertainly at her employers.

"The carriage!" Cindy said.

"Go back upstairs, Annabelle."

"Miss Midge, she crying in her room."

Cindy, torn between her daughter and her son, glanced toward the stairs. "Get me the carriage and then go stay with her." She raised her fist and advanced on her husband. "Get out of the way, Henry, or I'll hit you."

Annabelle ducked around him and out the door while Henry grabbed Cindy's wrist. "You aren't going anywhere. That boy's going to take his medicine."

Cindy yanked her arm out of his grasp. "Don't think you can bully me, too." With an effort she kept her voice even. "Frank's made a mistake, but you're making it worse. You can't be a martinet to your family. What's the *matter* with you?"

"I pinned all my hopes on that boy," Henry said, despair suddenly washing over his face. "This is Mike Holt's fault."

"Frank's fault, Mike's fault," Cindy said grimly. "Probably my fault, too. Everybody's fault but yours, Henry, is that it?"

"What do you mean by that?"

"You want everybody else to be wrong, so *you* don't have to take any responsibility for what's happened. When you're ready to stop blaming Mike, Frank, the anarchists, and everybody else but yourself and willing to make peace with your son, then *I'll* talk to you. Right now I'm going to find our boy!" She whipped past him, slamming the door in his face as he tried to stop her.

It was fully dusk when Frank came to the rail depot and stood staring at the timetables posted outside the ticket office.

"Well?" The ticket clerk looked at him irritably. The depot was crowded with travelers. "You want a ticket or not?"

"Uh, how much for a ticket to New York?"

"Twenty dollars." The clerk pushed his gartered

sleeves higher and tapped his pencil on his pad when Frank stood silent again. "You want it or not?"

"I only have five dollars," Frank said. He had been too angry to think of taking any money with him. All he had was the money in his pockets.

"Then you ain't going to New York," the clerk said. "If you don't want a ticket, get out of line."

Frank turned to look at the people behind him. A man with a heavy leather portmanteau thumped his walking stick on the floor in annoyance. Behind him, a woman in a sealskin cloak had two wailing children by the hand.

"Move aside," the clerk said.

Frank stepped out of line. *I won't go back*, he thought. But where was he going to go? He went inside and sat on one of the wooden benches in the depot's waiting room, where it was warm, and tried to think. Travelers milled around, each with a known destination. Frank could hear the chuffing and whistles of the steam engines, the bang and crash of cars being coupled outside. A conductor's voice shouted the names of cities: New York, Trenton, Columbus, Cincinnati.

Frank envisioned himself pawning his ring for a ticket to New York, telling Rachel and Pyotr and Mike and Eden that his father had thrown him out. He was being treated like a kid, like a damned baby who couldn't take care of himself. Like the fool his father said he was. Even his mother had lectured him as if he were a stupid child. Frank's eyes spilled over with tears again, and he brushed them away angrily.

Travelers bustled past him and went out to trains while he sat huddled in his greatcoat, elbows on his knees, staring at the floor. It was made of marble tile, in squares like a chessboard. For no reason he counted them.

The ticket clerk watched him from his window as night fell and the depot emptied. Frank was alone on his bench when he looked up to find a railway agent looming over him. The burly man stood, thumbs hooked in his vest, glaring suspiciously.

"Get up, kid. You can't sleep here."

"I wasn't sleeping."

"Nobody sleeps in the depot. Nobody rides free." The agent was not treating him with the deference he was usually accorded. Frank realized that the confrontation with his father and the resulting feeling of abandonment had robbed his face of its look of privilege, of certainty and position. "You got the money for a ticket, kid?"

"I—no."

"Then get out. If you're on the bum, you can't sleep here."

Frank stood up. "I'm not on the bum."

The agent scrutinized him, then softened a bit. "You look too clean for it, but these days you can't tell. I see more of you boys every day, trying to cadge a ride. Get out. And stay out of the freight yards, too."

Frank started to protest, but he knew it wasn't going to do any good. He hunched his shoulders into his coat collar and went outside into the cold. The wind cut through even his heavy coat.

From the platform, beyond the disappearing caboose lights of a receding train, he could see the squat, oblong boxes of the freight cars waiting to be coupled. A brakeman walked along the line, his lantern swinging. He shone it into the darkened cars, then slammed their doors together and pulled down the bolt with a heavy thunk.

Frank was shivering with cold when there came into his mind some recollection of his cousin Tim's riding the boxcars during the American Railway Union strike. Frank looked over his shoulder for the railway agent. The man was standing in the depot doorway, watching him. Frank straightened his shoulders and walked down the platform. At its end he turned into the darkness of an unlit corner and waited, huddled against the wall out of the wind. Across the yards, the brakeman finished his rounds, and the lantern vanished.

Frank slipped across the tracks and into the shadow of a single empty boxcar, then looked behind him again.

Nothing moved. He ran across more tracks, toward a
line of coupled cars behind an engine. His dark coat
blended into the night as he ducked behind the last of
the coupled cars. The depot water tower, darker than
the sky, loomed above him. Frank peered at the boxcar
and saw that there were doors on that side, too. He tried
one, fiddling with the bolt until it came loose with a
creak. He froze; but when no one shouted at him, he slid
it open. It was too dark to see what was inside, but he
jumped up anyway and scrambled onto a dusty floor.

Feeling around in the darkness, Frank found
wooden crates at one end, mail sacks at the other. A
whistle suddenly split the air, and he heard voices
shouting indistinguishable words. Frantically he wrestled the open door closed. He was enveloped in utter
darkness. The floor shivered as another car was coupled
with a bang to the far end of the line. He waited,
petrified, his heart pounding, for the brakeman to come
back and find him; but there was only silence. Frank
crouched wearily on the floor and finally, when nothing
else happened, lay down on the mail sacks. They were
lumpy, but their bulk rose comfortingly around and
above him, giving him some protection from the cold.
He closed his eyes wearily and slept. He didn't wake
when the cars began to move.

They drove up and down the streets of Alexandria,
checked the hotels and hospital, every place she and
Jerome could think of that Frank might have gone. He
had been at the depot, but the agent said he had left,
though not on a train.

She returned home late at night, lips blue and dark
smudges of fatigue under her eyes. She came back only
because Jerome, concerned for her well-being, finally
refused to drive her any longer.

Beaten, she pushed her way through the front door,
gave her wet coat to Annabelle, and trudged upstairs to
comfort Midge. The girl was asleep, so Cindy lay down
beside her. Henry had locked himself in his study.

V

Sunlight slapped Frank in the face, blinding and nearly as vicious as the railway policeman who banged the boxcar door open. Frank sat up on the mailbags, shocked out of sleep. The policeman launched himself through the doorway.

"Get the hell out of here!" He grabbed Frank by the collar and threw him. The edge of the boxcar caught his ribs as he fell.

Frank landed sprawled in the cinders, his ribs on fire. He gasped. The air was dry and sunny and cold enough for his breath to condense in front of his face. "I wasn't doing any harm."

"Get out of here before I shoot you." The cop slapped the holstered pistol at his belt, and Frank began to run.

The train had stopped on a siding skirted by a ravine of scrubby trees and brush. Beyond the gorge was a tumbled shantytown of the sort that always grew along the tracks on the outskirts of any city. Ahead, rising above trees, he could see the depot water tower.

The policeman fired a bullet after him for good measure, and Frank, his heart pounding, stumbled across four lines of tracks, threw himself down the side of the ravine, then rolled and slid into the scrub at the bottom.

Frank lay there for a long time, listening for the sounds of gunfire or footsteps. He heard nothing, and finally he sat up cautiously. He had come to rest in a trampled clearing hidden from the tracks above, and he was not the only one to have found it. The remains of a fire and an empty bean can spoke of human habitation. No one was there now, but the older marks of other fires and a packing-crate shelter told him that the refuge was used regularly. Maybe someone would come, he thought, feeling desperately alone. His stomach was knotted with hunger. He remembered the five dollars in his pocket and thought about the shantytown. It would certainly have a store, he thought. Frank rubbed his hands over his face, trying to clean the dirt from it. He brushed at his clothes and found a triangular tear in his coat, caused by the fall from the boxcar. Then he climbed the far side of the ravine and ducked through a sagging fence.

Frank walked down a narrow alley, and at its end, he came to a street. He faced a saloon that stank of urine and stale beer and, next door, a weathered store with an equally faded sign proclaiming Dry Goods. The tin sign was punched through with bullet holes in the exact center of both Os.

Frank went inside, grasping the five dollars in his pocket. The proprietor inspected him, taking in the soot-streaked face and dirty hair.

"You hoboes get younger all the time," he muttered. "Got any money, kid? I don't give handouts."

"I have money," Frank said. He looked at the shelves, trying to think what he could cook on an open fire. He remembered the empty can in the ravine. "Give me some beans. Three cans. And a can of tomatoes. And some ground coffee. And matches."

The proprietor produced them and narrowed his eyes as Frank gave him the five-dollar bill. "Where'd you get that?"

"It's mine," Frank told him.

"Yeah, sure. What you going to carry this stuff in? You got a bedroll?"

"I . . . ." Frank looked at the pockets of his great-coat.

"Here. Two cents." The proprietor added a sturdy

bandanna to the pile. "You just fell off the turnip wagon, didn't you, kid?"

"I just fell off a boxcar," Frank muttered.

The man looked at him curiously, eyes lighting on the gold ring. "You got a home to go to?"

"Nope." He gave the word a little swagger as he said it, more to bolster his own courage than to bluff the proprietor. He tied the cans into the bandanna and pocketed his change.

"If you got a home, you go back to it," the proprietor called after him.

Frank turned in the doorway and looked back at him. "Where am I?"

"Dayton."

Back in the ravine, Frank used his pocketknife to cut open the can of tomatoes and a can of beans. He made a fire of scrub wood and dried leaves, then set the beans in it and stirred them with his knife. He hadn't thought to buy a coffeepot or ask where water was, so the coffee was useless. He ate the tomatoes and drank the juice instead. As night fell and the cold intensified, he shivered and wrapped his arms around his knees and cried.

But when that jag was over, it seemed to have washed something away on the salt tide of tears. A firm resolve hardened his features. He felt more in control. He knew he was strong. He wasn't helpless; he could work. His father didn't think he knew anything about life? Well, Frank decided he would keep going until he did. The things he didn't know about survival were already beginning to haunt him with his hunger and the cold. But those were things his father didn't know, either, or had forgotten in the days since his hardscrabble boyhood. They were the lessons that the people in the tenements and the hobo jungles had learned only too well. *I'll find out,* he vowed sleepily. *I'll find out what I don't know.* Despite his fear, he felt exhilarated.

Frank slept by his fire and woke in the cold dawn when the last embers went out. He struggled to his feet and flexed his muscles to relieve a momentary stiffness.

His ribs still hurt, but his body would put up with a lot.
His stringent training at Hargreaves was standing him in
good stead.

The sound of a train in the distance made him
scramble up the side of the ravine and crouch in the
shrubbery where he could watch the tracks. If other
hoboes caught boxcars from here, then so could he. He
would just have to wait until after the cars had been
searched, he thought, and felt proud of his growing
knowledge of the world.

The roaring engine came down the line, shaking the
ground. Frank had never looked at a ten-wheeler from
below before, and his immediate impression was of
weight—awesome weight driven by unbelievable power.
It slowed and was shunted onto the siding. Beyond it,
Frank heard the rush and roar of a passenger express
speeding in the other direction.

A brakeman climbed down from the stopped freight
and used the time to inspect his cars and throw the bums
out before the train pulled into Dayton. The man
slammed a boxcar door open and climbed inside. After a
moment he climbed down again and went on to the next
car. Apparently nothing was amiss, Frank thought, since
no bodies came flying out. When the brakeman had
disappeared down the line, Frank crept from his hiding
place. The engine ahead was beginning to whistle, and
Frank wrestled with the boxcar's heavy door, which the
brakeman had fastened again. Finally it slid open, but
the train had already begun to move. Frank flung his
bindle inside and ran beside the car, still holding on to
the door frame, trying to outpace the train, to get up
enough speed to jump.

The train moved faster, and Frank was afraid to let
go. Those iron wheels were too heavy and too close; he
might slip and be injured or killed. Terrified now, he ran
faster and faster, gasping for breath, hampered by his
greatcoat. He had to jump—it was now or never.

Frank launched himself upward at the car, scrab-
bling with knees and elbows as the train picked up
speed. He hung, half in, half out, kicking frantically,

fingernails digging into bare board, as he felt himself slipping backward. The great iron wheels wanted to draw him down and pull him under.

A hand abruptly reached out and grasped his, and another hand grabbed his coat collar. Frank was dragged inside, over the rough floor. On hands and knees he looked up at a man in tattered overalls. Under the stubble and the dirt, he appeared to be about thirty-five. His eyes were startlingly blue under bushy, dark brows, and the expression on his square-jawed face was wary.

"Thank you," Frank said, gasping. "I didn't think there was anybody inside."

"When I saw your bindle come in, I figured somebody was behind it," the man said. "Didn't figure you was going to leave it, either."

"No." Frank sat up and leaned against the wheel of a new buggy. The car was full of them, lashed down to boards nailed to the floor.

The other man closed the car door. "They see that, they'll be all over us in Dayton," he commented.

"Why didn't the brakeman throw you off?" Frank asked. "I saw him check the cars."

The other man spat. "I bought my ride, that's why."

"Bought your ride?"

"Paid off the brakeman. Gave him two bits." He studied Frank's face. "You're green, ain't you?"

"I'm not as green as I was," Frank said.

"Seems like I bought your ride, too. What you got in the bindle? I ain't eaten today."

Frank produced another can of beans and the coffee. It seemed fair to feed the man; Frank *was* benefiting from the man's bribe. "I don't have water, though."

"Listen, kid. Always carry water. You can be in one of these cars two, three days."

"Oh." Frank started to open the beans with his pocketknife. "My name's Frank Blake. What's yours?"

"Bill." The man looked at him. "And you don't go telling your name to every 'bo you meet on the road."

"Oh."

Bill caught sight of the signet ring on Frank's right hand and narrowed his eyes. "You're on the run, ain't you, kid?"

Frank finished cutting the top of the can, but he didn't answer.

Bill seemed to approve. "That's right. Don't go telling everybody your business. But you put that ring in your pocket. Some folks would roll you for it. And you catch it on a boxcar door while you're jumping, you're like to tear your finger off."

Frank looked at the ring, and for an instant his father's angry face glinted out of it. He tugged it off and stuck it in his pocket. "It's nothing special," he said. "I was going to hock it."

Bill produced a spoon from his own bindle, and they took turns eating out of the can with it. Bill ate ravenously, gulping down the beans. He reminded Frank of a stray dog he had once found. Frank had given it a piece of meat, and the dog, starving and half-feral, had swallowed it whole.

The train slowed for Dayton, and Bill motioned to Frank to get under one of the buggies in the darkness at the back of the car.

"Will they check again? I thought you bribed him."

Bill didn't answer until they were wedged under a surrey at the far end. Then he said in a low voice, "Look, kid, if you're going to go on the bum, you got to learn that nobody's your pal. The cops could check 'cause they don't trust the brakeman. The brakeman could roust us out of here 'cause his boss is watching, and he wants to look good. He could throw us out for fun. Nobody's your pal, kid. Not even if you've bribed him."

They emerged after the train had rolled out of Dayton. Bill opened the boxcar door six inches for light. He produced a grimy pack of cards from his pocket and began to deal out solitaire. He cocked his head at Frank. "You play poker, kid?"

"Some," Frank said. Not well, he knew, but learning seemed a part of this adventure.

Bill's face was unreadable. "Got any money?"

"A little."

Unexpectedly, Bill laughed, a grating noise almost like a cough. "You better keep it. We're going to get hungry again."

Frank looked out the open door. Winter-bare corn-fields rolled by. "Do you know where we're going?" he asked Bill.

"Indianapolis," Bill grunted. "Springfield. Does it matter?"

Frank wondered if it mattered to Bill. How many times had he been down this line to know it so well? "I have to find work," he said. "Make some money."

"You don't look like the panhandling type," Bill said with a grin. It was the first smile Frank had seen. "You might find something in the stockyards at Indianapolis. I've done okay there before."

"Then why didn't you stay?" Frank asked, and then knew that he shouldn't have.

"I don't stay anywhere too long," Bill said, and went back to his solitaire.

They got off the train in Indianapolis, Frank because he was determined to find work, Bill for reasons of his own. The stockyards, next to the freight yard, produced an overwhelming aroma of steer and steer manure and the sounds of constant lowing as well as milling of thousands of hooves. But there was no work.

"We don't hire 'boes," the stockman in the office said.

"I'm not a bum. I'm just out of work," Frank said.

"He is." The stockman jerked a thumb at Bill. "Both of you scram."

"They don't need anybody," Bill said, dragging an indignant Frank out the door. "They hire anybody quick enough when they need them."

"He talked to us like we were animals," Frank protested. He remembered the "No Jews" and "No Irish" signs in New York. "It's not right to treat people like that."

"Kid, where have you been?" Bill turned out of the

stockyards up the street, and Frank followed him. Warehouses and rail yards gave way to tumbledown houses and then gradually to a city park with better houses beyond it.

"Where are we going?" Frank finally asked.

"You want work, don't you?" Bill was studying the houses on either side of the dirt road. They were painted and clean but unpretentious, most with vegetable gardens in the back, plowed over for the winter, some with rosebushes in the front. "This is where you go, kid. People in shantytown can't afford to hire you; people on Snob Hill are too highfalutin." He stopped, looked at a white gate in a picket fence, and grinned again. "This one feeds 'boes, too."

Frank saw an odd chalk mark on the gatepost as they went in and wondered if that was how Bill knew. Did transients signal the easy marks for one another? It seemed logical.

Bill went up the walk and had to grab Frank as he started toward the front steps. Bill pulled him around to the back door, where the man knocked and then took off his cap and held it in both hands.

A woman wiping her floury hands on an apron opened the kitchen door. She seemed to know what they wanted. "You boys can split wood for me," she said. "But I can't pay but a nickel apiece. Times are hard here, too."

"We're right hungry, ma'am," Bill said.

"I'll feed you." She pointed at a stump in the bare garden. "The ax is over there." She studied Frank closely and looked as if she might question him but then changed her mind. "Split me that wood, and I'll give you chicken and dumplings."

Sawed-up lengths of an oak tree lay on the ground beside the ax. Bill picked it up and took the first turn, standing the limbs on the stump and bringing the ax down on them raggedly. After two logs he stopped and rubbed his forearm. "Got it cut up in a fight couple years back," he explained. "Hurts like hell now when I use it."

"I'll take a turn," Frank offered, wondering whether there was really anything wrong with Bill's arm. But he liked chopping wood, enjoyed the clean way the blade hit into the log and split it open. It had been his chore at home, and he had never minded.

Frank split most of the rest of the wood and finally gave the ax back to Bill with three logs to go. He wanted to see if he could make him take it. Bill gave him a long look and then picked it up.

When they knocked at the door again, the woman handed them two plates and two glasses of cold buttermilk. Frank found himself bolting it the way Bill had consumed the beans. He had never been this hungry, and it tasted wonderful. They put the plates on the back steps and at the well filled the canteen from Bill's bindle. Neither one of them mentioned that Frank had earned most of Bill's nickel as well as his own. Bill had known where to go; he had been the one who could read the symbol on the gate.

In the late afternoon they walked into the hobo jungle hidden in the trees beside a stream, a tributary of Eagle Creek, outside the Indianapolis rail yards. Three hoboes were gathered around a fire, under a makeshift shelter of packing crates and salvaged tin roofing. Beyond it was a tent and another fire, and above that, in a big poplar, a platform supporting a kind of tree house with a canvas awning. Cleats had been nailed to the tree below it. A painted board nailed to the tree read City of Lost Souls.

The weather must have been fair for a few days, Frank decided, for this many hoboes to be encamped. When it froze or snowed, they would surely seek somebody's barn or hop a freight. He looked at them curiously and realized that he and Bill were being inspected, too.

"Where you from, brother?" asked one of those squatting by the fire. He wore a wool cap pulled down over his ears and wool gloves that were frayed at the fingertips. A drooping mustache masked the gaps of missing teeth.

"Dayton," Bill said. "Me and my pal." He stared at them, and they stared back—warily at Bill and almost hungrily at Frank. "You got some room by the fire? We got a little coffee."

"Always room for another lost soul, brother," the man in the wool cap said. "I'm Preacher John, and this here's Saskatchewan Ed and Loco."

"Digger Bill."

"Ain't I heard of you?" Loco turned ferretlike eyes on him.

"Reckon maybe. The kid here's my pal."

"Sure."

Frank kept quiet, watching them with interest while Bill brewed the coffee. He could feel Loco's eyes sliding toward him.

"Hey, kid, you ever been this way before?"

"No."

"That's a fine coat."

"It ain't for sale!" Bill snapped.

"Sure."

Frank was beginning to understand certain things. He stood up and peeled off the coat. "It wouldn't fit you," he said quietly. "I'm a lot bigger than you." He gave them a moment to take in the width of his shoulders and the size of his muscular forearms, and then he put the coat back on.

"Strong as an ox," Bill said. "Split a whole load of wood this afternoon." His eyes met Preacher John's in a kind of unexpressed wink that was not lost on Frank. All the same he knew he'd gotten his point across to Loco.

The coffee in Bill's tin pan boiled, and he poured two cups. Frank wrapped his hands around his cup for its warmth. The coffee tasted of grounds and left a sediment in the bottom of the cup, but Frank didn't care. Dusk was falling, and the hot, bitter brew helped keep the cold away.

The hobo in the tree house swung his legs over the platform and pulled a harmonica out of his coat. After a moment Frank recognized the tune. It was a hymn, an old one, "Revive Us Again."

The harmonica faded away, and the hobo above them began to sing:

"Oh, why don't I work like other men do?
How the hell can I work when there's no work to
*   do?*
I went to a house, I knocked on the door.
The lady said, 'Scram, bum, you've been here
*   before!'"*

Saskatchewan Ed pulled out his own harmonica and took up the melody:

"Hallelujah, I'm a bum,
Hallelujah, bum again!
Hallelujah, give us a handout
To revive us again!"

"That's downright sacrilegious," Preacher John protested.

"So's starving to death," the hobo above them said. "I am a musicologist. I sing songs. I do not critique them."

"Give us another then, Harry," Ed said.

"Might stir out them two," Loco said, pointing at the tent.

"Naw," Harry said from the tree house.

"They keep themselves to themselves. For a cup of coffee, though, I will favor this gathering with 'Red River Valley.'"

Frank passed him up a cup of coffee, and they sang dolefully, accompanied by Harry's harmonica.

"From this valley they say you are going,
We will miss your bright eyes and sweet
*   smile. . . ."*

The words lingered in Frank's head after the men turned in, wrapped in their coats and blankets and lying around the fire. Was anybody missing him? he wondered. He felt certain that his father wasn't but hoped that he was. He hoped they were all scared to death. His mother would be if she knew where he was, Frank thought with satisfaction. One day he'd go back, older, experienced, sure of himself, a man of the world, able to hold his own with his father across the dinner table. And then, because he was not entirely starry-eyed, he wondered if these men sleeping around him had felt that way once.

Where had they come from? Loco, he thought, looked too crazy to have ever held a job; but Saskatchewan Ed claimed to have been fired in the American Railroad Union strike of 1893 and blackballed by all the railroads since then. Harry, the musicologist, was an enigma—an educated bum. Preacher John claimed to spread the Word, but Frank suspected that it was the collection plate that fired his oratory. How had they started on the bum? Despite the hardness of the ground and the noise of Harry's snores, Frank was too weary to think about it for long. He drifted off in midthought and awoke only when Bill's tight, menacing voice snapped him out of sleep.

Frank, heart pounding, looked around him in the darkness and made out the crouched shape of Loco. Bill was sitting up beside him, a pocketknife in his hand.

"Make another move, I'll cut your liver out."

Loco had stopped, frozen, on hands and knees. Now he lifted his hands carefully and settled back on his heels. "I was just going to pee."

"Like hell. You don't need to climb across us to pee. I warn you: Try it again, and you're dead."

Loco stood and backed carefully away. They heard him in the bushes making good on his explanation.

"What happened?" Frank whispered. They had kept their voices low, and none of the other hoboes was awake. Or they were pretending not to be.

"He's crazy," Bill said. "He wants your coat. Don't you get alone with him."

"But how could he—" Frank bit off the question as Loco came back and lay down on the opposite side of the fire. The man had intended to kill him—for a coat. It was the only way Loco could have gotten it.

Frank balled himself up and inched a little closer to Bill—Bill had heard Loco once and doubtless would wake again if anything else happened. All the same, he counted two thousand, four hundred and eleven sheep before he slept again.

Frank woke with the dawn. He was stiff and cold but alive. He decided he wasn't going to spend another night camped with Loco, though. He looked around for Bill to tell him so and saw him coming out of the woods, rubbing his mouth with the back of his hand.

"I'm ready to move on," Frank said.

Bill gave him that crooked grin. "Reckoned you might be."

Frank picked up his bindle and then set it down again. Suspicious, he untied it and saw only his matches and coffee. There had been another can of beans in it the night before. He looked slowly at Bill and caught something in his eyes. Bill opened his pocketknife and began trimming a ragged fingernail. It wasn't a pretended nonchalance so much as it was a closing down of all communication.

Frank slowly retied his bindle and started for the woods. The two hoboes from the tent were up and making their own fire. The larger glared at Frank as he passed them, and the other, kneeling over the fire, turned his face away. Something about the shape of the little man's neck and chin caught Frank's eyes, and when he passed the tent, he turned and looked back, whether they liked it or not. He was almost certain the smaller hobo was a woman. No wonder they kept to themselves. *I won't hurt you,* he wanted to say, but it wouldn't allay their fears. And rightly so. What was it Bill had said? *If you're going to go on the bum, you got to learn that nobody's your pal.*

Bill had claimed to be Frank's pal, but he suspected that Bill had stolen the can of beans from his sack. Frank went on into the woods in the direction from which Bill had come. He stood urinating and looking across the withered leaves and dead grass that covered the ground under bare trees. Something stuck up and winked back at him in the slanted sun. Frank buttoned his pants and went to stand over it. It was the lid to the can of beans. Frank poked around with the toe of his boot and found the can, too, hastily hidden in a mound of leaves.

I would have shared it if he'd asked me, he thought, feeling angry and betrayed. The thief hadn't been Loco or Ed or Preacher John—not with Bill sleeping so lightly next to him. He knew it was Bill. His first impulse was to take the can back to camp and say so. But something about Bill's expression when he had seen Frank find the can missing made him reluctant.

He kept Loco away from me, Frank rationalized, looking for reasons to forgive his friend. *If you're going to go on the bum, you got to learn that nobody's your pal.* Bill knew how to find work, although Frank had done the bulk of it. Bill was wise in the ways of the hobo world and could read the signs on gates. He had been hungry.

But I would have shared it with him.

Frank was hungry, too, but it seemed useless to spit accusations. He scooped out a little hole in the leaves, put the can in it, and covered it back up again. He had a little money left, enough to buy them breakfast until they could hop a freight and find work.

When he went back to the camp, Bill was boiling water for the coffee that Frank carried in his bindle. He looked up at Frank, his face expressionless. Gradually he relaxed a little, probably because he realized that Frank wasn't going to say anything about the beans.

Frank thought again of the stray dog. The family had kept it and fed it well; but it had always eaten anything it could find—including birdseed spilled from the feeder or berries off the pyracantha bush. It never came to understand that it was no longer starving.

VI

San Francisco, February 1896

Tim Holt stood with his hands in his trouser pockets and stared out the third-floor city-room window onto Kearny Street. "I don't know where the hell else to look for Frank," he said to Hugo Ware and Raphael Murray. They were perched behind him in silent sympathy on Hugo's desk. "My aunt seems to think I have miraculous powers of divination."

"We've all had our ears out," Rafe Murray said. "We're good, mind you, but we're not the Pinkertons."

"His old man's a *spy*, for heaven's sake," Hugo said. "*He* ought to be able to manage it."

"Shhh! We don't use that word in the family," Tim said. "And in any case, except for a smoking telegram to my brother Mike blaming him for the whole mess, Uncle Henry doesn't seem inclined to chase after Frank. It's my aunt Cindy who's determined to find her baby."

"You don't sound overly sympathetic," Rafe commented, "to the plight of the poor lost lamb."

"The poor lost lamb is nearly as big as I am," Tim said, "and he was boxing champion of his military academy last year. If my uncle wasn't an immortal idiot, he'd know not to march around roaring ultimatums if he doesn't expect the kid to call him on them."

"Mr. Holt!" Tim saw a copyboy galloping across the city room with an envelope. "This just came for you, Mr. Holt!" The boy's eyes gleamed in anticipation.

"Thanks, Clyde, but I don't think it's earthshaking news. It's from my brother." He unfolded the sheet.

FRANK NOT HERE STOP NO WORD EITHER STOP YOU TELL
UNCLE HENRY STOP I HAVEN'T THE NERVE TO   MIKE

"Aw," Clyde said, "I was hoping we was at war with Spain."

"That'll come on the AP wire, you ninny," Rafe said. "If you want excitement, you can come with me to the hanging and run the story back. Big John Gianetti's supposed to pay his debt to society today—assuming the police haven't been paid off or that crazy woman of his doesn't try to bust him loose. And this election's got the telephone system so overloaded it's about ready to fry itself. I couldn't get through to the city room at all this morning."

"That's because you were drunk and asleep in the pressroom," Stu Aggrams, the city editor, said without looking up from two desks away.

"Untrue!" Rafe said.

"The telephones are screwy," Hugo confirmed. "I tried them, too." They both knew Stu didn't mean it. Rafe drank like a fish, but he never missed a story. It was claimed by the young and worshipful copyboys that he wrote better drunk than sober.

"Well, get over there and take Clyde with you, then," Stu said. "Try not to get shot if Crazy Kate comes after her darling. I haven't got enough reporters to go around today as it is. Ware, what the hell are you still doing here?"

"On my way," Hugo said, picking up his hat. In Stu's eyes a chat with the newspaper's owner was no excuse for not being on the street.

"Kate can't aim anyway," Rafe said, putting on his own hat. "Last time she hit a judge. In the next room."

"What else do you need, Stu?" Tim asked. "I can give you part of my afternoon." Tim knew he could go back to his office and be the boss and worry about bumping into Rosebay while Hugo wasn't there, or he could be out on the street pretending he was Rafe—a carefree man with nothing but hangings on his mind.

"Seeing as you're bored," Stu said, "I need some color on the mayoral election."

"That's what comes of putting up reform candidates," Tim said. "No color." But he decided to go anyway. Rosebay couldn't seem to understand that it wasn't an insult that he avoided her. She had cornered him that morning, already riled over his failure to court the latest nice girl she had dug up for him.

"I just don't understand you, Tim Holt." She had trapped him in his office even before he had been able to down his morning coffee while reading the first-edition proof pages. "You acted just like she had leprosy. She's a *nice* girl."

"I didn't do anything to her," Tim protested.

"Then why did she act like I'd set her down next to Frankenstein's monster when I went to ask her afterward how she liked you?"

Tim threw up his hands.

Rosebay folded her arms. "I don't know what you're doing, but you scare them to death. You ought to talk to Hugo or Rafe about how to court a girl."

"I don't *want* to court a girl!" Tim discovered that he was yelling. "And Rafe mostly courts them horizontal. I gather these specimens of yours are too pure for that approach."

"Tim Holt!"

"Rosebay, why do you keep shoving these women at me? How can you be so thick? You know it hurts just to look at you every day and know I can't have you."

Rosebay's eyes filled with tears and slowly brimmed over. She was the only woman he knew who was beautiful when she cried. "I can't stand it, either, and I'm scared to death I'll do something bad. And—"

"And you want me safely married, is that it?" Tim shook his head in exasperation. "And you think that'll make me safe? Or you, either? You've got rocks in your head."

"At least I'm trying to find a way," Rosebay said. "At least I ain't running away from my problems."

"Hah! You said 'ain't.' You don't ever do that unless you're practically hysterical."

"I am not hysterical," Rosebay said with dignity. "And I'll say ain't if I got a mind to."

Tim folded up the proofs that he had been trying unsuccessfully to read. "I am not running from my problems. But given the nature of our situation, it doesn't strike me as the best notion to snuggle up too close to it all the time, either." He gave her a long look, letting his hunger for her sit plainly on his face, just to be sure she got the point. He saw with satisfaction that she flinched.

Rosebay took a step backward. "I don't know what's got into you."

"Yes, you do." He wouldn't take his eyes off hers. Finally she backed through the door.

Tim went back to his proof pages. Five minutes later the telephone rang at his elbow.

"Holt here."

"You're coming to us for dinner tomorrow anyway," Rosebay's voice said. "And don't give me any excuses because I won't listen to them." She hung up before he could argue.

All of which had a great deal to do with his decision now to hide out in the precinct houses, entirely male citadels. He rang the bell for the elevator, and the brass doors slid open.

"Street, Jim."

The elevator boy pulled the handle, and the car slowly descended. The trouble with Rosebay, Tim thought, was that she had an irritating urge to put everything, people included, in a proper place. She seemed oblivious to the fact that putting people in the right compartment didn't necessarily make them stay there. They pulled themselves loose with distressing regularity and ran away with the iceman or shipped out on a whaler for Newfoundland. Tim had been a newspaperman long enough to know that.

The elevator boy stopped the car. "Ground floor, Mr. Holt. You going to vote for Jimmy Phelan?"

"I reckon," Tim said.

The *Clarion* had endorsed him. But despite the reforms achieved over the past two years by Adolph Sutro and the promise of further progress under Phelan,

Tim harbored a sneaking yearning for the bad old days of Blind Chris Buckley, whose political machine made up in flamboyance and graft what it lacked in moral fiber. There had been an endearing wickedness to the Buckley days that spoke of the city's youth and exuberance. Maybe it was Tim's reaction to Rosebay and her determination to see him married, but everything seemed to have grown too respectable lately. He sauntered down Kearny Street and passed a doorway advertising Mme. Gounod, Celestial Phrenology, and was somewhat cheered.

At Phelan's headquarters he found the usual blue atmosphere of cigar smoke and triumphant profanity—Phelan was clearly winning.

"Holt!" Someone recognized him and waved a hand. "You voted yet?"

"On my way to," Tim replied. "Suppose you boys tell me for the record what a vote for Jimmy Phelan's going to get me—besides lower gas rates and all the other nonsense you've been promising the public."

One of Phelan's politicos chuckled and offered Tim a cigar. "We're going to throw the rascals out, is what."

Tim raised his eyebrows and sniffed the cigar. "Which rascals? The ones who bribe the press with Cuban cigars?"

"Hell, if one cigar'll buy you, Holt, then you're a bargain. No, I mean unreachable rascals. The ones that have been burrowed like mites into the body politic. We're going to convey upon His Incipient Honor the power to appoint and/or remove the police commission and the board of health and other such octopi as may be in need of trimming."

"That'll take a new charter," Tim pointed out.

"Yep. And James Duval Phelan's the man to get it through. He has the workingman's rights at heart."

"And how does James Duval Phelan feel about the workingwoman's rights?" a feminine voice inquired. Tim recognized Virginia Barstow of the *Bulletin*.

The campaign worker laughed and clapped her on the back, not too gently. "When the workingwoman can vote for him, Jimmy'll care a lot. Have a cigar—all the boys have one." He thrust it into her hand and went off chortling.

Miss Barstow stood looking at it for a moment and then presented the cigar to Tim. "I don't smoke," she commented.

"Don't take it to heart," Tim said, embarrassed. "They're all just full of high spirits today."

Miss Barstow gave him a thin smile. "Boys will be boys, of course. Even when they're fifty."

Tim ducked out before she could get down on him, too. His track record with women didn't seem to be getting any better. He thought he would go vote for Jimmy and see if there were any good fights at the polling station. Election Day could usually be counted on for at least a dozen nitwits to settle their political differences with empty bottles and jackknives. Half the male population of the city got drunk on the free beer dispensed at victory parties and the torchlight parades that always enlivened election night.

A beer wagon rumbled down Kearny Street, bringing more fuel for the celebration that was just cranking up in Phelan's headquarters. Fireworks went off under Tim's feet, and a horn blew in his ear. As dusk fell, Kearny Street was ablaze with torchlight and noisier than the Fourth of July. Anyone who wasn't too drunk watched the bulletin boards outside the neighborhood's saloons, where the tallies from each precinct were posted. Loud cheers went up at every new count, drowning out even the peddlers who made their livelihood hawking therapeutic shoes and rheumatism bracelets.

The street was choked with celebrants on foot and horseback, while others were hanging out of buggies, sulkies, and hacks. A cable car insistently butted its way through the crowd, and the mob in the street parted and swirled around it like water, then, in a high-spirited mood, pulled hapless passengers off the rear steps.

"Think of woman—lovely, defenseless woman—in the midst of this!" opponents of female suffrage had exclaimed two years before when the matter had come up for a vote in California. The measure had lost.

Tim had to admit as he wriggled his way through the melee toward his home precinct that he wouldn't much like to have his mother or sisters caught in this crowd. With all that beer running freely, though, Tim decided he wouldn't mind having a drink himself, to numb the image of Rosebay that lay just beneath his eyelids. He veered toward a saloon doorway from which the faint notes of a ragtime piano floated above the firecrackers.

When he got to the door, he stopped. It was accepted wisdom in the newspaper game that reporters drank; but lately Tim had begun to keep track of *why* he drank and had discovered that it was a form of anesthesia. That realization made him nervous. So far as he had been able to discover, men like Rafe Murray had no particular reason to drink other than a love of liquor. They would either burn themselves up with it in a fine flame or quit when they got old enough for their bodies to complain. But Tim found himself using whiskey to blot things out, and he wondered how long it might take him until that was habitual, until he grew so unhappy that life itself would require deadening. Disgusted, he swerved away from the saloon.

He went on up the sidewalk and stood bemused before a medicine show on a corner of Market and Kearny streets. Above red, white, and blue bunting loomed a monstrous sign:

WONDERFUL DISCOVERY

Are You Suffering from Neuralgia? Are You Afflicted with Dyspepsia? Is Your Liver Torpid? Is Your Blood Impure? Are Your Hands and Feet Cold? Have Bad Habits Injured Your Health? If So, Then Try

RICHARDSON'S MAGNETO-GALVANIC BATTERY!

Tim wondered if the battery, guaranteed to infuse electricity into the system of man, woman, or child, could cure a broken heart. The sign bore the image of a stern-faced young woman wearing the battery directly over hers, so perhaps it might. Electricity was the latest thing—a cure-all born of the public's fascination with electric lights and motors—providing the public with gadgets that seemed to run on magic. If this force could light a lamp, it might just as effectively cure a liver. In the last twenty years every fly-by-night operator in the country had developed electric belts, electric socks, electric corsets, and any other item of apparel that might draw a profit from a gullible consumer. None of the garments was electrified in the least, which was just as well.

Tim turned up Market Street to cast his vote in the political medicine show. He reflected that politics fed on many of the same urges that prompted people to buy electric socks. There was a police wagon outside the polling place, so he quickened his steps, glad to abandon philosophy in the hope of mayhem and good copy.

"What's up?"

The driver of the wagon yawned. "Some loony thinks she can vote."

Tim raised his eyebrows. "Quiet night?" he inquired sarcastically. He ducked into the polling place and, grinning, pushed his hat back on his head. A woman who might have been in her twenties and might have been handsome if she hadn't been so obstinate looking, was glaring at an outraged precinct worker and a befuddled police sergeant.

"Go ahead," she urged. "Arrest me for the crime of wanting to vote. I dare you!"

"Lady," the cop said with elaborate patience, "if you'll just go home peaceably, we won't have to do anything like that."

"I have no intention of going anywhere," she said, "until this man allows me my rights as a citizen of the United States." She pointed a finger at the precinct worker, who leaned forward, fuming.

"You're a female. Females don't vote."

"Now why do you suppose that is?" Tim drawled, standing in the doorway. He was enjoying himself immensely. He couldn't have asked for better "color."

"Because women don't know enough," the precinct worker answered. "Because they got men to do the voting for them." He glared, pop-eyed, at the woman, an alien invader of his dominion. "Because it ain't natural."

A drunk fell through the door with perfect timing. "Of course," Tim said. "With stout fellows like this one, the ladies can rest assured that they can leave the voting to men."

A general chuckle went round, but no one except Tim seemed inclined to take up the woman's part. The room was stuffy with cigar smoke and the warmth of human bodies, all male except for the intruder. The voters and precinct workers alike seemed uneasy with her presence.

"Get her out of here," the precinct worker told the sergeant.

"Come on, miss. Let's just leave, all right? You don't belong here. Things get rough downtown election night."

"Not as rough as they're going to get if women are not accorded their rights. I'm not leaving."

The sergeant looked unhappy. "Lady, I don't want to have to drag you out of here."

Tim decided he didn't blame the sergeant. The man would be a laughingstock. The woman wasn't small—she was nearly as tall as Tim—but she was only half the sergeant's size if you counted width. She had brown hair pinned under an elegant black felt hat, with a curling black feather that dipped rakishly to frame her chin. Her walking suit was elegant but cut in a style that did not require tight corseting, and hemmed to reach no lower than her ankles—dress reform with style. She had a straight nose and arching, dark brows. Her oval face tapered to a determined chin. Tim thought she might be his own age, on the late end of her twenties. She gave the sergeant an icy glare and an ultimatum: "Arrest me, or let me vote."

"Lady, *I* can't let you vote," the sergeant said with exasperation.

"Arrest her!" the precinct worker demanded. "Now!"

"Hell, yes!" one of the voters said, chuckling. "Come on now, Sergeant, she done *asked* you to."

They crowded around her now, eager for her to be

humiliated or for some retribution for her stepping out of place. To them, the voting booth was both a private club and a refuge. Tim could almost feel a kind of vicious hunger emanating from the men. It came on suddenly, but he knew that some of them would go home and hit their wives. He stepped forward, feeling almost protective.

"I'm Tim Holt, of the *Clarion*. Why don't you come on out with me, and we'll talk."

"I am not going to be lured away like a child," she informed him, "promised a sack of peppermints or a new doll."

"I wasn't trying to," Tim said. "Don't be so touchy."

"Well, what are you trying to do?"

"Interview you. What's your name?"

"Elizabeth Emory," she said. "Interview me in jail. It will make a much better story."

"You ever been in jail?" Tim demanded.

"Get her *out* of here!" The precinct worker hit the limits of his temper. Voters were lining up, but nobody was voting. In a few minutes everything would be so confused that the precinct's final tally would be suspect. "Get her out *now!*" he shouted at the sergeant.

"Come on, miss." The sergeant put his arm under Miss Emory's and propelled her toward the door.

"Let her come with me," Tim said.

"No!" She dropped to her knees suddenly, nearly toppling the sergeant with her.

"Get up, lady!"

"I have a right to vote. I will not leave voluntarily."

"Oh, goddamn it." The sergeant got his arms under hers and hefted her to her feet. "Riley!"

The driver from the police wagon came to the door.

"Help me, damn it." Together they managed to dodge the drunk and drag Miss Emory, her black kid boots trailing on the sidewalk, to the wagon. A crowd had gathered outside and offered helpful advice.

"Lock her up!"

"Marry her off!"

"I know what *she* needs!"

Tim caught a glimpse of her tight, furious face as Riley

pulled open the door of the wagon and the sergeant shoved her through. The sergeant slammed the door, then locked it and climbed up on the seat with Riley.

Tim followed as the wagon lumbered into the street, inching through the crowds. Elizabeth Emory was the best story that had happened that day—knife fights were a dime a dozen. Besides, he didn't quite trust the police. If that sergeant was riled enough, he was likely to pick up a drunk or two and shove them in the wagon with her.

Tim, easily keeping pace, followed along on the sidewalk where they could see him. At last the wagon drew up outside the police station. The men let Miss Emory out and, under Tim's observant eye, marched her without undue force up the steps.

"Mr. Holt. Still with us, I see." She gave him a disdainful glance.

"Why do you do this to yourself?" Tim inquired. He knew that the vulgar remarks shouted at her in the street had stung. He could see it in the tightness of her mouth.

"I'm going to book her, buddy," the sergeant said. "Scram."

"I wish to make a telephone call," she said.

"Later. When we get through the paperwork. You asked for this."

There was a bench in the lobby of the police station, and Tim sat down on it to wait. The police were going to put her through the whole booking process to rub her nose in it, and there wasn't any way he could stop them. He didn't feel much inclined to anyway. She *had* demanded it. If she spent a few hours in a cell with some drunken floozy from the Battery, no one could say she didn't have the courage of her convictions.

He watched as another wagonload of election-night celebrants arrived, drunk and flailing and throwing up. A man with his cheek slit open stood weaving, the blood falling in soft plops on the floor. No one seemed to notice. Lawmen, beefy in their uniforms, milled through the station while the booking officer, behind a high counter, laboriously entered the names of the wicked in a large book.

Elizabeth Emory had vanished. Tim decided they must be through with her by now. He was about to slip the lieutenant in charge a five spot for an interview with her when a tall, dapper man with the patient air of a scholar entered the station. He waited for a lull in the roar of activity, then said to the booking officer, "I am here to post bail for my daughter."

Tim pricked up his ears and got off his bench. "Mr. Emory?"

"Dr. Sidney Emory." He raised his brows in inquiry.

"Timothy Holt, the *Clarion*. I'd like to interview your daughter, sir, with your permission."

Emory laughed. "Elizabeth doesn't need my permission. And I rather expect that's the purpose of this escapade."

Tim blinked. "Then her protest had your approval?"

Emory presented a hundred and fifty dollars in crisp bills to a sergeant. "I wouldn't say approval exactly," he murmured.

Elizabeth appeared in a moment, disheveled but with dignity. "Still with us, Mr. Holt, I see."

"He wishes to interview you," Mr. Emory said. "This was extremely expensive, my dear. I trust you intend to pay your own fine."

Certainly this was not the demeanor Tim would have expected from a father called from his dinner table to bail a daughter out of jail. He stared at Emory. "Did you know your daughter was intending this, sir?"

"Let us get one thing straight, Mr. Holt," Elizabeth Emory said icily. "If you wish to interview me, you will interview *me*—not my father, who is not my keeper, nor more intelligent nor rational than I simply by virtue of his being male. Do we understand each other?"

"Perfectly," Tim said. "Why did you do it?"

"Aggravation, Mr. Holt," Elizabeth Emory said. "And sheer frustration. The women's rights movement has gone nowhere during the last two years. In 1894 we had a chance to adopt woman suffrage in California, but it was voted down. The momentum of the movement has come to a screeching halt. And that is women's fault for growing too comfortable. We have won *some* rights, but we will never be free until we have the vote. I felt the need to dramatize that fact."

"By trying to vote illegally." Tim was scribbling in his notebook.

"There is no other way for women to vote. And vote we must, or we remain slaves. My action was an attempt to stir some life into a movement that has grown complacent. Otherwise, the men have won. They have handed us a few small toys and chuckled in their beards when we were content to play with them."

Tim grinned. "Tell me more." Miss Emory was excellent copy.

Elizabeth looked at him haughtily, as if unsure whether he was being sympathetic or patronizing. "It is almost a new century. If we don't wake up, Mr. Holt, we will find that we have been stuffed like a taxidermist's sample and set decoratively in the parlor, permanently smiling."

Tim wrote it all down. Dr. Emory seemed prepared to wait. Tim envisioned a hysterical mama at home, with smelling salts under her nose as she sank onto her couch. Maybe there was no mother. That might account for Miss Emory's unconventionality.

"Miss Emory, wouldn't you like to go somewhere a little less, er, noisy?" That was a euphemism for the drunks rollicking through the door. They were far gone, and it was hard to decide whether their language was more shocking than their odor.

"I am quite all right, thank you. Since the male political machine has seen fit to drag me here, then here I shall stay."

"I posted your bail," her father remarked. "I trust you aren't planning to take up residence in the corridor."

The lobby doors opened again, letting in the bang and flash of fireworks. Rafe Murray appeared, with his hat on the back of his head and one black curl drooping between his eyebrows. He skidded to a stop when he saw Tim's companions.

"Evening, Dr. Emory. Out slumming? Or are you studying the social condition of the city on election night?"

"On the contrary," Sidney Emory said genially, shaking Rafe's hand. "This is Elizabeth's adventure."

Rafe tipped his hat. "Didn't see you, Elizabeth. That's a fetching dress." He crinkled his eyes at Tim in a grin and disappeared down the hall toward the press room.

Tim waited for Elizabeth Emory to explode, but she didn't. He scratched his head, puzzled. Rafe seemed well acquainted with the Emorys, odd enough in itself since Rafe mainly was acquainted with people the police were looking for. And the phlegmatic calm with which Dr. Emory received the arrest and jailing of his daughter argued a domestic arrangement beyond Tim's ken.

"Tell me more about your views on woman suffrage," he suggested.

"I'm for it," Elizabeth snapped. "If you want to discuss the movement further, I will do so after I have seen what your newspaper prints about me tomorrow. I have learned not to give too much ammunition to male journalists who wish only to ridicule us."

"Fair enough," Tim agreed. "Where can I reach you?"

Elizabeth unbent a little. "My card." She handed him a square of pasteboard from her small beaded bag. It bore an address on Van Ness.

Tim put it in his pocket and bowed. After he watched Sidney Emory escort his daughter down the steps of the police station and into a waiting carriage, he returned to the voting place to cast his ballot, as was his right. Then he strolled back toward the *Clarion* building, which was still ablaze with lights and would be all night. The *Clarion* was an evening paper, but it printed an extra the morning after every election day. Miss Emory was articulate and pretty, and she espoused a controversial issue. She was just the thing to boost circulation:

WINSOME POLITICAL REFORMER
ARRESTED ON ELECTION NIGHT

No election night in our fair city can be expected to pass without a full jail, but last night the San Francisco Police Department added to its haul a most unusual specimen: a respectable woman. She was a lady, in fact, of undisputed virtue. What was her crime? Attempting to vote in the mayoral election.

Miss Elizabeth Emory, a flashing-eyed, brown-haired beauty, maintained that women, or rather the women who espouse the cause of feminine rights, have grown too complacent, too comfortable and too grateful for the few reforms that we males have seen fit to grant them. Therefore, she set out last night to stir things up a bit at the downtown precinct. . . .

"Well, I never heard of such a thing!" Miss Lewis, the nice girl to whom Rosebay introduced him, shook her head. Blond curls bobbed as she spread her hands to indicate complete befuddlement. "I can't imagine being actually put in jail. It must have been the most horrible experience for her."

"Well, I believe she did exactly what she set out to do," Tim said.

"That's what I mean," Miss Lewis explained. "I don't understand how anyone—any *nice* girl—could be so, well, insensitive as to subject herself to that." She gazed earnestly around the rest of the people at the dinner table for assurance. "Mrs. Ware, would *you*—?"

"Certainly not," Rosebay said. "I think we've got a right to vote, but I wouldn't go downtown on election night, much less into that jail, for all the tea in China."

Tim noted that Rafe Murray, who boarded with Rosebay, was staying out of the discussion. He made a mental note to grill Rafe about the Emorys later. For the moment Tim studied his dinner partner. Emmeline

Lewis was undeniably pretty, with soft, honey-colored curls framing a heart-shaped face. She had light green eyes, a turned-up nose, and a full, pouty mouth. She smiled at Tim over her wineglass, from which she took a delicate sip.

"I enjoy the *Clarion* very much, Mr. Holt. It has such—such joie de vivre."

She wasn't a teetotaler, and she read the news. Tim let himself hope that maybe this introduction was going to develop into a relationship. Despite what he maintained to Rosebay, Tim wanted desperately to find some other woman to love. For a while he had gone to every party he was invited to, danced with debutantes, and allowed himself to be inspected by their mamas. But nothing ever worked out. He was both too intense and too uncertain a prospect, and the girls took to their heels like startled sheep.

"What do you enjoy most about our newspaper, Miss Lewis?" Tim asked, testing the waters.

"Well, of course I always read the national news."

Out of the corner of his eye, Tim saw Rosebay nodding approvingly. He wondered how much coaching she had done.

"One is so sympathetic to those poor souls in Cuba," Emmeline added.

"And do you favor our intervention, Miss Lewis?"

"I would leave that to the President, of course. I'm sure he knows best. But it does seem that we ought to be protecting people who are fighting for their freedom. This General Weyler from Spain is a brute. Of course the Spanish are all very haughty."

Tim flicked an eye at Rosebay, who beamed at him encouragingly. He wondered if Miss Lewis knew any Spaniards or was drawing her opinion from the popular characterizations of American theater and vaudeville. It didn't matter; she really wasn't any more shallow or less informed than most people. She was just making the best of a stilted conversation. She seemed to be trying to please him, which he knew must be a nuisance for her.

"What do you really like to do, Miss Lewis?" he whispered.

"Curl up in the sun and read novels," she whispered back, and then giggled, startled. "I must sound awfully lazy."

"Not at all." It was the most refreshing thing she had said yet, and it sounded unrehearsed.

Rosebay was serving apple cobbler, which sent a steamy, aromatic cloud of cooked apples and cinnamon over the table. "Emmeline made the dessert," she announced proudly.

"It smells wonderful," Tim said. He was beginning to feel as if his collar were strangling him. Hugo Ware and Rafe Murray were both studying him as if they had some kind of bet on the outcome. He glanced at Miss Lewis again, trying to make something work, and produced only a surge of physical desire to explore that slim-waisted, full-breasted body. She caught his eye and looked unnerved. *Oh, hell*.

After dinner he fled into Hugo's study, where Hugo and Rafe were already in residence. He left Miss Lewis in the parlor with Rosebay.

"You're supposed to be out there," Hugo said mildly. "Rosebay banished us to give you courting room."

"I'm not courting anybody," Tim said grumpily. Why couldn't he fall in love with Emmeline Lewis? he wondered. It should have been easy. He sat down in a chair by the fire and helped himself to Hugo's whiskey. "Tell me about the Emorys," he said to Rafe. "Sidney Emory seems an odd duck."

"With an odd duckling," Rafe said. "And another one at home, and a strange mama duck, too. I'll take you calling."

If I can get out of the house alive, Tim thought. He knew Rosebay was going to be lying in wait for him.

VII

An election always meant at least a week of chaos at the newspaper, both before and afterward. It was two weeks before Tim thought to hunt down Rafe Murray in his lair at the courthouse pressroom and request a further introduction to the Emorys.

"How do you come to know them anyway?"

"Sidney Emory's a noted writer on social reform," Rafe explained, taking Tim's elbow and steering him down the corridor. "You uneducated ignoramus."

"You being such a pillar of society," Tim murmured, "I didn't exactly envision your sitting at the feet of anybody who might want to reform *you*." He could smell whiskey on Rafe's breath.

"Social reform," Rafe said loftily. "Not my personal habits. He reads my stories, and I find his criticism useful." Rafe, an aspiring author, had sold several stories about San Francisco to magazines. "It's refreshing to converse with someone whose soul and literary vision are unhampered by the conventions of journalism—the need to pander to the desire for sensationalism and the maudlin appetites of the man in the street." He strode briskly along, waving his arms for emphasis.

Tim didn't argue. He lengthened his stride to keep pace. "You've had a snootful. Does Miss Emory let you call on her in this disgusting state?"

"I don't call on Miss Emory," Rafe said. "She finds me feckless."

"I find you feckless, too," Tim muttered. Rafe was, however, the best writer on the *Clarion* staff.

* * *

Rafe led Tim up a set of steps that rose imposingly past a stone retaining wall and between twin hedges of boxwood to a pale yellow clapboard house with a round turret at the corner. The wind off the bay caused a pennant at the turret's top to snap. Yellow crocuses were poking up in the flower beds below the porch. A well-used swing hung beside the front door.

Rafe thumped the knocker, which was hung just below a small pane of glass set into the door at eye level. Something erupted from the depths of the house—there were the scrambling of claws on hardwood and the thump of a body hurtling against the door.

Rafe flinched as an enormous yellow dog looked at them through the glass. "She always does that," he said to Tim. "But I never get used to it."

"Down, Alice!" Tim heard Elizabeth Emory's voice, and then the door opened. Miss Emory had Alice by the collar. Even on all fours the dog was impressive.

"Good afternoon," Tim said. He knelt and held out his hand to the dog. "How do you do, Alice?" Alice panted at him in a cloud of moist dog breath. Her tail thumped the floor, and she gave him her paw.

"As you can see, she's not dangerous," Elizabeth said. "She just likes visitors. If you don't look out, she'll—"

A huge tongue slurped across Tim's face, and Alice's nose sent his hat toppling off the back of his head.

"If you don't look out," Elizabeth said unnecessarily, "she'll lick you."

"I see." Tim retrieved his hat and stood up. "Did you find my account of your adventures in the voting booth sufficiently laudatory to allow me to come in?" he asked. "I'd like to know the next chapter."

"They haven't set a trial date," Elizabeth said. "I don't think they want to. Come into the parlor. I found your description of my physical appearance in your columns to be irrelevant, but other than that, it was fairly well balanced. Perhaps it was a trifle flip and fatuous, but I suppose it would be too much to ask to be taken seriously."

"I take you as seriously as I do anybody with a political cause," Tim commented.

"I'll keep that under consideration," Elizabeth said gravely.

Tim gave her a suspicious look. He thought *she* was making fun of *him*. She took them into the parlor, where the rest of the family had gathered, and introduced Tim. Rafe was obviously an old acquaintance.

Sidney Emory greeted them warmly, and Elizabeth's mother and sister said hello with polite curiosity. Mrs. Aurelia Emory was in her early sixties, a tall, elegant woman whose clothes reflected practicality as well as a sense of slightly unorthodox style. She had the most beautiful voice Tim had ever heard, low and vibrant and clear.

The sister, Madeleine Emory, possessed the undecided, coltish beauty of a girl in late adolescence. Tim guessed she was about eighteen.

There was, he learned, a son in between, who was a lawyer for the American Railway Union. Another young man, whom Tim mistook to be a son, proved instead to be another aspiring writer, Jack London from Oakland, across the bay. He and Rafe and Sidney Emory were soon wrapped up in a low-voiced argument concerning the necessity of a moral purpose in literature.

Tim and the Emory women discussed feminism. Occasional counterpoints from the literary debate interrupted when the men's voices rose to a sufficient level.

"The only solution to the inequities of marriage," Madeleine said, "is free love—a true partnership, rather than the legal bondage that woman is subject to presently."

"But what about the safeguards that marriage affords a woman?" Tim asked.

"Many wives have husbands who beat them or desert them," Elizabeth told him, "and yet they have extreme difficulty in obtaining a divorce from these men. Very few of these women feel very safeguarded."

"Have you ever been married?" Tim inquired.

"I have not. So far I have seen no advantage to that state."

Alarmed, Tim eyed Mrs. Emory. Most mothers of his acquaintance would have been writhing in horror if such sentiments issued from their daughters' lips.

"—absolute necessity for education to prepare our citizens for a life of service to one's fellow man!" Dr. Emory's voice intruded.

"But one's fellow man isn't always appreciative," London said, and Rafe chuckled. "There are other schools, too, Doctor."

Tim thought this family's school unorthodox enough. It was the most peculiar afternoon Tim had ever spent, but it seemed to be normal for the Emorys. "Do you ever worry," he asked Mrs. Emory, "that your daughters' upbringing in radical ideas will rob them of a chance at normal domestic happiness?"

Elizabeth sat bolt upright, eyes flashing, and Tim decided he hadn't phrased that very well.

"You must understand, Mr. Holt," Aurelia Emory said before her daughter could leap in, "that I myself married very late in life, and then not until I had found a man with whom I felt I could live in harmony. If my daughters do not marry until late, or do not marry at all, I shall be content so long as I know that they are happy in their chosen state."

"My sister didn't marry until she was nearly thirty," Tim said, hoping to smooth things over a bit. "She's a doctor." He glanced at Elizabeth. *Hah. Put that in your feminist pipe and smoke it.*

"I did not wait so long deliberately." Mrs. Emory smiled. "It was more a matter of its taking so long to find a very rare breed of man." She smiled affectionately across the parlor at her husband, still deep in his discussion. Alice had followed them in and was asleep on the hearth. She lay on her back, legs in the air, and London idly scratched her stomach while he talked. The room was warm and inviting but more like a very comfortable library than a parlor. Bookcases lined every wall, and books and magazines covered the tables, which were without the usual fashionable clutter of wax flowers and photograph frames and china shepherdesses.

"My children have all been brought up unconventionally," Mrs. Emory said gently. "I suppose we may all seem as odd as a tribe of monkeys to you."

"Not at all," Tim said gallantly while thinking that indeed they did. His father's household had been considered to be unconventional by some of their acquaintances on the grounds that Alexandra sometimes rode astride and Janessa had acquired a medical degree. But in comparison to the Emorys, the Holts were the soul of conformity.

He learned that Aurelia Emory, at fifteen, had helped to organize the first Woman's Rights Convention at Seneca Falls, New York, in 1848. Her husband had been raised a Quaker, in an abolitionist family. Their barn had been a stop on the Underground Railroad before the war. He was a noted freethinker and author of several books on social reform and the labor movement.

Their house appeared to be a kind of salon for progressive thinkers of all stripes, and the girls had grown up running tame among them. Eugene Debs, whose acquaintance Tim had made during the railway strike two years before, visited them, and so did Elizabeth Cady Stanton and Susan Anthony. Tim pictured Elizabeth, and then Madeleine, as young girls awake past their bedtime, sitting on the Turkish cushions that were piled on the floor and listening until the small hours of the morning to discussions about free love, free thought, socialism, feminism, and populism, with avantgarde art and literary theory thrown in. They had probably been weaned on arguments that flamed with the intensity that reformers could produce, civil but impassioned. No wonder the daughters weren't conventional. But they were marvelous copy. Tim had been writing down their conversation, pencil flying in his own personal shorthand.

"So you are in legal limbo?" he asked Elizabeth. "A criminal with no trial date?"

"They don't seem to find me dangerous enough to

hurry with," Elizabeth said with a half smile. "So I suppose I shall have to hurry *them*."

"You *want* to go to trial?"

"Of course. What do you think I did it for?"

"Publicity," Tim answered promptly. "But you already got that."

Elizabeth was curled in an overstuffed chair. She put her chin on her hand and smiled at him sweetly. "I want more."

"I was planning to publish a second interview," Tim said. "But since you're so blatant about it, it's a little embarrassing."

"All the male politicians are blatant about it, and you interview them every time they call a press conference," Elizabeth said not so sweetly.

Madeleine cocked her head at him. "Are you saying that only men are allowed to be straightforward?"

"Not at all," Tim said. "You're a menace. How old are you?"

"Eighteen."

"Maddy's decided to skip girlishness and go straight to her forties," Rafe said over his shoulder. Madeleine didn't retort. Apparently Rafe was exempt.

"California voted down woman suffrage two years ago," Tim said. "How long do you think it will be before you can get it on the ballot again?"

"Did you vote for it, Mr. Holt?" Maddy asked.

"My personal opinions are irrelevant to this interview." He wasn't going to butter up the little devil.

"They aren't irrelevant to me," Maddy told him.

"I'm not interviewing you." Tim grinned at her. "If *you* want to be interviewed, go get arrested."

"The Sixteenth Amendment is designed to eliminate the necessity of fighting this battle state by state," Elizabeth said.

"The Anthony Amendment?" Tim asked. "Even if you could get it through, it would still have to be ratified state by state." And so far the amendment's supporters had been able to get it out of committee only one time, and then it had died on the Senate floor. "My father's a senator. I'm afraid he doesn't give the Anthony Amendment much chance. Not from personal conviction, mind you," he added hastily. "I believe he would vote for it. But he says sentiment in the Senate is very much against it."

Maddy's eyes blazed. "That's because the Senate is comprised of men."

"They are still the legislative body of this country," Tim said. "If you want to change a law, you'll have to deal with them. Or vote them out."

He realized as soon as he had said it that that was an idiotic remark. Maddy glared at him, and Elizabeth gave him a pitying look.

"We can't vote, Mr. Holt," Mrs. Emory reminded. "Which does make things difficult."

"We are subject to laws we have had no say in," Elizabeth said as if she were explaining a basic principle to a moron. "And for redress we are forced to go to the men who have made those laws in the first place and convince *them* to allow us into what has hitherto been their private club."

"Some of them are afraid that if they give you ladies the vote, you'll make liquor illegal," Tim said. "Would you care to comment on that issue?"

"A great deal of poverty would be eliminated in this country if husbands did not have the option of drinking away their pay in the corner saloon," Elizabeth remarked. "And then returning home to beat their wives because there is no money left."

"A great deal of drinking would be eliminated if we saw to it that every man could earn a decent wage and didn't need to anesthetize himself to face the bleakness of his life," Tim retorted.

"And what about his wife," Elizabeth demanded, "while we are making the country comfortable for men? *She* does her work without the 'anesthesia' you speak of."

"You ever take a nip of old Lydia Pinkham?" Tim inquired. "That 'home remedy' is about forty proof. Plenty of fine, upstanding housewives stay soused on one kind of snake oil or another."

"If they resort to tonics it is because their lives are otherwise unbearable."

"And what did I just say about men and saloons?" Tim pressed.

"The women are unaware of the amount of alcohol in those potions, I assure you."

"So it's fine and dandy to be a drunk if it's not on purpose? Miss Emory, you are losing ground here, and you know it."

Elizabeth looked at him thoughtfully. "I will give you Lydia Pinkham, Mr. Holt. But very few women who drink abuse their husbands as a result. It is not alcohol that I am against so much as it is the behavior that it produces in men—violent behavior that is almost always directed at some woman."

"Very well, and I will grant you that point. But the morals of it aside, most men aren't going to want to give the vote to a group of women who outnumber them and who are likely to cork their bottle for them as a first move."

"The women's rights movement has its origins in the temperance movement," Mrs. Emory explained. "In fact, the males within the movement were reluctant to allow women delegates an equal place. That attitude angered many women enough to strike out on their own. But still it is very difficult to disassociate suffrage from temperance entirely, when so many women believe in the cause so strongly. As Elizabeth has said, their conviction is less a matter of morals than of personal safety. A drunken man is a terrifying enemy to most women."

Elizabeth peered at his notes. "Perhaps you could include that I take a glass of wine with my dinner, Mr. Holt, and am not planning to board up the saloons. We are freethinkers. We do not seek to ban any behavior that does no harm to other people."

"That's not a sentiment shared by all women in the movement," Tim said.

"Of course not. We aren't identical reproductions of

one another. We are individuals. What we share is a determination to order our own fate."

Tim certainly found these three women capable of it, and their home had a warmth and a freedom that was inviting. They seemed to encourage their guests to be as they were—not as social convention decreed that they should behave. He folded his notebook and stood up. "I'm grateful for your time. I'll probably run this the day after tomorrow. If we get a lot of letters on it, I may want to do a couple more interviews, to let you respond to the letters, that sort of thing."

"I shall attempt to be controversial enough to hold your readers' interest," Elizabeth said. Her eyes glinted with a faint sheen of steel.

"I don't espouse causes; I print the news," Tim said, unrepentant. "But I did vote for woman suffrage two years ago."

At the end of the week, as Tim approached the Emorys' gate again, he felt dubious about how much that vote was going to be worth now in Elizabeth's eyes. The gate was splattered with eggs, and someone had scrawled "Ha-Ha" across the top. He knew that the *Clarion* interview was responsible for the vandalism. Tim had received forty letters. A few were approving; some were disapproving but reasonable; others were vicious: frothing and hysterical, invoking God's judgment and declaring the Emorys a nest of unnatural females and Sidney Emory an anarchist.

Tim knocked with some trepidation at the door. It was answered again by Elizabeth, in a voluminous canvas apron and shirtwaist sleeves rolled up.

"Is it safe to come in?" Tim asked sheepishly.

"Certainly," Elizabeth said. "You're just in time. I'm going to scrub the front gate."

Tim noted the bucket of soapy water and brushes on the porch and picked them up. "Let me do it. Please. I feel responsible."

"You quoted me quite accurately," Elizabeth said good-naturedly, "but you can help anyway. The gate's no trouble, but Alice is a two-man job. She went out to bark at them, and they got egg in her coat."

"Where is she?"

"Out back, tied to a tree. She hates to be bathed. I can't so much as fill a scrub bucket without tying her up. Otherwise, she vanishes for the rest of the day."

"Can't say I blame her," Tim said. It was cloudy, and the air moved with the uncertain jumpiness of early spring.

"I'm sorry about this," he added as they tackled the gate.

Elizabeth's face suddenly took on a bleak expression, and she turned away from him. "It's not important."

"You look as if it's important," he said gently. "You don't deserve eggs on the gate for your political opinions."

"A great many people don't deserve the things that happen to them," Elizabeth said tightly. "It's just that it's depressing sometimes, being a pariah."

"Worth it, though, do you think?" Tim asked. He gave the gate a final swipe with the brush.

"Certainly," Elizabeth said. She shook soapsuds off her hands, put them on her hips, and studied him. "Am I bullying you into helping me wash the dog because you're feeling guilty?"

"Of course not," Tim said. He refused to feel guilty either for printing her interview, which she had asked for herself, or for being male. His gender did not make him the equivalent of those egg-throwing idiots. He couldn't say he much wanted to wash a dog, though.

Tim and Elizabeth carried a tin washtub from the basement and two cans of hot water from the kitchen boiler. They filled the tub with cold water from the pump and added the hot. They found Alice still tied to her tree, mournfully awaiting her fate.

Elizabeth loosened the rope and pointed at the tub. "Get in, Alice." The dog didn't budge. "Miserable animal." Elizabeth got her arms around Alice's barrel-shaped chest, and Tim hefted the dog's back end. They managed to tip her into the tub, where she stood, ears drooping, looking like some hapless French aristocrat in a tumbril on the way to the guillotine.

Tim shed his jacket and donned the apron Elizabeth provided. He felt that he looked vaguely like someone's butler, and he didn't think the apron was going to provide much protection. Elizabeth used a tin cup to dip warm water from the tub. She poured the water over Alice while Tim ruffled the dog's coat backward so that it would get down to the skin. Alice moaned in misery, making a sound like a faraway freight.

"I told you to stay away from those hooligans," Elizabeth chided. "You're lucky they didn't throw rocks. What do you think you are, a Doberman pinscher?"

Alice moaned again, and her ears drooped sideways.

"What *is* she anyway?" Tim asked, rubbing a bar of laundry soap into her dripping tail.

"Labrador retriever mostly," Elizabeth replied. "With maybe some mastiff." Alice was bulkier and bigger than most labs, but her temperament had plainly bypassed the fiercer mastiff. Soaking wet, she looked so miserable that Tim and Elizabeth both started to laugh. Alice pricked up her ears. Her tongue lolled out, and as they loosened their grip, she gathered herself together, bunching her shoulder muscles.

"Oh, no!" Elizabeth shouted. "No, Alice. Don't do it!"

When Alice waved her dripping tail, Tim and Elizabeth stopped trying to dissuade her and started to run.

Alice shook. She put her back into it, and a spray of dog-scented soapy water whirled around her. She vibrated like an electric motor, and when she was done she looked around and saw that no one was within grabbing distance. Unrestrained, she hopped out of the tub.

"Come back here!" Elizabeth gave chase. Alice lolloped around the backyard and cavorted in the flower beds, every now and then pausing to shake. Elizabeth, apron strings flapping, her hair coming out of its knot, ran after her. "Alice!"

Tim decided that chivalry was probably in order. He circled, and when Alice came prancing around a cypress tree, he grabbed her. She was collarless and slippery, and Tim's hands slid along her back. He gave up all hope of staying dry and wrapped his arms around her. They toppled over together.

Tim found himself on his back in the flower bed, clutching a dripping dog to his chest. Alice slurped her tongue affectionately across his face.

Elizabeth, holding her sides, came panting up to them. She looked at Tim with horror. "Mr. Holt! I'm dreadfully sorry, I—oh, Alice! You terrible dog! Get up this minute!"

Alice smiled unrepentantly and shook again for good measure. Tim still had hold of her front paws. He let his head loll back in the zinnias. "That's a strenuous dog."

Elizabeth seized Alice by the scruff of the neck and heaved her off Tim. "Mr. Holt, I'm mortified. Please get up and let me do something about your clothes."

Tim propped himself up on his elbows. "Let's finish the dog first." He stood up and inspected the muddy tracks down the front of his apron and the parts of his shirtfront that the apron didn't protect. He suspected that his backside looked much the same.

Elizabeth groaned. She still had Alice by the scruff of the neck and one ear. "I am horribly sorry. Your nice trousers."

"They can be cleaned," Tim soothed. It dawned on him that she was embarrassed, and he was not inclined to let loose of that advantage. "If you think you can hold that feckless animal, I'll go get a bucket of rinse water."

When he came back from the pump, Elizabeth had managed to get Alice in the tub again. Alice had the sheepish look of a dog that has been scolded. She hung her head when she saw Tim.

"It's all right, Alice. You can't help being a pea brain."

"True, but at least her heart's in the right place," Elizabeth said, holding the dog's head while Tim poured rinse water over it. "She's very fond of children and cats."

"I'm sure she'd rescue either one from a burning building," Tim said, "if she didn't get confused and carry it back inside by mistake."

Elizabeth chuckled. Her laugh was low and musical like her mother's. It was the first time Tim had heard her laugh. Alice hung her head lower. "She knows we're making fun of her."

"She owes us the entertainment," Tim said. He poured the final bucket of rinse water over her. "Ready? Okay, one . . . two . . . three!" They let go of Alice and fled. They were barely out of range when flying spray erupted from the tub.

Elizabeth looked up at the sky. Darker clouds were rolling in. "We'd better dry her off in the kitchen." She whistled to Alice and beckoned to Tim. Alice shook again, cavorted through the grass, and streaked for the warmth of the house.

The Emorys' kitchen was floored with red flagstone and warmed by a fat stove and its attendant copper boiler. Elizabeth had laid out towels on the table, then Tim and she enveloped Alice in them, thus adding a layer of wet dog hair to the mud on their clothes. Tim surreptitiously studied Elizabeth over Alice's towel-muffled head. Elizabeth's hair hung damply in her face, and most of her chignon had fallen loose and dripped down her back. She had mud on her nose. He decided that any woman who could look that good while washing a dog had a natural talent.

When Alice was reasonably dry, they turned her loose and pulled off their aprons. Elizabeth bundled them up and threw them in a laundry hamper on the porch. "I'll make you some tea. Would you like to change into a suit of my father's clothes?"

"I'll do fine," Tim said. "Your father might not care for it."

"He'd never miss them," Elizabeth assured him.

"He wouldn't remember to *wear* clothes if my mother didn't remind him. He and my mother took the ferry across the bay to give a lecture at the Oakland Library." She poked up the fire in the stove and put the kettle on to boil. "I think Maddy is lurking upstairs. She hates to wash Alice. I expect she'll come down if I make some tea."

Tim wondered if Miss Emory was carefully assuring him that they were chaperoned. In spite of her age and her political views, she might still care what her neighbors thought. Maybe those eggs on the gate bothered her more than she would admit.

Elizabeth went to a shelf over the sink and took down a tin canister of Chinese tea and a teapot shaped like a Chinese dragon, with long whiskers and splayed toes. "Have you ever had green tea? I like it very much." She opened the tin and showed him the tightly curled green leaves.

"Seems appropriate for the teapot," Tim said, peering at it. The dragon curled all the way around the pot, and its open mouth was the spout.

As the tea was steeping, Elizabeth put a plate of almond cookies on a tray, and Tim carried it into the parlor. Maddy didn't seem inclined to appear. Alice was asleep again in front of the fire, adding a faint odor of wet dog to the aroma of burning eucalyptus. Outside, the sky had darkened ominously. Elizabeth came in and lit the parlor lamp, and the room flowered into a saffron glow. Tim settled in a leather armchair and turned his toes appreciatively to the fire. Thunder rumbled overhead, and in another moment rain poured down outside.

Elizabeth poured him a cup of tea and seemed to be trying to figure something out. "Do you have any female reporters on your newspaper staff, Mr. Holt?" She kept her eyes on the teapot, as if to convey that the question was casual, unimportant.

"Well, no," Tim admitted. "My business manager is a woman, though. Mrs. Ware is extremely competent."

"Almost as competent as a man?" Elizabeth murmured.

"Now quit that. She is more competent than the man who preceded her. That's why my first manager hired her, and why I kept her on."

"Oh." Elizabeth nibbled a cookie thoughtfully. "So you weren't the one to hire her?"

"I wonder why it is," Tim mused, "that I want to strangle you when you get like this?"

"Men always want to strangle women who make them uncomfortable." Elizabeth watched him through narrowed eyes as a crack of lightning spat overhead.

"And how do you know you make me uncomfortable?" Tim inquired. "Maybe I just think you're unreasonable."

"Men think any woman who wants to step out of her place is unreasonable."

"I don't think you're unreasonable for wanting to vote," Tim pointed out. "I think you're unreasonable for calling me 'men' as if I were a composite of my sex—as if everything any man ever did to you was my personal fault."

"Men do that to women," Elizabeth said, infuriating him.

"Oh, yeah? Do you hear me complaining to you that the first woman I ever courted was a vapid dolly who jilted me because her father told her to? Or about the one who married somebody else while she was in love with me, and then went all tragic and keeps trying to be my sister?"

"Men blame things like that on the next woman they court," Elizabeth said. "That's different. You're not courting me."

Another spear of lightning sizzled just outside the window, and the reverberation of its thunder shook the house.

"I sure hope not," Tim seethed.

"He's courting you," Maddy said. She watched from an upstairs window as Tim made his way through the storm, shoulders hunched into his coat, a borrowed umbrella over his head.

"He is not," Elizabeth said irritably. "We spent the whole time arguing."

"He helped you wash Alice."

"He felt sorry for me." She sat down on the log-cabin quilt on Maddy's brass bed and picked dog hair off her skirt. "I looked like a scullery maid, I had eggs on my gate, and he felt sorry for me."

"Nobody feels sorry enough for somebody to wash a dog unless he's courting," Maddy said. "Particularly not *that* dog. I expect his trousers are ruined."

"He's just like all the other men." Elizabeth brooded. "He thinks he owns the world."

"Goodness, what a storm," Maddy said. She peered out, her nose against the glass. "Look at that wind. It's nearly taken his umbrella away."

"I'm *not* going to stare out the window at him," Elizabeth said. "He's a business acquaintance. There are tea and almond cookies downstairs if you want to come down."

Maddy folded the corner of the book she had been reading and put it on the wicker table beside her bed. "I would have come down earlier," she said, "but I think the two of us together intimidate him."

"So you eavesdropped instead," Elizabeth said.

"Not exactly. You were both pretty loud. If I happened to be in the hallway I couldn't help hearing you."

"And exactly why are you so interested?" Elizabeth straightened her hair, using Maddy's brush.

"Because if it had been anyone else, you would have combed your hair as soon as you came in after washing Alice," Maddy said. She studied her sister as if she were a scientific specimen. They were ten years apart in age, but now that Maddy had grown up they had begun to be close. "I'm trying to figure out why you want to make yourself look as awful as possible when you see this man."

"I don't!"

"Well, you comb your hair for Jack and Rafe," Maddy said. "You know you do. And you put on lip rouge." She padded down the stairs in search of the almond cookies, and Elizabeth followed her. Alice woke up as they went into the parlor.

"His sister's a doctor," Maddy said, apparently considering Tim Holt's list of recommendations.

"She isn't involved in the movement," Elizabeth said darkly. "Rafe told me that she goes home and bounces twins on her knees every night."

"What's wrong with twins? Do you think that's overdoing motherhood? Too showy?"

"Don't be an idiot. Nobody plans to have twins. But I think it's selfish to be a pioneer and then not use your position to better other women's circumstances. It's unconscionable to get what you need and ignore everyone else."

"That's not fair," Maddy protested. "Just by being a doctor she makes it clear that women are capable of that profession. And if *you* had twins, how much time would you have, to go around getting arrested?"

"That's just what I mean." Elizabeth ate a cookie and ignored the fact that Maddy was feeding one to the dog. "I suspect that Mr. Holt is the sort of man who wants a woman who'll have twins for him."

"You're letting this idea of twins get out of hand, if you ask me," Maddy said. "They're becoming some kind of metaphor for some nameless ill-treatment you expect Mr. Holt to inflict on his wife."

"I have no idea what Mr. Holt may inflict on his wife, and I'm not interested."

"If you're not interested, then why are we arguing about it?" Maddy inquired.

"You brought it up," Elizabeth said. The wind was howling outside the house now, and through the windows they could see a hurricane wind tossing the trees and driving the rain before it. Elizabeth stared at it. "They won't run the ferries in this," she murmured. "The folks'll stay the night in Oakland, I imagine."

"I expect." Maddy was unworried. The Emory family relied upon its members to exhibit good sense. If the bay was stormy, one stayed in Oakland and assumed that those left at home could take care of themselves, too.

"If I marry," Elizabeth said, searching for some way to explain why the Holts made her feel disgruntled and uneasy, "I want the kind of marriage that Mother and Father have—a partnership. I can tell just from talking to Mr. Holt that he believes that his mother is allowed a great deal of liberty. But his father rules the household. I have the feeling that is exactly the way Mr. Holt would behave if he married."

Maddy bit into a cookie and shook her head at the dog. "I already gave you one. You think his wife would have some freedom but not enough? And be expected to be grateful for it?"

"I strongly suspect so," Elizabeth said.

"Oh, well, then, you should marry Rafe. His wife would have all the freedom she wanted."

"Along with a great many other inconveniences," Elizabeth said dryly.

Maddy mulled it over. "Maybe he can be educated," she said. "Mr. Holt, I mean. Not Rafe."

"Maybe he can't, too," Elizabeth said. "It might be easier to educate someone you have to start from scratch with than someone who thinks he already knows everything."

"I'm not sure he thinks he's educated," Maddy pointed out. "He may just think you're aggravating."

"What sort of woman is Miss Emory?" Rosebay looked up from the *Clarion*'s latest interview with Elizabeth, the one that had provoked the eggs on her gate. Rosebay had clipped and saved it.

"Aggravating," Tim said. "She thinks all men are universally to blame for the oppression of women."

"So do I," Rosebay said. "Except for you. And Hugo. And men like you-all."

"Miss Emory makes no such distinctions," Tim said.

"Well, what's she like to talk to? Do you think she's pretty?"

"She didn't like my saying so in the first article. Said her personal appearance was irrelevant."

Rosebay regarded him with suspicion. "That wasn't what I asked you."

"Well, yeah, I think she's pretty," Tim said. "She's tall, and when she looks at you, you know there's somebody there."

He strolled out, and Rosebay bit her lip. That didn't sound pretty to her, but it bothered her that Tim thought so. *She's not the right woman for him,* she decided. *She'll give him an awful time.* Rosebay reminded herself that she had wanted to find Tim a nice girl—but not this one. Rosebay was counting on someone who wanted to make a home for him and would be a friend, and would think it was all right for Rosebay to see him sometimes. . . . No, not this one. She looked miserably at the clipping in her hand. Elizabeth Emory would not do at all.

VIII

Yellow Mountain Oil Field, April 1896

"Be glad to have you watch, Mr. Blake," Harkness said from his high stool under the cable-tool drilling rig. He didn't look particularly glad. "Just be sure you stay out of the way of the beam. She's heavy."

"Don't worry." Peter glanced respectfully at the walking beam above him. The cable-tool rig was a refinement on the old spring rig, which had consisted simply of a drill bit slung from the end of a green sapling. In its modern incarnation it was powered by a monstrous steam boiler and engine—nothing Peter wanted to tangle with. The engine's iron drive wheel, big enough for a small locomotive, turned an even bigger wooden band wheel, which, in turn, ran the walking beam that raised and lowered the iron drill bit in the shaft. Peter hefted a spare drill bit and nearly dropped it on his foot—to Harkness's amusement, he thought.

From the end of the walking beam hung the drill cable, adjusted by a four-foot iron temper screw and tended by Harkness, perched on the tall stool beside it. The walking beam was supported at its center by a samson post and counterweighted from behind by a box of rocks. Positioned between the samson post and Harkness was a freestanding "headache post," which kept the samson post from falling on the driller's head when it occasionally worked loose from its moorings. The rig floor was noisy, slippery with the water that lubricated the drill, as shuddery as a railroad trestle in use. Between the boiler and the forge, it was as hot as hell's antechamber in the well house, and the harpoonlike fishing tools with which Harkness pulled broken drill bits from the shaft added to Peter's impression that he had stumbled into the boiler room from which the devil ran his kingdom.

Boyne, the tool dresser, hoisted worn drill bits to the forge for sharpening. For this he was paid two dollars a day. Harkness made four dollars, and the company considered both men overpaid.

Peter watched the cable slowly unwind, punching the drill deeper into the earth. He understood mechanics, although the rig didn't hold the same fascination for him that it would have for his cousin Tim, who took things apart just from curiosity. He realized that he needed to know every inch of the Sierra Oil operation, learn everything, if the other directors weren't going to eat him alive.

That much had been made clear at his first board meeting, when he assumed the position that his heavy investment in the company had bought him. Sanford Rutledge, the Sierra Oil president and general manager, was locked in a power struggle with William H. Kemp, the former president and the most powerful of the directors. They fought over everything, including the proper reinvestment of profits, where and how much land should be bought, and which products should be marketed. Whatever Rutledge wanted, Kemp did not, and vice versa. Board meetings took on the atmosphere of a perpetual dogfight, with Kemp and Rutledge growling at each other's throats, thrashing in the dust while the other directors leaped out of the way.

Most particularly, however, Rutledge and Kemp made war over the refinery on the San Francisco Bay, at a location fancifully named Oleum.

Peter's investment gave him enough clout to swing votes either way, and he had taken to his heels when Rutledge and Kemp began to lie in wait for him, lurking around corners to expound their views. The men's

beards wagged as Rutledge and Kemp each offered
solemn assurance that his was the only proper
perspective—and then the adversaries demanded Peter's vote. But he would make no decisions until he could
back them up with facts.

Fact number one was that an oil company drilled
where the oil was. The best wells that Sierra Oil had
sunk were in the upper valley slung high in the mountains between Ojai and Sierra—nowhere near the San
Francisco Bay.

Fact number two was that the refinery in Sierra was
more than decrepit. But how much of its decay was due
to simple wear and tear and outmoded machinery and
how much to deliberate neglect, Peter wasn't sure.
Rutledge dug in his heels every time any repairs to the
Sierra operation were proposed—Oleum was Rutledge's
baby. Kemp fussed and fumed about the expenses of
shipping crude oil north to Oleum, yet he was willing to
spend any amount to shore up the most dilapidated
sections of the Sierra operation. Josiah Welty, Sierra's
veteran refinery man, found himself receiving conflicting orders daily, to pack and move to Oleum, then to
stay put in Sierra.

Fact number three, which also troubled Peter, was
that most of the other refinery workers in Sierra couldn't
transfer to Oleum because they couldn't afford to move.
The company certainly would not be willing to pay their
way; roustabouts were a dime a dozen in a country still
struggling with an economic depression.

Peter mulled over these problems as he rode back
to his lodgings in Sierra. It was still the tail end of the
rainy season, and fat black clouds were boiling up over
the mountains. Peter pulled his slicker off the back of his
saddle just as the clouds broke open and a cold rain
sheeted down around him. Struggling through the folds
of dark oilskin, he looked with some sympathy at the
cattle pastured beside the dirt road. They lowered their
heads and turned their backs to the rain. Peter's hired
horse seemed inclined to do the same, so he gave it a

good kick to indicate that he had no intention of standing under a tree till the rain let up. They plodded along.

There was something else bothering Peter, however, something that had nothing to do with Sierra Oil: Where the hell was Frank? Was he out somewhere in the rain, soaked and miserable? Cindy was frantic. How could Frank have done anything so idiotic and put his family through such pain? Sure, their dad could be stiff-necked, but that was no excuse for Frank's running away. *If I ever catch up with him,* Peter thought, *I'll . . .* Actually, Peter didn't know what he would do. But he couldn't shake the idea of Frank, alone, naïve, and in trouble or in danger.

Rain sloshed over the brim of Peter's hat and down the neck of his slicker. He shivered, feeling as cold as he imagined Frank to be. Anger seeped into his concern. *The hell with Frank,* he decided. The kid was probably lolling on a beach somewhere, warm and fat and not giving a damn that the family was in an uproar, that Midge was miserable and his mother and father were fighting. Although Cindy's letters were guarded in this respect, Peter was astute enough to read between the lines. Damn stupid kid! Peter's hands clenched angrily on the reins. Frank ought to be thrashed, and it was a shame that their father hadn't done it. But where *was* he?

Horse and rider were soaked by the time they came down the mountain into Sierra. The rain was just letting up, and moments later the sun came out in a splash of brilliant yellow, folding itself into the hillsides and between the clapboard houses. Flower gardens glowed behind picket fences.

The horse snorted suddenly and swiveled its ears. Peter turned in the saddle at the clatter of a gasoline engine behind them. He grinned. Here was progress— the automobile had arrived in Sierra. A gaggle of children in the street pointed and shouted, and the curious poked their heads out of windows. The motorist, as soaking wet as Peter, beamed proudly, obviously pleased with the stir he was making. And better yet from Peter's point of view, the man was driving a Blake. The little silver Diana stood up jauntily on the hood, her bow drawn, as the car chugged by. A barking dog pursued it, and Peter's horse rolled its eyes and jigged at the smoke and noise.

"Get used to it," Peter informed the horse.

Curious, he followed the Blake, intending to ask the driver where he was from and how he liked his motorcar. The Blake turned in at the gates of the Sierra Oil refinery several blocks away. By the time Peter had caught up and looped his horse's reins at the post, the driver was out of the Blake and talking to the refinery's office manager.

"None?" The driver's expression was peevish. Aggravated, he looked from his expensive new machine to the manager.

"Not a drop." The manager shrugged. "Sorry, bud. We only refine gasoline once a week. Won't have any for you till Thursday."

"This *is* a refinery, isn't it?" the motorist demanded. It was a rhetorical question.

"We don't get much call for it," the manager explained.

"Well, I'm not sitting here till Thursday." The driver snorted in disgust.

Peter stopped in his tracks. This was probably not a good time to introduce himself.

"'A plentiful supply of good, cheap fuel,'" the driver muttered, obviously quoting from the Blake Company's sales brochure as he passed Peter. He cranked the Blake over and chugged away.

Peter headed for the refinery office. "What do you mean, we don't have any gasoline for sale?" he demanded.

The manager started to say "Not till Thursday" and then recognized Peter. "We don't sell enough to make it worthwhile, Mr. Blake," he said apologetically.

"Maybe if we *made* some, we'd sell it," Peter said. "I suppose you know that was one of my company's automobiles."

"Bit of luck he didn't recognize you then, wasn't it?" the manager said sympathetically.

"What exactly *do* we sell here?" Peter inquired, exasperated.

"Fuel oil, lamp oil, kerosene," the manager said. "Asphalt," he added.

"I'll let you know when I invent a motorcar that can run on asphalt," Peter said. "Hair pomade," he muttered disgustedly, eyeing the display of petroleum products advertised in a glass case in the front office. "But no gasoline till Thursday."

"Maybe you ought to talk to Mr. Rutledge and Mr. Kemp," the office manager suggested. "I don't set the refinery schedule."

"Oh, I intend to," Peter said.

"It's all I can do to keep the place functioning," the manager said gloomily as Peter headed for the door.

Infuriated, Peter mounted his horse again and headed back into town. He wasn't going to argue with anybody until he was dry, but just wait until the next board meeting. . . .

Two blocks down the muddy main street, the sun was just beginning to dry the water from the wet road. A crowd of children had gathered, interspersed with the loungers who inhabited the feed-store porch. A farmer in bib overalls was maneuvering a pair of mules into position, and as Peter drew abreast he was appalled to see the farmer was hitching them to the front of the Blake.

"Get a horse!"

"He's got mules now. He don't need no horse!"

The crowd of wags on the sidewalk slapped their thighs in hilarity while the much-tried driver of the Blake, his motorcar out of gasoline, stood with arms folded and attempted to ignore the hecklers. Peter reined his horse around them and resisted the urge to pull his hat down over his eyes. He was immensely grateful that he hadn't been the one to sell the man his Blake.

Peter returned his horse to the livery stable, then

walked the three blocks to the furnished cottage he had rented when he decided he had better stick around for a while to be sure he knew what Sierra Oil was doing with his money. And be sure *they* knew what they were doing with it, he thought grumpily.

Peter shucked off his wet clothes and threw shirt and undergarments into an already overflowing hamper. The cottage came complete with a Mexican gardener who spent his time moving plants around according to some undisclosed plan and understood not a word Peter said to him, and a cleaning woman who came once a week, muttered something about bachelors, and told Peter not to put his feet on the sofa. Unfortunately the cottage did not include laundry services.

After he had changed into fresh clothes, Peter picked up the hamper and set out to find a laundry before rain fell again. The sky was looking very threatening. Rain seemed to come and go in minutes. He pushed his way through the door of the Fine French Laundry on Alvarez Street just as the skies opened.

The air inside felt nearly as wet as outside, but a warm cloud of steam enveloped him. A red-haired girl in a white canvas apron came from the back when she heard the bell ringing over the door. Peter peered at her over his basket, and she reached out for it.

"Put it on the counter then, and let's see what you've got." Peter decided that the "French" designation was a frill for elegance's sake. She sounded American to him, perhaps with a touch of Irish. Her hair was pinned into a knot on her head, but the steam caused stray tendrils to curl appealingly around her face. She wore a blue gingham dress, with the sleeves rolled nearly to her shoulders, revealing muscular forearms and hands reddened from her work. Peter thought she was awfully pretty.

She seemed to notice that he did. "You're new here, aren't you?" she asked, sorting his shirts. "You work in the oil fields? My brother Sid's a jackline tender in Avenal Canyon."

"Not exactly," Peter said. "I, uh, I own part of the company."

She peered at his clothes more closely. "I guess you do. I didn't look at that shirt good."

Peter glanced uncomfortably at his custom-made laundry. Did she think he was showing off? "My name's Peter Blake," he said, trying to sound friendly and not snooty.

"I'm Peggy Delaney," she said, stuffing his shirts into a canvas sack. "You going to be a regular customer, Mr. Blake? I'll give you your own bag if you are."

"I expect I'll be here for a while."

She wrote "P. Blake" on the bag with a laundry marker, then tossed the sack onto a pile behind the counter.

A three-quarter partition separated them from the laundry room in the back. Peter could see steam rolling up above it and hear the *thunk* of a pressing machine. It was still ice-cold and wet outside, and the warmth of the laundry was inviting. "Do you own this place?" he asked.

"I run it," Peggy said. "Me and the hired girls. Me dad owns it, such as he is." Her lips compressed in annoyance. "Wherever he is."

Peter looked at her longingly. She was the first pretty woman he had met here, and he was cold and lonely.

She cocked her head at him. "Your shirts'll be ready Wednesday."

Embarrassed, Peter looked at the floor. He couldn't think of a reason to stick around. "I—I like a little starch in them," he said, feeling foolish. "Not too much."

"Right you are."

The door banged open again, jangling the bell, and a burly man came in, shaking water from himself like a dog. He looked about forty-five, was red in the face, and had a plaid wool cap jammed down over his forehead. Sprigs of ginger hair stuck out from under it. He stomped behind the counter and reached for the till.

Peggy tried to slap his hand. "You've had enough."

He pushed her away. "It's cold out there. I need a bit to warm me up."

"You're pickled already," Peggy said, but she didn't try to fight him. Her lips tightened as she watched him stuff a handful of bills into his coat pocket. "Now there won't be enough to pay the girls."

"There's plenty." He glared at her and then at Peter for good measure. "Plenty if you were out hustling work instead of mooning around with the men. That Chinaman bastard's getting half our trade."

"He wouldn't if you'd turn a hand to the work," Peggy snapped. Neither of them seemed to care that Peter was listening.

"Washing's not a white man's work. Goddamn Chinese coolies trying to undercut prices, robbing white folk of their livelihood. They ought to be shipped out." He clumped around from behind the counter in a moving cloud of rye whiskey and the smell of wet wool. He glared at Peter. "Who the hell are you?"

"This is Mr. Blake," Peggy said. "He's from Sierra Oil."

"Well, get back out to the field and leave my daughter to the wash, damn you. We got a living to earn."

"He's an owner," Peggy said angrily. "You're stinking drunk."

"Don't sass me, or I'll clip you one." Delaney glowered at them both. "I'll be back for dinner. It better be hot."

He slammed out the door, his head down into the rain, and Peggy, biting her lip, looked at Peter. "That was my pa," she muttered.

There didn't seem to be much to say to that. Peter wondered where her mother was. Did Peggy Delaney have any defense against that old devil, or was Peggy her mother's defense? He couldn't think of any way to ask that without sounding like a supercilious rich man trying to tell the poor how they ought to live. He'd known a bunch of goody-goodies and never could understand why the poor didn't up and throw rocks at them.

"I guess you need to get back to work," he murmured.

Peggy snorted. "Somebody'd better." She picked up the pile of laundry bags and marched around the partition, her back rigid with embarrassment.

Peter stood for a moment in the empty room and then went out into the rain. There was a board meeting the next morning, and he had some notes to prepare before then. No gasoline until Thursday—he was going to give them hell for that.

There was a grocery store on the corner two doors down, and Peter ducked in to see if he could wait out the rain in there. Maybe he would try cooking his own dinner that night instead of going to a restaurant. He wasn't much of a cook, but it would be something to do. He was bored. And while he ate he could work on his figures for the meeting.

He peered around the shelves, trying to think what he could manage to cook. A fat black-and-white tomcat was asleep on sacks of rice in the window. At first Peter thought the cat was stuffed until it opened one green eye. When Peter hefted a sack of rice from beside it, the cat stretched and spread out its toes, claws extended.

"That's Hiram," the woman behind the counter said. "He's a fine mouser."

"I'll bet he is," Peter said. He didn't mind a little cat hair in his rice; it was far preferable to mouse droppings. In a small-town grocery, one or the other was inevitable.

"What can I do for you?" The woman was round and motherly looking, and she gave Peter a smile.

"I was trying to decide what I could cook without burning it," Peter confessed.

"Well, now, rice is easy. Twice as much water as rice. Boil it about twenty minutes. I could give you a fresh chicken to go with it. A nice young hen. I raise them myself."

Peter smiled back, glad to have someone friendly to talk to. "That would be fine."

"You just wait here, Mr. Blake, and I'll pluck it for you. Won't be many folks coming in till this rain lets up."

She disappeared into the back of the store, and Peter heard a door open and close.

He wondered how she knew his name. He supposed word got around a small town fast when the oil company was its biggest industry. In a few minutes he heard a furious squawking and then a thud and silence. Apparently the chicken was *extremely* fresh.

She returned in a few minutes with a headless carcass—already gutted, he hoped, eyeing it uneasily. She poured a pot of water from a kettle that was already hot on the wood stove and dipped the chicken in it by the feet.

"How do you like Sierra, Mr. Blake?" She perched on a chair and began to pluck feathers.

"Uh, very much," Peter said.

"I hear you're from San Francisco. Are you planning to live here permanent?"

"Well, not forever," Peter answered. "It's a very nice town, though."

"You're not seeing us at our best in all this rain. We do need it, though. Won't be any more till next winter." She hesitated, squinting at him over the chicken, her fingers automatically yanking feathers. "Mr. Blake, tell me: Is it true they're closing down the refinery?"

"I don't know," Peter said honestly. "I'm new on the board, you know, and—"

"Mr. Blake, I'll tell you for a flat fact we got to have that refinery. Can't you make 'em see the light?"

"Well, it's a business decision," Peter told her. "The new facility at Oleum is much better equipped." He felt like a cad.

"My husband's a boiler tender," she went on. "We couldn't make it without his pay. Us nor half the folks that buy from us here." She shook feathers off her fingers. "We're doing about all we can now, what with the store and the chickens. I just don't know. . . ." Her words trailed off, and she bent her eyes on the half-plucked chicken. "I know I shouldn't be putting you on the spot like this, but I was just feeling flat desperate, and you looked so friendly-like," she murmured.

"It's all right," Peter said, embarrassed.

"Well, no one can talk to Mr. Rutledge or Mr. Kemp. They don't take the time. And they don't shop here in town anyways."

"I don't think it's really been decided yet," Peter said. "Not for certain."

She finished plucking the chicken in silence, then rinsed it in the pot again. "You want the feet?"

"No," Peter said. "Not at all."

"I'll take them off for you then." She disappeared into the back room once more, and Peter heard the hatchet *thunk* twice. She emerged with the dressed chicken and began wrapping it in butcher's paper. "No point in having the feet if you don't use them," she said. "I make soup with them. Sometimes I give them to Hiram for a treat. He likes them."

The cat meowed at the sound of his name and got up off the sacks of rice to see if this was one of those times. Nose twitching, he twined around Peter's ankles.

"Mr. Blake." The woman looked at Peter, determination in her eyes. "I want to show you something." She took a lined notebook from under the counter and opened it. "This is my credit book. Times like these, some folks won't give credit; but then they lose customers, so I don't know as they're better off. All these folks *intend* to pay me, and they will, too, if they can. But every single one of them but two has a husband or a boy in the oil fields. How are they going to manage if the company shuts the refinery down?"

Peter looked at the book "It would just be the refinery," he said, trying to sound optimistic. "The pumping operation won't stop."

"Not till the wells go dry," she said. "They could, too. Oil wells are like throwing dice. And the refinery accounts for over half the jobs anyhow. We figured with the refinery here, there'd always be work, no matter what."

"I'm sorry," Peter said. He didn't know what else to say.

"They don't care," she said, and her voice was edged

with bitterness. "Rutledge just wants to have a pretty new place in San Francisco, and Kemp doesn't care, either. He just wants to spite Rutledge. He doesn't care about *us*. I know I shouldn't be talking to you like this about them, but you looked to me somehow like maybe you *would* care. Can't you make them see? Can't you make them see that *we* matter, too, that we aren't just pieces of the drill rig?" She looked at Peter with fierce hope in her eyes.

"I don't know," Peter said, feeling helpless. "I'm new, and I don't understand it all yet. I'll look into it."

She nodded, her hope fading. But she managed a smile as she handed him his chicken. "Enjoy your dinner, Mr. Blake. Come back and trade with us some more. I put an onion and a couple of carrots in here to go with your chicken."

Peter regarded the chicken dubiously. Plucked and naked it looked reproachful to him. The rain had stopped by the time he left the grocery, and the other hens had come out into the yard to cluck and fuss and look for worms. They were oblivious to the fate of their companion, going by in a white paper parcel.

At the cottage Peter found a Dutch oven in his kitchen cupboards, put the chicken in it with the carrot and onion and a cup of water, and gratefully set the lid on top.

The stove was wood fired, cast iron, and as black as soot. Peter opened the firebox to see how the fire he had laid was doing and discovered that it was about to go out. He never had gotten the hang of building a fire in a stove. His house in San Francisco possessed a gas stove, and it was the delight of his housekeeper's heart. The last time Peter had tried to wrestle a wood stove into cooperation had been in the bad old days in Guthrie, Oklahoma, when he had been running the business end of Tim's first newspaper and taking turns burning the beans with his cousin. He didn't think his culinary skills had improved any since then.

Peter poked at the fire and muttered, "Burn, blast you."

He thought wistfully of Peggy Delaney, who would probably have gotten this old wood stove whipped into shape in no time flat—and for a hell of a lot more appreciative audience than her old man. Of course Peter couldn't invite a nice girl to dinner and expect her to do the cooking, or even invite her to dinner at his house without a chaperon, not in Peter's world. Upon reflection he suspected that Peggy's world might be different. She had a competence about her that he liked. He pictured her shapely, muscular arms bent over a laundry tub or building a stove fire just so. He could invite her out to a restaurant. He'd bet she didn't get much chance to eat in restaurants.

Suddenly the fire began to smoke, billowing around the firebox door. Peter swore and yanked it open with a towel. It wouldn't do to get her hopes up, of course. She would have to understand he wasn't serious, just looking for a friend. It would probably be better not to do it at all. . . .

He managed to cook the chicken and boil the rice. He discovered that two cups of raw rice turned out to be about six cups cooked, enough to last him until doomsday, he reflected—although most of it was burned. He took a plate of chicken and rice to the kitchen table, opened his notebook on Sierra Oil's finances, and settled down to something he did know—figures.

The chicken wasn't too bad, he thought, with liberal additions of salt and pepper. But the rice definitely had a burnt taste. After he had finished eating, Peter tried chipping the rice out of the pot and finally filled it with water and set it out on the back porch. He went back to his figures, hoping he hadn't given himself indigestion. Kemp and Rutledge were going to do that for him on their own.

"Unnecessary. Perfectly good equipment here, with a little repair." Kemp glowered across the table at Rutledge and laced his fingers like a breastplate across his ample midsection, as if Rutledge might be planning to fire grapeshot at him. Kemp was a series of circles: a round, red nose on a round bald head, trimmed at the edges with a fringe of gray hair like a monk's tonsure. Two hamlike haunches supported a spherical middle, atop peculiarly small feet, so that he looked as if he were about to topple over and roll down the street.

"Hah! The place is falling apart. Progress is at Oleum, but you're too blind to see it." Rutledge glared back with fiery eyes above his patriarchal whiskers and preached his doctrine of salvation through new machinery to an uncomfortable congregation—he was a corporate evangelist promising brimstone to the unconverted. John D. Rockefeller's Standard Oil figured as the forces of darkness in this scenario, Peter had discovered. "Waiting to devour us!" Rutledge waved bony arms. "Waiting to gobble us up!"

"Nonsense!" Kemp boomed. "Nothing at all to worry about." His wide mouth opened and closed with a snap.

"Mr. Blake will back me up on this."

Peter started. "Huh?" Rutledge was pointing an accusing finger at him.

The other three men on the board, Morris, Hatch, and Simpson, were studiously examining their notes, unwilling to let either of the combatants catch their eyes. Individually none of them had enough power to sway the question either way, and not one of them wanted the wrath of either Kemp or Rutledge on his head.

"Well, Mr. Blake?" Rutledge boomed again. "What's all this?"

Peter got a grip on himself and dug in his heels. He was by far the youngest, but he had enough money in Sierra Oil now to give him seniority. "I've been studying the question, gentlemen," Peter said carefully, "and I don't think we should make a hasty decision."

"Hah!" said Kemp.

"One that would be irrevocable, either way."

"Hah!" said Rutledge.

"One issue no one has discussed," Peter said firmly,

"is what will happen to the town of Sierra if we move the entire refining operation to Oleum. Don't we owe our workers some security and consideration?"

"Good heavens, man," Rutledge said. "There's plenty of labor at Oleum. Tramps come in on every train looking for work. The country's full of them."

"Too many of them down here," Kemp said. "Panhandlers and thieves. Disgraceful. Not the sort of men we want." He laced his fingers across his middle. "No man needs to be poor if he's willing to apply himself."

So much for paternal concern for the refinery workers, Peter thought. "Mr. Kemp, if the situation of our workers doesn't trouble you, then what *is* your objection to the move to Oleum?" Peter asked.

"Rutledge," Kemp said. He gave Rutledge a derisive snort. "Wants to move us all up with the swells of Frisco. Go to the opera. God knows what all."

There was more to it than that, Peter decided, but obviously this quarrel was not entirely based on economics.

"What the hell did you two want to go into business together for anyway?" Hatch muttered, which was exactly what Peter wondered. "You've been fighting for ten years."

"Don't like swells," Kemp said. "I'm a country boy myself. The country's good enough for me."

"You're a hayseed," Rutledge accused.

"Oh, for God's sake," Simpson grumbled. He went back to his notes.

Peter peered out the corner of his eye at what Morris was writing, since he had not spoken yet. The sheet said "Dear Mother . . ."

"Not the time to go off building new facilities," Kemp said.

"It's already built," Rutledge said.

"Over my objections. Chicanery." Kemp looked accusingly at Morris, Hatch, and Simpson, who shuffled papers and refused to look back at him. "Time to retrench, not expand. Can't even sell oil in Los Angeles now. Every idiot with a pick and a spade has a well in his damned backyard. Now they're oversupplied. That's what comes of letting amateurs into the business."

"We aren't trying to sell oil in Los Angeles," Rutledge said with elaborate patience. "And the business is already full of amateurs!"

Kemp was a local man, with an orange grove and a cattle operation. Rutledge came from Pennsylvania, where he had prospected for oil before—and been forcibly bought out by Standard Oil, as Peter recalled.

Peter tried to get the meeting back on track. He wasn't going to vote for anything before they had voted on his own private gripe. If Rutledge and Kemp could use this approach, so could he. He coughed. "Gentlemen, before we pursue this further, there is a matter I wish to bring to your attention. And that is the refinery schedule."

"Refinery schedule?" Rutledge seemed to be considering whether or not that could be turned to a discussion of the superior virtues of Oleum.

"Yes, indeed," Kemp said, apparently with similar intent. "Now the repairs I am proposing—"

"It's not a matter of repairs," Peter said. He smiled. "I am afraid I cannot come to any conclusion regarding the rival merits of Oleum and Sierra until we adopt a refining schedule to meet our customers' *current* needs. Gentlemen, I have some notes here on our gasoline production. . . ."

IX

At the board meeting of Sierra Oil, Peter insisted that the refinery schedule be geared to producing gasoline three times a week, at twice the present quantity. When Kemp attempted to conclude that motorcars were a newfangled fad fated for oblivion once the novelty wore off, Peter presented him with the impressive—and still growing—sales statistics from the Blake Company. When Rutledge, still promoting the move to Oleum, protested that there were no motorcars in the area, Peter gave a harrowing description of the Blake's driver being turned away from his only local source of gasoline, then humiliated in public.

Peter concluded with a concise primer of corporate-customer relations. It would probably be a cold day in hell, he told the directors, before that driver, obviously well off if he owned a Blake, bought any fuel oil or kerosene manufactured by Sierra Oil, either.

The other board members wriggled on the hook, and the subject of Oleum surfaced regularly; but Peter steadfastly refused to consider any other issues before his own was settled. The directors had accepted Peter on the board because Sierra Oil badly needed the infusion of his cash. Now they were stuck with him, he pointed out, and would have to trust his business acumen. The vote was taken, and Peter accomplished his goal. As soon as the board agreed to his terms, Peter announced that it was dinnertime, and he would have to study his notes further before he could commit himself to any decision pertaining to the refinery. He escaped before either Kemp or Rutledge insisted that he dine with *them*.

Now, having made his getaway, Peter looked around his empty cottage and wondered if he ought to bolt the door. Kemp and Rutledge were as determined as a pair of bloodhounds. Peter honestly didn't know what he thought about Oleum. The pleas of the woman in the grocer's shop still troubled him, but Oleum was already built, a fait accompli. A tour of the Sierra refinery had convinced him of the truth of Rutledge's statement that the equipment was falling apart. It could have been repaired with the money spent on Oleum, but it hadn't been. Peter wasn't at all sure that the company could survive the expense now. At some point hard finance had to be considered along with the human suffering that a move would create.

A clattering ring from the parlor reminded him that the cottage was equipped with one luxury—a home telephone. The caller was undoubtedly Rutledge or Kemp, with further arguments that Peter was not willing to hear on an empty stomach. He picked up his hat and fled.

It was one of those beautiful spring afternoons that southern California produced after a rain had washed the land, and Peter stood on the sidewalk soaking it up. The air was thick with the scent of orange blossoms from the single tree in the backyard, and the hum of bees was loud in his ears. It was still daylight, the sun hanging over the western mountains. Peter had a longing for company less whiskery and argumentative than Sierra Oil's board of directors, and he found himself strolling— without really meaning to, he told himself—toward the French laundry.

Peggy Delaney was just locking the front door as Peter walked up. She smiled at him but shook her head. "Those shirts won't be ready till tomorrow, Mr. Blake. I hope you weren't needing them. They was promised for tomorrow, and I don't ever seem to get ahead."

"I wasn't looking for the shirts," Peter said diffidently. "I thought . . . well, I thought maybe you'd come and have dinner with me. I get awfully tired of eating alone."

She studied him as if trying to figure out what he had in mind. She had her apron folded over her arm. Her blue gingham dress—the same one she had on the day before, Peter thought—clung to her, damp with the steam of the laundry. It was faded and frayed at the hem, the day dress of a workingwoman who probably didn't own much else.

"Just dinner," Peter explained. "Please. There's a nice place down the street." And not too fancy, he thought. She wouldn't be embarrassed in there.

Peggy grinned. "I know there is, but nobody ever took me there. I'd admire to go with you, Mr. Blake, but I got to get dinner for my pa."

Who probably wouldn't be home to eat it until after the saloons closed, Peter thought. "Could you leave it for him?" Peter asked. "Would he mind if you ate dinner with me?"

Peggy snorted derisively. "You saw my pa, Mr. Blake. There's not much point in me pretending he's a church deacon. He wouldn't notice, long as he gets his supper. All right then. I've got soup on the stove already. You walk me home, and I'll get things ready for him."

"Good." Peter gave her his arm, and she took it with a glance of mild surprise. She led him to a side street, then down nearly ten blocks into the area where she lived. It was a neighborhood of narrow, rutted streets and tiny weathered houses whose porches sagged and whose shutters hung askew—rental houses with landlords who saw no point in repairs, and tenants who didn't have the money or the energy for them.

But there was something about the environs that Peter liked, with its smell of cooked cabbage and its lines of wash and the gamboling herds of children playing ball in the dirt. It was alive in a way that the block where Peter's cottage stood or the wide streets where the rich people's houses sprawled was not. This was the heart of the town, its underpinnings, the human machinery that kept the place running. This was where the gardeners, the waitresses, the laundresses, housekeepers, and mechanics lived. The rich people provided the money, but the work of making the town move came from this neighborhood.

Peggy turned up a dirt path to a tiny house with a missing front step and a single camellia in the flower bed. "Come on in if you've a mind to," she said. "I won't apologize, but it's not much to look at."

Inside was a tiny room that served as both kitchen and parlor, warmed by an ancient stove. The furniture consisted of a sagging sofa and a heavy kitchen table with four chairs. A shelf of plates on the wall was arranged to give a place of honor to a blue-willow pattern tureen and a rose-flowered cup and saucer of the kind bought at fairs. The interior had an air of shabby pride and was spotlessly clean, in comparison to the weatherbeaten exterior.

Peggy stirred a soup pot that bubbled on the back of the stove, then expertly banked the fire in the firebox. She set the table for one, then sliced a loaf of bread and put it on the table. "That's good enough for him," she said.

She looked down at her dress. "Would you mind if I changed out of this?"

"Go right ahead," Peter said. "I'll wait for you." He watched her hurry down a narrow, dark hall that he supposed led to the bedrooms. There couldn't be more than two, he thought, and they must be tiny, boxlike. While he waited, he looked around. On one kitchen wall was a picture of a fluffy kitten, a bow around its neck, in a basket of roses. On the opposite wall was a souvenir plate with a fanciful volcano spewing flame into the sky and a kneeling native girl in some kind of sarong making obeisance to it.

"That's my Hawaii plate," Peggy said proudly when she came out. "A customer gave me that when I found his pearl studs he'd lost. I always wanted to see Hawaii for real."

"Maybe you will one day."

"Someday," Peggy said grimly, "I'm going to see

something besides this town." She had changed into a white shirtwaist and a black taffeta skirt. Peter suspected the shirt was also a gift, from a customer who didn't want it anymore. A black felt hat with a faded yellow rose was pinned to her red hair.

"You look very nice," Peter said.

"Well, I wanted to do you proud," Peggy said. "I never had anybody take me to dinner before." She wrapped a brown wool shawl around her shoulders.

They walked back toward town and the restaurant Peter had selected. Peggy beamed and waved when they passed a woman she knew. The restaurant was small but cheery with red and white tablecloths. It served a workingman's dinner—plain food and plenty of it. Peggy settled happily into a chair and arranged her taffeta skirt around her knees. She looked at the menu and with sudden shyness told him to order. Peter ordered steak, deciding that was probably what she usually had the least of.

"Where would you go if you left Sierra?" Peter asked her. The waitress set down a plate of hot bread, and Peter held it out to Peggy.

"As far away from these oil fields as I can get myself," Peggy said. "I should have lit out when Mama died, but she made me promise I'd take care of Pa and Sid. I reckon I've about paid up, though."

"I didn't realize your mother was dead," Peter said. "I'm sorry."

"It was different when she was around." Peggy bit hungrily into the bread. "We ran the laundry together, and Pa didn't drink so much. He's been sour as a bad apple since she went, and Sid lit out himself when he couldn't stand it anymore. He mostly sleeps in the barracks up at Avenal Canyon. He and Pa fight like weasels now that Mama's gone."

"Your father must have loved your mother a lot," Peter ventured.

"He was mad as fire that she died," Peggy said. "He had to hire another girl for the laundry." The steak arrived, and she cut into it. "Lord God, this is good," she said after she had luxuriated in the taste, then swallowed. "And no dishes to wash."

Peter smiled, enjoying her appreciation. "I expect you see all the soap and water you want to at work."

"That's a fact. But it's the oil I hate, you know? It gets into everything. You can't hardly keep clean, and I hate trying to wash it out. It's like trying to scrub sin off the devil. I've never known anything in my life but the oil fields; but when I get a stake together, by God I'm gone. I got a bit put aside already." She leaned confidentially across the table. "Pa doesn't know."

"It must be hard to save from your pay," Peter said, sympathetic.

"I don't get paid," Peggy said flatly. "Not that we pay that much to the hired girls. I skim from the till when Pa doesn't get to it first. I got a sock in my mattress he don't know about. If he don't find it first, one of these days I'm going to give him an awful surprise."

"Just go off on your own?"

"You bet." Peggy looked at him. "Tell me about some places to go. You been all over, I bet."

"Well, I've been to Germany."

Peggy laughed. "Lord, that's too far afield for me. I've got to go where they speak English. What's it like, though?"

"Very old," Peter said. "Old castles, old towns, old churches, old dukes. Grevensburg, where my mother came from, hasn't changed much since the sixteenth century. I think some of the inhabitants are actually that old."

"Your mother's German?" Peggy looked fascinated.

"My real mother," Peter said. "She died when I was very young. I was raised over here by my father and stepmother. And I must say I prefer the States. I've lived in Washington, D.C., and San Francisco." Feeling that sounded rather tame, he added, "I was in the Oklahoma land rush in '89."

Peggy sighed wistfully. "You been places I don't even know enough to wish for. Tell me where I'd like to go."

"Miss Delaney, I haven't the foggiest idea," Peter said, smiling. "What are you looking for?"

Peggy's eyes glowed with appreciation when he addressed her as "Miss Delaney." She rested her elbow on the edge of the table and her chin in her hand. The steak was forgotten momentarily. "I don't know," she said dreamily. "A place I could make an opportunity for myself. And where everything don't turn black as pitch from rock oil."

"Oil's a valuable commodity."

"It keeps a laundry going, that's a fact. It's just so—all over. When Sid and me was kids, we used to get dirty as the devil just playing up the canyon where it drips out of the rocks. Used to make my mother crazy trying to keep us clean. You reckon the laundry's my comeuppance for that?"

"When you get married and have children, they will be your comeuppance," Peter predicted. "They all get dirty. I used to get filthy just walking around our backyard. Nobody could figure out how I did it. Dirt just jumped out and stuck to me."

"I won't get married around here," Peggy declared. She stuck her chin out to show she meant it. "I won't try to keep some driller clean all my life."

Peter had been going to ask if he could take her to church on Sunday but decided maybe he'd better not. It wouldn't do to let her think he had serious intentions.

Peggy seemed to have an inkling of what was going through his mind. "Now you, you'll marry some nice girl who never did a load of laundry in her life," she said matter-of-factly. "When you get ready to settle down. And you won't expect her to, neither. She'll be getting a catch, I reckon. I can't look for that kind of ease. I just want a man who'll treat me decent and not drink up all his pay. I'll settle for that one of these days, I suppose." She didn't sound thrilled at the prospect, just resigned.

"Do you have a fellow?" Peter asked. "I wouldn't want to make trouble for you, taking you out like this."

"Not a steady fellow. There's one or two come calling. If they don't like what I do, they can go

somewhere else. Tonight's the best fun I ever had since
Sid and a pal took me down to the fair in Ventura last
year."

"I'm glad you're enjoying yourself," Peter said. She
didn't seem to be making any unwarranted assumptions,
so he relaxed. "It's nice for me to have the company. It's
lonesome in a new place when you don't know anyone."

"I never had anyone treat me like a lady before,"
Peggy said frankly. "Mostly they want to go sparking
somewhere." She gave him a sidelong glance and went
back to her steak.

Peter wasn't sure whether she was warning him off
or indicating that she wouldn't mind going sparking with
him somewhere. She didn't act like a girl you couldn't
kiss, and the longer he looked at her, the more he
wanted to. She had a turned-up button nose and a pretty
mouth, and eyes that were a pale aquamarine in color.
Her skin was lightly freckled. Girls like Peggy didn't
have time to fool with bleaching creams and protective
veils. Peter had always liked freckles and could never
understand why all the girls he knew wailed whenever
they got one. He finished his steak and noted that Peggy
had eaten all of hers. He liked girls who didn't poke at
their food like canaries, too.

"Will you have some dessert? I saw a good-looking
apple pie over there."

Peggy looked hungrily at the pies and cakes lined
up behind glass. Her eyes twinkled. "Could I have ice
cream on it?" she whispered.

"Certainly, Miss Delaney. Two kinds, if you like."

"Plain vanilla," Peggy said. "That's what I want. On
hot pie."

Peter waved the waitress over. "Hot apple pie,
please. Two slices. With vanilla ice cream."

"Yes, sir."

Peggy put her chin in her hand again and sighed
contentedly. "This is the best dinner I ever had."

"Oh, come now, Miss Delaney, I can't believe you
don't know how to bake a fine pie."

"Of course I do," Peggy said. "I'll bake you one, too,

for a thank-you if you'll let me. But it won't taste near as good to me as this one that I didn't have to do nothing but stick a fork in."

"Your frankness is endearing," Peter said. "I'll have to take you out to dinner again."

Peggy grinned. "You just ask."

It was dark and getting chilly when they left the restaurant. Peter turned the other way down the street toward the livery stable.

"Where are we going?" Peggy asked.

"To get a buggy. It's a long walk back."

Peggy didn't protest that she walked it every day. She stood on the wooden sidewalk, hugging her shawl around her while Peter dragged the stableman away from his own dinner and ordered a buggy.

"It's after hours," the stableman warned. "It'll cost you double. I got to come out after and rub him down again."

"That will be fine," Peter agreed placidly. His voice carried the unconcern of a man who had enough money to hire a buggy whenever he wanted one.

He handed Peggy in, and she bounced gently on the upholstered seat while Peter shook out the reins. "I feel like Cinderella," she said with deep contentment.

"I think her coach was much more elaborate," Peter said. "But this one does have the advantage of not turning unexpectedly into a pumpkin and mice." And if a buggy ride made her feel like Cinderella, he wondered how she would react if he brought her flowers. It was really very gratifying to spoil a woman who was so appreciative. Most of the ones Peter knew would have regarded a livery stable buggy as a marginal conveyance at best.

The horse, already fed for the night, clip-clopped sleepily down the street. Peter reined it past the shuttered storefronts and into Peggy's neighborhood. She sat up proudly beside him and waved jauntily at a young mother out gathering her children for bed. "I'll be the talk of the block tomorrow," she said, then giggled.

"Am I making you a scandal?" Peter asked seriously. He didn't want to damage her reputation. It wouldn't be fair.

"You're making me the envy of every woman I know," Peggy replied.

Most of her neighbors seemed to be sitting on their porches. Peter could make out their dim figures in the dark. Peggy leaned out of the buggy and waved again to be sure they noticed her.

Peter drew the buggy up in front of Peggy's house and got down to help her out. There were no lights on inside. Her father was presumably still at the saloon.

"Mr. Blake, I thank you."

"Miss Delaney, it was a pleasure."

Peggy looked at him expectantly.

Peter hesitated. He was dying to kiss her, and she seemed to expect it. "Um . . ."

Peggy put her arms around his neck and kissed him instead. She was undeniably good at it and kissed with the enthusiasm of someone who liked kissing. Apparently the neighbors' opinions were not a consideration. Peter put his arms around her waist and kissed her back. It felt so good that he went on doing it for longer than any of the carefully brought up young ladies of his acquaintance would have stood for. Peter had a healthy young man's appreciation for the feel of a willing girl in his arms, and the scent of soapsuds that clung to her was as heady as any perfume. She smelled faintly of perspiration, too, and of bleach and laundry starch. He found it oddly attractive, like smelling a real girl instead of a bottle of Florida water. He nuzzled her neck experimentally, and she wriggled closer. He wasn't sure exactly where this was going and was leery of letting it go too far. He stood back and smiled at her.

"Shall I walk you to your door?"

"Naw," Peggy said. "I reckon you saw enough of Pa the other day to last you."

"Is he home?" Peter looked nervously at the dark house. "I don't see a light." He had visions of the man emerging, wrathful, to ask his intentions. He shied a little and ducked toward the buggy.

"Passed out most likely," Peggy said. "That's his boots by the door. He knows I'll give him hallelujah for it if he tromps mud on my floor. Sometimes he's sober enough to notice."

"Oh. Well, good night then."

"Good night," Peggy said happily.

Apparently she wasn't going to ask if she would see him again, which made Peter feel a little easier. "I'll see you tomorrow," he called from the buggy. "For my shirts."

"They'll be waiting."

Peggy turned up the dark path, and Peter reined the horse around. He drove away with the sensation that every housewife on the street was out on her porch watching him. It made the back of his neck prickle, and he knew why—it was an instinct that he was out slumming and someone was going to tell his mother. He felt embarrassed by that, but he couldn't quite shake the feeling. As he drove home, he told himself that Peggy was a nice girl, and he was a cad to think about her that way when he liked her so much. He wanted to see her again, and why shouldn't he?

To make up for his ignoble thoughts, Peter, with a box of candy under his arm, picked his shirts up at closing the next day and walked Peggy home, blatantly by daylight.

She held the candy box in front of her, where she could admire the picture on it, of a woman in an improbably diaphanous dress, and the huge yellow ribbon bow. Smiling from ear to ear, she turned to him. "I'm going to save the box," she vowed. "Put it on the knickknack shelf with my cup and saucer."

It was only a box of drugstore chocolates. It was so easy to please a girl like Peggy, who had never had anything, that Peter felt uncomfortable. "I'm glad you like it," he said.

"Where'd they ever get the idea for that dress?"

Peggy asked, marveling. She giggled. "Wouldn't I just be a scandal in something like that?"

"Well, you know," Peter said seriously, "women used to wear dresses like that, back at the beginning of the century. That picture is a bad copy of a famous painting of Madame Récamier."

"Who was she?"

"A famous Frenchwoman. She knew all the political and literary men of her time and—"

"French," Peggy said. "Well, no wonder." She took his hand and pulled him up the steps to her house. "Come on. Let's open this." Inside, she took the ribbon off the box with the greatest care, then lifted the lid. "Oooh. Here, you pick."

Peter gravely selected a chocolate and bit into it. Peggy picked the same kind that he had and put the lid back on. "I'm going to make them last." She turned toward the narrow hall.

"I thought you were going to put the box on your shelf," Peter said, smiling.

"Not till it's empty. Pa would wade through them as fast as you can say Jack Robinson. He's not going to get a sniff of these."

Dubiously, Peter followed her into her bedroom, wondering how Peggy's father would like that. The room had a narrow dresser and a rusting iron bedstead painted white. Peggy pointed to the corner of the threadbare quilt that covered it. "You just lift the mattress up for me."

He did so, and the mattress rustled as he bent it. He thought the worn stuffing had been padded out with straw. Smiling sheepishly at him, she slid the box under it. "Kind of like a bank, you know."

"Safety deposit box," Peter agreed.

The shabby quilt had been a good one once, lovingly pieced together in a pattern of hearts and stars. He supposed that her mother had made it. A voice from the front of the house startled him into attention, and Peter shot like a rabbit from the bedroom, with Peggy behind him.

It was Peggy's father, bawling for his dinner as he came through the door. Peter blanched as Mr. Delaney shot him a bloodshot glance from under the peak of his cap. "What are you doing here?"

"Mr. Blake walked me home," Peggy said icily. "He come to the laundry to pick up his shirts." She pointed at the paper package Peter had left on the table. "And he was just going."

"Where's my supper?"

"It ain't time." Peggy shooed Peter out to the porch. He clutched his shirts under his arm. "Try not to mind Pa. I hate it when he's got a snootful."

"That's all right." Peggy, he realized, seemed more worried about his impression of her father than the man's impression of him or the fact that his daughter and a young man had been in her bedroom. Mingled relief and uneasiness made him shuffle his feet uncomfortably. "Do you, er, ever get a day off from the laundry?"

"I get Sundays when I put my foot down with Pa," Peggy said.

"Maybe we could go on a picnic." He wanted to see her. Damn it, he would see her, he decided, and the hell with her father.

"Where's my supper?" Mr. Delaney bellowed.

"Sunday morning," Peggy said, and Peter departed with as much grace as he could muster.

By Sunday morning Peter was whistling with anticipation. He dressed in white trousers, a striped blazer, and his best straw hat. The dream he had enjoyed for two nights running was still in the back of his mind, settled in a suitable niche where he could revel in the sensation and not have to think about its ramifications. He had woken this morning and the morning before with his arms around his pillow and the very clear memory that in his sleep the pillow had been Peggy.

As long as he didn't dwell on it for too long, he had almost quit worrying that a light romance wouldn't do. With a wary eye out for the gardener, Peter quickly cut a handful of yellow jonquils with his pocketknife. Then, a blanket and basket in hand, he set out for the livery stable.

Within minutes he was in front of Peggy's house. She was waiting on the porch with a basket on her arm. She had on a yellow dress that Peter thought must be her one and only best. The sleeves were big and balloony and stiffly starched.

Peter climbed down, tucked the jonquils into the basket, and handed Peggy in to the buggy, settling her basket beside the one he had brought.

"I baked that pie I promised you," she said, and sat back contentedly to watch the road unspool between the horse's ears, through the outskirts of the town, up the mountain, and into the high valley. The fields were yellow with mustard flowers, and the sky was cloudless. She took the jonquils out of the basket and braided them into a crown.

The road narrowed between high banks where the oil seeped blackly out of the rock. An overpowering smell of sulfur warred with the perfume of orange blossoms floating up from the orchards. Peggy wrinkled her nose.

"We'll be past it in a few minutes," Peter said. He had grown familiar with the road by now. He laughed. "When I was a kid, I lost an Easter egg once. It rained that Easter, and my parents had to hide the eggs inside the house. About a month later the whole parlor started to smell like this, and my mother wouldn't let anybody leave the house until we had found that egg. She took it out with tongs and made my father bury it."

They came out into the upper valley, and Peter turned the buggy down a dirt path through an orchard, where he stopped and helped her down. They spread the blanket under apricot trees, where there were only the heady scent of grass and the low, slow hum of bees. Peggy, wearing her crown of jonquils, took a deep breath and tilted her face to the sun. Peter stared at her, soaking up her prettiness, feeling wonderfully wicked to be in an orchard with her instead of at church. She lowered her face and stared dreamily back at him.

"What are you thinking about?" she asked. "You look awfully solemn."

"Do I?" Peter asked. "I was thinking how pretty you are. Lots prettier, for instance, than old Rutledge and Kemp." The day before, he had spent another trying afternoon in yet another board meeting and felt like a tightrope walker, determinedly on his wire above them while they all poked at him, trying to push him off the rope onto one side or the other. He knew he needed to and would have to make a decision about the refinery but couldn't. Economics and practicality spoke loudly for the move to Oleum, but Peter didn't want to be the man who gave the final word. He didn't want the suffering of the townspeople on his conscience. What a relief Peggy was, he thought, pretty Peggy with jonquils in her hair.

They ate until they were stuffed, devouring ham sandwiches made with fresh rolls from the bakery; oranges; bottles of sarsaparilla from the drugstore; and Peggy's pie.

"This is heaven." Peter sighed. "I wish we could just stay out here." He took his hat off and rolled over on his stomach, propping his chin in his hands. Peggy was stretched out beside him, picking Johnny-jump-ups from the grass at the edge of the blanket. He turned to watch her. She twisted half a dozen of the little wild violets together and stuck them in his buttonhole.

Peter reached up and brushed her face with his fingertips. "You're a pleasure to take on a picnic, Miss Delaney," he said softly. "In fact, you're a pleasure altogether."

Peggy wriggled a little closer, and he wrapped his arms around her. He kissed her, letting his hands explore the curve of her spine. When she pressed closer yet, he let them drop to the crest of her hip. Her breasts were warm against his shirtfront, and slowly he drew his hand up and touched one. She seemed to like it, turned a little in his arms, and stroked the hand that fondled her. He could make love to her, Peter thought, desperately wanting to. Her dress buttoned down the front. He tweaked the buttons open with his fingers, then slid his

hand inside warm folds of cloth that smelled like soap
and orange blossoms. His mouth fastened on hers,
harder now, and she parted her lips. His fingers rested a
moment on her chemise, then burrowed down inside it.

He knew that what he wanted must be obvious to
her, and she seemed happy with that, accepting his
physical attentions with the same uncomplicated pleasure with which she had taken the candy and jonquils.

Peter's hand slid out from her dress and down her
hip, stroking her thigh, lifting dress and petticoats,
coming to rest between her legs. Peggy sighed and
twisted under him so that he lay on top of her. She began
to unbutton his shirt.

What he was doing suddenly hit him like a brick.
He jerked his hand out from under her skirt. "I'm sorry,"
he said, gasping. "Peggy, I'm sorry." He sat up, breathing hard.

She looked at him, puzzled. "It's okay. I don't
mind." Peter was buttoning his shirt, so she buttoned
her dress, watching him curiously.

"It wouldn't be right," Peter said. "I'm sorry. I got
carried away."

Peggy seemed content with that answer. "Easy to
do," she agreed with a little chuckle, "on such a pretty
day." She put his hat back on his head and touched his
lips with a finger.

"We'd better go." Peter began packing the remains
of their lunch. Peggy, still smiling, picked up her jonquil
crown and hummed to herself.

Safely back in the buggy—and upright—Peter felt
his heart gradually stop thumping. He looked furtively
down at his trousers and tried to will that evidence away,
too. Maybe it would have been all right. He didn't think
she was a virgin—she'd been having much too good a
time. The notion of stopping the buggy, pulling Peggy
onto some soft grass, and starting over again banged back
and forth in his head. It wouldn't be honorable to give
her false hope, he decided. But she knew he hadn't any
notion of marrying her. She'd as good as said so. And she
wasn't in love with him. She wasn't showing any signs of

falling in love with him, although she obviously liked his attention and gifts. She had other beaux; she had told him that already. So why shouldn't he make love to her?

Peggy laid a hand on his arm. "Don't you worry about Pa," she comforted. "He won't even know I been gone."

Peter flinched, horribly aware that underneath it all, Mr. Delaney was exactly what he'd been worrying about. Peggy wanted out—away from her father and away from the laundry, and Peter couldn't shake off the question of what she might be willing to do to accomplish her goal. If she had been with other men, he assumed that she knew how not to get pregnant—and also that she knew how to be sure that she did.

Peter bit his lip, ashamed of himself for harboring such suspicions. Peggy was much too nice a girl to trap a man that way. But just how well did he know her, and how sure was he of that? A vision of himself facing her father and brother and the business end of a shotgun flooded his mind all too clearly.

"I'm sorry," Peter said. "Please forgive me."

"Sure," Peggy said, while Peter prayed that she wasn't astute enough to see what it was that he was asking forgiveness for.

He patted her hand. "You're much too nice a girl to treat that way."

"Aw," Peggy said. She seemed to be touched. "I swear you're the nicest man I ever went with. You make me feel like a real lady."

"You are a real lady." Peter smiled at her, relaxing again. By the time they got back to town, he had just about convinced himself that it was moral scruples that had stopped him.

sitting in here with him, although she obviously liked his attention and gifts. She had other beaus. She had told him that already. So why should he make love to her? Perry laid a hand on his arm. "Stop! If you move...

X

Topeka, Kansas, May 1896

Frank could feel the change of speed the moment the train started to slow. His eyes were squeezed shut against the wind of the freight car's movement and the whirling cinders that blew down the track beneath the cars. Then, without shifting his grip on the rods, he cracked open his soot-caked eyes to check the landscape. Ahead he could see the outline of Bill's head and shoulders under the next car—the cars had all been locked; no cushy ride this time. Both he and Bill rode slung in the precarious hammock of rods that braced the underside of the boxcar.

Frank was a "road kid" now, the hoboes' term for the younger ones, some only twelve years old, who often traveled in packs from train to train, city to city. They scrounged meals more often than they found jobs, and they hooked up with an older hobo whenever they could, for protection—although the protection often had its price. Frank had seen hoboes, rough arm possessively around a road kid's shoulder, leading him off to pay for his dinner in ways that Frank had recently become aware of. At least Bill hadn't wanted any of that. Frank was too big to be easy prey, and by now he was also too wary.

The train slowed some more, and Frank, bedroll on his back, got ready to jump. By reputation Topeka was a bad town. The railroad bulls shot hoboes from off the rods or tops of cars as often as not. If you wanted the odds in your favor, you got off the train before it pulled into the yards.

Frank gathered himself into a crouch, heart in his mouth as always. When the train lost a little more speed, when the hammering clamor of the wheels and linkages shifted a note, he jumped, flinging himself outward, arms spread, clutching at air, away from and past the thundering wheels that ate up track and anything that fell beneath them. He landed with a thud in knee-high grass and black-eyed Susans, then rolled over in time to see Bill flying in after him.

Bill hit the ground hard, harder than Frank had, and lay facedown for a moment, grunting. There were hoboes as old as seventy who still rode rods, but it got harder for those men with every passing year. Frank, with the springiness of youth still in him, regarded Bill now with a certain amount of pity.

Bill looked up and caught him at it. His blue eyes were as hard as marbles in his soot-streaked face. "Get up and get moving, kid."

They picked themselves up and began to trudge down the dry ditch.

"Might get work here," Frank said, starting a conversation by way of apology.

"Might."

"Stockyards," Frank said, sniffing the air. Stockyards were unmistakable, and always near the railhead.

"Railroad shops, too," Bill said, softening a little. "Might get on."

Frank glanced at him with curiosity. Railroad shops, where engines were built and refitted, didn't hire bums. That was skilled work. Had Bill been a rail-shop worker? Frank wondered. He must have been something—he had once let it slip that he had not started bumming until he was thirty. But by now Frank knew better than to ask.

Most bums had once had some training and still practiced their skill whenever they could get the work—transient trackmen of the railroads; railroad boomers, out-of-work brakemen or firemen; fruit canners laid off in hard times; sheep shearers whose work season was only four months long as the wool harvest shifted through the Southwest. The rest of the time they were whatever they had to be. Frank had learned that contrary to public opinion, most of them would rather work than panhandle, if only there was work to be found. They were handymen, jackleg carpenters, mule drivers, ice harvesters for the refrigerator cars on the fruit trains, and sewer hogs who dug ditches and roadbeds. Bill had decided that he and Frank would head for California and the summer harvest.

But first was sleep. You couldn't ride the rods and sleep, or you'd fall under the wheels. The railroads ate their passengers regularly with wrecks and derailments, and the bums were killed most frequently of all. It was too easy to fall, or be tossed off by a railroad bull, from the rods or the top deck or from the "death woods"—the narrow plank above the couplings of a boxcar. And inside the cars, freight could shift and sway when the train was highballing and kill or crush a rider. No experienced hobo was tempted to sun himself in the open doorway. Frank had tried it once and been yanked back by Bill as the train lurched around a bend and the huge sliding door rolled shut like a guillotine. "Want to keep your legs?" was all Bill had said.

Sneezing with soot and spring dust and pollen, they climbed out of the ditch and tramped through undergrowth along a barely visible path—a hoboes' track that Frank could follow now almost as well as Bill could. Frank unbuttoned his heavy coat and slung it with his bedroll over his shoulder. He had acquired a blanket and a thin pillow, which he had scavenged from a trash heap. The temperature was rising as the sun came up, and he was not only sticky with sweat and coal dust but itchy from the insect life that inhabited all his clothes.

They arrived in the jungle as a handful of other hoboes appeared from the opposite direction. These men had been riding east instead of west. Deep in the shrubbery and scrub trees, insulated from the thunder of the rail line, they could hear water. When the sound reached his ears, a bum wearing a railroad boomer's thousand-mile shirt of black sateen whooped and began to unbutton his garment, and in a moment they all were racing, howling and chortling, toward the stream.

Waist-deep and not too fast, the stream flowed just beyond the jungle, then pooled out gurgling and cool, under a stand of cottonwoods. Frank, stripping his clothes as he ran, went with the rest of the men. It was the first chance he had had in weeks to wash all over, and his filthiness was suddenly more than he could bear. He dropped his bindle on the stream bank and shucked off his boots and stinking socks, then his soot-blackened shirt and trousers and long underwear. He dropped the greatcoat on his bindle where he could keep an eye on it. Then he scooped up the clothes and went dancing into the water.

The river was full of naked men, laughing and splashing one another, dunking their pals under the pool, diving, and spluttering. The water was cold and clear, and it washed over Frank like a hymn, like a shouted hallelujah. Frank threw his clothes into the water, then dived under the water and came up shaking water from his ragged hair. Bill surfaced next to him, and Frank splashed a handful of water at him, then ducked again as Bill dived for him. They wrestled underwater, writhing like otters, in a flurry of loose clothes, and came up spouting and thrashing.

"I'm going to drown you, kid!" Bill yelled. But the water had made him happy, too, and he gave Frank a rare grin. He scooped up water in his hat and whirled it at Frank and everyone else nearby.

Frank made a grab at a sock that was floating downstream. He clutched his clothes to his chest. "I'll take your socks if you lose me mine, you bastard," he yelped. "I'm going to wash them out. Drown these bugs."

"Hell, you can't drown bugs," Bill said, chortling. "They're like 'boes—in-dee-structible!"

"Well, I'm going to try. They've had enough lunch off me." Frank stuck the rest of his clothes under one arm but spread his shirt to let the water flow through it.

He swirled his socks and trousers in the water, muddy now from the men's splashing, then held out his long underwear so the current could fill them. The water carried the legs away from him, washing out whatever was living in there. Then he turned the underwear inside out and repeated the process.

All up and down the stream, the other hoboes were washing. Finally they hung their clothes on the over-hanging limbs until the pool looked like a good wife's washday. Outraged columnists in small-town newspapers called them vermin, derided their dirt in the same tone they accused the vagrants of being jobless through their own doing; but in truth none of them liked to be dirty. No one enjoyed living in filth. The men washed whenever they could find water, whenever no switchmen chased them from the depot water tank or farmwives from their wells.

Frank hooked his socks on a twig above his underwear and went back to swim some more. Every now and then he craned his neck to check on his coat. He wasn't overly worried. It would be difficult to make off with it in broad daylight, and all the other hoboes were naked. They weren't going anywhere until their clothes dried. Besides, he had Bill with him, and most of the others seemed to recognize Bill, if not by previous acquaintance then by the aura he carried with him. They wouldn't tackle Bill in daylight, either.

Frank leaped like a porpoise in the pool, dived and leaped again, and saw that some of the others were watching him. He had grown taller and even more heavily muscled in the last months, but there was still a youthfulness about his body. He knew what they might be surmising about him and Bill. Frank dived again. They could think what they wanted—there was a certain protection in that, too. Bill was splashing like a puppy, but the years on the road—and whatever had occurred in the years before that to drive him to the road—showed on his body. There was a roll of fat just beginning to form above his waist. It was not the fat of indolence but the rearranging of the body with age. A jagged scar like twisted lightning ran down his cheek, and Frank, with his newly wise road-kid's perception, thought that probably the broken neck of a beer bottle had made it.

His right forearm looked odd, slightly thinner than the left and with an odd indentation, as if it had been twisted or smashed and not quite straightened. The injury must make it difficult for Bill to perform heavy work, Frank thought; Bill hadn't been lying when he'd told Frank in Indianapolis that he couldn't split wood any longer. But it wasn't scarred, and Bill had said he'd had it cut up in a fight. He had been lying about that. Frank wondered why. How had he hurt it? In a rail yard? The link and pin couplers that hooked the freight cars together cost many railroaders a finger or two. It was conceivable that a man who slipped could get his arm caught as well.

Bill noticed Frank looking and turned away, sliding underwater so that the arm was hidden. Frank shrugged again and, feeling as sleek as a seal, went back to his swimming, luxuriating in the sensation of the water sliding over him. Most of the other hoboes had climbed out now and, wrapped in the ratty blankets from their bindles, were crouched around a newly built fire. Coffee was boiling in one tin pot, and a hoboes' mulligan stew simmered in another.

Mulligan was a staple of the jungles, a communal concoction of anything handy, including hoppins, which were vegetables from gardens and market trash bins, and gumps, which included meat of any kind—bacon rinds, butchers' scraps, the occasional chicken straying by the road or stolen outright from a henhouse. Stealing food made Frank feel guilty, but he had been hungry enough to do it more than once. Their last job, stringing fence outside Kansas City, had broken a long spell of unemployment and hunger. Now they had a little money again, and Frank had a turnip and three onions for that night's mulligan in his coat pockets. Bill had a ham bone.

Bill climbed out, shook water from himself, and bent over Frank's coat for the vegetables. Frank floated lazily on his back and watched a patch of cloud drift through blue sky. A lark circled above him. Frank had almost come to believe that a life on the road was a prerequisite to appreciating how very beautiful America was; only with hardship could one revel in the softness of new grass; only by sleeping on the ground or riding on a boxcar was a hobo entitled to perceive the natural grandeur that the passengers riding on the plush inside could glimpse only through glass. Frank yawned and wondered if his father, devoted to the cause of duty all his life, had any knowledge of how magnificent America was. Had he ever taken the time to find pleasure in its loveliness, or had he been satisfied just with serving it, according to his lights?

The lure of the road was insidious, and in Frank's youthful enjoyment of it he had almost forgotten the great plans he had made to become a socialist and reform the world—almost but not quite. He had come to understand, though, that no system, no matter how just and humane, would reshape into respectability the lives of men such as Bill if it meant living boxed within the four walls of a single house.

Frank wasn't even sure by this time that he himself would want respectability, at least while he was young. There was too much out there to see—too many open roads and trains to ride—to give up the adventure for an office and a cause. Anyway, he told himself idly, paddling with his hands to stay afloat, cradled in cool water, he had come to learn about life, to understand what his father had claimed he didn't know. Frank yawned again. Still too much to see . . .

His eyes closed, with the memory of the lark fluttering behind his eyelids . . . and he woke to find himself sinking with his face full of water. It was time to get out. He swam strongly for the bank and climbed up, then pulled his blanket from his bindle to wrap himself in. He lay down under a tree with the coat for a mattress and his scavenged pillow under his head. Bill was already asleep and snoring.

Frank woke at midafternoon, stretched, and walked down to the riverbank for his clothes. They were dry now and smelled of sun instead of stale sweat. He pulled them on after shaking a beetle out of his shirt, and hopped around trying to send his foot into the stiff leg of his trousers.

Bill was awake, propped against a tree, looking at nothing. Frank stood over him. "You want to hike in, see what there is?"

"Too late in the day," Bill answered. "Tomorrow."

Tomorrow was fine with Frank. More hoboes had come into the jungle, and one of them had a guitar in a battered case. The smell of mulligan, hot and savory, and the wood smoke hung in the breeze. The stew's contents were by now unidentifiable. Anything might be in it, and Frank had learned not to ask. He was perfectly happy to eat a possum if nobody told him about it beforehand. He wandered over and after folding up his coat to sit on, hunkered down by the fire. He was still stiff from spending a night on the rods.

The others inspected him, gave him room, and asked no questions. The only credentials required in the jungle were that you contribute something to the pot— dandelion greens if you had nothing else—and put some wood on the fire. Their talk went on around him.

"Big Joe Jospey . . ." one of them said. "Yeah, I seen his moniker on the tank in Fargo last week. Might catch up with him here."

A depot water tank was the hoboes' mailbox, chalked with names of the men who passed that way, the date, and the towns where they were heading. Hoboes passing through town memorized the information and became walking grapevines, passing on the whereabouts of pals and acquaintances, towns that were hostile or not, rumors of work to be had in San Francisco or St. Louis.

"Going to go up the Indian Valley line this summer," the railroad boomer in the black shirt said. "Nothing around here." Indian Valley was the railroad bum's slang for the high end of the tracks—the railhead frontier up in Montana or the feeder lines in the Dakotas—where fewer questions were asked about a man's credentials. A railroader who had been blacklisted in the strikes of the eighties or in 1894 might still be able to work there.

"I was on the Sevier Valley line last summer," another man said. "Nothing there but jawbone pay— food and tobacco and scrip for the goddamned company store."

"Can't get a winter stake on jawbone pay," the man with the guitar said. "Never did get one last year. Tried to hole up in Florida but ended up on the county work gang." He scooted closer to the fire, took out his guitar, and strummed it dolefully. As the sun set, the afternoon was getting cold.

Frank got up off his coat and put it on. The wind shifted, blowing smoke and ash in his face, and he began to cough. Eyes streaming, he reached into his pocket for his bandanna, and then froze. His burning eyes forgotten, he reached deeper, fingers searching the lining, feeling for his gold school signet ring, but finding nothing. He jerked the bandanna out and shook it. Nothing fell from it. Nothing was in the other pockets, neither the inner nor outer ones, except for an onion skin.

"What's the matter, kid?"

Frank jerked his head up and then shook it grimly. "Nothing." He mopped his eyes with the bandanna. "Smoke."

His ring was gone. He felt quickly through the other pockets of his greatcoat again, but he had never kept the ring in any but the first one he had searched. He had sewn it by the band to the lining and never took it out. But he had a habit of stroking it, turning it in his fingers in the pocket. It had been there when he had come off the train. Now there was just a loose strand of thread. Frank turned his head slowly and looked at Bill under the tree. Nobody else knew he had had it; nobody else had touched the coat. Frank replayed the picture of Bill rummaging earlier in the coat for the onions.

As if he knew, Bill turned finally and looked back at him. After a long, slow stare, he turned his head away, blue eyes sinking closed.

"Here, kid." The railroad man, sensing some trouble, passed him a bottle—cheap hooch, raw and stinging. Frank took a deep gulp, which left his throat as hot as his eyes.

Frank stared at the fire and beyond, at the callused fingers plucking the guitar strings, a hobo tune he had heard before, as melancholy and brutal as life on the road. Suddenly life didn't seem as idyllic as it had before, nor so uncomplicated. Frank remembered an empty bean can in the woods—food that he suspected Bill of stealing from him—and of his analogy of the stray dog he had owned. That didn't seem so uncomplicated now, either. The dog had stolen to eat. It hadn't pilfered money; it had no understanding of money. But the ring was solid gold.

Nobody's your pal, kid. Not even Bill? Frank agonized. Not even now? Was that the price of the road? Other road kids paid a price. Because Bill hadn't tried to exact sexual favors, Frank had grown sure of him. But that *was* the price of the road, he realized now with a leaden thud like someone hitting him. You went it alone, or you paid up. Miserable, he huddled by the fire.

Another hobo had joined them, a "wolf" in hobo parlance, with his punk in tow, a thirteen-year-old boy with a thin, pinched face and a shock of wheat-colored hair covering his big ears. The wolf and his boy sat next to each other, and the man's attitude of ownership was obvious. The other hoboes glanced at them, then quickly looked away. They knew what had been transpiring between the pair, yet it wasn't their business to intervene or protect the youngster from the wolf. Frank flushed. Just now he felt not greatly different from that boy.

It wasn't the loss of the ring itself that upset him; the ring spoke of everything Frank had wanted to leave behind. It was his last link to his father's ambitions, not his own, and he was better off without it, freer without it. Instead, it was the sense of being manipulated, being owned—as surely as the boy across the fire would go panhandling tomorrow for the wolf and think that he was being loved and protected . . . and as surely as Frank knew he wouldn't say anything to Bill about the ring because he had grown both disillusioned and a little afraid of him.

After Frank, ignoring Bill, had eaten the mulligan out of a sardine-tin plate and drunk more whiskey, he wrapped himself in his coat and blanket and went to sleep.

In the morning he got up and found that Bill had slept the night under the tree, in a kind of silent dare to Frank to come and confront him. Frank walked over and looked down. Bill's hand moved a little under his bedroll, and Frank knew it was wrapped around the knife Bill carried with him.

"I hear there's work," Frank said. "We need a stake to get on to California."

Bill's dark, guarded face lost its tautness. He sat up, scratching leaves from his hair. "Ambitious, ain't you?" He grinned.

"I have to be," Frank said with meaning. "I haven't got anything left to hock."

Bill scrambled out of his bedroll, chuckling, and Frank thought he saw a certain amount of relief in his face. He slapped Frank on the back. "Makes a man free. No ties to bind. Kind of does you a favor."

"I expect it does," Frank allowed. In the morning, and with Bill whistling sunnily as he rolled up his bindle, the ring didn't seem to matter so much. If there was a dark undercurrent to life on the road, then maybe it was a favor to have been taught it. His head ached from the whiskey, and he felt more grown-up than he had the night before. By daylight he now recognized a distinction between himself and the little road kid who had drifted in last night. He could have fought Bill for the ring; he might even have won, although he doubted it. But then he would be alone, with no teacher to show him the rail lines, to hold the intricate web of track that knitted the country together in his head . . . no one to catch his hand if he slipped jumping for a car . . . no one to stand off a railroad bull with a club in his hand.

Last night he had wanted to cut loose from that. But this morning, with the opportunity to do so, he couldn't. If he had somehow traded his father, along with the ring, for Bill, it wasn't a concept he was ready to grapple with yet.

Things were different between Frank and Bill after that, though. They had reached some unspoken agreement, but it, too, had its price. Frank began to sleep with his boots tied around his neck even when there were just Bill and him, a hobo habit he had never bothered with before if no one else was around. Bill said nothing about it, except once, when he remarked, "You're learning." But that remark was offered offhandedly and might not have referred to the boots, had Frank chosen to ask.

They bummed from Topeka up to Omaha and then to Cheyenne, working a cattle drive in Cheyenne to increase their stake. Frank sewed what money he had in the lining of his coat and the bottom of his necktie. Frank had no idea whether or not Bill still had the ring, but he suspected Bill did. Frank thought the ring might be Bill's insurance against the day he finally lost a foot or a leg under a six-wheeler or met a bull strong enough to throw him off the top of a highballing mail train.

"Anyone looking for you, kid?" Bill asked him once. Parents sometimes sent the Pinkertons after their runaways if a road kid actually chanced to come from a family that cared. Frank imagined that Bill might not want to be caught with the ring on him but wasn't willing to give it up without good reason.

"Nobody's looking for me that's found me," Frank said, taking a perverse pleasure in being noncommittal. Let Bill worry. Runaway road kids dragged home by the Pinkertons and then rescued by their wolf were the stuff of hobo legend. But what happened more often than not was that the wolf got the hell beat out of him, and the kid ended up in a reformatory.

The jackallike packs of road kids who traveled on their own were frequently more savage than the older hoboes and made their stake by stealing and by rolling drunks. The Pinkertons and the railroad police were no more fond of them than they were of the seasoned tramps, although they might be somewhat more reluctant to throw a youngster off a speeding train. But a road kid who had been in a military academy and displayed solid-gold rings might be another matter.

Frank was no punk, and he made a point of proving it. His background gave him a bit of an advantage with Bill, and he used it, becoming less tractable as he grew more seasoned. When they played cowboys for five days in Cheyenne and Bill's arm gave out while fighting a green-broke horse, Frank, who rode expertly, pretended not to notice and let the beast toss him. Nor did Frank share his day's pay with Bill, after the manner of younger boys and their protectors. That was the price Bill had to pay for the ring.

The next day, battered and limping, Bill quit, and they moved on, catching a short-line freight to Laramie. They got into town after dark and tumbled out of an empty boxcar to run for it through the shadows on the edge of the railyard.

Bill, familiar with the Laramie jungle, said it would be full at that time of year. Western towns were less vicious than the Eastern ones or those in the Midwest. He said that too many Westerners had been nearly on the bum themselves when they had arrived here and hadn't gotten so civilized yet that they had forgotten about it. They were less prone to scare tramps or to smash jungles or to put bullets through the cook pots.

The Laramie jungle had the down-at-the-heels air of a frontier wagon train that had given up hope and stopped where it was. Shelters of packing crates and pieces of old tin roof, scavenged fragments of broken boxcars, and canvas tents were clustered around seven or eight fires. The air smelled of wood smoke and mulligan stew and the stench of unwashed men and open latrines.

Bill found a crew he seemed to know and went off to drink with them, leaving Frank to entertain himself.

They had fallen into that habit since Topeka, and it was as much Frank's doing as Bill's. Frank was a little afraid of Bill despite his sometimes sunny companionship; but Frank had begun to suspect lately that Bill was growing a little afraid of *him*. What the man might do about that, Frank wasn't sure. Bill was an enigma, as unfathomable as a boulder of coal with some fierce inner core forged in a fire that Frank could not imagine. He had begun to think he might cut loose from Bill when they got to California.

Frank settled himself around a fire where there was room and put a chunk of fatback and a carrot, carefully sliced with his pocketknife, into the mulligan.

The hoboes scooted over to make him welcome after a quick but careful inspection. "That your pal over there?"

"Yeah," Frank said.

"He got a moniker?"

"Goes by Digger Bill. I'm Frank." He had learned to leave off the last name.

"Heard of him. Not you."

"Reckon not."

They studied him some more and possibly revised their opinions of his age. Frank had begun to look older. His face had grown weatherbeaten, and he was beginning to acquire the feral look of the road.

When most of the hoboes were asleep and Frank was nearly out, too, Bill came stumbling back to camp, threw his bedroll on the ground, and fell on it. Bill had a taste for whiskey, Frank had discovered, and had begun to go on more and more benders. He started to snore, so Frank pulled his coat collar up over his ears.

When the sun was high enough to wake even Frank, who possessed the adolescent's capacity to sleep through anything, Bill was still out but no longer snoring. Sleeping it off, Frank thought with some disgust. He packed his bedroll and put his boots on before he shook Bill awake.

Bill was inert, his hat over his eyes, the blanket up to his chin. Still dead drunk, Frank thought. The other

hoboes were up and about their business, breaking camp
or boiling up their clothes in a tin washpot over a farther
fire. Frank shook Bill again, and when Bill didn't respond, Frank patted his face none too gently.

Bill's cheek was cold—colder than it should have
been even in the morning chill. Frank touched it again,
let his hand rest there a moment, then yanked the
blanket back.

"*Bill!*"

Bill didn't answer, and the brown pool of dried
blood on his chest told Frank that he wasn't going to.

"Bill!" Frank began to shiver, and the other hoboes
gathered around, staring.

"Jesus God."

"Dead!"

"He's been knifed."

Staring, they drew closer to Frank and muttered
ominously.

"Get up, kid."

Frank looked up, staring back at them. "I didn't kill
him."

"Somebody killed him, kid, and I don't reckon
nobody he didn't trust could get next to Digger Bill."

There was no time for mourning or even for deciding whether Bill warranted it. He certainly hadn't warranted being murdered. Grim-faced and accusing, they
stood around Frank. There was law, unwritten but as
clear as crystal, in the jungles. Rolling drunks was one
thing, although it might get you beaten up; killing was
another. If the brotherhood of tramps began to prey that
savagely on its own, there would be no refuge for them
anywhere, and they knew it. Frank knew it, too. He
thought fast, and before they could stop him, he dug
Bill's knife out of his bedroll—a better knife than
Frank's.

"Get away from me." He stood slowly, knife in
hand. "I didn't kill him. You better look for the man who
did."

"We know the man who did, punk," a burly hobo
growled.

"I'm nobody's punk," Frank retorted. "Not his, not yours. Why the hell should I have killed him?"

"Reckon you know, punk." Road kids, enslaved to a brutal jocker, occasionally got desperate.

Frank fingered the knife. "Call me that again, and I'll show you I'm not."

"This is murder," another man said. Young and earnest-looking, he was not much older than Frank. "If we countenance murder, we are truly beyond civilization."

"That's right, Doc."

"We are outcasts," Doc said. "We aren't trash."

"I didn't kill him," Frank repeated. He backed a step away from them.

"Nobody else could of."

"He was dead drunk," Frank told them.

"Didn't look drunk to me," another man said. His glinting eyes were framed between a whiskered chin and a slouch hat. "I was drinking with him last night, and he was near sober when he left. I known Digger Bill some years," he added. He spat on the ground and glared at Frank.

"He could hardly walk," Frank said. "Anybody could have gotten near him."

"But nobody did, 'cept you. I was awake near all night." He pulled his slouch hat down deeper over his forehead, and light flashed briefly from his fingers. Frank narrowed his eyes. The man quickly stuck his hand in his pocket, then brought it out again, bare; but Frank knew what he had seen. His Hargreaves Academy ring.

"You bastard," Frank seethed.

"Murdering scum." They were all bunched behind the man who had worn the ring, even the boy called Doc. These men knew one another. No one except the dead man knew Frank. Frank knew exactly how much chance he would have of convincing them of his innocence.

He took a good grip on Bill's knife. He picked up his bindle with the other hand. They took a step toward him, then stopped. "Try it," Frank challenged. He knew he was young and big and muscular. They all might take him, but no one wanted to be the first to try.

"Get him, boys," the man in the slouch hat said, but he didn't seem inclined to do it himself.

"Let him go," Doc said. "He hasn't anywhere to run to now." He looked almost sorrowful. "You're marked, fellow. You've cut yourself off."

"I didn't kill him," Frank said again. He looked at the man in the slouch hat. If he accused him, the man would be forced to jump him, and then the rest would follow. He moved another step away. "I'm gone." He walked ten paces backward, and no one followed. In a flash of vitriolic defiance, he flung at them, "I'm gone, but one of you's a killer. You all better sleep light till you figure out who he is!"

He turned and ran, bindle in one hand, knife in the other, stumbling through the underbrush. Tears suddenly streamed down his face. A low whistle announcing a train was crying up the tracks a quarter mile away. Frank slung his bindle and stuck the knife in his belt and sprinted for it. He didn't care where the train was going.

The jungle was on the west side of Laramie, and the train, outbound, was picking up fast. Frank lurched into the open as it came puffing up the tracks. He started to run, holding his hand to the side of the cars. Flying faster, they brushed past his fingers. When he felt a step rail smack his fingers he dived for it, praying. His chest slammed hard against the side of the car, and his arms felt as if they would pull from their sockets and send him rocketing, limbless, backward again. But he held on, breath smashed out of his lungs, ribs aching as if they had been crushed.

Christ, I made it. . . . He hung for a moment, waiting to throw up. When he didn't, he climbed, pulling himself over the top, then lay spread-eagled on the slanted roof. The wind whirled by, cooling the sweat on his face.

His heart was pounding. He lifted his head and saw the land rushing away behind him, faster and faster.

Ahead the train uncurled like a bright snake, a cannon-ball mail train hurling itself westward.

Crying, bereft, he rode flattened to the top of the car. The thunder of the wheels beneath him rumbled. *Gone, gone, gone* . . . Bill was gone; now Frank was gone, too—westward, finally alone, able to trust no one. Never again would he sleep in the camaraderie of the jungle without a knife beneath his pillow. Doc's words came back to him over the roar of the wheels. *Marked.* Tagged with the name of murderer on every water-tank grapevine. Now he was truly an outcast. The sunlight splattered on the rails ahead and sprayed back at him in fiery flashes, just as it had from the lost ring.

XI

Frank's self-pity lasted until the train rolled into Ogden, Utah, and he could climb down off the roof. There, he caught the eye of another hobo alighting from the car ahead. The look he gave Frank was veteran to veteran—no greenhorn rode the roof of a cannonball mail, at least not successfully—and Frank felt as if he had passed some test, some unmarked and vital way station on his journey.

He spent the night in the Ogden jungle. He was edgy but reminded himself that hoboes didn't use the telegraph. In any case he gave his name as Fritz, a childhood nickname his brother, Peter, had once concocted to annoy him. In the morning he struck it lucky and found a boxcar filled with sacks of wheat bound for Sacramento. It was a mixed train with Pullman cars ahead of the freights, but Frank hadn't enough of a stake to spend any money riding the plush—and he wouldn't have spent it if he had. He was pigheadedly proud of the fact that he hadn't bought a ride yet.

In Sacramento he caught a train going down through San Francisco to Salinas. The urge to stay awhile in San Francisco and see the sights was strong. But San Francisco was the location of his brother's motorcar company and his cousin Tim Holt's newspaper. Better to go to bucolic Salinas, he decided, where Tim and Peter were unlikely to stray. The train was as thick with hoboes as a ship was with barnacles. The grapevine said there was work in Salinas, bringing in the first lettuce crop. Between Sacramento and San Francisco,

171

and from San Francisco down to Salinas, was farm country. The air was so thickly scented with new-cut hay and wet fields, not even the smell of hot grease and coal smoke could overwhelm them.

Because Frank was young, it wasn't in him to stay pessimistic for long. He let himself mourn Bill briefly and grapple with whatever it had been in Bill that had prompted him to steal the ring and then to show it in some fit of drunken bravado to a man who would kill him for it. Frank came to no conclusions but managed finally to bury Bill in as shallow a grave in his memory as the hoboes in Laramie had probably buried his body—if they hadn't just dragged it away and dumped it far from the jungle for the police to find. One tramp more or less rarely bothered the authorities enough to investigate. Sometime he would think more about Bill and maybe reach an understanding.

For now, he picked lettuce in Salinas with a migrant crew, mostly Mexican, and stayed for a week in the labor camp on the edge of a farm. By then he had collected three dollars in pay and a backache that made him feel eighty years old. Most of the rest of his earnings had been docked for the unsavory mess that the field crew's cook served up, as well as "rent" for a bed in a bunkhouse made of packing crates and empty oil cans.

"There's got to be something better than this," he grumbled to no one in particular, devouring whatever nameless substance was on his plate. Maybe fruit picking, he thought. At least he could do that standing up.

He joined the swarm of men moving south again, traveling on to the next farm, the next orchard, the next rumor of work. But the trains proved to be well guarded. There were too many bums, too many free riders, and railroad management was going through one of its periodic fits of exasperation.

After a bum who was thrown from a roof and fell under the wheels died, Frank took to the dirt road instead. His boots were still in good condition. The weather was fair. Even with his greatcoat rolled into his bindle, he didn't have much to carry. He had not yet become like some older hoboes who lugged every conceivable scavenged necessity—four cookpots, three hats, two coats—their own snail shell on their backs.

He tramped south from Salinas to Monterey, worked a week in the canneries there, and then set out through the lovely South Coast country with enough food to last a couple of weeks and a tent for which he had paid hard cash. He was no longer comfortable in the jungles. The stark beauty of the coast—jagged rock and the tall spires of redwood groves, with the ocean, green and turbulent, below—gave him part of what he had come away from home for. This was an opportunity to be alone, utterly alone in the night, with the flung diamonds of the stars overhead and no other voice but a coyote's in the distant hills. These places induced a kind of contemplation that caused Frank to realize that although he wasn't perfectly sure of anything anymore, he wanted to see it all.

He hiked on, repaired a barn roof in the Carmel Valley, and built a chicken coop in Jolon. He was proud of that chicken coop. He had never built anything from scratch, and the way it rose under his hands and the smooth, obedient feel of wood under ax and saw were a pleasure to him. When he was finished, the coop leaned a little, but it was solid. It looked jaunty, he thought, and the chickens seemed to like it. They settled in, clucking and chuckling to themselves in the straw, while the rooster strode back and forth in front, crowing.

"Must think he built it himself," the farmer said approvingly. "I've got more work," he offered, "if you want to stay on."

Frank was tempted. He had exchanged his work for a huge, delicious breakfast. The little farm was cozy, the sort of place that hired hands dreamed of, with a plump farmwife making biscuits at dawn every day and a Jersey cow lowing contentedly in her field, chin resting on the top rail of the fence and morning mist wreathing her ankles.

"No," Frank decided. "Thank you, but I'll be moving on."

"You're young," the farmer said. "I used to go tramping myself. Went clear to Arkansas once. But at my age a man stays put when he finds his place." He glanced affectionately toward the farmhouse, where his wife was doubtless baking bread or putting up preserves.

Near Paso Robles, Frank caught a train again and traveled south of San Luis Obispo before the authorities threw him off. The train wasn't going very fast, and he jumped before the railroad bulls could toss him. He landed in a ditch. The road south ran near the tracks, and he started down that. He thought of the farmer in Jolon. Frank was tired of the trains and the luckless bums who rode them. He daydreamed that some driver on a hay wagon would pass and give him a ride.

If wishes were horses, then beggars would ride. His mother used to say that whenever he or Peter or Midge expressed a desire for something unreasonable or otherwise out of reach. In this case, to Frank's delight, the wish came true some quarter of a mile later, when a huge, empty freight wagon clattered past him and stopped.

"You want to earn a ride, bud?" the driver called over his shoulder.

"Sure." Frank trotted up.

"Then climb on. I got a pile of furniture to load. You help me out, I'll take you clear to Santa Maria with it and pay you two dollars for the work. Throw in a good dinner."

"Sure!" Frank said again. He threw his bedroll into the back of the wagon and hopped up beside the driver. The sides of the wagon said Mission Moving and Hauling in fading paint.

"I could use some more muscle," the driver said, whipping up his team. "Got an old lady in Guadalupe, she's selling up the farm to move in with her son. Won't go without her granny's breakfront and dining table and all her whatnots."

Guadalupe was another farm town, a single, two-block-long main street, surrounded by fields of cabbage and the feathery gray leaves of plants the driver identified as artichokes. The farmhouse was weathered and old; the fields were overgrown with weeds or gone to seed. The woman who met them at the door was at least in her sixties and as weathered as her house. Widowed, Frank thought, with a son in the city and a farm that was too much for her. The "whatnots" proved to be massive oak and mahogany pieces, a bedstead with a monstrous headboard, and a three-tiered sideboard with a marble top. The dining table was five feet across with a pedestal base and gigantic claw feet.

"You be careful with that," the woman warned as they lifted each piece.

"Yes'm." Frank got hold of his end of the marble slab, and he and the man staggered out the door with it. It was like lifting a tombstone.

"And you crate that!" she called after them. "I don't want it cracked."

They loaded the sideboard and the table, carefully tying into cloth bags the screws that assembled the pieces. In the parlor were a settee of hideous antiquity, with carved wooden roses, and a grand piano.

It took all morning, and midway through their labors, the son arrived to supervise. He wore a natty banker's suit, a derby, and spats.

"Now you watch it with the piano," he cautioned.

"I ain't planning to drop it," the wagon driver grunted as he and Frank maneuvered it with great difficulty through the door. "You didn't mention no piano," he added.

"I certainly did," the son protested. "What do you think I hired help for?"

"Reckoned it was so you didn't get no rupture moving that goddamned breakfront," the driver muttered under his breath.

Frank wondered what the driver had planned to do had he not fortuitously come upon Frank walking down the road.

The old woman's son didn't seem inclined to lend a hand with any of it. He followed them out to the wagon to make certain they padded all the furniture properly and to argue with his mother over a set of china, apparently sent on ahead.

"Maisie doesn't think there's going to be room for it," he said. "She's got her own dishes, brand new."

"There'll be room," his mother said, "or I'm not coming, Clem. If you'd stayed and run the farm like your daddy wanted, I wouldn't have to be moving."

"We've been through that, Mama," Clem said, surveying the farm with dislike. "And I got you a good price."

"Land company!" His mother snorted. "Pretty soon there won't be no family farms. Country's going to the dogs."

Frank and the driver went back in to get another load, and she followed. Frank thought she wasn't going to like her new home one bit, and he was reminded of the hens in Jolon, secure and happy in their spruced-up habitat.

He and the driver got to Santa Maria as the sun went down and unloaded everything in the dusk, wriggling the heavy pieces into the spaces that a disapproving Maisie had begrudgingly cleared for them.

"You got good muscles, kid," the freight driver said as they hauled the ungainly bedstead up two flights of stairs. "You from around here?"

"No," Frank said.

"Where are you from?"

"Lots of places," Frank grunted, setting the bedstead down. "Off and on."

"I thought so," the driver said. "You got the look."

By the time the piano was brought in, a process that drew observation and advice from a gaggle of small boys on the sidewalk, night had fallen. The driver headed the team out of the residential neighborhood where Maisie and Clem lived and into the town. In full darkness he drew rein outside a restaurant near the stockyards and gave Frank a nickel. "You go on in, kid, and have them rustle us up some coffee. I'll find some water for the team, and then we'll eat."

The restaurant was plain and homey, closed up

against the night chill of the coast. Frank sat at the counter, surrounded by the smell of hot grease, and gave the nickel to a Mexican waitress with a voluminous canvas apron over her red dress. He put his bindle on the floor.

"Two coffees. My pal will be in in a minute, and then we'll want hot dinners."

She brought him the coffee, which was horrible but hot, and he drank it greedily, warming himself. The other customers were mostly farmhands and field workers, many of them Mexican, like the two waitresses. Frank cocked his head to listen to the fast flow of the conversation, liquid and lilting and strange, around him. He finished his coffee and when the driver didn't come in, started on the other cup. He had finished the second cup by the time it dawned on him that the driver wasn't coming in.

Frank jumped off his stool and yanked the door open. There was no wagon or team to be seen, no activity to be heard in the dark street at all except for the muffled lowing from the stockyards. Frank groaned and limped wearily back to his warm stool in the restaurant and put his head in his hands.

"More coffee, señor?"

Frank shook his head morosely.

The waitress hovered over him. "You sick?"

"He stiffed me," Frank said, outraged.

The waitress looked puzzled. "Your friend?"

"He cheated me!" Frank seethed. The whole world was a cheat. He felt embarrassed to have been duped so easily and was furious over the hard work he had done. "He owes me a day's pay. You know a Mission Hauling Company?"

She shook her head. She took his coffee cup and refilled it.

"I can't afford any more," Frank said.

"Refills are free."

The other waitress was older, with the same dark eyes and cinnamon-colored skin. The younger one beckoned her over while Frank thought unhappily about his lost dinner and two dollars' pay. If he could find the bastard, he could go and try to shake it out of him; but in this part of the country, the "Mission" in Mission Hauling didn't mean any more than calling yourself Colonial would have meant in Virginia. There were Spanish missions all up and down the coast. They were local landmarks. Every other business was the Mission something or other. Frank felt through empty pockets and looked hungrily at the pies under glass on the counter.

The waitresses watched him sympathetically and talked to each other in quick, chirruping Spanish. "*Niño pobre*," one of them said.

"You have a place to sleep?" the young one asked him.

"I have my tent," Frank said. At least he'd had enough sense to bring his bindle in. He had been afraid that someone might steal it out of the wagon, distrusting an unknown person while the acquaintance beside him was getting ready to stiff him. He looked down at it, hurt and furious. "No money, though," he muttered. A stranger wasn't going to care about that. That was his problem. Another lesson learned. Frank put his empty coffee cup back in the saucer and started to get up.

"No, no." The young waitress looked over her shoulder into the kitchen, and then quickly, while the older one watched, cut a generous wedge of pie and set it in front of Frank. "Don't tell," she whispered.

Frank stared, and then he grinned. "Gracias," he whispered back. He picked up a fork and ravenously ate the pie while they watched him maternally.

"I wish I could pay you," he said when he had finished.

"It's okay." With another furtive glance at the kitchen, the older one slid a paper-wrapped parcel across the counter. "It is just scraps. We have to throw them out anyway."

Frank put the parcel in his coat pocket and found two cents at the bottom. He put them on the counter. "It's all I have. You take it."

"No, no." They pushed the coins back at him.

Frank picked up his bindle and let himself out into the dark street. The package might have been filled with scraps, but he knew they wouldn't have been thrown out, not in a restaurant like that. Families were too big and money was too scarce to waste food. The scraps would have gone home with the cook or the women who had given them to him. He looked back through the lighted window. Behind its film of dust and grease, the women were already back at their work.

Frank felt as if someone had held him upside down and shaken him, rearranging all of his notions. A man he had trusted had cheated him, and unknown women had given him pie as well as meat from their own dinner.

He trudged south out of the town and pitched his tent in a fragrant eucalyptus grove. He fell asleep, mulling everything over while a pair of courting owls hoo-hooed to each other in the branches above him.

Two weeks later Frank had gotten as far south as Ventura and begun to look for work in the fields there. Not here, they told him. But maybe around Ojai, or maybe farther south in Oxnard. Frank turned his steps inland. He didn't know where he was going, but it didn't matter. He had the whole world to explore, and the more he saw of it, the more rich and strange it became to him. Like a sponge he wanted to soak it all up, and someday, eventually, he might come to understand it. For now he would work his way through it, pick the things that grew from it.

The Ojai Valley enchanted him. A mountain, stratified like a layer cake, with faint traces of the winter snow still on the top, rose above the east end. Below it the valley, still green from the winter rains, rolled out. He redug irrigation ditches washed out by winter storms, then moved on, drawn upward out of curiosity, to the apricot orchards and oil fields. He stared at the drilling rigs until someone asked if he was looking for work. He was directed on again toward Sierra and Sierra Oil.

He presented himself at the hiring hall, and the boss inspected him.

"Got any experience, bud?"

"Sure," Frank said, undeterred by the fact that none of it was with oil wells. After all, it was only another kind of harvest, another crop to be pulled from the ground. The drilling rig on Yellow Mountain had fascinated him. He wanted to see if he could make one go.

"What have you worked at?"

"Jackline tender," Frank said, proudly bringing forth a term he had heard.

"Two dollars a day and a bed in the bunkhouse. Wagon's waiting." The boss jerked his thumb at the side door. "Next."

Frank stared around him, still fascinated, as the wagon lurched up the steep track into Avenal Canyon. The lush, emerald hills' knee-deep grass was beginning to seed. On the higher reaches was manzanita scrub, the red branches twisting in the sunlight. At the end of the road a tramway climbed steeply, shooting still farther into otherwise inaccessible country—a railroad to the sky. Frank grinned, delighted as the breeze caught his hair. The wind was hot, dusty, and smelled of sulfur. He climbed out into a wooden city on the mountaintop. Derrick spires and the low roofs of drilling sheds and bunkhouses sat below.

"Delaney, show him the ropes."

Frank followed, still turning round and round as he went to take in the sights. The "ropes" seemed to be literal ones—a dozen lines strung out from pulleys, high above a single shed to pumps clustered like moored boats around it. Frank, gawking, craned his neck up.

Delaney scratched his red head and gave Frank a look of deep suspicion. "You run a jackline before or not?"

"Well . . . uh . . ."

Delaney chuckled with what seemed to be genuine amusement.

"I can learn," Frank said in a hurry. "I can learn anything."

"Well, hell," Delaney said. "It's no skin off my nose if you can't."

Surprised and gratified, Frank hastily assured him that he could.

"Serves 'em right for not paying attention," Delaney said, laughing.

"I took an engineering course in school," Frank told him.

"College boy?" Delaney raised his eyebrows.

"Well, no. High school."

"Silly bastards," Delaney muttered. "Who the hell they got on at the hiring hall?"

"I don't know," Frank said.

Delaney grinned again with an amusement Frank didn't quite understand. "Well, if you blow the sucker up, it's more work for me. I like a little job security. Come on."

Delaney took him into the shed. A single eccentric wheel revolved inside, pulling and releasing cables that ran through the roof and fanned out to the surrounding wells. It was powered by a steam boiler that hummed and buzzed like a horsefly and had to be kept stoked with coal.

"They been trying to come up with an oil burner to fire the damn thing, but they ain't yet, praise God," Delaney said. "They already blew up a ferryboat trying to run it on oil. Now, you take a twelve-hour shift, alternating with me, and you get Fridays off if you ain't blown the rig to hell by the end of the week. You got to keep the firebox stoked right and watch your gauges. Too much steam, and she'll blow. Not enough, and the wheel won't turn right, and you're like to snarl the lines."

Frank was inspecting the rig, more absorbed by the irregular revolutions of the eccentric wheel than by the needs of its boiler. But he went over and dutifully let Delaney instruct him in the reading of the gauges.

Whatever arcane machinery might be run by the steam, the boiler was the heart of it. The kitchen boiler that had heated his parents' house in Alexandria, the boilers that drove the incredibly fast six-wheeler mail trains, and the monstrous boilers that ran the canneries in Monterey were all members of the same family. Frank had a healthy respect for them. A mistreated boiler could explode, and given the proximity of uncounted barrels of oil, that was an unnerving prospect.

"That's right," Delaney said. "You pay attention. If you ain't scalded to death right off by the steam, you'll go up in hellfire."

"Yes, sir," Frank said. "I have fired a boiler before. Truly."

"All right. Now take a look at these cables. She'll run like clockwork if you keep the boiler going. But if a cable snaps or slips, you shut down pronto. You got that?"

"Yes, sir."

"I want to be sure of that," Delaney said. "You take your first shift with me."

At the end of the day, weary and grimy with oil, they took turns under the pump in the yard. Delaney stuck his head under the water while Frank worked the pump handle. "I reckon you'll do all right, kid." He came up shaking water from his hair and scrubbing his face with a towel.

Frank stuck his head under the pump, feeling as if he had been fried in petroleum. The inside of the jackline shed was as hot as Hades, and he was black from head to toe.

"There's a shower in back of the bunkhouse," Delaney said.

"Tomorrow," Frank said. "Tonight I'm too tired to care."

He ate a meal of stew, provided by the oil-field cook and only marginally more palatable than mulligan, then fell into his bunk. He slept the rest of his twelve hours off and was ruthlessly prodded out of bed by Delaney to take the first shift the next day.

Frank watched the eccentric wheel ratchet its way

around, stoked the boiler, read the gauges, and wondered why on earth he was enjoying this. It seemed incomprehensible to him at first, but he truly did like this job. There was a satisfaction in the oiled precision of the engine and the wheel.

At the end of the week he picked up his timecard and rode the tram down the mountain with Delaney to pick up their pay at the oil-field office.

"You're on your own, kid," Delaney said. "I got business to tend to. Just don't miss the tram in the morning."

"I want to buy some clothes," Frank said. He thought maybe he'd stay awhile, get off the bum, and pull a stake together. A week of sleeping under a roof had left him reluctant to give it up. "And get the things washed." His clothes were stiff with oil.

"Down the street," Delaney told him. "My pa's laundry, if he ain't dead yet. Tell my sister, Peggy, I sent you." He set off in the other direction, apparently harboring no desire for a visit home.

Frank bought a pair of denim jeans and a new work shirt in the dry-goods store, then talked the owner into giving him permission to put them on in the back room. He took the discards to the laundry, feeling that he might be better served by simply burning them—a sentiment echoed by the laundress when he handed them across the counter.

"This ain't all going to come out," Peggy Delaney said. "You know that?"

"Anything you can get out will be an improvement," Frank said.

"No kidding. We'll boil them and see."

"I don't suppose I could get them back today? Sid said to say he sent me," Frank added, giving her what he hoped was a winning smile.

"Well, considering you're the only thing he's sent me in months, and that includes money, I guess I can try," Peggy said. She smiled back at him with a look that made Frank glad he was wearing new clothes and not the revolting bundle on the counter. "You don't talk like an oil-field roughneck. Where you from?"

Frank shrugged, reluctant to intrude his old life into his new one. "All over."

"Tramping? Lots of men are these days. You were lucky to get on at the company. They just fired a hundred men for unionizing, or you wouldn't have been hired."

Frank looked dismayed. His sympathies were with the unions.

"It ain't your fault," Peggy said.

Frank stared at her, reluctant to leave. "Would you take a walk with me, if I pick up my things when you close?" he asked, a little startled by his own boldness and newly acquired confidence. He had never asked a girl out before. And Peggy wasn't really a girl. She was older than he was.

"How old are you?" she asked, apparently considering the same question.

Frank looked at the wilted calender on the wall. "Eighteen," he said with a sudden and dazzling smile. "Today. It's my birthday."

"Many happy returns," Peggy said skeptically. She cocked her head, considering. "Well, I don't see why not," she said. "Seeing as it's your birthday. I never went with anyone younger than me, but to tell you the truth, I took you for twenty at least. What's your name?"

"Frank. I'll be here at five," he said happily.

At five, Peggy had his clothes, stained but washed and smelling of bleach, under one arm. She was waiting by the door as he sauntered up, hands in the pockets of a new denim jacket, the wind ruffling his sandy hair.

"I wish I could take you someplace nice," he said ruefully. "But I spent all I had on clothes."

I must be crazy, Peggy thought. She felt untethered, at a loose end, straining to get away from the oil fields but taking up with another roughneck. This one had something different about him, though, the same quality that Peter Blake possessed, of knowing things beyond her experience and still thinking she was a lady. This one wasn't rich, of course; but on the other hand he was better looking than Peter. In fact, he was better looking than nearly anybody she had seen, with the muscular sexuality and the friendliness of a young tom-cat.

"What did you do with yourself all day?" she asked him.

"I spent it in the library," Frank answered.

He showed her the book under his arm. *An Anthology of Modern Verse*, it said. *Well, good Lord,* she thought. "You don't have to take me out. It's your birthday. I'll cook you dinner if you want. I cook better than those chuck-wagon cooks."

"Anybody does," Frank said ruefully. "But I bet you're great."

"I never read any poetry," Peggy said as they walked.

"I'll read you some," Frank offered. He opened the book. "Wait a minute." They were passing a house with a flower garden in front. He vaulted over the picket fence and snagged a tiger lily and vaulted back. He gave Peggy the lily and began to read:

> *"The blessed damozel leaned out*
> *From the gold bar of Heaven:*
> *Her eyes were deeper than the depth*
> *Of waters stilled at even;*
> *She had three lilies in her hand,*
> *And the stars in her hair were seven."*

He looked up at her and smiled. "That's Dante Gabriel Rossetti."

"Stars in her hair?" Peggy murmured. "I like that." She looked over her shoulder at the garden. "That's old lady Miller's. If she saw you, she'll be after us with a broom."

"Nothing ventured, nothing gained," Frank said. "And anyway, she didn't see me."

"You're terrible," Peggy said, laughing.

"Oh, I'm a desperado," Frank admitted, then joined in the laughter. "No garden's safe."

Peggy sniffed the lily. "Read me some more?"

She took him up the street to her house, where she lit the lamp and put the lily in a glass of water. Frank, meanwhile, leaned against the wall with the book open in his hands.

They ate nearly half the chicken pie that was in the warming oven, and Peggy produced two bottles of beer from the little root cellar that had been dug outside the back door. She decided that if her father came home drunk enough, she could convince him that he'd had them himself. Anyway, she knew he wasn't likely to come home. He hadn't been home in three days, and when he was on a bender like that, it always lasted an entire week.

"You're not only better than the chuck-wagon cook," Frank said, "you're wonderful." He drank the last of the beer and looked fully content. Peggy got a pan of water from the pump and put it on the stove to warm for dishwater.

Frank got up and stood beside her. "I'll wash those for you."

Peggy blinked in surprise. Peter Blake might bring her chocolates, but he never washed the dishes for her. Funny how they had the same last name, but it was a common one.

"You got any kinfolks?" she asked while Frank washed the dishes.

"Not around here."

"One of these days I'm going to be able to say that," Peggy said. "I swear to God."

"You don't get on with Sid?" Frank swiped a dish through the rinse water and put it on the table for Peggy to dry.

"I get on fair enough with Sid when he's around. It's Pa and this oil field I'd like to show my heels to. If I was a man I'd just catch a freight like you done."

"Women do now and then," Frank told her. "But it's a bad life for them. Don't you try it."

Peggy dried the last dish. He was protective of her, as if he were the older one. "No, I reckon I'll be here awhile yet, till I get enough put by to start out new somewhere."

"A woman as pretty as you needs to be careful," Frank cautioned.

Peggy smiled at him. "Careful of what?" she asked, her eyes dancing.

On an instant's impulse, Frank bent down and kissed her. "Careful of people like me, maybe."

"I'm older'n you," Peggy reminded him, her eyes twinkling. "I can watch out for myself—if I get to feeling like I need to." She reached up and traced the outline of his lips with a fingertip.

"What do you feel like watching out for right now?" Frank whispered. "Me or your pa?"

Peggy giggled. "Pa don't care what I do, long as I keep working. He's going to get a surprise one day."

Frank, seizing the opportunity, put his arms around her.

Peggy moved a little closer, just letting herself drift into it. Why not? He was awfully nice and very handsome, and kissing him blocked out the oil field and the long, dreary days working for just what she could skim from the till. His strong arms felt good. Frank was something she could skim from the till, too—a little bonus that life held out every now and then . . . a chance to be warm and cuddled and loved, even for only a night.

Kissing, they walked down the dark hall, then climbed into Peggy's bed, the straw in the mattress crinkling under them. Frank's eyes glowed, and his breath came faster as it became clear what she was offering. His hands roved over her, quick and hungry, undoing the buttons of her dress, feeling for the strings of her chemise. Peggy unbuttoned his shirt and buried her face in his chest, inhaling the scent of sizing and new cloth and the warm smell of his body. The buttonholes on the new jeans were stiff, and both she and Frank fell to laughing trying to get the buttons through them.

Frank wriggled his jeans down over his narrow hips, then kicked them off the bed.

"You feel so good," he murmured, stroking her.

His hands were callused and hot, and their touch made her nipples stand up. She wondered dreamily, fitting her hips to his, if he had ever been with a woman before and decided that if he hadn't, he had a pretty good idea what to do about it. Being wrapped in his arms was like being in a warm cocoon. It felt good being wanted this much, just for herself.

"You can sleep here tonight," she whispered afterward, cradling him. "I'll wake you in time for the tram."

Frank floated now as he had in the stream, halfway between sleeping and waking. "That was the first time," he whispered back. "Thank you."

Peggy cuddled him, liking the solid, muscular feel of his broad shoulders. "I thought maybe it was," she murmured. "But you got a natural gift for it, honey." She giggled in the darkness. "Happy birthday."

Frank propped himself on one elbow, eyes heavy lidded. "Good teacher." He kissed her throat. He felt as far from Washington and the Hargreaves Academy as he was likely to get.

"I never knew any boys that read poetry before," Peggy said.

"Do you want to hear some more?" He was beginning to wake up now, to be reluctant to sleep and miss anything. He was also feeling an interesting stirring that could lead to more lovemaking.

"Okay."

He got out of bed, padded into the kitchen for the book, then came back. He lit a stump of a candle on the crooked nightstand by the bed and sat cross-legged in the tangled bedclothes.

> "Sunset and evening star,
>   And one clear call for me!
> And may there be no moaning of the bar,
>   When I put out to sea."

"Who wrote that?" Peggy asked.

"Tennyson. It's called 'Crossing the Bar.'" He read the rest while she listened, twining a strand of her tumbled hair around one finger.

"That's about dying, isn't it?" she asked when he had finished.

"Yep," Frank said. "I like it a whole lot."

"Who would have thought of writing a poem about dying?" Peggy said wonderingly. "Death in the oil fields is common enough, and no one gives much thought to it. It comes when it comes, and often it ain't pretty." She sighed. "I like it, too, though. 'I hope to see my Pilot face to face.' That's almost like church, isn't it?"

"Mmm-hmmm." Frank smiled as he leafed through the pages. The light from the candle made a yellow circle, encompassing them both. "Poets have trouble with the church, though. Poets think too much." He flipped another page and came upon Edward FitzGerald's translation of Omar Khayyám. "This is by a Persian fellow. He believed in living for now. . . ."

He lingered over the verse, shaping it into magic in the candlelight while Peggy listened to the foreign-sounding words and mysterious visions.

> "Iram indeed is gone with all his Rose,
> And Jamshyd's Sev'n-ringed Cup
>   where no one knows;
> But still a Ruby kindles in the Vine,
> And many a Garden by the Water blows."

The candle fluttered and dimmed. Frank laid the book down and pinched the small flame out. He quoted from memory, "'We are no other than a moving row, of magic shadow-shapes that come and go. . . .'" He slid down into the bed, reaching for Peggy, twining one ankle around hers. "'Round with the sun-illumined lantern held, in midnight by the master of the show.'" He kissed her, his heart thudding, and abandoned himself, like Khayyám, to the here and now.

With the feelings evoked by the Persian poetry still singing in their heads, they made love again, more slowly now that the first hungry edge was gone, then slept finally when the sun began to splinter the darkness.

"Oh, my Lord!" Peggy sat up suddenly, throwing the covers off them both.

"What?" Cold air on his bare skin rocketed Frank out of sleep.

"Look at the sun!" Peggy, trailing hairpins in the bedclothes, scrabbled for her chemise and petticoats. "Look at the time! You're going to miss that tram. Get *up*!"

Frank sat up and dived for his pants.

"I ought to be at work *now*!" Peggy pulled her dress over her head and twisted her hair into a knot, jabbing pins into it. The sun stared accusingly through a cracked windowpane. "You're going to get fired."

"No, I'm not." Frank, hopping on one foot, pulled a boot on. "I'll make it. You've got your dress on inside out."

"Oh, hellfire!" Peggy yanked it off again and pulled it on correctly. "I *always* wake up on time. Oh, Lord!"

They dressed and ran, Frank hurrying back again to retrieve the book. His touseled hair stood up on end like exclamation points.

"You're a sight," Peggy said. The warm, magical cocoon of the night before was split open by the day . . . but just a trace of it lingered, enough to soften her expression as she unbolted the door. "You look like—like—" Suddenly she burst into giggles as quickly as she had wakened to indignation. "Like you been helling around all night," she said in helpless laughter. "Come *on*. You got to catch that tram." She pushed him out the door.

Frank bolted down the path. At the gate he yelled over his shoulder, "It was worth it. Even if I miss it, it was still worth it!"

He took to his heels up the street with the book under his arm.

XII

Washington, D.C., July 1896

The Holts had invited the Blakes to come to the District to dine, ostensibly to discuss politics—the Democrats had just nominated the flamboyant and controversial William Jennings Bryan for the presidency—but actually because Alexandra Holt, suspecting that Cindy Blake was on the thin edge of a breakdown, wanted to visit her sister-in-law.

"Well, Toby, are the Republicans going to get in this time? Or are we going to have that madman for a president?" Henry Blake cast a disapproving glance at a copy of the *Washington Post*, which lay on the dining room sideboard. They had all read Bryan's "cross of gold" speech, and irreverent political cartoonists were already caricaturing him as Jesus.

"I don't expect Toby knows any more than we do," Cindy told her husband. "I don't know why you always expect people to know these things." Her voice was thready, and she twisted the stem of her wineglass between her fingers.

"I don't," Henry said with elaborate patience. "I was merely asking for an opinion."

"When someone gives you one, you're irrationally angry when it doesn't turn out to be accurate," Cindy said, then looked away, not at anything in particular, just out the window.

She's going to snap, Alexandra thought, *if they don't*

191

find Frank soon. Cindy's only interest in the political discussion was to express anger at Henry over his concern about it. And Alexandra wasn't sure how much of Henry's calm might be put on. He had always had a streak of the martinet in him; but he loved his son, and he must be agonized with worry. Alexandra thought Cindy looked brittle. Her dark purple dinner dress would have better suited a much older woman, and the huge balloon sleeves seemed somehow threatening, as if the dress were in the process of swallowing the woman wearing it.

She hadn't been to her gallery, which had always been her passion, in two months. The responsibility of owning a business, on top of her worry and guilt about Frank, got to be more than she could stand, and she had hired a manager to run the gallery. He always wore a velvet smoking jacket, and his hair curled around his ears, so he looked the part; but Alexandra doubted that Cindy had the faintest idea whether he was doing a good job or could even add two and two together.

Midge was also feeling the strain. Cindy said that the girl had been plagued with nightmares. Tonight her freckled face looked pinched. Alexandra proudly noted that Sally, who generally considered Midge an archrival, was being solicitous and had lent her cousin a fancy belt with ribbon laces and metal mountings, to which Sally was much attached.

Alexandra leaned toward Cindy and left the men to talk politics. Toby's career in the State Department was uncertain, depending upon whether Bryan or McKinley won, and she knew her husband had some decision making to do; but she couldn't concentrate on their future in the face of her sister-in-law's misery. "Have you had any word at all?" she whispered.

"None," Cindy said. "Nothing at all. I've had letters from Tim and Janessa and Mike—" She dabbed at her eyes angrily with a napkin. "And I don't blame Mike. I know exactly who's to blame. And Peter's tried, too, of course. But none of them has been able to learn anything."

"What about the detective you hired?"

"I'm still paying him. He was highly recommended. But there are so many boys out there. So many. . . ." Cindy's eyes welled over.

Alexandra sympathized. Two years before, she had watched Coxey's Army, unemployed, ragtag, and footsore, a "protest in boots," march into Washington to demand that someone somehow find them jobs. Since the stock market crash of 1893 and the railroad strikes the next year, the tide of unemployed had grown steadily greater. They flowed through the Midwest for the wheat harvest, then to Oregon and California for the fruit picking. Eulalia hired one or two transients a year for the Madrona—one of the few ranches that kept year-round hands—and, softhearted, she could never bear to turn them out again. Every year there were more of them, some younger than Frank, boys who had realized that the best they could do for their families was give them one less mouth to feed. How could anybody find one boy in the nameless throngs?

"Dear, surely he will come home." Alexandra patted Cindy's hand uncertainly. Cindy was the older. In the years after Toby's first wife had died and before he met Alexandra, Cindy had taken care of Janessa and Tim. Tough and capable, Cindy had weathered Henry's jilting her, as well as the death of her first husband. And she had come through it all in the same stubborn, squarejawed way the Holts always did. Now, however, she seemed lost in the face of too much uncertainty. It seemed to Alexandra that Cindy might have withstood it better had Frank simply died. It was the not knowing that was so excruciating.

"When he's had his fill of adventure," Alexandra murmured, "then he'll come home."

"Oh, God, I wish I could be certain of that." Cindy sneaked a glance at Henry, then looked away. "Frank and his father may never speak to each other again. He may never come home. Do you know I can't get that awful song out of my head? It's maudlin and dreadful, but it just tears me apart."

"Where Is My Wand'ring Boy Tonight?" was among the current popular ballads, sung with affected pathos at soirees and recitals, generally by "musical" young ladies who hadn't a clue as to what they were singing about. It had been the selection of a friend's daughter at a musicale two nights before, and it had made Alexandra and Cindy writhe. Alexandra remembered the lyrics:

Oh, where is my wand'ring boy tonight,
The joy of his mother's pride?
He's treading the ties with his bed on his back,
Or else he's bumming a ride.
He's on the head end of an overland train,
That's where your boy is tonight.

Cindy put her knuckles to her lips. "Alex, I can't even talk to Henry about it anymore. He refuses to discuss it."

"Maybe he finds it too painful," Alexandra suggested, watching the men. Henry definitely looked ragged.

"It isn't pain, it's anger," Cindy said brutally. "Someone's had the nerve to stand up to him."

"Oh, no," Alexandra said. "Henry loves that boy. He was so *proud* of him at Christmas."

"But that was when Frank was living up to Henry's expectations."

"Darling, you know Henry loves Frank. When Frank comes home, Henry will be so glad to see him, he'll forgive everything."

"I don't know. . . ." Cindy looked down the table at the men. Her eyes narrowed. "But I'll tell you this, Alex: If Frank doesn't come home, I won't ever be able to forgive Henry."

Alexandra flinched, unnerved by the look in Cindy's eyes. Henry Blake had been her first love, and most certainly her deepest love. When they had finally found their way around their differences and married, everyone in the family had been overjoyed. What was happening to them now?

"Try to understand Henry. I'm sure he wouldn't—"

"I don't want to understand Henry!" Cindy hissed. "In our entire married life, Henry has made no effort to understand *me*! I'm tired of doing all the understanding. I want my boy back!" She buried her face in her hands and burst into tears.

San Francisco

"You don't understand me at all." Elizabeth Emory accorded Tim Holt a haughty glance from under her parasol. Elizabeth had Alice on a leash, and the huge yellow dog, enthralled by the sights and smells of a country fair, was trying to tow Elizabeth away. As a result, Elizabeth leaned several degrees off the vertical, like a drunk on a lamppost.

"I don't want to understand you," Tim retorted. "You drive me crazy enough as it is."

"Hmmmph." Elizabeth inspected their surroundings while Alice barked at a goat in a pen. "You certainly know how to entertain a lady."

"I brought you here so you could see what you're up against," Tim explained. He jerked his thumb at a line of farmers wearing bib overalls and waiting to see the bearded lady. "Take a good look at these old boys and how they live. They're the ones who're going to vote on giving women the vote." They passed the rarie-show booths and strolled past an adolescent boy washing a red and white steer. "Him, too."

"And exactly what does that mean?"

"It means that the man in the street—or the man in the pigpen—outnumbers the man in the library. They're the ones you've got to convince, not the advanced thinkers you grew up with."

"I'm perfectly aware of that," Elizabeth said. "I am not as cloistered as you think." She got a firm grip on Alice and bent outside the fruit and vegetable tent to inspect a giant squash that had won a blue ribbon. "Do you suppose they're any good to eat when they're that big?"

"I doubt it," Tim said. "Their virtue is in being large, like the seven-foot man or the *Great Eastern*."

"I see. Mass for its own sake."

"Exactly. Want to ride on the carousel now?"

"It's what I came for." Elizabeth had admitted somewhat sheepishly to this passion when they had walked through the gates and heard the musical tinkling of the carousel's calliope in the distance. Tim found it an endearing trait, one that made her more human.

They strolled down the midway, passing up the livestock ring and the tents full of virtuous housewives' summer canning and intricate quilts. The sun was setting, and Elizabeth folded her parasol. Tim slipped her hand into his, and she seemed content to let it stay there. They had progressed that far, to a certain grudging admission that they were courting, although seasoned with firm distrust on her side and exasperation on his.

What her parents made of it, neither of them knew. They were standing back, Maddy reported, so as not to be wounded by shrapnel. Tim suspected that the Emorys liked him—but then they also liked Rafe Murray, Jack London, and the numerous other rebels and iconoclasts who frequented their parlor. Whether they would care for him as a son-in-law he had no idea. He did know they wouldn't push Elizabeth toward any match; they would leave the decision to her.

Besides, Tim wasn't sure he even *wanted* to marry her. He had found himself calling on her more often than mere journalistic inquiry would warrant, then she crept into his thoughts at odd times. Finally, he realized with a start that when he daydreamed, Elizabeth Emory's face, not Rosebay Ware's, flitted into his vision. That was the clincher. His heart still tightened a little when he saw Rosebay, but the sensation was no longer agonizing—now it was more of a wistful affection, a yearning he could live with.

Okay, so he loved Elizabeth. The idea had unnerved him in the beginning. First, he wasn't sure he was prepared to take on a wife who would make a spectacle of herself whenever her conscience called for it, especially since her principles seemed to call for action unnecessarily often. Second, he had always assumed that his enlightened views would still leave him entitled to rule the roost. With Elizabeth that was no sure thing. But she certainly was fine company, and that compensated for all of his uncertainty.

They passed a display of garlic, a local crop whose growers staged a yearly contest for the best recipe fortified with their product. A painted billboard proclaimed it good for catarrh, jaundice, poor eyesight, and general debility, and the air outside the tent was strong enough to stagger a goat.

"I hear you sent poor Rafe to be a judge for the best garlic," Elizabeth said. "It will be weeks before anyone will get near him."

"Better him than me," Tim said, unrepentant. "The *Clarion* has a duty to its subscribers. We must all bear the burden."

"Well, at last report he'll be safe from vampires," Elizabeth said.

"True. They've been so bad this year." The *Clarion* was joyfully following the trial of a merchant seaman who had found another man in bed with his true love and stabbed her in the throat with a toasting fork, proclaiming afterward, possibly under the influence of Bram Stoker's recent novel, that the culprit had been a vampire. The bloodsucker had flown in the window, the seaman claimed. Rafe brought them daily accounts from the courtroom, including the bits that couldn't be printed.

The cloud of garlic slowly thinned to a faint scent as they left the farm displays and came to the concentric circles of rides and penny-a-play games that made up the carnival midway.

Tim stopped to peruse the carny booths clustered gaudily along the outer ring. A man in a bowler hat and plaid trousers of electric intensity held out a pink stuffed rabbit with one hand and beckoned the suckers in with the other.

Tim squeezed Elizabeth's hand. "Would you like a toy rabbit?"

"Just a penny a pitch, a penny a pitch! Win your best girl a prize! It's easy! Just watch the gentleman here!"

The "gentleman here" was a shill who tossed his rings unerringly over the pegs, winning rabbits with magical ease. Everyone else had less luck.

"I have no earthly use for a rabbit," Elizabeth said.

"You could give it to Alice."

"I expect she'd enjoy it—before she ripped it to shreds. But nobody ever wins those things."

"Hah," said Tim, rolling up his sleeves. He handed the barker a dime for ten rings, settled himself behind the chalk line, and eyed the rows of pegs. The front row entitled the winner to a rubber snake and the middle row, a plastic kewpie doll. Tim decided to go for the rabbit.

"I'll have another ten rings," he said when the first were exhausted, with only a snake to show for them.

"You're never going to get the silly thing. It's a scam." Elizabeth cast a knowing look at the barker, who was enticing a group of farm boys to lose their money.

"I know it's a scam. But it's still possible to win. Here, you, give me ten more rings."

"You're wasting your money, Tim."

"Will you be quiet? There! *Hah!* Success!" Tim turned triumphantly to the barker and demanded his rabbit.

"See how easy it is, folks?" the barker called out, handing it over. "This gentleman just won. Anyone can win. Penny a pitch!"

"What did you spend on that rabbit?" Elizabeth asked. "Thirty cents? You can *buy* them for twenty."

"Don't be so miserly. It's a present for Alice. You can have the snake."

He presented it to her and gave Alice her rabbit. Elizabeth tucked the snake into her pocketbook, but

Alice was delighted with the rabbit and carried it retriever-fashion, dangling gruesomely from her jaws.

"Why on earth are you so stubborn?" Elizabeth demanded of Tim.

"I might ask you the same question," Tim murmured. "All I spent was thirty cents."

"Don't start that again," Elizabeth said warningly.

"Start what?"

"You know what."

"No, I don't know what. Is this a guessing game?"

"No, this is a fight. We could probably work it up to a pretty good one." She softened. "Or we could ride the carousel."

"The carousel. By all means."

At the red and gold booth, Tim bought three tickets, which included one for Alice. The ticket agent didn't care who rode the attractions, as long as he got his nickel. Alice jumped up onto one of the swan boat benches and chewed thoughtfully on her rabbit while Tim and Elizabeth climbed onto horses behind her.

The steam calliope tooted, and Tim admired Elizabeth's profile as they began to turn. She tilted her head back dreamily and watched the midway lights glide by in the dusk as the horse rose and dipped on its brass pole. Maybe a couple of rides would soften her up, Tim thought, deciding to talk to her about her court date. He didn't want her to give up her cause; he just wanted her to be reasonable and not make a fool of herself.

"And what exactly is that supposed to mean?" she inquired a half hour later, when he had broached the subject. She was unsoftened by either carousel rides or subsequent cotton candy and a souvenir teaspoon with her name on it.

"It means there's no possible reason why you should put yourself on display in a courtroom and act as if you were Joan of Arc. You tried to vote illegally, and you know you're going to lose. Why don't you just pay the fine and be done with it?"

"Because I don't want to," Elizabeth said, her voice

strong. "Because the whole point of protesting in the first place was to call attention to the cause."

"You got attention," Tim said. "You got plenty."

"And I'm not going to knuckle under now. If women don't stand up for their own rights, nobody else will—obviously." She glared at him.

"You look just like that silly snake," Tim accused. "You've got just the same expression—indiscriminately venomous. Don't bite me just because I don't want you held up to public ridicule. You haven't got any more leg to stand on than that dingbat and his vampire defense."

"I see," Elizabeth said icily. "And I suppose your revered publication is planning to say so?"

"Not at all," Tim said. "I'll try to make you look as little like an idiot as possible."

"Oh, well, thank you very much for your consideration."

"Any time. Look, damn it—pardon me—look, the more the *Clarion* sticks up for you, the more the *Chronicle* will play it for laughs. Protesting in the first place is one thing; standing up in court and trying to pretend it was your right to do so is another. The prosecutor is going to get mad because you're wasting the taxpayers' money—"

"I don't have any say in all the other ways it gets wasted," Elizabeth snapped. "I might as well seize the chance while I have it."

"—and you're still going to lose and pay the damned fine."

"I have no intention of paying any fine."

"If you don't, you'll have a stay in the county jail," Tim said, "and I doubt if they serve tea."

"That is precisely my intention."

"*What?* Have you lost your mind?" Tim stopped in the middle of the midway and turned to face her while fair goers bumped around him. "You are not going to jail!"

Elizabeth took a bite of cotton candy and pinched off one for Alice, who had dropped the rabbit and was looking hopeful. "I don't know what you have to say about it," she informed him.

Tim picked up the rabbit. It was damp and smelled of dog breath. Grudgingly he tucked the toy under his arm. "Everyone else will have plenty to say about it," he snarled. "I won't need to. Do you have any idea how much I put up with?"

"Do I embarrass you?" Elizabeth demanded. "I'm terribly sorry. Perhaps you'd better not be seen with me."

"Of course I'm not embarrassed!" Tim yelled, because he was but didn't want to admit it. Waldo Howard and Stu Aggrams thought his courtship was absolutely hilarious. Even Hugo Ware had asked with exaggerated innocence if Elizabeth intended to promote dress reform at the wedding by clothing the bridesmaids in bloomers. There was no wedding planned, Tim had snapped, and they all nodded their heads in sympathy and said that they would think twice about committing to Miss Emory for life, too.

"I just don't see why you have to make a spectacle of yourself," he said, lowering his voice.

"I see," Elizabeth said loftily. "When a man stands up for his rights, he's a hero. When a woman does, she's a spectacle. A dislike for serving as a doormat is unfeminine."

"Nobody," Tim assured her, "would take you for a doormat. But you're wasting your time. This ploy isn't even new. Susan B. Anthony tried the same thing in 1872, and she didn't get any further than you're going to."

"She did what she felt she had to do." Elizabeth's eyes narrowed. "I don't see why you can't respect my need to do the same."

"I don't respect your need to put yourself on display like a rarie show," Tim said. "These men you see"—he gestured at the crowd—"and they're ninety percent of the voters, are going to come and gawk at you as if they were watching the bearded lady. As if you were a curiosity but not someone they'd want to give the vote to."

Elizabeth's eyes sparked. "And that's exactly how you

feel about me, too, isn't it? Well, I won't waste my time telling you what's wrong with *you,* you supercilious—" She broke off for want of a respectable word to call him. "Here." She shoved the cotton candy at him and snatched Alice's rabbit. "Please take me home."

"You look like you ate a lemon," Hugo informed him the next morning when Tim appeared at the *Clarion* offices.

"Wedding's been postponed while the bride does a turn in the slammer?" Rafe asked genially.

"There isn't any wedding," Tim growled at them. "And if you need someone to make fun of, go interview the vampire." He stalked into his office and slammed the door. Unfortunately it had been a long drive home the night before, and one conducted in angry silence. Tim had deposited Elizabeth on her doorstep, shaken hands with Alice, and solemnly thanked the dog for the nice evening. Elizabeth had dragged Alice inside and shut the door in his face.

Now Tim glared at the page proofs waiting for him on his desk. He read the lead story three times without any comprehension of what it was about. Finally he gave up and turned his back on the proofs, swiveling his chair around and propping his feet on the bookcase behind his desk.

Hugo watched from his desk as Rosebay bounced up to Tim's office door and opened it. She took due note of what she recognized as Tim's favorite brooding position and backed out again.

"Tread ye carefully," Rafe advised.

"We fear the boss has been crossed in love," Hugo told his wife with exaggerated sadness.

"What do you mean by that?" Rosebay demanded.

"Miss Emory has declined to pay her fine or otherwise accommodate the law of the land," Rafe said solemnly. "She prefers instead to be pilloried in a public courtroom. We are all shocked by this unwomanly behavior, and poor Tim is embarrassed."

"Well, I don't blame him," Rosebay said. "I wouldn't get up there for all those men to poke fun at me. And don't you tease him, Rafe Murray, or you'll get beans for supper, you hear me?"

She disappeared down the hall to her own office—a little too quickly, Hugo thought as he heard the door close. Whistling thoughtfully, he started down the hall after his wife.

"What's troubling you, Rosebay?" Hugo's upper-crust British drawl had lost its accustomed light tone and sounded tight, constricted.

Rosebay looked up from her books. The skin of her face seemed stretched taut, he thought, and the green eyeshade was pulled down low, as if she were hiding under it. "I don't know what you mean," she said airily.

"I mean for the last two years you've been trying to fix Tim up with every unmarried female who is still breathing. What's the matter with this one? Are you peeved because you didn't pick her out?"

"Of course not. It's none of my business."

"Agreed," Hugo said. "But you've been making it your business. You've made a whopping effort to enter Tim in the marriage stakes, and now that he's out the gate, you've gone nervy." He leaned in the doorway, arms folded, watching her. He wasn't going to go away. "It seems to me," he said slowly, "that back in the wild old days, you always had a soft spot for Tim."

"I was right fond of all you boys," Rosebay said. "You all kept that crazy Rowell from killing me. Especially you, Hugo. You were going to hang for me."

"I still would," he told her. "But I can't help you over this."

Rosebay looked at him warily.

Hugo came and sat on the edge of her desk. He took her hand.

"Hugo," Rosebay protested, "Tim didn't care two cents for me back in Guthrie. I mean we were pals, but there wasn't nothing—anything more."

"Stop it," Hugo said. "I'm not interrogating you."

"Well, what do you call it then?"

"I'm suggesting that it might be time for you to let go of Tim Holt," Hugo said.

Rosebay started to say again that she didn't know what he meant, but then she looked as if she couldn't quite bring herself to lie.

Hugo patted her hand and carefully lifted off the eyeshade. He scooted over so he could cuddle her shoulders against him.

"You're sitting on the ink pad," Rosebay said.

Hugo extracted it and closed the lid. He draped an arm around her shoulders. "Now see here. There's one thing I've got to know. Do you love me?"

"Yes." Rosebay sniffled.

"Did you love me when you married me?"

"Not as much as I do now." Rosebay sniffled again. "I just don't deserve you."

"Now don't start acting guilty. I don't think I could bear it." He cleared his throat. "You can't help how you feel. What's important is what you do about it. It seems to me you've been trying to do the best you could."

Rosebay didn't say anything. She twisted the ring on her finger, the plain gold band Hugo had bought her in Guthrie. Their initials were engraved inside, her two and Hugo's whole string of them. In Hugo's family the sons each had four or five names.

Hugo had been a remittance man, paid by his father and his own brother to follow his own wayward course in America, far from England. Then he had married Rosebay. She had made all the difference in his life. He had written England to let his family know and to inform them with newfound pride that he didn't want any more bank drafts from home.

They had stopped the checks but never acknowledged the marriage. It was exactly what they would have expected of him, he supposed, marrying a penniless Appalachian girl with wayward grammar. But how utterly that failed to describe Rosebay!

Hugo stroked her hair. "I just want to know one thing. I can stand your being in love with Tim; I always thought you were. But I need to know what's happened between you."

Rosebay sat up straight, suddenly outraged. "Since I been wed to you? Nothing at all, Hugo Ware, and don't you dare to think it!"

She was so explosive he hid a grin. Rosebay was the most moral person he knew. If she said nothing, then indeed it was nothing.

He continued to stroke her hair. "You had it pretty good, didn't you, until this Emory woman came along?"

"That's not fair," Rosebay protested. "You said yourself I'd been trying to marry him off. I have, too, Hugo. Honestly I have. I just want him happy."

"You want him happily married to a woman you picked out," Hugo said baldly. "But that's kind of like getting to keep him for yourself, isn't it?"

"This one's just not right for him," Rosebay said stubbornly. "She'll make him a laughingstock and not have any respect for him."

"You've never even met her."

"I know what I read in the paper," Rosebay said.

"And you've been around long enough to know that what you read in the paper is never the half of it."

"I was right happy when I saw he was courting somebody," Rosebay said. "I purely was, after he'd been scaring off all the girls I tried on him. But she's not making him happy. He's mad as fire half the time."

"That's his business," Hugo told her. "I know you've been trying to be happy for him, and you're going to have to continue putting on a good face."

Rosebay's eyes spilled over. "You're better'n I deserve. I do love you, Hugo, truly I do. I just was hoping Tim's wife would be somebody I could be friends with."

"Well, she probably won't be," Hugo said. He might as well shake her out of that notion right now. "You don't get to pick anybody's mate but your own, and you don't get to straighten out anybody's life but your own." He hugged her close to him, circling her with both arms. "And you don't get to have Tim and me both, my love. I'm sorry."

XIII

The Emorys took stock of the situation with the academic curiosity with which they generally approached life. Having raised their daughters to think for themselves, it seemed a little late, as Mrs. Emory said, to send Elizabeth to deportment classes.

"We deliberately brought her up to question the status quo. I hardly feel we can tell her one should only have the courage of one's convictions until it becomes inconvenient."

"Rafe says jail is very uncomfortable," Maddy observed. "She'll probably be in a cell with drunken tarts and those women who roll sailors down on the Barbary Coast."

"A life of sin isn't contagious, dear," her mother said.

"Of course not," Maddy replied. She plopped down on the hassock by her mother's chair. "Those are the women, poor things, who really need to stand up for their rights. I can't imagine any woman living like that if she had an alternative. Rafe says it's all to the men's advantage, even if the drunken ones do get their billfolds stolen now and then."

"Rafe has a certain amount of firsthand experience," her father murmured. "Maddy, you aren't getting too attached to Rafe, are you?"

"I like Rafe," Maddy said. "If you mean am I falling in love with him, not on your tintype. He drinks too much, and he chases women."

Sidney Emory chuckled. "You seem to have a grasp of the situation. Just keep those facts in mind."

"Don't worry about me," Maddy said. "I probably won't ever get married. Worry about Elizabeth."

"Worry about yourself," Elizabeth said, marching in. "If you can spare the time from talking about my business."

"You're the only one who's going to jail," Maddy pointed out. "Rafe says it has rats."

"So does our cellar," Elizabeth said.

"You don't sleep in the cellar."

"Maddy, I believe we can carry on without your review of the accommodations," Dr. Emory said. "Elizabeth, if you are committed to going through with this, I've found you a lawyer. He can't win, but he'll plead your case eloquently. That is your goal, isn't it?"

"My goal is to acquire the right to vote," Elizabeth said with an edge to her voice.

"I sympathize with you," Dr. Emory said. "Stop talking to me as if I were young Mr. Holt."

"She has to take it out on somebody," Maddy said. "Since she's not speaking to Tim."

"Maddy, please mind your own business—"

"He's bound to be at the trial," Maddy pointed out. "Rafe told me that Tim plans to report on it himself."

"He *what*?" Elizabeth's eyes flashed. "I refuse to have him there!"

"I'm afraid you can't do anything about it, dear," her mother said. "When you take action to attract public notice, you can't pick and choose. I'm sure Mr. Holt will give a fair account."

"Well, I'm not!" Elizabeth said, outraged. "He'll be condescending and sarcastic."

"How do you know?"

"I just do. If he wasn't cooking up something horrid, then why didn't he tell me he'd planned to be there?"

"Because you aren't speaking to him," Maddy pointed out.

"With excellent reasons," Elizabeth said. "Now if you will excuse me, I need to prepare myself. Should Mr. Holt call, please tell him I'm not at home."

"She's in love," Maddy said after Elizabeth stomped upstairs. "We'd better watch out."

"At least she doesn't appear to be blind to his faults," her father remarked.

Mrs. Emory picked up her knitting. "I had hoped she would fall in love with a scholar," she murmured, casting on a row of stitches. "It would have been more restful."

"But that's the trouble with scholars," Dr. Emory said, chuckling. "Remember Junius Cavanaugh? A most worthy man."

"And almost entirely soporific," Mrs. Emory agreed. "Half your charm, Sidney, was how much fun we had arguing politics. Poor Junius put me to sleep. Perhaps *scholar* wasn't the word I wanted. 'Intellectual' then."

"Mr. Holt seems well educated and is highly intelligent," Dr. Emory said. "I'm afraid that isn't their problem."

"It's his attitude," Maddy said. "He believes in women having rights; he just assumes that those rights are kindly granted to us by men."

"As opposed to being ours by nature, you mean?" her mother asked.

"Exactly. We get the rights, but men get the credit."

"That's a rather subtle distinction," Dr. Emory pointed out.

"Not if you're a woman," his wife and daughter said simultaneously. They looked at each other, smiled, and solemnly shook hands.

"Forgive me, my dears," Dr. Emory murmured.

"Then I understand why Elizabeth mistrusts young Mr. Holt," Aurelia Emory said. "I'm afraid they have a rocky road ahead of them. You don't think she'll do anything foolish, do you, Maddy?"

"She'd have to start speaking to him again first."

At Elizabeth Emory's trial, Tim took pains to sit with the other newsmen and not with the Emorys several rows to the front. Maddy waved at him over her shoulder, though. Elizabeth glared at her and pulled her arm down.

The *Chronicle* and every other paper for miles around had sent reporters. Virginia Barstow of the *Bulletin* wore an expression of weary resignation and refused to be baited by the male reporters. The men, however, were in irreverent form and prepared to enjoy themselves.

I told her so, Tim thought. Except for the *Bulletin*, every other paper would get the most jokes they could from the story, and even the *Bulletin*'s copy editors might liven up Virginia's copy. If Elizabeth wanted publicity, she would get it; but she wouldn't like it. And, Tim thought glumly, she would probably blame him for it even though he had warned her. Blast the woman. Already all the vacant seats had been taken by yokels getting ready to watch the show.

"All rise."

Elizabeth moved to be with her attorney at the defendant's table as the judge came in and sat down. He looked annoyed at having his time wasted on nonsense. He glared at Elizabeth and announced that he would hear this case without a jury and settle it speedily. She could rely on his impartiality.

"I would sooner send a rabbit to carry lettuce," her lawyer said in a laconic drawl. "We'll have a jury." He sat down.

The judge ordered the prosecutor and Elizabeth's lawyer into his chambers for a conference.

Virginia Barstow bent her head toward Tim's. "Jimmy Phelan's sent the word down to the court to make it short and snappy," she whispered. "Seeing as it was his election she tried to vote in, His Honor's not hot to have any questions of validity popping up."

Tim chuckled. San Francisco politics being what they were, the opposition was capable of claiming, if the notion occurred to them, that half the voters had been disguised as women and cast votes illegally.

"I'm afraid the defendant's set on a jury trial," Tim said.

"I reckon you'd know," Virginia said. "I fell in love with a fellow I wrote a story about once. Terrible mistake."

"Thank you for your kind advice."

The lawyers and the judge returned, and a jury was impaneled before the luncheon break. Tim, deciding he had a headache, went and had a medicinal whiskey and a roasted beef sandwich from the free lunch counter at the nearest saloon, then returned to the courtroom. He sat and glared at the back of Elizabeth's hat and tried to ignore the other reporters' running commentary, which was growing increasingly scurrilous under the influence of their own lunchtime refreshment. Tim wasn't sure any of them had bothered with the sandwich.

The judge, under the instructions from His Honor the mayor, did his best to keep Elizabeth off the stand, but he finally had to give in. With a brief glance at the row of reporters, Elizabeth settled in to testify in her own defense.

"Miss Emory, do you have anything to say that you feel might justify this unlawful and deplorable behavior?" The judge looked as if he considered it highly unlikely.

"I have this to say: To deny the vote to half the population while subjecting them to laws made by the other half of the population is essentially slavery and thus unlawful in itself. Therefore, as far as I can see, I've committed no crime."

The reporters all wrote that down verbatim. Elizabeth was always good for a quote, and most of the journalists were rebels enough themselves to appreciate her logic. They didn't want anything to come of it, but they would admit to its logic.

The judge was less impressed. He smacked his gavel and read the charges again, portentously, then eyed his jurors to make certain they were with him. "Elizabeth Emory is accused of knowingly, wrongfully, and unlawfully attempting to vote and disturbing the peace. The said Elizabeth Emory being then and there a person of the female sex . . ."

"'Then and there'?" a juror mumbled. "Ain't she still?"

A bailiff glared at him. "Be quiet."

"But—"

The bailiff leaned over, nose to nose. "Be quiet."

There were snickers from the reporters' row.

"This behavior," the judge continued, "was contrary to the form and statute of the peace of the city of San Francisco and the United States of America."

"Against the peace?" a man of the spectators' bench hooted. "Ain't they ever seen an election night?"

"You going to try to clean up election night, Your Honor?" another spectator inquired. "Hell, this little gal couldn't even make a dent in what goes on through election night. What do you want to go bothering her for?"

"Silence!" the judge bellowed. "Order in the court!"

"*Be quiet!*" The bailiff put hamlike hands on ample hips and bent forward to glare at the spectators. "One more peep out of any of you, and I'll clear this courtroom."

"Thank you," the judge said dryly. "I was just going to say that."

When the courtroom had been subdued into a refractory silence, the judge continued to enumerate the dangers posed to the peace and stability of a nation when its female citizens believed they could vote whenever they felt like it.

"Laws are the bulwark of civilization. Without laws we let anarchy loose upon the land. The jury is instructed to consider this."

"Is he running for something?" Tim whispered to Virginia Barstow while the jury was doing its considering.

"Lord, I hope not," she said. "I think he just likes to hear himself speechify. He does get carried away."

"'Anarchy let loose upon the land.'" Tim grinned. "She's a more dangerous woman than I thought."

"You might just mull that notion over now and again," Virginia suggested, "before you do anything final.

There's more truth to it than you've really considered."

"Aw, come on, Virginia. You're a suffragist. What are you talking about? Anarchy, my foot! Maybe we ought to have the police go around and check to make sure everybody wipes their feet on the doormat, too, and doesn't sing bawdy songs on Sunday."

"Now I know why she's mad at you," Virginia said.

"And exactly what's that supposed to mean? And why don't you stay out of my business anyway?"

"Which question do you want me to answer?"

"Oh, all right. Why is she mad at me, since you're so all-fired omniscient?"

"Because you're trivializing what she's doing," Virginia explained. "You're equating wanting to vote with pretty little peccadilloes that don't matter and saying the court ought not to punish her because of that."

"I'm sticking up for her," Tim protested, stung.

"You're sticking up for her by saying what she did is so unimportant that the court shouldn't bother with it. That's demeaning and, in my opinion, inaccurate. If you marry her, you're going to find out that not only does *she* not think it's trivial—"

"I know she doesn't think it's trivial," Tim muttered. "She's been quite clear on that subject."

"Believe me, Mr. Holt, it's *not* trivial. Elizabeth Emory is a fire-in-the-eye reformer, and she's capable of raising untold hell. Once women can vote, they'll set in motion a series of changes in this society you can't even begin to imagine. Miss Emory is trying to start that engine moving, and she's about as dangerous to the status quo as the socialists. Worse, maybe."

"I thought you wanted to vote."

"Oh, I do. And I'm all for the changes that it's going to bring. But I've got enough brains to know I won't like all of them and that it will be a wild ride."

"Well, who said I was going to marry her?" Tim demanded, harking back to Virginia's original warning.

"Everybody," Virginia told him. "The betting at the Press Club is running five-to-one for a wedding before the year's out."

"How do you know? They don't let women in the Press Club."

"And you wonder why I'm not content with my lot in life," Virginia retorted.

"I *don't* wonder, damn it! And since you have such a good grip on the grapevine, tell my ostensible pals to keep their noses out of my life."

"I'm going to put a bet on," Virginia said. "After further study of the racing form, I don't think *she'll* have *you*."

The jury returned to announce that after much deliberation it had decided that Elizabeth Emory was indeed a female and had indeed attempted to vote and that the two were incompatible.

The judge announced that he would mull over the criminal's character and past record and pronounce sentence in the morning.

The spectators stood up, and the journalists dashed off to the courthouse pressroom to telephone in their copy for the evening editions. Tim thought about trying to get a quote out of Elizabeth and decided that he probably couldn't print it if he got one. Maybe she would calm down a bit after she read his story and found out he wasn't trying to make fun of her—if she would be able to figure that out. Lately it seemed as if no matter what he said, Elizabeth found some way to be insulted by it.

When the evening *Clarion* hit the Emorys' walk, Maddy and Alice went to get it. Maddy wanted to read Tim's story first, before she handed it over to Elizabeth. She unfolded the paper and perused the city page as she walked back to the house. "Well, I think he's done us proud," she told Alice.

She picked the afternoon mail out of the box on the way and found Elizabeth in the downstairs parlor. "Have you given any thought to how useful it would be to have a publisher in the family?" Maddy inquired of her sister.

"Give me that." Elizabeth snatched the newspaper.

"You got a letter, too, from Mrs. Catt. Which one do you want first?"

Elizabeth was reading Tim's column and didn't answer. When she had finished, she read it again.

"You won't find anything nasty," Maddy said. "I really think you ought to consider him. Think of the voice it would give the movement."

"And then he could feel proud of how much he was indulging me," Elizabeth said scornfully.

"You aren't going to give him any credit at all, are you?" Maddy said. "That's not like you, Liz."

"I know it's not." Elizabeth sighed. "And I don't suppose he can help it. I'm just not sure I'm up to a lifetime of trying to explain to him that being patronizing is insulting."

"Well, *I* think he'd be worth the trouble," Maddy said. She cocked her head at the newspaper again, reading upside down over the top of it. Her eyes had a thoughtful gleam. "You could get editorial support for the movement and all the publicity you wanted."

"That would be utterly despicable," Elizabeth said.

"Lots of women marry for money," Maddy said cheerfully. "What's the difference?"

"Oh, never mind. Give me the mail." Elizabeth opened the envelope, then read the letter.

"Of course if you're in jail, he may be too embarrassed to propose," Maddy said.

"Will you be *quiet*?"

"I could bake you a cake with a file in it."

The much-tried Elizabeth stood up, the letter clutched in one hand, its envelope in the other. "I swear you haven't got any sense. You have no idea what I'm going through. I hope you fall in love with the first man you see tomorrow, like Titania. Now leave me alone. I have to talk to Mother about this letter."

She swept out of the room. Maddy, undaunted, followed her.

"You may come in, Madeleine," Mrs. Emory said when she saw her younger daughter behind Elizabeth at the sitting-room door. "But you may not open your mouth." She sat and slowly read the letter while Maddy fidgeted and Elizabeth paced.

"You see the problem?" Elizabeth asked.

"Certainly," Mrs. Emory said. Maddy opened her mouth, and Mrs. Emory forestalled her. "Mrs. Catt needs Elizabeth to help with the suffrage campaign in Idaho this summer. Organizers are needed very badly, and that is your sister's strong point."

"But if I go, the devils here will think they've won!" Elizabeth explained.

"Oh, I see!" Maddy said. "You can't go if you're in jail. Well, golly, who'd want to pass up a chance to go to jail?"

Mrs. Emory smiled. "Admittedly, dear, most people would prefer Idaho. But Elizabeth has a point. She's drawn attention to the cause and has publicly stated her intention of going to jail. If she pays her fine instead . . ."

"It will look as if I haven't the nerve to follow through," Elizabeth said. "But how can I turn Mrs. Catt down?"

Carrie Chapman Catt was the youngest vanguard of the movement, a woman both open-minded and skeptical. She had had it written into a contract before her marriage that she was to have two months off from all matrimonial obligations each fall and spring to campaign for the cause. She was a tireless and efficient organizer who had revolutionized the National Association for Woman Suffrage, occasionally over the complaints of its older members. She had seen woman suffrage passed in Colorado three years before, possibly because she had won over hard-bitten miners with a hair-raising descent down a precipitous railroad grade on a brakeless handcar, so as to catch the only train that could get her to a scheduled speech. Nobody in Colorado forgot her act of bravery, as reported by the railroad crew that had witnessed it, and Mrs. Catt remained convinced that it had won Colorado women their vote. Carrie Chapman Catt was legendary.

"This is an honor, and you are clearly needed," Mrs. Emory said. "How would you feel if you gave up the Idaho campaign, which may succeed with your help, in order to make an essentially fruitless gesture here?"

"Very foolish," Elizabeth said. "And unreasonable. I'll go to Idaho and let Mr. Holt have the last laugh."

Mrs. Emory laid a hand on Maddy's arm as Elizabeth left the sitting room. "If Mr. Holt wishes to further his acquaintance with your sister," she whispered, "he had best *not* laugh at her. And if the opportunity arises, you might mention that to him."

Tim thought that Elizabeth looked particularly grim the next morning and put it down to her decision to go to jail. If she thought he was going to write pathetic stories about her hardships there, she was dead wrong. Looking nearly as grim as she did, he sat, arms folded, and waited for the judge.

"You look like a viper." Maddy shook his elbow. "Move over. I need to talk to you."

"Are you supposed to be associating with the enemy?" Tim asked, but he scooted over.

"You're as bad as Liz. I ought to wash my hands of both of you."

"Then why don't you?"

"Because Mother told me to warn you. Mrs. Catt has written to Liz to ask her to go to Idaho right away and help organize the women's suffrage campaign there. It's a wonderful honor, and Liz is the best we have besides Mrs. Catt at public speaking. She *has* to go, so she's going to pay her fine instead of going to jail. And Mother says you are not to laugh at her."

"Can I chuckle quietly to myself in the privacy of my own house?"

"No," Maddy said. "I'm certain she'd hear you."

"All rise."

Tim rose and slipped out of the spectators' gallery while the judge walked to his bench. In the courthouse pressroom he dislodged a sleeping reporter and called his city editor on the telephone.

"It's a fizzle, Stu. She's not going to jail; she's going to carry the word to Idaho instead. My guess is two hundred dollars—that's what the judge always hands down for anything short of ax murder—but I'll let you know later."

He caught a cable car and then walked the rest of the way to the Emorys' house. Alice, as usual, flung herself at the front door. Tim ignored her and sat down to wait in the porch swing for Elizabeth. Across the street, gardens of red geraniums, purple heliotrope, and yellow marguerites looked cheerful and gaudy against the pale clapboard houses. A strong breeze made the Emorys' house feel as if it sailed like a galleon on its hilltop, pennant snapping from the round turret.

It all looked cheerful, but an unaccountable depression had taken hold of Tim, and as he waited, he felt no real hope that their meeting would solve anything.

Half an hour later the Emorys appeared in the family carriage. Elizabeth descended, as stiff as a mannequin, and marched up the walk while her father turned the horse down the alley to the carriage house.

"Good afternoon, Mr. Holt. Please excuse me—I am quite tired." She continued past him to the door, but the dignity of her stride was marred by the explosion of dog as soon as the door was opened.

Tim collared Alice. "Get down, you monster. Look, Elizabeth, I just want to talk for a minute."

"I don't know what there is to say. I'm sure you were amused by my meekness to the judge."

"I wasn't there," Tim said.

"I saw you."

"I left before the end. How much did he fine you?"

"Two hundred dollars, and I paid it. I hope you're satisfied."

"Why the hell should I be satisfied? Excuse me."

"Because I took your advice and didn't refuse to pay."

"You didn't take *my* advice," Tim said. "Are you going to ask me in?"

"No."

Tim folded his arms and glared at her. "I hope you have an excellent trip to Idaho, Miss Emory. Success in all your ventures." He tipped his hat and was gone.

"Why didn't you let him in?" Maddy asked as Elizabeth stalked through the door.

"Because there is absolutely no point in it," Elizabeth answered. "If we continue to see each other, we'll have an excellent chance of making each other miserable for life. Now I have to pack."

Elizabeth took a carpetbag and a trunk down from the attic and opened them. She looked wistfully at her comfortable room. Besides a brass bed, washstand, and wardrobe, it contained one whole wall full of books, and a "Turkish corner" with crossed drapes hanging above a pillow-strewn divan. Beyond, screened by a hanging curtain of seashells, was a writing room with a tall secretary and a second wall of books. The hotels she could afford in Idaho would contain no such amenities. She would be lucky if they contained indoor plumbing. Despite her best intentions, the thought crossed her mind that if she married Tim Holt, they could travel together, and that might be fun. He seemed like an adventurous person, not the sort to complain when meals were meager or trains were late. Elizabeth liked to travel with an amenable companion and loathed doing it alone. *I'm not going to marry him just for company*, she thought, furious at herself, and began folding shirtwaists.

That night, Tim settled himself in a boxcar, his back against a bale of alfalfa hay and his feet on his carpetbag. He was paying for the privilege of traveling with his horse. Trout tended to kick its stall apart on trains when unaccompanied and to bite the groom when attended. No one but Tim and White Elk, the Madrona Ranch's foreman, had ever been able to ride Trout successfully, although nobody else had much wanted to try, either.

At the other end of the boxcar, Trout snorted at him with mistrust. Not liking the accommodations, the horse's eyes rolled wildly, and steel-colored ears flattened down against its mane.

The train began to roll, then picked up speed with little chuffs of steam. Trout blew down its nose.

"You're a nuisance," Tim declared. "I don't know what I want with you."

But, in fact, he did. There were plenty of horses on the Madrona if he wanted merely to ride, but galloping across the landscape on Trout appealed to him just now. This horse in particular embodied the same furious aggravation and bewilderment (Tim suspected that Trout was intelligent enough to realize that it was not natural for men to ride horseback) that had laid hold of Tim. Going home to the Madrona—Holts in trouble always went home to the Madrona—and riding Trout through the ranch's green valleys and pouring out his uncertainties to his grandmother might bring him to some kind of solution or peace. He hadn't told Eulalia he was coming.

At the station in Portland, Tim led Trout down the ramp into the lantern-lit railyard. As he did he noticed that a bum had slid off the rods beneath the car.

"I'd have let you inside if I'd known you were down there, friend," Tim told him.

The bum eyed Trout, who was weaving back and forth without moving its feet, its big head thrust out like a snake about to strike. "Thanks all the same, Captain, but I'd sooner chance the rods."

"See? Nobody likes you." Tim tied his carpetbag on behind the saddle, then led Trout down between the rows of boxcars, out of the yard, past the lamp-lit depot, and into the open street. He knew better than to climb into the saddle in the railyard. Trout always opened their rides by trying to throw him.

Tim put his foot in the stirrup and was up in the saddle before Trout could rebel. Trout's rear elevated in a furious, thrashing kick, and Tim pulled the horse's head around, snubbing Trout's nose into its shoulder. Trout spun like a top, and the horseshoes sent up sparks from the cobbles.

After the horse had spun around enough, it slithered to a stop, head still pulled around, eyed Tim balefully from its left eye, and bared its teeth, finally trying to sink them into Tim's knee. Tim jerked Trout's head the other way, and they set off down the street, their opening routine accomplished.

The Madrona, a kingdom unto itself, lay outside town and was built on the first land grants to Oregon settlers who crossed the continent in covered wagons. Tim's grandparents had been among them. He took a deep breath of the fish-and-sawdust-scented air that blew from the Portland docks—timber and canned salmon waiting to be shipped. The air was wet, not as salty as San Francisco's but with the clear, cold smell of river water.

Portland sat at the confluence of the Columbia and the Willamette rivers, between the Coast and the Cascade ranges, in the heart of farm country. Tim's childhood had been spent there, baling hay on his father's ranch, picking apples in the summer, and green-breaking three-year-old cavalry remounts, born on the Madrona, for the army.

Tim kicked Trout into a gallop as soon as they were out of the city and onto dirt road. The night air smelled like the river and the lushness of the farms to either side. Trout lengthened its stride. The horse loved to run. Trout never tried to throw Tim as long as Tim gave Trout its head. Tim's theory was that Trout got bored at low speed.

There were still lights on in the big house when Tim came up the long drive beneath the double row of madrona trees. He pulled the bell and waited until the door slid open a cautious inch. An eye peered out at him from beneath a white nightcap, and Tim peered back, recognizing Amy Givens, the housekeeper.

"It's me, Amy. Tim."

The door opened farther. "I'll be darned if it ain't," Amy said, pleased. "Well! Guess I don't need this." She was clutching a nine-inch rod of brass as big around as her thumb, with a solid lump at one end. Tim recognized it as belonging to a decorative mortar and pestle set that adorned the hall table.

"I guess you don't," Tim agreed. "I always wondered what use that thing was."

"It does fine to whomp a prowler with," Amy said, returning the pestle to its brass mortar. "With no one but us females in the house now, it pays to be careful."

"Of course it does," Tim said, glad that he wasn't a prowler. That thing would crack a man's skull. "Is my grandmother still up?"

"Just barely, "Amy said. "She's putting in her curl-papers."

"Tim? Is that you?" Eulalia pattered down the stairs in slippers and robe.

Tim kissed her, dodging the paper-wrapped curls that waved on her forehead. "I've left Trout outside. I'll go to the stable for a few minutes if you'll wait up for me."

"By all means," Eulalia said. "Remove that animal from my garden."

She was in the kitchen with a pot of tea when he came back. Amy was nowhere to be seen. Eulalia had the gift of knowing when her children and grandchildren needed to talk. She poured him a cup of tea, and Tim was concerned when he noticed her frail hands shaking slightly.

"Do you want some whiskey in this, dear? The decanter's in the pantry."

"No, thank you, Gran. Lately I've been getting the feeling I've been hopping into a bottle a little too quickly when things go sour."

Eulalia looked at him thoughtfully. "You may be wise to notice that, dear. Our family has always gone at everything with great intensity, and I'm afraid that behavior includes our vices as well as our virtues."

"That's us," Tim said, grinning. "Overboard on all occasions."

Eulalia nodded, sipped her tea, and waited for him to tell her what it was that had "gone sour."

Finally he looked up from his cup. "I'm in love, Gran," he said plaintively, "and I don't know what to do about it."

"Something is stopping you from doing the usual

thing?" his grandmother inquired. "Maybe you'd better spill *all* the beans."

Tim spilled them, and when he had finished, Eulalia sat silently thoughtful, her curlpapers nodding like sea anemone tentacles as she pondered. "Well, I'm relieved you aren't in love with someone else's wife," she said frankly after a few minutes. "To tell you the truth, I did suspect it might be that."

"It was that," Tim said, flushing with embarrassment, "but I'm over it."

"That accounts for why you were so peculiar at Christmas, I expect," Eulalia said. "It's an extremely unpleasant situation, believe me."

Tim raised his eyebrows in surprise.

"Many, many years ago your grandfather Whip and Grandpa Lee's first wife, Cathy, were in love with each other before Whip married me. Lee and I never were sure how much emotion remained between them. They were killed in an avalanche together, you know. Sometimes I think it was appropriate that Lee and I married after they died . . . to even the well, not the score— the equation, maybe."

Her voice grew soft as she wandered backward into the past. Tim followed as best he could, contemplating with love and fascination the tangled threads of his family's tapestry. Eventually she came back. "This new woman, dear. I think I understand the difficulty. You may simply have to give each other a very light rein."

"That's the problem," Tim said. "I'm not sure we can."

"And you want *me* to tell you if you can?" Eulalia asked, incredulous.

"Well, yes," Tim said.

She laughed. "Oh, no, I wouldn't dream of it."

Tim chuckled. "I thought grandmothers' specialty was giving advice."

"Only when they know it won't be taken," Eulalia said firmly. "I have no intention of taking responsibility for anything of that sort. Your grandfather Whip and I were very different, so I know a marriage of opposites

can be successful. But I haven't the foggiest idea of
whether or not *you* can do it."

"Well, who's going to tell me, if you aren't?" Tim
demanded.

"Frankly, if you can't tell yourself, I suspect the
answer is no," Eulalia said.

No easy answers, Tim thought as he followed Eulalia upstairs to the bedrooms. *You always hope there are,
expect there to be, demand them, in fact. But they never
come along.*

He climbed into bed in the room that had been his
as a child. Now it served as the repository of things that
no one knew what else to do with. His mother's treadle
sewing machine and wire dress form stood in one corner.
The dress form loomed against the windowpane. A
headless female as sievelike as a colander . . . no answers there.

Tomorrow, he thought sleepily, he would go out
with White Elk, out on Trout across the land, the
enduring, unchanging part of his clan's heritage. He
would look at the new crop of foals and admire White
Elk's children, and ride the fence lines until he knew
something. What he might come to know he had no
idea, but he went to sleep with the conviction that some
knowledge was there in the land, deeper than the plow
could go.

XIV

Idaho, August 1896

The Patrick Henry Hotel in Hailey, Idaho, dated to the city's silver boom days of the early eighties. Since then, practicality had replaced the opulence for which new nabobs had been willing to pay, and the Patrick Henry's spacious suites had been partitioned, and then partitioned again, until the resulting single-room accommodations contained barely enough space for a chest of drawers, a wardrobe cupboard, and a bed.

"Not enough room to swing a cat, is there?" the bellboy remarked cheerfully.

"I'm unlikely to want to," Elizabeth murmured. She opened her pocketbook and gave the boy a nickel, and he deposited her carpetbag and trunk, then left.

Elizabeth unpinned her hat and set it on the bureau, pausing to evict a spider from the washbasin. She opened the trunk, which had miraculously followed her on her wanderings and resisted the railroad's best efforts to ship it to Spokane or Salt Lake City. Since the Equal Suffrage Association convention in Boise in mid-July, she had traveled ceaselessly for two weeks, circling through the Mormon farm towns of the Bear Lake country, the sheep and cattle country of the Snake River, and the mining towns of the Salmon River Range. Her route followed the political organization pattern that Carrie Chapman Catt had developed and with which she had won the vote in Colorado: Form a suffrage club in every city and a team for every precinct; poll the vote and convert the doubtful. The latter was the business of the local club. Elizabeth's jobs were to show the like-minded in Idaho how to do it and to give a speech persuasive enough to introduce the suffrage amendment into the public mind and grease the wheels.

Elizabeth extracted her "speechifying dress," a black silk of impeccable propriety and Paris design, from the trunk. The room's wardrobe cupboard was tiny, but she hung the dress up to get out some of its wrinkles by morning. Then she yawned and spread her map out across the bureau top. Her mind was already moving beyond Hailey and on to the next town. Her destinations were all beginning to look the same to her: She was greeted by the same club president, usually the town banker's or judge's or mayor's wife, a woman with influence and enough money to spend time on the cause; the welcoming committee expressed the same civic pride in the town's ornate courthouse, church, meeting hall, and up-to-date improvements; the same resolute women, determined to have their own voice, hung on her every word; and the same audience gathered at her evening speeches—mostly the young and the already converted, farmers and their wives with their babies in baskets, having driven twenty miles in a buckboard to hear her.

The fact that this sameness never conveyed itself to her hosts was a mark of her ability. Elizabeth was good at what she did . . . and her activities consumed her attention to a degree that she had had very little time in the previous two weeks to think of Tim Holt. When he did cross her mind, he would be tucked away to be worried about later. She would have to employ the same method if she married him, too, of course. There would be times when the cause came first. He wouldn't put up with that, she suspected.

Although Carrie Catt's husband had been accommodating, Elizabeth thought that George Catt was a different breed from Tim Holt. In fact, Elizabeth had heard that the marital contract freeing Carrie to pursue her biyearly suffrage campaigns had been George's idea.

If Elizabeth proposed an agreement, Tim might sign it. But she knew that a man who had been persuaded into an idea was horribly unlikely to stick to it. Better not to risk it, she decided. Better simply not to marry.

Elizabeth peeled off her grimy traveling suit and set the skirt and basque aside to be sponged and pressed the next day. She pulled on a nightgown and wrapper and took her toothbrush to the bathroom at the end of the hall. The convenience was clean enough after she decided to ignore whatever it was that scuttled down the drain in the claw-foot tub. Quickly she brushed her teeth and washed her face and departed, her eyes carefully averted to avoid noticing if whatever it was had crawled back up.

She locked her room door, unpinned her hair and brushed it, and prepared to go to bed.

Elizabeth was collected in the morning by Laura Johnston, who proved, predictably, to be the mayor's wife. She was a thin woman with hair and skin the color of wheat straw and a face creased with the lines of someone pioneering a harsh country. She was dressed in a skirt and jacket of taupe gabardine and a velvet hat, lush with roses, from a San Francisco milliner—the reward of having stuck it out.

"Goodness," she said, eyeing the room. "I do wish the movement could afford to give you better accommodations. If I had known, I would have asked you to stay with me."

"It's quite all right," Elizabeth assured her with more conviction than she felt. "I slept very comfortably. The movement needs to pinch its pennies, but I truly do fare better in hotels. I have a habit of staying up at night to rehearse my speeches, and I pace quite irritatingly while I'm doing it."

"Well, if you're sure then." Mrs. Johnston escorted her downstairs to the hotel dining room and then, fortified with eggs and coffee, to the Hailey Woman's Club. On the way they admired the handsome façade of the Blaine County courthouse and the Gothic Revival splendor of the Emmanuel Episcopal Church. A maze of wires overhead crisscrossed the sky like a cat's cradle.

"We had the first telephone system in the Idaho Territory," Mrs. Johnston said proudly. "And the first electric lights."

"Very impressive," Elizabeth said politely.

"Oh, we're very up-and-coming in our conveniences," Mrs. Johnston said. "Now if we could just bring our politics up to the same mark—"

"How many women do you have on the committee?" Elizabeth asked.

"Twenty workers. The ones that can be counted on, you know. That doesn't take in the ones who'll miss their canvassing for a hairdresser's appointment or because the husband is in a temper. Or the temperance members—they're rather uneasy allies, I am afraid."

Elizabeth nodded. The suffragists couldn't afford to alienate the Woman's Christian Temperance Union, from which they drew many of their members. Nor could they afford to speak too loudly for the temperance cause. It was a ruling precept of Mrs. Catt's that one should not tell men what the women were going to do with the vote before they got it. The liquor industry was already convinced enough of the danger to be opposing the suffrage amendment.

Elizabeth found the twenty workers awaiting her in the club office. They ranged in age from eighteen to sixty, from miners' wives to judges' wives and a few widows and spinsters who earned their own way, paid their own property taxes, and were bitterly resentful over the little they got for it.

"Look at this editorial." Mrs. Hammond, who ran a stamp mill almost single-handedly, shoved a folded newspaper at Mrs. Johnston. "I know the whiskey distributors have been wining and dining that man, but this is too much!"

"The *Star* never has supported us," Mrs. Johnston said. "It remains a font of unenlightenment among the newspapers of this state." She passed the column to Elizabeth to read:

The better class of women do not wish to
vote. While women are intellectually superior
to a class of voters upon whom the franchise has
been for some years conferred, the minds and
constitutions of the ladies are too delicate, too
refined, and too sensitive to be brought into
immediate personal contact with election
roughs and plug-uglies. We oppose it because
we firmly believe that God Almighty did not
ordain that horse racing, prize fighting, or
voting for sheriff should be embraced within
woman's sphere.

"And who in tarnation do they think is running that
mill?" Mrs. Hammond demanded. "I got an invalid
husband can't hardly walk. They want plug-uglies, let
them come and see what walks into that stamp mill every
blessed day."

"To tell the truth, it's not you they're worried about,
Hattie," Laura Johnston said. "It's the Mormons." She
looked at Elizabeth. "People are afraid the Mormon
women will vote as their husbands tell them to."

"They only got one wife apiece these days," Hattie
said. "Puts them even with the rest of us."

"Actually it doesn't," Elizabeth said, having done
her homework. "There are far more women in the
Mormon towns than in the rest of the state. And there's
been so much trouble between Mormons and outsiders
that no one trusts anyone else. The Mormons in Mont-
pelier built a fence right down the middle of town to
separate themselves from the 'gentiles.' It will be part of
your job to convince people that adding so many Mormons to the vote will not threaten them."

"And just how are we supposed to do that? Everybody's got some bee in their bonnet the Mormons are
going to vote in plural marriage again."

"These are misconceptions it is up to your committee to set straight. Now then, I have brought you some
ammunition." Elizabeth opened her carpetbag and
pulled out neatly tied stacks of leaflets. "These are from

the national office and should help you reason with the unreasonable." She set the leaflets on the table, and the women immediately began to sort through the titles: "Objections to Woman Suffrage Answered." "Twelve Reasons Why Women Want to Vote." "Woman Suffrage in Wyoming." "How Women Voted in Colorado." The last was an attempt to defuse a potential problem. Women in Colorado, who had been given the vote by a largely Populist legislature and governor, had then turned around and voted Republican, defeating the governor. Idaho's Populist miners were going to take some convincing.

"Use the Colorado pamphlet judiciously," Elizabeth advised. "In canvassing mine workers, it may be best not to bring up the subject unless someone forces you to it. And then you may use the argument that this simply proves that women do *not* vote as their husbands tell them to but will cast their own ballots."

"We don't have quite so much anger over that here," Mrs. Johnston said. "But it's an issue up in Coeur d'Alene. You'll find out when you get there."

"It is no part of our job to promise that women will vote one way or the other," Elizabeth said. "Beware of that. It's like putting your foot in glue; you'll never get it out. Our goal is to convince the population that a woman will vote her individual conscience as men do, and with the same responsibility."

"More, in a lot of cases," Hattie Hammond said, then snorted.

"And that women have the *right* to vote for the government that controls them. That is the key point. Stick to that, and you won't go wrong. I can't express enough how important it is to maintain our dignity and refrain from verbal rock throwing. It's *men* we have to convince, unfortunately. If we make them feel threatened, they'll vote the amendment down."

"We do have a number of men in our organization," Laura Johnston pointed out.

"Excellent. Now what you want is a male adviser from the hierarchies of each of the political parties. I'm aware that you don't need advice, but suffrage mustn't be seen as the property of any one party. And after the voters have been polled, ask your *men* to canvass and convert the most opposed. The holdouts will listen to other men when they won't listen to you."

"No kidding," one of the women muttered. "They can start off by converting my husband. He hasn't listened to me yet."

"You should know, Miss Emory," Laura Johnston said, "that some of us are here against the wishes of our husbands. Not myself, fortunately, but a number of our most dedicated workers have paid dearly for it in one way or another."

Elizabeth nodded grimly. That wasn't news to her, either. There were almost always a few defiant souls who joined the movement in spite of their husbands. Most endured only angry quarrels as a result, but she knew of a few who had been beaten. There was nothing to be said in response—it was life as they all knew it and another reason why they wanted the vote.

"Next," she went on, "you need a committee to poll all the clergy on the subject, then ask those in favor of the amendment to preach on it. Without," she added dryly, "putting a similar notion in the minds of those opposed."

"Most of them haven't got the gumption to be opposed," Hattie Hammond said. "Asking the Lord's pardon, but I believe in speaking truth as long as we don't rock the WCTU's boat. The preachers know where their congregation and their bread and butter come from, and it ain't from the bachelors."

"Good. Now, there are certain to be dozens of political speakers in Hailey between today and the election." This, she knew, was an understatement. By late October, candidates and party men would be moving across the state by rail, road, and riverboat, as unstoppable as a plague of locusts and far more loquacious. "Your job is to send your most, uh, *tactful* workers to convince each of them to say a few words for the amendment when they speak."

Elizabeth glanced at Laura Johnston, who nodded minutely, conveying that she had received the message inherent in "tactful." It was an unfortunate fact that devotion to a cause did not necessarily render one sensible or even articulate. Movement history was rife with horror stories generated by someone's having let just any idiot loose with the press and the politicians, then finding the movement pilloried the next day as a band of radical revolutionaries and lunatics.

"Next . . ." Elizabeth could automatically recite the battle plan from memory, a talking machine allied with the body of a good war-horse. She derived a kind of physical pleasure from keeping a grueling schedule, thus showing the unbelievers what women could do.

By eight o'clock that evening she was ready to face down even her own kind. An angry-faced woman in the front row waved a placard: WE DON'T WANT TO BE MEN. The meeting hall blazed with electric lights—Hailey's pride—and Elizabeth noted that nearly half the people in the chairs were men. This was a good sign. Sunflowers and yellow ribbon, the badges of the movement, blossomed fairly thickly in the men's buttonholes and on the women's hats. The woman with the placard stood out like an infuriated geranium, red faced and glaring around her.

There were always "remonstrators," dedicated, Elizabeth thought, to keeping their own sex imprisoned so that they themselves would not have to venture beyond the ground where they had grown comfortable. She pitched her voice to the back rows. "Thank you for making me welcome."

"You aren't welcome!" the woman in the front row shouted as she stood and held her placard high. "Decent women don't want to vote." She turned to face the rest of the audience. "These suffragists are out to turn women into men and break up decent women's homes! Man was made to deal with worldly matters, and a woman's purpose is to be a gentling influence within the home. If there is discord between them over politics, if the woman goes out among the rabble, if our protections are stripped away from us in the name of equality, you're letting Satan get a toehold! My man's vote is good enough for me!" She was obviously a practiced speaker.

"Then you are fortunate," Elizabeth told her and the audience. "Many of us cannot say the same and are compelled to seek our *own* voice."

"Women have no business taking on men's work! Any decent woman would be ashamed to go out to a voting booth!"

"The editor of your newspaper appears to think so, too," Elizabeth responded forcefully. "He finds us too delicate to handle such a weighty matter as a paper ballot. Perhaps you both are limited in your experience. Listen to the words of a woman who has been through troubles you have never dreamed of, Sojourner Truth, who was born a slave." She glanced at her typewritten script, but she knew the quote almost by heart:

> "The man over there says women need to be helped into carriages and lifted over ditches and to have the best place everywhere. Nobody ever helps me into carriages or over puddles or gives me the best place—and ain't I a woman? Look at my arm! I have plowed and planted and gathered into barns, and no man could head me—and ain't I a woman? I could work as much and eat as much as a man—when I could get it—and bear the lash as well! And ain't I a woman?"

"You sure as hell are!" came a shout from the back row. "'Scuse my language."

"Lottie," a woman also in the front row said, "if you want to let Seth do your thinking and your voting for you, that's your privilege. But sit down and clam up about it."

Hands in the second row reached out and pulled the placard-bearer into her seat.

* * *

"You had them eating out of your hand," Laura Johnston said, her eyes bright. "Lottie doesn't understand how privileged she is. Seth worships the ground she walks on, and he wouldn't ever do anything she didn't approve of. That's where she gets all that sweet domestic influence claptrap. She has no conception that thousands of women in this state are married to men who're completely immune to the Sunday-school platitudes she's so enamored of."

Exhilarated with success, they were walking back to the Patrick Henry. The night was crisp, with a hint of coming autumn in it, and Elizabeth was still keyed up with the sense of power and the alertness that making a speech always gave her.

"We're conditioned," she said fiercely. "We're conditioned to believe that subjugation is protection. That's what we're fighting. Getting the vote won't end that struggle."

Laura left her in the lobby of the Patrick Henry, after promising that a carriage would take her to the station in the morning. Elizabeth, still thinking about Lottie, went upstairs. It was Lottie's own cocoon of pampering that rendered her unable to see other women's desperate need. The Holts pampered their women, too, Elizabeth thought. Tim Holt would pamper her. And it would make him incapable of seeing her need.

Tim Holt again? Elizabeth was annoyed to discover that he had crept into her thoughts. Dodging past Lottie and Laura and Sojourner Truth, he was a discomforting masculine presence that was as insistent as it was disturbing. Elizabeth's being unmarried was a result of the conscious decision that she could not bear the restrictions such a union would place on her. It had nothing to do with a dislike for men or a fear of masculine sexuality. The Emory daughters were far better educated in the sphere than most "nice" women of religiously and socially conservative households, although certainly no better than most women from the opposite side of the tracks, where there was more inclination to acknowledge the world as it was.

Elizabeth was uneasily aware that her strong attraction to Tim embodied a dangerous combination. He entertained her intellectually—when they weren't fighting—and he attracted her physically to an extent that told her quite clearly that if she ever let the barriers down with him, that would be it. Elizabeth had never been to bed with a man, but that was because she had never been in love. Her inexperience had nothing to do with lack of desire, which she knew would come on her when the right man and opportunity presented themselves.

Social convention in Elizabeth's class decreed that a woman who had a sexual relationship with a man and was not married thereby cast herself into outer darkness. She hadn't yet been willing to risk that. Would she be ready to risk that for Tim, she wondered, rather than take the step of marrying him? With mild surprise at her own wickedness, Elizabeth contemplated that notion for a moment and decided that she didn't know. Anyway, what was he doing bothering her, when she was working? She pulled the sheets on her bed down and slapped the pillows with some feeling that she was smacking her life back into order.

In the morning Elizabeth caught the spur line for Ketchum, some twenty miles away. Ketchum lay tucked down where the jagged banner of the Sawtooth Range strung itself along the skyline. It was a mining town not greatly different from Hailey, although its women's club was far less organized than that run by Laura Johnston and her twenty fighters.

Upon arriving, Elizabeth realized that Ketchum's women needed to see exactly how political activism was done, needed to learn that they wouldn't go up in smoke for daring to stand on a street corner and argue with men. Elizabeth gladly gave them a demonstration. She was armed with printed samples of the text of the suffrage amendment as it would read on the November ballot, and she hailed passing men outside the Ketchum post office and distributed the leaflets.

"What do *you* think of the woman suffrage amendment, sir?"

"The what?" A miner in overalls of impressive proportions looked at the paper in his hand.

"The woman suffrage amendment. That's its text there in your hand."

The miner grinned. "Heck, I can't read. What's it say, honey?"

By now two or three other chuckling men were standing around to see what she would do. Elizabeth took due note of them.

"It says that women ought to vote along with men."

The miner scratched his head, amiable but disapproving. "Is that so? Then I'm agin it. Women don't know enough to vote."

"But *you're* going to vote?"

"Sure am," the miner said proudly.

"If you can't read, how do you know what you're voting for?" Elizabeth demanded.

"Well, I just kind of take a stab at it, like. I get somebody to show me the important stuff, like who's going to be president. Them's always the big boxes. I don't worry about the little ones too much."

"Thank you," Elizabeth said dryly. "You're an inspiration to all of us."

"Well, I figure it's my duty," the miner said kindly. "But you don't need to do it. You go find yourself a feller, honey. You ain't too old yet."

As the miner hefted a mail sack into his already laden wagon and set out toward the mountains, Elizabeth turned to the chortling men behind her. "Now who would you rather have voting on an issue that was going to affect you personally?" she inquired sweetly. "Me and these other ladies who read the newspaper daily, or that galoot who just left us, who doesn't worry about the little boxes? If you ever run for mayor, gentlemen, I assure you you will be in one of the little boxes."

"I *am* the mayor," one of them said, tipping his hat while his cronies doubled over behind him. "And I assure you that I shall vote for your amendment."

"You see how it's done?" Elizabeth asked the women with her. "It's all grist for the mill."

"I got you!" the club president said. "If they're agin it, you make them look like the durn fools they are!"

Once the Ketchum women had the notion, they took to it naturally and with enthusiasm. These were residents of the frontier, and they had been through harder times than their eastern sisters. Like Sojourner Truth, they had plowed and planted, and the luxury of being a delicate female was mostly one they had had to discard. The club president stuck a pile of leaflets in her pocketbook, picked up her skirts, and marched down the plank sidewalk to set up shop outside the saloon. The secretary invaded the bank with hers, and the treasurer went to the dry-goods store, where the perpetual backroom checker game was a male stronghold.

That night Elizabeth made her speech and left with the feeling that Ketchum could hold its own. She was less certain of Idaho City, the next on her circle of stops, which would bring her back to Boise and a meeting with Mrs. Catt in mid-August. Although Idaho City's newspaper had for several years come out in favor of equal suffrage, the city was a boomtown that had never quite lost its boom. It had burned down four times; its bank was robbed regularly; and only twenty-eight of the two hundred souls in Pioneer Cemetery had died of natural causes. It was wild, it was woolly, and it was proud of it. Understandably, the liquor interests wielded a great deal of influence in Idaho City.

Nevertheless, Elizabeth gave her pep talk to the suffrage workers and her speech to the populace. She flatly refused to share the podium with the president of the WCTU's Idaho Chapter.

"I'm not against your work," Elizabeth said firmly. "But you are going to scuttle mine if you can't be patient."

"You won't have much audience anyway," the WCTU president predicted irritably. "They're all going to the hanging."

"The hanging?" Elizabeth echoed, wondering if she had heard that correctly. It was 1896, for goodness' sake.

"The sheriff sent special invitations," the other woman said. "Fellow shot two deputies and the sheriff's dog."

Elizabeth departed the next morning with no clear sensation of having made a dent in the small audience that had gathered in Idaho City. As the train picked up speed past the mine works where, having depleted the stream gravels, Idaho City was now using hydraulic hoses to blast away the hillsides, she saw the previous night's gallows draping its depressing shadow across the tracks.

"Civilization!" Elizabeth grinned at Carrie Chapman Catt from the depths of a monstrous feather bed in Maryanne Whitman's house in Boise. She propped herself up against the headboard, wriggled her toes, and scrunched herself deeper into the nest of feather pillows. Mrs. Whitman, president of the Boise club, had refused to hear anything about Carrie or Elizabeth staying in a hotel.

Mrs. Catt sat on the edge of the bed. Her brown braids hung over her shoulders. "You've done excellent work, dear. I believe we have a chance of taking this state this time."

"We will now that you're here," Elizabeth said.

Carrie Catt was only thirty-seven, but she had already shaken the dust out of the national organization and run one successful state campaign. She tucked her cold toes up on the bed and pulled her lawn nightdress over them. Then she rested her arms on her knees. "I feel as if I've been trying to harness a mule and a pronghorn antelope to pull in tandem with a buffalo and a giraffe," she said. "If we can't squelch our differences long enough to get the vote, we don't deserve it."

"Who's been set off now," Elizabeth asked, "besides the temperance faction? And the socialists. And the—"

Carrie frowned. "It's more annoying than it is important. I had a flaming letter from a worker in Washington who must have been asleep in a hollow log all year. She just heard about the Bible Resolution at the national convention and wanted to put in her two cents' worth."

"For or against?" The Bible Resolution, Elizabeth

well knew, revolved around the national convention's disavowal of any connection with Elizabeth Cady Stanton's "Woman's Bible," a commentary on those passages of Scripture that referred to women. Mrs. Stanton questioned the divine inspiration of those sections that were derogatory toward females.

"She thinks Mrs. Stanton is headed for hellfire. *I* wish she'd go canvass voters and let Mrs. Stanton worry about it."

"What do you do when you disagree with George about something?" Elizabeth asked suddenly. "I mean, political divisions are all very well for people who don't have to live together, but—"

"Ah-ha!" Carrie said. "You're thinking of marrying that newspaperman."

Elizabeth groaned. "Does everybody in the world know my business?"

"Well, we're all very concerned when one of us marries, you know, for fear the movement might lose her."

"Did you ever think of not marrying? Of just, well, um . . ."

Carrie laughed. "I thought of 'well, um' several times. But I decided that a commitment to each other was important. If he meant so much to me that I'd want to make love to him, then he was important enough for me to marry. And in that case, either I wasn't as committed to the cause as I had thought or else he was compatible with it."

"Well, how on earth can you tell?" Elizabeth demanded.

Carrie raised her eyebrows. "You want some magic test? Like true love's kiss? It's really quite simple: If you don't know, then don't marry him. And if you think you do know, you can still end up being wrong. Susan Anthony has sat on the fence all of her life, afraid to get married to a man while staying married to the cause. I won't blame you if you do, too. I know I was one of the lucky ones."

XV

Sierra, September 1896

Frank's "few weeks to get a stake together" had turned into months. He had traveled clear across the continent, and the itch in his foot subsided a little more with each night he slept in a real bed—particularly the nights he slept in Peggy's bed. He had been delighted to discover, on reaching the jackline camp, that he had left his laundered clothes behind at the Delaney residence—certainly a fine reason to call on her again.

They soon fell into the habit of Peggy making dinner for him every Friday night, and even if he couldn't get into town in time for dinner, he was certain to appear by ten or eleven, sometimes climbing in the back window for form's sake if Mr. Delaney was home—not that the man cared, so far as Frank could tell. Mr. Delaney tried once to inveigle Frank into a poker game and skin him of his pay, but that was as far as his attentions went. Sid didn't seem to mind Frank's intimacy with Peggy, either.

"You don't knock her around, and you ain't a sissified snob like that other fellow she hangs around with. She won't even introduce me to him."

Frank supposed that Peggy was spending time with a town fellow. Well, more power to her, he thought. He had no special claim and certainly nothing to offer except a determination to get her in bed every chance he got and an occasional bouquet of stolen blooms from someone's garden.

In some ways it was, Frank decided, the best time

of his life: He had a pretty girl he didn't have to marry and a job he was getting good at. The little steam boiler and the eccentric wheel were completely familiar to him now. Every hiss and click, every whine of the cables, was a known sound, which fell into a known pattern. One wrong note was capable of jerking him out of daydreams in an instant. His contentment was multiplied because he had pay in his pocket on Friday morning and all day to spend in town, this being his day off. The librarian in the Sierra library recognized him now. She had apparently transformed him in her own eyes from an oil field roughneck to a "nice boy." She saved special books for him and didn't mind that they were going to the jackline camp.

On Friday afternoons there was the news to catch up on in the Drillers' Repose, a flophouse with rooms on the second floor and a saloon bar and perpetual poker game on the ground level. For a nickel Frank could make a lunch of beer and a sandwich of smoked ham and argue about whether or not the United States ought to go to war with Spain.

"We went to Nicaragua, didn't we?" a refinery worker demanded, thumping his beer on the counter.

"That was just to protect our own folks," a driller retorted. "That ain't like getting into a shooting war."

"I ain't afraid of a shooting war."

"You ain't in the army, either."

"I would be if we had us a war. Any red-blooded fellow would be."

"Do you think we've got the right to stick our nose in Spain's business, though?" Frank asked.

"Hell, she's right off our coast, ain't she? Spain ain't got no right to carry on like that in this hemisphere. I know what I read in the paper. Them Cubans is fighting for freedom, trying to throw off a king just like we done."

"We tried to tell Spain how they ought to behave," another driller said, "but they wouldn't listen. They're asking to be taught a lesson, and we ought to go and do it."

Privately, Frank doubted that the issues and their

solution were that simple, and he was well enough acquainted with his cousin Tim Holt's opinion of the "yellow press" magnates—William Randolph Hearst, for example, who was printing any incendiary arguments he could think up in an attempt to push the country into war—to know that what a fellow read in the papers wasn't either the whole truth or nothing but the truth. But it did seem as if the country was headed that way anyhow. Teetering on the brink of war gave life a tinge of excitement that was hard to resist, despite a healthy skepticism of the motives behind all the flag-waving.

"I suppose it depends on who wins the election," Frank said to Peggy. He was propped up in her narrow bed and reading the newspaper he had brought with him.

"Romantic, aren't you?" Peggy teased, snuggling beside him. "A fellow that reads the newspaper in bed is a new one on me."

Frank leaned over and kissed her. He fondled one bare breast. "I didn't read it *first*, did I? Listen to this: The gold Democrats have nominated their own fellow for president. That makes four candidates now." He flattened out the paper on his knees. "The Republicans have got McKinley; the Socialist Labor party has got Matchett; Prohibitionists have got Levering; the silver Democrats have got Bryan. But the Populists have nominated Bryan, too, and so have a renegade bunch of Republicans."

"What does that mean?" Peggy asked.

"Damned if I know," Frank admitted. "Politics are a mystery to me. But whoever wins will decide whether or not we have a war."

"Would a war be so bad, Frank? Don't we have to show Spain they can't fool with us?"

"They aren't fooling with us," he said.

"But they're butchering those poor people," Peggy retorted. "Isn't this country supposed to stand for freedom? I say we ought to give them what for."

"I expect we will," Frank said. "Even if it's not the

right thing to do. I don't run the government, thank God." He tossed the newspaper to the floor and pulled Peggy, giggling, over on top of him. "Come here and give me what for instead," he suggested.

He never got much sleep on Friday nights, but he never missed the tram, either. Friday nights with Peggy gave him something to look forward to all week long, and the pleasant anticipation carried him through the next workdays. At midweek he enjoyed the bunkhouse boys for company. Some fellow always had a guitar or a mouth organ to help pass the time, and since the workers had varying days off, someone was always fresh from town with news for the others to chew over around the dormitory stove.

Late in September Sid came back to the bunkhouse to announce he had been transferred to the refinery as a boiler tender.

"You going to let them do that, bud?"

Sid didn't look happy. "I got no choice. If I won't do it, there's plenty more where I come from. I go where they'll pay me."

"But they're closing the refinery. Then what? You ought to fight them on this. You been working for Sierra five, six years."

"I said I'd take it," Sid growled. "It ain't your business." Something not quite right about his expression made Frank watch him closely—and cautiously, lest Sid catch him at it.

Sid pulled off his cap and scratched his head while the others continued to mutter their indignation and reiterate that it was a damned shame.

"Hell, maybe I'll light for Canada," Sid said suddenly. "I hear they found gold up there."

"Gold? Where'd you hear that?"

They leaned toward him quickly, avidly, and Frank thought he saw a flicker of relief pass over Sid's face.

"Just scuttlebutt," Sid said. "Some old sourdough in the Repose heard it from a pal who heard from a pal who came down on a train from Seattle."

"I ain't seen nothing in the papers."

"I told you, it's just scuttlebutt."

"Rumors on the snowstorm," Frank said, laughing. "Gypsy gold."

But he crowded around Sid with the rest of the men, warming their hands and imagining. The bunkhouse was clapboard, not too solidly built, with newspapers tacked over the inside walls to keep out the drafts. Over the newspapers the jackline crews had pasted their own adornments: picture cards advertising patent medicines, ladies' faces cut from magazines, a two-year-old poster advertising that the Ringling Bros. Circus would pass through Ventura. And above each bunk were photographs, flyspecked and dog-eared from being carried in bedrolls: girls left behind; girls who had said "Get lost"; childhood homes; pictures of dogs, blurrily photographed, tongues lolling; old pals long dead.

"I'd go to Canada in a shot," one of the boys said. "Get me a couple of thousand together, then come back and buy the farm back from the bank."

"If I went north, I'd stay till I was rich," another man said. "I'd build me a house with an indoor bathtub and gold faucets; that's what I'd have."

"You don't bathe but once a month anyhow," someone hooted.

"I would if I had me a nice indoor tub with hot running water. Then I'd marry me a nice little wife to scrub my back."

"You'd *have* to be rich to get a nice lady to scrub a warthog like you."

"How about you, Frank? What would you do if you made a strike up there?"

"I expect I'd try to reform this country's society some," Frank said. "Spend it working out a way to see that one percent of the people don't have ninety percent of the power and money."

"He's a socialist," someone said, laughing. "One of them foreign anarchists."

"Take it from me, kid. Don't waste your time trying to reform nothing. Just get yours."

"But that's what this country's supposed to be about," Frank said. "Opportunity."

"Yeah, for who?" said the boy whose family farm had been lost to the bank. "I don't want to get rich. I just want things like they were." He sounded bewildered that such adversity could have befallen his clan.

"I ain't seen much opportunity knocking on *my* back door," another man said. "All I got is just a fair shot they're going to shut down the refinery and throw me and half the town out of work."

"That's right. We ain't safe, either."

"Like I said, don't waste your time feeling sorry for me," Sid said with a quick grin. "If they shut down the old refinery, I'll come looking for your job. Get it, too. I got seniority."

"Seniority don't make no difference without a union. They do whatever they feel like."

"What company doesn't? You want to play poker for some of that gold you think you're going to dig up?"

They dealt out the cards on an empty cable spool, and the talk drifted to other things. It was all talk anyway. Unless a man was desperate, he wouldn't pack up and go to the Yukon on a rumor. And none of them could do anything about the refinery. It would close, Frank thought, despite the intermittent repairs that were being made. An acquaintance from the Drillers' Repose, who coopered barrels at the refinery, said that Mr. Kemp would order improvements or repairs, then Mr. Rutledge would countermand them when they were half-done. It made the newest refinery superintendent near crazy. Rutledge had sent the experienced superintendent to Oleum. Kemp had fired his first replacement.

Frank let himself be dealt in. His cousin Tim had taught him to play poker and advised him never to draw to three-card straights. Frank had refined his technique over five months in the hobo jungles and was a match for most of the fellows in the bunkhouse. He was uneasily aware that he was beginning to feel more at home in the company of oil-field roughnecks and migrant laborers than he would be now at some Washington dinner party.

Am I fixing it on purpose so I can't go back? he wondered.

The oil-field crews acknowledged something in his speech and manner that indicated education and privilege, but they accepted him without question. That might be more than his parents' society would do now. He envisioned himself wearing a stiff-bosomed shirt, drinking good port, and listening to his father's cronies, stout generals and well-padded steel men. They all supported ample stomachs that betokened their prosperousness. If Frank had told those well-to-do gentlemen about the hungry children of Cherry Street and the jobless men who clung to speeding trains, they would tell him the poor were lazy and ask him if he didn't agree. And in order to keep the peace in his father's home he would assure them that he did, while stoically enduring the itch that came from the hooves concealed beneath his patent leather shoes.

The next day a new man replaced Sid. Frank, the old hand now, showed him the ropes and ruthlessly assigned him the night shift, which had previously been allotted to Frank by Sid.

Frank didn't see much of Sid after that, not at Peggy's or when he hitched a ride down the canyon on occasional evenings to prowl through the bars and hear the news. He mentioned Sid's virtual disappearance to Peggy.

"He's got weird," she said. "I don't hardly never see him, either. He came in the laundry and had a row with Pa last week, but I don't know what over."

"Something's in the air," Frank said. "Everybody's feisty."

"It's because of the refinery," Peggy told him. "Wild stories are flying all over, and nobody knows if management is closing down or not. I got a friend—well, he's got a piece of the company—and even he don't know." She gave Frank a sideways look. She kept her two beaux separate and never named them to each other. "Least he says he don't," she added thoughtfully. She pulled the sheet up a little higher and tucked it under her arms. It was getting cold at night.

Frank pulled the sheet down again and nuzzled her. It was hard to worry about jobless families or Sid or even who else she was seeing, with Peggy naked in the candlelight beside him.

He forgot all about Sid until a week later, on his Friday off. Frank bought a newspaper and wandered into the Wellhead Saloon, out of his normal orbit, to read.

The Wellhead was less homey than the Drillers' Repose, an atmosphere hard to achieve. But where the Repose had the seedy comfort of a familiar sprung chair, the Wellhead's smoky interior held a slight air of inhospitality, as if it might be some kind of private club. It was too early for the evening crowd, and the fact that the Wellhead was nearly empty did nothing to dispel this sensation.

The bartender didn't bother to look up when Frank came in. The man was wiping down the counter with a greasy rag that smeared the spilled ashes and beer into a film. A couple of roughnecks in oil-stained overalls were sharing a bottle of whiskey at a table. There was no sound except a bluebottle fly buzzing loudly above them, unattracted by the sticky paper that dangled limply from a beam.

Frank, who just wanted to read undisturbed, ordered a beer, carried it to an isolated table in the corner, then buried his nose in the newspaper. Sunlight slanted through the grimy window, and he held the paper up to it. Frank noted items of local interest: A housewife complained that her chicken house had been decimated by coyotes, "bold as brass in the middle of town," and a bounty was declared; the dry-goods store announced a shipment of "fine French dress goods"; the fire department was holding a pancake breakfast; and a brawl at the Wellhead Saloon the night before had resulted in the loss of an earlobe by one participant—cut off with a knife, Frank assumed, although the article didn't say. He was reminded of a hobo who had claimed to have bitten a man's ear off. He knew that at night the Wellhead was where the men went when they wanted a fight. For some of the oil-field roustabouts, a fight was recreation.

The Wellhead slowly started pulling in its evening clientele. When several men sat down at the table a few feet from his, Frank didn't bother to look up from behind his paper. He had turned to the national page and was following the political news, most of it Readyprint shipped preprinted from the East or from San Francisco. The Sierra paper was too small to subscribe to an Associated Press franchise. Only gradually did he realize that while half his brain was reading the newspaper, the other half, without his particular permission, was eavesdropping on the next table. One of the voices was Sid's, and it was that recognition, together with an odd tautness in the man's tone, that had drawn Frank's ear.

"Not much trouble to it," one of the other men was saying. "A little fancy work in the right places, and boom."

"Not much trouble for who?" Sid grumbled.

"Why, for you."

"I don't like it. And my pa ain't reliable."

"You can't back out now," a third man said. "Besides, Mr. Rutledge, he's reliable. You better bet on it."

"Why don't he do his own work then?"

A chuckle. "Swells don't do their own work. Rutledge nor Kemp never lifted a hand to wipe their own butt. That's what the likes of you and me are for."

Frank sat, stuck behind his newspaper, not entirely comprehending what he was listening to. Something about the last time he'd talked to Sid, in the bunkhouse, made Frank reluctant to advertise his presence.

"Goddamn it," Sid said, and Frank froze, thinking he had been discovered. But Sid wasn't talking to him.

"Gimme a dollar." Mr. Delaney's voice, Irish and demanding, his brogue slurred with whiskey, was easily recognizable.

"Ah, Christ, he's drunk," Sid said. "Get out of here, Pa."

"Gimme a dollar. You got lots." Mr. Delaney evidently planted himself, bumping into the table. "Lots more where that came from."

Frank could hear Sid's chair scraping back. Or somebody's. *Oh, hell,* he thought. If he sat out a fight between Sid and his pa, it would be obvious he had heard it all—whatever "it" was. He peeked cautiously around the paper and decided it was time to have a beer somewhere else. He saw Sid stand up and grab Mr. Delaney by the collar.

"Go sleep it off, Pa!"

"Don't you be sassing your old man, Sid Delaney. I'll lay you out. You're an ungrateful bastard just like your sister."

When Mr. Delaney swung at his son, the two other men at Sid's table closed around him. They gave the impression of intending to beat Pa into silence.

No one in the saloon made any attempt to intervene. As the other patrons stared stolidly and the bartender gave his attention to stacking up a row of beer glasses, Mr. Delaney swung at Sid again. Sid knocked him down, which was no easy task. The older man was shorter than his son, but he was solidly built and fueled by alcohol. He half rose, kneed Sid in the stomach, and readied himself for another assault. Sid smacked him again, then gagged as his father's fist connected with his Adam's apple.

Frank decided it was high time to get out. He folded his paper and stepped around the combatants as casually as he could. Behind him Sid and his father thrashed on the floor.

"You're as twitchy as a cat." Peggy prodded Frank in the ribs in the darkened bedroom. "What in Mother Mary's name is the matter with you?"

"Sorry." Frank rolled over on his back and folded his arms behind his head. "I'm just restless, I guess."

Neither Sid nor Mr. Delaney had shown up at Peggy's house after the fight, but Frank couldn't quite shake the feeling that he had overheard what he ought not to. He didn't know what to make of what the men had been saying, but the feeling that it was dangerous stayed with him.

"You jump every time an owl hoots," Peggy informed him. "How am I supposed to sleep through that?"

"I'll try to be still," Frank said. He slipped one arm under her head and cuddled her down onto his chest. Maybe that would calm him. "I haven't seen Sid lately," he remarked casually. "You have any notion how he's doing over at the refinery?"

"No. I don't see him, either," Peggy said sleepily. "I think he was daft to take that job. What's he going to do when they shut the refinery down, you tell me that?"

What indeed? After this afternoon, Frank believed that Sid might have been employed there to make certain that it *did* shut down. *A little fancy work in the right places,* one of the strangers had said, and boom. The mention of Mr. Rutledge's name didn't help any, either. Rutledge was one of the owners. Wasn't he the one who was reputed to want the refinery closed? And who was Frank going to ask about it? Not Peggy, certainly. Did Peggy know anything, he wondered, and if she did, would she tell him? How much affection did she have for her brother and her father? And if Frank went to the owners or even the midlevel bosses, would he get anywhere or just get fired? Who else might be involved? And what *was* it they were planning? Frank didn't have the answers to any of it and didn't know where to get them. Just now keeping his mouth shut seemed to be a pretty good plan.

It continued to seem like a logical strategy to him the next day, when he caught the tram up Avenal Canyon to take his shift on the jackline. He wasn't a company cop; he was a two-dollar-a-day jackline tender, and that didn't pay for services as a spy. For all Frank knew, Sid and his buddies might be planning a shutdown, which could give the union a toehold. If that was the case, Frank would stay out of it. He didn't entirely approve of what they seemed to be planning, but his sympathies were too strongly pro-union to rat on them.

He mulled over the problem all day and kept tripping up on the name of Rutledge. Rutledge was no union man—that was as sure as sunup. Frank was still thinking about it when he came off his shift.

"Watch your gauges," he said automatically to the new man, the same admonition Sid had handed Frank every night until he had gone down to the refinery to work—as a boiler tender. Oh, hell. *Watch your gauges*, Sid had warned him. *If you don't watch them, they'll blow you to hell*. You and whatever else is handy. *Damn*.

The day shift was just sitting down to supper. Frank grabbed a plate and filled it with chili and corn bread. The chili was greasy and swimming with lard, but he wolfed it down anyway. He was young enough to digest anything.

Feeling a little better with a full stomach, he went to the bunkhouse. He found the rattlesnake when he turned down his bed. He leaped backward, halfway across the room.

"Jesus!" One of the other men picked up a stove lid and advanced cautiously on the snake. The reptile didn't move.

"It's dead," someone else said. He looked at Frank and snickered. "Someone's putting you on, kid."

Frank straightened. His heart was pounding. "Well, they did a good job," he said sheepishly. He picked up the dead rattlesnake and flung it out the window. "Which one of you morons do I have to thank for it?"

They all looked at him blankly, and no one smothered a laugh.

"Not me."

"Me neither."

"Maybe it was Sid. He was by this afternoon."

"Yeah," Frank said quietly. "Sid's a real joker." He slid into bed, and when he felt under the pillow, he found what he had expected. He pulled out a piece of paper. Printed on it in block capitals were the words, KEEP QUIET. That answered at least one of Frank's questions. Sid had seen him in the Wellhouse, all right.

XVI

"Reluctantly, Mr. Rutledge, I'm afraid I have to agree with you about moving refinery operations to Oleum." Peter looked from Rutledge to Kemp and shook his head to emphasize his unwillingness. "Had I come into the company earlier, I would have strongly recommended that funds be spent instead to repair the Sierra facility."

"Exactly what I'm proposing," Kemp snapped.

"But the money has *already* been spent," Peter said wearily, "on the Oleum facility. You can't spend it twice."

"You're a whippersnapper." Kemp's wide mouth opened and closed with a snap, and Peter thought of frogs.

The other three directors—Morris, Hatch, and Simpson—sat quietly and looked from Kemp to Rutledge to Peter.

"Now see here." Peter stood up to give himself the advantage of height over Kemp—it took Kemp awhile to heave his girth out of his armchair, and it was not a dignified process. "You invited me—and my funds—into this company. I'm a busy man with no time for infantile name-calling. So let's stick to the facts."

"Sound man," Rutledge approved. "Youthful blood. Knew it was a good idea."

"It wouldn't have been such a good idea if you hadn't already built your damned plant," Peter informed him.

Rutledge chortled in his whiskers. "Too late, eh?"

"The plant's a fait accompli," Peter said. "I don't like

it, but it's been built, and this company can't afford two refineries."

"Rubbish!" Kemp bounced in his chair. Peter wasn't sure whether he was trying to heft his weight from it or was merely impelled by the force of his own convictions. He snorted. "I think we should sell that monstrosity in Oleum if we can't afford both."

"Standard Oil would swallow us whole!" Rutledge protested.

"Selling the plant at Oleum would hardly be a practical solution," Peter said, resisting the temptation to add, "Pipe down." "It's an unfortunate fact of business that one never gets out of a facility what one has put into it, particularly if the competition suspects it's a distress sale." He nodded at Rutledge. "You're quite right in that."

"Of course I am." Looking proud of himself, Rutledge stroked his beard.

"I want to bring up the question of our moral commitment to this town, however," Peter said. "We can't just fold the refinery and leave the local residents in the lurch."

"Don't see what the locals have to do with anything," Rutledge said angrily.

"We're pulling their economy out from under them," Peter, incredulous, explained. "Most of our workers have families. I propose that the company agree to pay moving and resettlement expenses for as many of our refinery workers as are willing to make the jump to Oleum."

"What?" All five of the directors stared at him.

"Never heard of such a thing!"

"Preposterous!"

"Wasteful! Criminal!"

"Well, how the hell do you expect them to get by?" Peter exploded. "Where are they going to find work?"

"That is not the company's concern," Rutledge said. "We are not a charitable organization."

Peter tapped his hands together, fingertip to fingertip. "In that case, I may need to reconsider my decision."

"Come now, Blake," Hatch said, energizing himself enough to join in the debate. He might not hold enough power to sway major decisions, but he had plenty of opinions, and by his expression, paying workers' moving expenses went contrary to all of them. "We're a business. We make money for our shareholders. We don't hand out free lunches."

"Spoils them," Morris chimed in. "Renders them totally unfit to work."

Peter raised his eyebrows. "Mr. Simpson? Would you care to comment?"

"Me?" Simpson, startled, rearranged his papers, squaring the corners. Nobody ever asked him for his opinion. "Bad for business," he said, giving Peter a puzzled stare, as if Peter might not have explained himself properly. "Surely you can't be proposing that Sierra Oil pay a crew of replaceable roughnecks to pack up their wives and dreadful children and go live it up in San Francisco. You aren't serious, are you? Of course you're not." He shook his head, glad to have explained it to himself. "Plenty of labor in Oleum."

"You gentlemen are missing the point," Peter said. He folded his arms. "I have no intention of voting for a move to Oleum unless some provision is made to ease the blow to our workers here."

"Hah!" Kemp said. He glared at Rutledge.

Rutledge stopped stroking his beard. He swung around to glare at Peter. "That's blackmail, Mr. Blake."

Peter grinned, slowly. "Yep." He sat back down and waited, arms still folded.

There was silence and at last Rutledge spoke. "Very well," he said balefully. "I will accede to this extortionate demand, but only to save a noble company from the clutches of that devouring bastard Rockefeller." He glanced up and down the table to see whether Morris, Hatch, and Simpson were wearing expressions of suitable watchfulness, vigilant against the dragon.

"I want a formal vote," Peter said. "The board agrees to pay moving expenses for Sierra refinery workers."

"All right, blast it!" Rutledge said testily. "I'll vote aye."

"Hah!" Kemp said triumphantly. "I won't."

"I beg your pardon?" Peter stared at Kemp.

"I wouldn't vote my *own* moving expenses if it meant moving the works to Oleum," Kemp said, then settled in his chair. "Extraordinary expenditures must be approved by unanimous vote of the board of directors. I wouldn't vote to pour water on Rutledge if he was on fire. Put that in your pipe and smoke it. Hah!"

"You'd sacrifice the well-being of the refinery workers and their families just to thwart Mr. Rutledge?" Peter demanded.

"Without hesitation," Kemp said. "But it doesn't seem to me that it'll come to that, being as you won't vote the move without the expenses."

"Don't bet on it!" Peter seethed, tired to death of the lot of them.

"Excellent. We shall not bow to pressure, Kemp." Rutledge adopted his most patriarchal expression.

"Don't you bet on it, either," Peter snarled. He picked up his leather-bound portfolio and stuffed it under his arm.

"Where are you going?" Rutledge demanded.

"Home," Peter said, disinclined to offer anything beyond bare civility.

He made his exit as gracefully as possible, but he still felt uncomfortably like the offended child on the playground who has picked up his marbles and gone home. It didn't matter, he told himself. Nothing would have induced him to go back into that boardroom until he had had a chance to be alone, to sort things out.

He was not going to be forced into a hasty decision by those weasels. It was bad enough to have to vote with Rutledge on moving the refinery at all, knowing that to do otherwise would be fiscally unsound. Having brought himself to cast that vote, to be waylaid by Kemp was maddening. He wanted to strangle someone. He also needed to decide who was the bigger hypocrite, he thought. There must be a way to get around Kemp. . . .

His mood lightened with the fresh air and distance from the Sierra Oil directors' room. Then he guiltily remembered that Peggy's brother, Sid, was a boiler tender in town now. Peter knew that Peggy wouldn't be very pleased with him if he put her brother out of a job. Maybe it would be just as well to break off that relationship, though. It was getting increasingly difficult for him to maintain self-control around her—she was too pretty and too willing. And Peter was too suspicious not to worry about both, although he felt ignoble about suspecting her motives. He couldn't just vanish from her life, of course. He would have to explain to her that he couldn't offer her any prospects, and it wouldn't be fair to her for him to go on like this, taking up so much of her time. . . .

Cheered by the realization that he naturally had to call on her to explain all that, Peter popped across the street to the stand from which Mrs. Gonzalez sold fresh vegetables and cut flowers. He couldn't undertake a delicate mission of ending the romance without bringing flowers. Peter tucked a cone of chrysanthemums under his arm.

Of course Peggy might talk him out of it, the back of his mind was murmuring. If she assured him that things between them were fine as they were, that she didn't expect more, then he could spend a pleasant evening in her company. And he wouldn't have to think about Kemp and Rutledge until tomorrow.

Having arranged all these possibilities to his satisfaction (and ducked the question of the moment, which was really Oleum and not Peggy), he set off whistling up the street.

It was dusk when Peter came up Peggy's walk. There was a light on in the house, but no one could be seen through the shades. Mr. Delaney was out getting saturated, Peter decided with relief. He far preferred the man during his absences. He knocked on the door and stood waiting, flowers jauntily draped over his shoulder.

No answer. Peggy never left a lamp burning when

she wasn't home; the house was a firetrap to begin with. Peter knocked again and heard stirring.

"Who is it?" Peggy called out.

"It's Peter."

"Oh, mercy, just a minute."

He heard some further muffled utterances and then there was silence. It was somewhat more than a minute before she opened the door, rosy in the face and apparently glad to see him. At least she was smiling, but she seemed skittish. "Peter, dearie! You're a welcome surprise. Come in. We were just having a beer and a little chatter."

"We?" Peter stepped inside cautiously, handed her the flowers, then froze. At the stove, pouring himself a cup of coffee with the exaggerated nonchalance of a man who has just pulled up his pants, was Frank.

"Coffee?" Peggy offered, correcting herself. "We were having coffee, not beer. I'll pour you some."

Peter stared at Frank. "What the hell have you been doing?" he thundered.

Frank flushed, but his lips twitched.

"Frank's a friend of mine," Peggy said, stepping between them. "You got no call to—"

"He's my goddamned brother!" Peter shouted. "My *kid* brother," he added, outraged.

"Lord God," Peggy said faintly.

"I thought that sounded like you," Frank said, managing to find his voice.

"And you just stood there waiting for me to walk in, when everyone in the family's been—"

"I couldn't find a window to slide out of," Frank said. "And it would have been disrespectful to Peggy."

"Peggy!" Peter turned to glare at her. "I suppose you just never got a chance to mention you were seeing my eighteen-year-old brother!"

Clutching the chrysanthemums in one hand, Peggy put her other hand on her hip. "No, I didn't, since you never seen fit to mention to me that you had one, nor Frank neither, and there being more people named Blake in the world than you could shake a stick at."

Peter and Frank glared at each other over the top of her head.

"Furthermore"—Peggy waved the chrysanthemums under Peter's nose—"you don't have a claim on me, Peter Blake. You know I have other fellows, and I'd just like to know where you get off climbing up on your high horse like—"

Peter backed away from the chrysanthemums, which pursued him. "All right. All right! Of course, you're entitled to— But my own damn brother? Frank, I ought to tear you limb from limb."

Peggy looked from one to the other—Peter, dapper and indignant; Frank, unkempt and sleepy eyed, his chambray shirt buttoned, she noticed, one button off over his muscular chest. Frank was a good four inches taller. "Maybe you better not try to do that," she suggested to Peter.

"Yeah, Peter," Frank agreed. He noticed the shirt and rebuttoned it.

Peter slammed his bowler hat down on the kitchen table, folded his arms across his chest, and clenched his teeth. Then he loosened his jaws slowly, like someone unsticking them from taffy. "You look like a bum," he said.

"I wasn't expecting company," Frank said, "or I'd have brought my derby hat."

"Quit it!" Peggy stamped her foot on the floor, and startled, they looked at her. "This is my house. I don't put up with Pa rampaging around, and I don't have to put up with you boys, either, growling at each other like tomcats. What do you think you're doing, carrying on like this? And you both educated men."

"It's the nature of the male, I'm afraid," Peter said sheepishly. "It's our instinct to fight over the female."

"Well, I don't hold with that. And I'm not any alley tabby, either, who'll go with the one that makes the most noise. So you just stop it now."

"Yes, ma'am." Frank swept a graceful bow, then straightened, shaking his sandy hair out of his eyes. It was somewhat less ragged than it had been, because

Peggy had been trimming it for him. "May I pour you
some coffee, Brother dear?"

"And since you don't live here, Frank," Peggy said,
"I'll pour the coffee. Now sit down, both of you, and
behave yourselves." She took the rose-flowered cup and
saucer from the display shelf and set it in front of Peter,
obviously   a   conciliatory   gesture.   "Now then."   She
poured it full and left the brothers glaring at each other
while she got a vase for the chrysanthemums, then
poured the last of a water pitcher around the stems.

The fact that the flowers had been intended as a
parting gift had vanished completely from Peter's mind.
Finding his brother with his shirt buttoned wrong,
casually pouring coffee in the kitchen, roused him to
unreasonable fury.

"Come on, Pete," Frank said. "Back off, will you?"

"How long have you been here?"

"That's not your business, Peter Blake," Peggy said
over her shoulder.

"I meant how long has he been in Sierra," Peter said
with irritable dignity. "As you say, it is no concern of
mine how long he's been in your house." He resented
Peggy's treating him as if he were a dog in the manger
after he had done the honorable thing by her. Worse,
Frank, obviously untroubled by sexual scruples of any
kind, had done the opposite.

Peggy fluffed the chrysanthemums out and set them
on the table so that Frank and Peter had to peer at each
other through them. "Now then," she said, looking down
at them as if they were errant urchins.

Neither brother, however, was prepared to appreciate her attitude.

"Nix on the schoolmarm bit, Peg," Frank said. "You
aren't our mother."

Peter exploded. "And what the hell do you mean
putting Mother through what you've done?" he demanded of Frank. "I asked you how long you've been in
Sierra, you son of a bitch, with never a word to me!"

"I didn't know you were here," Frank explained.

"Do you think I'd have hung around town, waiting for you to put the arm on me, if I had?"

"How did you get here?"

"Trains mostly," Frank said. "I hoofed it some."

Peter stared at him suspiciously. "Where did you get the money?"

Frank folded his arms across his chest, in much the same gesture that Peter had used. Neither of them was aware of having acquired the stance from their father. "I didn't pay my way, you dumb stiff," Frank said with elaborate patience. "I rode the rods, boxcars some. It's not a bad way to go."

"It would be a bad way if Mother found out about it," Peter said. "It would scare her to death. Why the hell did you do it?"

"Didn't you hear the story?" Frank asked sarcastically. "I figured everybody in the family and all the cousins-by-marriage had heard it now—a thorough account of my iniquity."

"I heard you had a fight with Dad," Peter said. "And took off like a damn fool into a snowstorm. That was really intelligent," he added.

"Dad said I didn't know anything about life," Frank retorted. "He won't be able to say that now."

"I imagine not," Peter murmured with a quick sidelong glance at Peggy. "You tack head, didn't you stop to think what you were doing to Mother?"

Frank looked uncomfortable. "Yes, of course," he muttered.

"But not very much?" Peter asked acidly. "Not enough to write to her to let her know you aren't dead. She's so frantic she's hired a detective to look for you."

"And you want me to write to her so she can set him on my trail."

"I want you to write to her out of common decency!" Peter shouted. He shoved the vase of chrysanthemums to one side so he could glare directly at his brother.

Peggy watched silently. "I should've known you were related," she informed them at last. "You're both about as crazy as coots. Frank Blake, you write to your mother right now. I thought you come from some family that didn't care a dime about you."

"Well, he doesn't," Peter said.

"It's not your business, Peg," Frank said, looking badgered. "And if I find out you ratted on me, Pete, I'll pull your goddamned ears off."

"If you think I'm going anywhere except straight to the telegraph office, you've lost your mind," Peter said, then added, "Fritz dear." He hated being called Pete.

"You'd better not."

"I have to, you moron. Someone has to let Mother know you're all right, and apparently I can't trust you to do it. In my opinion you need to be taken home and spanked."

Frank shot up, and his chair skidded backward. "You better be ready to do it yourself."

"Glad to." Peter stood, too, shrugging off his jacket.

"Don't you dare!" Peggy said, trying to get between them.

"Get out of the way, Peggy." Peter lunged at his brother, rocking the table.

"Don't you fight in here!" Peggy snatched the rose-flowered cup and saucer to safety and clutched them to her bodice.

Neither paid any attention. Peter grabbed Frank by the collar, and Frank shoved him hard, toppling him over a chair. In a moment they were half under the table, rolling on the floor and trying to strangle each other.

Peggy set the cup and saucer in the sink. The table rocked again, and the chrysanthemums slid down its tilted surface. She caught the table as it was about to go over, but the vase bounced off, hit the heaving bodies, and rolled into the corner.

"You boys stop that!"

Oblivious, they thrashed at her feet. Frank's hair was dripping and full of yellow petals. Peter's shirt was torn across the shoulder seam. Peggy snatched up the flowers and vase and retreated with them to the sink. Her eyes lit on the coffeepot, still simmering on the back of the wood stove. She wrapped a towel around the handle and hefted it.

"You quit fighting!" When that didn't get any more response than her previous admonitions had, she lifted the pot and poured.

Scalding coffee hit Frank between the shoulder blades. Peggy held her skirts out of the way and poured the rest on Peter, catching him on the buttocks. Peter seized the opportunity to roll Frank over and pummel him. They howled and bumped their way out from under the table. The fighting stopped for a moment.

"You go at each other again, and I'll get Pa's bird gun," Peggy threatened. "Now sit down and act civilized."

"He's got no business handing off orders," Frank said, his chest heaving.

Peter bristled. His hair hung in his eyes, and there was blood on his mouth and chin. "After the way you behaved, you irresponsible puppy, you—"

"You two need a nursemaid!" Peggy shouted. "Now sit!"

They sat unwillingly.

"Now shake hands," Peggy ordered.

Each looked as if he would rather clasp a porcupine. Finally, Frank said grudgingly, "All right. Pax. But I won't shake hands." Eventually Frank spoke again. "And what are *you* doing in Sierra?"

Peggy's eyes were wide. "How long since you boys talked? Frank, your brother's an owner," she said proudly.

"Of Sierra Oil?"

"Of a piece of it," Peter said. "Are you working for my own damn company? You're fired."

"I quit," Frank said. "Jackline tending isn't such a plum of a job I can't bear to part with it. I'm hitting the road before you rat on me to Mother's detective."

"Peter, are you going to let him quit?" Peggy was indignant. "Winter's coming on."

"Winter in southern California wouldn't freeze a frog," Peter retorted. He considered his brother. "It's not my business to hire and fire roughnecks," he growled. "Stay on if you want to."

"Oh, thank you, thank you, boss." Frank tugged his forelock. "And how long until you wire Mother?"

"Tomorrow if you don't do it. I'm not backing down on that, Frank."

"Look," Frank said, "just give me a month. If you give me a month I can get a stake together, and I'll go home. I want to do it myself, when I'm ready, and not be dragged back by the scruff of the neck by some Pinkerton. I'm not a baby."

Peggy looked at him thoughtfully, but she didn't say anything.

"No one would know it from the way you've been acting," Peter said.

"Goddamn it, Pete—"

"All right, all right." Peter flung up his hands. "One month." Peggy's thoughtful gaze turned to Peter now, but he ignored it. "If you haven't arrived home in one month, I'm sending a wire. You got that?"

"Sure," Frank said. He folded his arms on the table. Peter did the same. Neither of them said anything else. They both turned toward Peggy.

She looked at them in exasperation. "If you think you're going to sit here trying to outwait each other, you ain't. I haven't got the patience. Are you going to shake hands?"

Grudgingly they stood and did so.

"Now go home," Peggy said. "I've had enough of your family for one night. My own's enough of a trial." She opened the front door for them and stood at the threshold, watching, while they negotiated the steps. It was not lost on either of them that they both knew where the missing step was, even in the dark.

At the street they stopped and regarded each other. Frank started to put his hand out again, but stuffed it into the pocket of his jeans instead. "How's Midge?" he blurted.

"She misses you," Peter said.

"Oh." Frank hunched his shoulders and turned away up the street, into a knifelike wind.

Peggy watched them go as the brothers turned their separate ways down the darkened street. Her neighborhood didn't have streetlights; the city council wasn't about to waste its electricity on the poor. She hoped Frank could find a place to sleep that night; he would know better than to try to get back in her bedroom.

She waited until their shadows had been swallowed by the night and then went inside, leaving the door unbarred for her father—if he ever showed up. Lately he had hardly been home at all, Peggy thought, and the one time he had been, he'd had Sid with him. They'd got into it again, although only God knew what about. Maybe her father wanted money out of Sid again, as if what he stole out of the laundry wasn't enough to keep him pie-eyed all day and night. Peggy hadn't cared enough to listen; she had just run them both out of the house when they got to yelling too loud. *I swear to God one of these days I'll have a house of my own, just mine*.

She got the pitcher and the vase of chrysanthemums out of the sink and went outside to fill them at the pump. An owl floated by overhead and then dived with a whap of wings, mousing in the overgrown backyard next door. Peggy cocked her head, listening for any further sounds in case Frank did decide to come sneaking back. She wasn't going to let him inside. It wouldn't be fair to make a monkey of Peter like that, not after he'd practically caught them in bed.

Peggy giggled at the thought. Frank's time on the road, she thought, had just about deadened him to feeling shame. Peter, on the other hand, hadn't in any way been prepared for what had happened that night— although she guessed Peter now had a wider view of the world than what he'd had before.

He had a right to be riled at Frank, though, she mused, as she took the chrysanthemums and pitcher inside. Not over her but over whatever was going on in their family. Odd to think about folks with money having all that trouble. When your own family was a trial, Peggy thought, you always assumed that everyone else's ticked along like clockwork. Well, of course they didn't, when you stopped to think about it. But what would have made a smart fellow like Frank duck out of a cushy life to go on the bum? Or work in the oil field, which seemed even less palatable than bumming to Peggy.

She sighed wistfully. She wouldn't take any bets now on how much longer Frank would be around. He would probably light out before Peter could wire their old man. Frank and Peter had both been lying to each other, as any fool could have seen.

There was no telling what Peter would take it into his head to do, given the shock he'd gotten. If she knew men, he'd probably come and try to get her in bed himself. Peggy set the chrysanthemums back on the table and mopped the water up off the floor. It had soaked into the threadbare rug, and yellow petals clung to the frayed fringe. She was fed up with men. She was angry with Frank and Peter because nothing would ever be the same between her and either of them. The lightheartedness had gone out of courting now. And she was aggravated with Sid for turning so sour and secretive. And with her father for all the reasons she'd been fed up with him ever since she realized what it had meant to her mother to be tied to him.

Peggy washed her rose-flowered cup and saucer and set them on the shelf next to the fancy box that had held Peter's chocolates. She went down the hall, hung her clothes over the chair, and slid back into the bed she had been sleeping in with Frank. It still smelled of him, and she buried her nose in the pillow and let a couple of tears roll down her cheeks.

Peter stalked up the street, his bowler hat pressed firmly over the rat's nest the fight had made of his hair. His polished shoes made a staccato *click-click* on the sidewalk once he had marched far enough from Peggy's house to be in a neighborhood that had sidewalks. He felt foolish and very nearly ready to erupt with anger. He was furious with himself for the certain knowledge that his own sensation of slumming, of carrying on with a girl who "wasn't the right sort" and feeling wary of her motives, had prevented him from doing as Frank had done. Worse, he suspected now that Peggy knew it. He was mortified and remorseful.

And he was nearly overcome with the desire to fight Frank again. Frank had split the whole family, driven a wedge between Henry and Cindy, and made Midge miserable. Even the Holt cousins had been affected by it. Toby had accused Henry of being stiff-necked, and then *they* had had a fight about it, too. But Frank didn't seem to care about what he had caused.

Peter had spent his whole life concerned about what people thought of him, worrying that he hadn't lived up to his father's expectations for an army career, and clinging to the conviction that Frank would assuage that guilt by doing it for him. And now where was he? He felt, irrationally, that Frank had pulled the rug out from under him, too.

Peter turned in at his own gate and shut it angrily behind him. In spite of what Frank might think, Peter planned to be at the telegraph office the first thing next morning. Frank didn't deserve a month's grace. Why should everyone else be miserable? Peter thought savagely. So Frank could play tramp as long as it suited him and go home when he felt like it? He hung up his hat and took a decanter out of the breakfront in the dining room. He turned the parlor lamp down to a dim, sulfurous glow, poured himself a shot of whiskey, then sat down to feed his anger with it.

Frank climbed the ladder to a hayloft near Peggy's home. He knew he could sleep there for the one night. The renegade hens who nested up there to hide their eggs from the farmwife clucked and jabbered at him and fluffed their feathers. When he didn't venture any closer, they settled down, murmuring to themselves in the darkness. Frank stretched out, pillowed his head on his arms, and thought about what to do. He knew how to be a roughneck now. He supposed he could always get a job in one of the other fields. It would be the first place the family would look for him, of course; but there were a lot of fields, and he could change his name. He hadn't any intention of going home. He would have to hit the road before Peter loused up his plans.

Another thing held him back: what he had over-heard in the Wellhouse. If someone was planning to blow up the refinery, there was a good chance that people were going to get blown up with it. Frank couldn't square it with his conscience to save his own hide by hopping a freight and just letting everything else go to hell. And if Sid and his father were involved, Peggy could get hurt.

Frank rolled over and tried to sleep. It seemed a shame to have seen Peter and fought with him without spending any good time together before going separate ways. But with Peter taking their father's side, there hadn't seemed any way around it. Frank turned over again, and something scrabbled away through the straw. Mice probably. There wasn't any other sound except for a few desultory clucks from the hens.

Frank felt as lonesome as hell. He sat up finally and wrapped his arms around his knees. A hen said *"Bawk!"* in an annoyed tone. The moon came up and poured a milky wash through the hayloft window. The second he had heard Peter's voice Frank had known it was his brother's. The recognition, the familiarity, had stabbed right through him with a longing for family that was tangible. If Peter hadn't been so steamed at finding him at Peggy's—Frank grinned in spite of himself and shook his head—their reunion might have gone better. If he thought he could get around Peter, he would be on his doorstep even now. Maybe it was just as well he didn't think so. The urge to cling to his brother, to kin, was overpowering. His reaction, he decided, was a sign of weakness, proving that he hadn't matured sufficiently to go home.

But Peter's having a stake in the company shed a whole new light on what Frank suspected Sid might be up to. Peter would know how to check it out. Hell, he was friends with Rutledge and the rest. They couldn't fire Peter. *I guess I owe him that much*, Frank thought, pulling his boots back on. Anyway, it was a reason to go see him on even terms.

He slid down out of the loft, accompanied by considerable clucking, and headed back toward Peggy's.

He scratched on her bedroom window, and she stuck her head out. "I'm not going to let you in, Frank, so you just—"

"I don't want in. I want to go see Peter. See if I can patch it up. I don't know where he lives."

Peggy eyed him suspiciously. "Truly?"

"What do you think I'm going to do, shoot him in his bed?"

"Of course not," Peggy said irritably. She had been asleep, and her tousled hair reminded him of the red hens' appearance. He half expected her to say *"Bawk!"* at him. "All right then, but you be mannerly, you hear?"

"Sure, Peg."

"I mean it, Frank. You boys don't want to be at odds with each other. That's an awful thing in a family, and I ought to know." She looked at him wistfully from the window and gave him the address.

A few minutes later Frank pounded on Peter's door. The yard smelled of newly mowed grass and late-blooming roses; the white porch rails gleamed in the moonlight. *Will I ever live like this again?* he wondered. And then, *Will the price I'll have to pay be worth it?*

Frank pounded on the door again when Peter didn't answer, then nostalgically observed the amenities that were so similar to the family home in Alexandria: the porch swing, the newly painted garden gate, the pots of geraniums by the steps . . .

"What the hell do you want?" The door slammed open, and Peter glared at him through the screen.

"I want to come in. There's something I need to tell you."

"What?"

"I'm not going to tell you on the porch," Frank said, exasperated.

"If it's crap about why I shouldn't tell Mom and Dad where you are, I'm not interested."

"How about you just bite your tongue for a minute and let me in? I promised Peggy I'd mind my manners."

"Did you go sneaking back there?" Peter demanded.

"I went to get your address, you jerk," Frank said, glancing around. "Nice place. I figured your little summer cottage wouldn't be in Peggy's neck of the woods."

"Why should it be?" Peter snapped. "I realize your socialist principles don't hold with my being able to afford a decent house, but unlike dear old Mr. Delaney, I don't spend every nickel I earn down at the corner saloon."

"You smell like you've been working on it," Frank said. There was a certain odor of Scotch whiskey about his older brother, although Frank didn't think Peter was drunk. "And Mr. Delaney isn't Peggy's fault."

"He isn't mine, either," Peter snarled.

"Nor is he ours!" a neighbor's voice yelled out of the darkness. "So maybe you folks would like to take it inside!" A window slammed, rattling the sash.

"Oh, come in," Peter said. He stalked into the house, and Frank followed. Peter sat back down in his chair in the parlor and picked up his glass. He didn't offer Frank a drink. "What do you want?"

Frank turned a side chair and straddled it, resting his arms on the back. "Since you're a corporate bigwig and all, I thought maybe you'd know what to do with this," he said.

Peter waited.

"I overheard something in the Wellhead that's been bothering me."

"If you overheard it in the Wellhead, you'd do better keeping your mouth shut about it," Peter commented.

"The fellow I overheard it from seems to think so,

too," Frank said. "I found a dead rattlesnake in my bed, and a warning note under my pillow."

"Don't expect me to bail you out. You asked for the life you're leading. Stay out of the Wellhead if you don't want trouble."

"It's not my trouble exactly," Frank said. "That's why I came to you. There was some talk of explosions and things going boom down at the refinery." He saw no reason to mention Sid, who was on the low end of the hierarchy. Nipping it at the top would cut Sid loose without costing him his job. Frank suspected that Sid might want to be cut loose.

"That's not unexpected, I suppose. Plenty of the boys are disgruntled over shutting down the refinery." Peter sounded bored; deliberately, Frank thought— making sure that Frank knew he was still a dumb kid, not to be taken seriously. "Stay out of the Wellhead, and you won't get all worked up over a bunch of roughnecks blowing off steam."

"These fellows were more than disgruntled," Frank said.

"Why the hell would they want to blow it up when they're mad over its closing?"

Frank was still young enough to be stung by Peter's condescension. "It might interest you to know," he said sweetly, "that one of your brother bigwigs was mentioned by name. Rather prominently, in fact, in connection with this imaginary scheme you're so blasé about."

"Sure," Peter drawled. "They're going to put a bomb in his mustache cup and strike a blow for the workers' paradise. I assure you we have adequate security to guard against that." Peter's tone of ennui was underlaid with a venomous anger.

Frank stiffened. "What I heard," he said between his clenched teeth, "gave me to understand just the opposite. Mr. Rutledge isn't the target. I think he's the author, and I came to you with this because I didn't know who else I could trust with it. I seem to have been wrong."

Peter leaned forward in his chair. "You were if you

thought you could cozen me with garbage like that. Rutledge may be wrongheaded, but he isn't criminal. And if you go spreading that story around, you'll find out just how deep a pit you've dug for yourself. I won't lift a finger to pull you out, either. That's slander, sonny boy. You back off, or I'll fire you if Rutledge doesn't."

"You don't believe me." Frank stared at him. "Why in the hell would I make it up?"

"I assume," Peter said viciously, "to distract me from your own conduct. Well, it won't wash. You're still going home."

Frank stood up, kicking his chair across the floor toward Peter. "I'll go where I damn well please. You're so pigheaded, you can't see what's in front of your face."

"I can see you," Peter said. "I can see what you've done to this family. I *can't* see any reason why I should trust you again."

"Fine," Frank snapped. "Don't. But if I were you I'd stay away from the refinery until you get less green about what bosses are capable of. You think the world's made out of marshmallow pudding." He looked at Peter with an exaggerated gesture of piety. "You see some fat cat singing hymns on Sunday, you just *know* he's looking out for all the poor little widows and orphans. Horseshit. Rutledge is capable of fleecing his own grandmother for another dollar, and so are Kemp and the rest of them. You'll be capable of it, too, in a couple more years, I expect."

"Get out," Peter hissed. "Get out of my house."

"Sure," Frank said. "I don't need you. Thanks for making it so clear. I thought I did for a while, and it had me worried." He banged the screen door, not bothering to close the other one, and, whistling, went out into the night, leaving Peter staring at nothing, his hands clenched on his chair.

Frank managed to keep up the whistling until he was out of earshot.

XVII

Idaho, October 1896

The little Northern Pacific engine was working up a full head at the Bonners Ferry depot, and its steam cloud provided the only warm spot on the platform. Elizabeth pulled her fur-lined traveling cloak around her and again blessed the fact that she had brought it. It was so bulky that she had nearly decided to leave it at home.

The secretary of the Bonners Ferry club, who had delivered Elizabeth to the depot, pressed a hot brick wrapped in flannel into her hands. "Now you take this and put it under your feet. And be sure not to go walking around in the snow. If the train stops, just sit tight until they get the track cleared. Otherwise, you'll get frostbite sure."

"Is it likely to stop?"

"It'll stop if a tree comes down on the track," the secretary said. "Or a rockslide. You never know what's going to drop off these mountains in the winter."

Elizabeth wasn't used to October being considered winter, but during her journey through Idaho she had come to understand that Idaho wasn't the California coast, either. A railroad journey, even in a train that was likely to stop for trees on the tracks, was considered a luxury by those who lived north of Boise. She had made her circuit through the northern two-thirds of the state mainly by stagecoach, riverboat, and occasionally a hired horse. Where her trunk might be just now, she had no idea. To simplify her journey, she had finally packed

271

what she could get into a carpetbag and sent the trunk back to Boise from the depot at Weiser.

Elizabeth, more than grateful for the hot brick, shook hands with the club secretary, climbed into the train coach, and settled into a seat by the window. Under her feet and insulated by a traveling rug and the hem of her cloak, the brick made a comfortable glow around her toes. Bonners Ferry was only thirty miles from the Canadian border and seemed nearly as cold as an igloo. It was the northernmost stop of her tour, and Elizabeth felt that perhaps she would begin to thaw now, by slow degrees, as the train steamed southward. She was scheduled to speak that afternoon at Sandpoint, forty miles south, then go from there to Coeur d'Alene, possibly the most important stop on her journey. The suspicions harbored by the miners of Coeur d'Alene still nagged at her. Labor troubles between the mine owners and the union had plagued the valley for four years. If miners thought that women would vote against the workingman, they would have none of the new amendment.

The engine let out a piercing whistle and began to move. Elizabeth, fighting to keep her eyes open, took out her notebook and read her speech through one more time. The rhythmic swaying of the carriage made her drowsy, and it hurt her eyes to read the typescript that jiggled on the page. Finally she gave up and slept, soon to be jolted awake by a bump and shriek of the whistle as the engineer hit the air brakes.

"What is it?"

The passengers hurled themselves against the windows of the bumping carriages and flung up the shades that had been lowered against the cold. Elizabeth, pressing her own face to the icy glass, saw trees and precipitous snowbanks whipping by above the rail bed. There was no apparent reason for the sudden braking. The whistle screamed like a banshee, wailing out across the valley below them. Then she saw what had happened—another train had derailed. Its broken cars were sprawled across both tracks down the hill ahead of her train, which was racing toward the wreckage.

"Lord God, we're going to crash!" the man in the seat behind her howled, and jammed his hat down over his ears as if for the dubious protection it afforded.

A child in the front of the car began to cry. Elizabeth whipped her head around and hissed, "Be quiet!" at the moaning passenger behind her. The brakes and the whistle shrieked, while steam boiled up in a cloud around the engine, visible ahead of them on a downward curve. There seemed to be plenty of room to stop, Elizabeth thought, but the train was probably going sixty miles an hour on a downgrade. Elizabeth gripped the armrests of her seat so hard, her knuckles turned white. Trees still zipped by the windows, but a bit more slowly now. When next she caught a glimpse of the wreck below, it looked startlingly near. She could see figures, dark against the snow, scattering from it before the possibility of its being hit by her train.

A conductor came through the door at the end of the car. His cap was askew. "Do not panic, ladies and gentlemen! Our engineer has the train under control." He darted a nervous glance out the window.

"Lord God, save us sinners!" wailed the passenger behind Elizabeth. "Save us from the flames of hell! We're all going to die!"

Elizabeth turned around again and grabbed the man by his shoulders. "If you don't be quiet right now, this second, I'll throw you off this train *before* it hits anything. Now what do you think of that?" When she reached for the man's window as if to open it, he sank back in his seat and stared at her from wide and terrified eyes.

The train swayed and shuddered around a curve, and Elizabeth could still hear the squealing of the air brakes. The train was driving straight at the wreck, so she couldn't see anything beyond it. But the snow-covered gorge was slowing in its flight past the windows. She heard another banshee shriek, and then the car bumped forward and rocked back. The conductor was toppled in the aisle as the train finally slammed to a halt. A series of clanging and thuds echoed down the line as each car behind them smacked into the one ahead.

"Hallelujah!" said the man in the seat behind Elizabeth.

"Ladies and gentlemen, please do not panic. Exit the car in an orderly fashion," the conductor, lying in the aisle, said as he wiped sweat from his pallid brow. "You will be notified as soon as you may reboard, as soon as it has been ascertained that there is no danger of fire."

"Dang," said a miner in a sheepskin jacket to his seatmate. "How can he keep up jawing like that when we just about got shot through the pearly gates?"

Elizabeth got up and dutifully joined the line of passengers filing out of the car. Their breath condensing around their mouths, they lined up on either side of the tracks. They stamped their feet in the cold and looked as irritable as a herd of mules.

"When are we going to get moving again?" a large woman in a felt bonnet demanded of a passing brakeman.

"When that other train gets hefted off the track, lady," he said over his shoulder. "Maybe you didn't notice all them cars lying on their sides," he muttered under his breath.

Elizabeth slowly slogged her way through the snow to the front of the train. The only way she was going to get more information was to go and see the situation for herself. She stopped abruptly by the drive wheels of her own train's engine. Ahead on the tracks, the engine of a northbound train lay sideways, nearly wrapped around a boulder that must have plunged from the cliff above the rail bed. The coal car and the mail cars behind it were overturned, and the rails were strewn with coal, broken slats, and spilled sacks. A knot of passengers, apparently unscathed, stood to one side, but a trail of blood, as shockingly scarlet as red paint in the snow, ran from the engine to a covered body by the rail bed.

"The engineer," someone said. "Poor soul. He

could've jumped, but I reckon he figured he could stop her. He near did. Fireman came through it all right."

A soot-blackened man, his clothing torn and bloodied, his cap in his hand, knelt by the body. A woman, certainly a passenger, was cleaning a gash in his forehead. He didn't seem to notice her.

They'll make a song for them, Elizabeth thought. Train wrecks and dead engineers, the more gruesome and bloody the better, seemed to inspire popular music. She walked past them with a murmured prayer and found a conductor from the wrecked train. She gently placed a hand on his arm.

"I'm sorry to bother you, but I need to know how long it will be until the track is cleared." She felt selfish and unreasonable even to ask.

"Tonight maybe," the conductor answered. "We've sent for a wrecking train. You'd better just go back and wait. They'll let you back into your own car in a minute."

"I can't wait," Elizabeth said firmly. She could afford to miss giving the speech at Sandpoint, but not at Coeur d'Alene—Coeur d'Alene was too important.

The conductor looked at her glumly, as if he were trying to talk to someone who didn't speak English. "Lady, you ain't got no choice."

"How far are we from Sandpoint?"

"Ten miles," the conductor said flatly.

"Could I walk it?"

"Not if you got any sense."

"I'm serious," Elizabeth told him. "Is the way passable? I'm not a shrinking violet, and I have warm clothes." She tried another tack. "Could *you* walk it?"

"*I* could," the conductor allowed. "If I was fool enough."

"Then I can." She turned back toward her train. She would follow the rail bed south.

"If it don't snow again," the conductor shouted after her.

Elizabeth ignored him, but when she was out of his sight she looked at the sky. It was clear and pale, with the thin winter sun riding at just about noon. There was more than enough time, she thought, to walk ten miles. She cast a wary eye about her and headed toward her own car to find her carpetbag.

"Get away from there, lady!" A brakeman who was trying to herd the passengers out of the way of the crew beckoned to her. "Just stay put, will you, folks? You can go back inside in a while. Stomp your feet if you're cold."

Disgruntled, they muttered at the brakeman, and the woman in the felt hat gave him what for over the whole situation, giving Elizabeth the opportunity to slip past, unnoticed. She was in and out of the car in less than a minute. She quickened her steps before anyone realized what she had in mind and tried to stop her. Beyond the smashed engine, she picked her way over the split mail sacks, then averted her eyes from the sheeted body of the engineer. A postal worker from the mail car, scooping wet envelopes out of the snow, didn't look up.

The conductor she had spoken to earlier paid more attention. He grabbed her by the wrist. "And where do you think you're going?"

"I told you. I must get to Sandpoint." Elizabeth detached her arm.

The conductor looked exasperated. "You'll get froze. You'll get et by a bear. Or a cougar."

"I have a pistol in my carpetbag," Elizabeth told him.

The conductor rolled his eyes. "You ever stop a grizzly with a lady's derringer?" he inquired.

"No, but I expect I could stop one with a forty-five," Elizabeth said, then stepped around him.

The conductor let out an angry breath in a little hiss of steam, not unlike the engine. "You been warned. You can't sue the Northern Pacific if you get hurt. You had an official warning."

"Fine." Elizabeth thought of Mrs. Catt and her hair-raising ride on the handcar. What Carrie Catt could do, she herself could do. She set off down the track.

Determination kept her warm for what she judged to be the first two miles. The snow was powdery, and she was wearing warm, low-heeled boots that were fine for hiking. The carpetbag didn't weigh much—at first. Through the third and fourth miles, she found the trek harder going. Both heels were blistered, but she gritted her teeth and ignored them. She counted her steps to measure the distance, throwing in an extra one every so often to counter what she feared was a tendency to be overly optimistic. It was nearly all downhill, which was more precarious than level ground and twice as tiring to her muscles.

When, by her watch and her counted steps she thought she had gone five miles, she sat down to rest on an outcrop beside the track. The hems of her skirt and cloak were wet and ice-cold, and her boots were soaked through. Her toes felt numb. For the first time, the club secretary's admonition about not stomping around in the snow came back to her.

She ate the sandwich that the club secretary had given her for her lunch and looked unhappily at the carpetbag. It seemed to have grown heavier. *I could take the leaflets with me and leave the rest here*, she thought. If she did, though, the passengers would see the carpetbag from the train when it finally passed by and conclude she had fallen victim to some mishap—the conductor's imagined grizzly bear, for instance. Elizabeth envisioned her father being telegraphed and every kind of hell breaking loose. *Mortifying. I only have five miles to go. Six, maybe. Please, not seven.*

The thought of having no dry, clean clothes to change into at Sandpoint cemented her decision. She hefted the carpetbag again and set out down the track. What if she met the wrecking train coming up the grade? Elizabeth wondered, looking apprehensively at the rail bed where it ran through a narrow gorge. She guessed that there was enough room for her to get out of the way. She was sweating. Odd, to be sweating when she was so cold. . . .

By the time she had gone another mile, she was light-headed and sought for some charm, some incantation to focus her mind on the tracks ahead, on putting one foot in front of the other, on not just sitting down in the snow. Maddeningly, all that came to her mind were the words to "The Frozen Girl," an old ballad about a silly wench too vain to wear her warm cloak out in winter weather.

"So what does that make me?" Elizabeth asked herself, her jaws clenched. How foolish a thing had she done by ignoring the conductor's warning? She couldn't go back now; the trek uphill would be very taxing, and she was certain she was more than halfway down. If she sat in the snow and waited for the wrecking train, she would freeze. *One foot in front of the other, one foot, two feet, hay foot, straw foot . . . march, Elizabeth. You are not a city slicker. You hike all the time.*

Her ribs ached. Breathing hurt. She stopped, dropped the carpetbag, then fumbled under the cloak and her wool basque to unhook her stays. She never laced tightly, but now she couldn't bear them at all. She wrestled with them and entangled them in her camisole. She cursed women's clothing until, by tearing the camisole from top to bottom, she managed to pull the stays out from under the basque. She looked at them with loathing and dropped them by the tracks. Let passersby wonder about that! Shivering, she buttoned her basque again and pulled the fur-lined cloak around her. Her neck was cold, and she wished for a muffler until it occurred to her to unpin her long hair and let it serve the same purpose. Finally, hair flowing around her shoulders, she tied her bonnet back on and trudged forward.

Around a bend the rail bed narrowed ominously into a wooden trestle over a meandering river. Elizabeth stopped and swore and pondered the danger: How fast could she cross the trestle? And from how far away could she hear an oncoming train? And why hadn't the conductor told her about the trestle? Not that she had asked, of course.

She slithered down the last slope and stopped again at the edge of the trestle.

Suddenly the wrecking train came shrieking up the grade, and Elizabeth jumped backward, her heart pounding. The train hit the trestle with a roar that shook the ground she was standing on and unnerved her so much she retreated farther up the embankment and crouched ten feet above the rail bed. Her hair whipped her cheeks as the train roared by under her. A startled white face in the cab turned up and stared at her. Then the train was gone, a black smoking snake chuffing upward into the snow, breathing live steam.

Elizabeth crept down to the trestle. The air around her knees felt warm from the heat of the train's passage. There wouldn't be another train coming behind the wrecker, she assured herself—not when they knew in Sandpoint that the line was blocked. She picked up her skirts and her carpetbag before the conviction could leave her.

Elizabeth ran out onto the trestle. She balanced carefully on the ties and stepped from one to the next. Soon she was suspended like a tightrope walker. Looking down at the river below made her dizzy. All the stories she had ever heard of hapless travelers who broke their legs on railroad tracks, who lay helpless while thundering trains smashed their bodies to bits, came back to her with appalling attention to detail. When she reached the other end of the trestle, she crawled off into the snow and threw up.

I could have been in a nice warm jail in San Francisco, she thought, scrubbing her face and mouth with snow.

She stood up again and hefted the carpetbag, which was beginning to feel like an anvil. What had the trainman thought, she wondered, when he saw her looking like a witch in the snow, clinging to the embankment above him? "I'm tougher than you think," she muttered, and slogged on.

She stumbled forward, and just as the sun slid out of sight she finally arrived, corsetless but uneaten by bears and still clutching her carpetbag, in Sandpoint.

The Sandpoint women, having heard of the train crash, had given up on her for the night. Summoned by messenger back to the depot, they bustled around her. The women expressed their horror, fascination, and admiration while she soaked bloody feet in the basin in the ladies' lounge, then changed into dry, clean clothes. They treated her to sandwiches and flasks of hot tea with whiskey and offers of a bed for the night.

"I've got to be in Coeur d'Alene tomorrow," Elizabeth said, wolfing down the sandwiches. "That's why I walked. I'm sorry I missed my speech here, but I can't stay. . . ." Her words sounded fuzzy, disjointed, to her.

"You look about half-dead," one of them said. "And don't you worry none about that speech. Once word gets out what you done, I'd like to find a man in Sandpoint who'll have the nerve to say women don't deserve to vote."

Elizabeth cradled the hot mug in both hands and drank more tea. Her hands were shaking, and some of the liquid spilled into her lap.

"You need a doctor, that's what."

Elizabeth shook her head.

"Well, we sent for one anyway." They nodded briskly at one another. "Being as we couldn't pry you loose out of the depot, he's coming here."

Elizabeth, too tired to move from the warm room and the overstuffed chair they had sat her in, nodded acquiescence. She had a vague memory of having pulled away from the women while refusing to budge from the station. "I have to catch a train," she said again.

"Well now, that's a problem. The last train's gone. Won't be another till morning."

"I have to *be* there in the morning." Elizabeth tried to sit up, to heave her bone-weary body out of the chair.

"There's the short line," one of them suggested dubiously. "But it ain't nothing but ore cars."

The main line, the woman explained, ran west across the state border to Spokane, Washington. But from there one could catch the electric excursion railway east to Coeur d'Alene or buy a ticket on the steamboat. The short line, however, went directly south on a narrow-gauge track that served the mines.

"I'll take whatever I can get," Elizabeth told them. "There must be someplace to put a passenger."

"Here's the doctor. You see what he says."

The doctor said, "Young woman, you have been extremely foolish," and thus produced in Elizabeth an instantaneous dislike for him. "Nor am I in the habit of examining my patients in a railway station."

"Then don't examine me," Elizabeth told him. "I am quite all right."

"Let me look at your feet."

"Why?" Elizabeth drew back her feet, clad in dry stockings, and tried to tuck them under her.

"To see if I am going to have to amputate your toes," the doctor said, grabbing an ankle and peeling her stocking down while Elizabeth tried to jerk her foot away.

The other women retreated tactfully to the end of the room.

Elizabeth glared at him. "You're hurting me."

"You have frostbite," the doctor declared, ruthlessly massaging her toes.

"I don't like you," Elizabeth said, the whiskey beginning to have an unfortunate effect on her temper.

"My dinner is at home on the table getting cold," the doctor retorted, "so I don't like you, either."

"Then why did you come?"

"I'm a doctor. I have to treat idiots as well as sensible people." He spread some salve on her toes and bandaged them. "You'll be lucky if you don't waddle like a duck for the rest of your life. Any woman who hasn't got sense enough not to walk ten miles through the snow hasn't got sense enough to vote, either, if you want my opinion."

"Well, I don't."

"You have it anyway."

"I suppose you've never treated a man who did anything foolish?" Elizabeth said.

"I've treated plenty of them. They don't have the sense to vote, either. But I can't do anything about them. If I were in charge there would be an intelligence test administered at the polls and three-fourths of the population wouldn't be allowed to cast ballots. Give me your other foot."

Elizabeth did so, unprotesting. The doctor was young and balding with a bristly black mustache and the much-tried look of a man who is missing dinner and wants his pie.

"I'm sorry if I was rude," she apologized. "I appreciate your coming out here at night. Are my feet going to be all right?"

"Probably, if you keep them warm. The nail's going to come off that big toe, I think. Make sure it stays clean and keep off your feet as much as you can. Stay in bed a few days, in fact."

"I have to get to Coeur d'Alene," Elizabeth said stubbornly. It seemed to be a litany—all she could say, as if, provided she said it often enough, some transportation would magically appear.

"Well, don't walk" was the doctor's parting shot.

"I got a nephew fires on the short-line Number Six," one of the women said. "They hook a passenger car on every so often for the mine bosses. They brung in scabs that way once, too, the dirty blackguards. But that wasn't Jemmy's fault. You let me talk to him."

She disappeared for half an hour while Elizabeth finished more tea and waited drowsily by the wood stove that warmed the lounge. When the woman returned, she reported that there was no passenger car hooked up for tonight's run, and Jemmy said it was as much as his life was worth to go fooling around with unauthorized cars. But the lady could ride in the caboose with the brakeman if she didn't mind some soot. It was plenty warm in the caboose, and they would set her in Coeur d'Alene by morning.

Elizabeth would have ridden a camel to get to Coeur d'Alene, and in her present state, the caboose sounded as luxurious as the Waldorf Hotel.

She put on her wet cloak and shoes and braved the weather once again. The narrow-gauge line ran past the other side of town, and its depot was no more than a tower and a water tank, dimly lit by signal lights.

As the Sandpoint women escorted her through town, she gave them what pointers she could for organizing politically. Then they went through the railyard to Number Six, and the brakeman, who was greasing the journal boxes at the ends of the axles, tipped his blackened cap and told her to hop on up and make herself to home.

The caboose was furnished with a table and benches, all bolted to the floor, plus a stove, a stairway to the cupola, and four bunks for the relief crew on longer runs. Elizabeth crawled gratefully into one of the bunks and pillowed her head on her carpetbag. The brakeman came in with an adolescent boy, an engineer's son who was deadheading—riding free—as was his privilege. He looked with curiosity at Elizabeth.

"This here's Miss Emory," the brakeman said. "We're giving her a lift to Coeur d'Alene, but you don't need to go mentioning it."

"Yes, sir," the boy agreed.

"This here's Georgie."

Elizabeth tried to sit up and put out her hand, but she smacked her head into the bunk above her.

"Don't get up, ma'am," the brakeman said. "You might want to sleep till we hit Coeur d'Alene." He looked as if he didn't know what to do with her and was wondering if he was going to have to entertain her.

Georgie was more interested. "Why you got to get to Coeur d'Alene?" he asked. "Somebody after you?"

Elizabeth managed to sit up without braining herself again. "Nothing nearly so interesting," she told Georgie. "I have to make a speech."

"Oh." Light dawned on Georgie. "You're the woman suffrage lady! My ma heard you talk down in Boise. She told my pa he'd better vote for that amendment, or she'd lay him out with the frying pan."

"I heard what you done to get 'round that wreck on the main line," the brakeman said. "Doggone if I ain't going to vote for it now. I wasn't going to, but I figure you earned it, ma'am."

Elizabeth started to say that *all* women had earned it but then decided to skip the party platform. If she had converted a brakeman by her idiotic heroics, she wasn't going to unconvert him by being pompous. "Thank you." She smiled sleepily at him and curled up on the bunk.

Another worker came in and took his place in the cupola. Elizabeth dozed as the train swayed into the night toward Coeur d'Alene. Her cloak was drying by the caboose stove, and the low voices of Georgie and the brakeman playing pinochle filled the car. Sleeping in the caboose bunk required much unconscious concentration; otherwise, she could have found herself flying out of bed as the train swayed around a curve. That it never quite succeeded in dislodging her was only because she slept with a death grip on the bed frame and her feet braced against the end.

The sunlight woke her, spilling through the high window. The brakeman and Georgie were putting away their cards, and the train was slowing. Elizabeth sat up creakily, her back and legs protesting the whole way. She felt as if she had been hoeing cotton.

"Thank you for the ride," she said when the train had stopped.

The brakeman and Georgie solemnly assured her that it had been a pleasure. She stepped out into the sun to discover that they were not at the Coeur d'Alene depot but at the mine yards, amid high piles of ore and slag.

She turned to the brakeman. "How do I get into town?"

The brakeman cupped his hands. "Hey, Jem!" The fireman stuck his sooty head out the cab window. "You reckon Abner's around this morning?"

"Saw him as we pulled up!" Jem yelled back.

"There you are," the brakeman said, proud to have solved her problem. "Abner—he does livestock hauling—ships up to Sandpoint on this line. You go around the front of that building over there and look for a wagon. He'll take you in."

Abner, she soon learned, had been hauling hogs in the wagon that morning. He was a vast man in overalls and a red-and-white checked cap. He called her "little lady" and dusted off the wagon seat with a handkerchief that was caked with hog-scented mud. At least he was gallant. He drove her proudly through downtown Coeur d'Alene while Elizabeth adopted as dignified an expression as she could muster and hoped that no one who came to hear her that evening would remember her arriving in a hog wagon that morning. Abner deposited her on the steps of the Palace Hotel.

Elizabeth expressed her gratitude, then nearly staggered with fatigue through the ornate brass and glass double doors and made a beeline across the plush carpet to the reception desk. She looked a wreck. Nothing but a hot bath and a feather bed were on her mind.

"He your new beau?" a voice behind her inquired, obviously referring to Abner.

Elizabeth spun around. Tim Holt was sitting in the lobby. He was wearing an exquisitely pressed frock coat and creaseless trousers. His polished boots rested atop the brass fender.

"He seems to be a homespun sort," Tim went on, "but they often make the best family men."

"He drives a hog wagon," Elizabeth said between her teeth. "He gave me a ride. What are you doing here?"

"I'm reporting the news," Tim replied blandly. He didn't get up. "This suffrage campaign is news. So are you. I hear you've been tearing up the state for the last month. Since I consider woman suffrage an important issue, I thought I'd like to be in at the finish."

"At the—" Elizabeth began to quiver with mingled fury and exhaustion. She was bone weary. Her feet hurt, her face was smudged with soot, and she had ridden in a hog wagon (and smelled like it, judging from the expressions of passersby). The sight of Tim, dapper and polished and toasting his toes at the fire, was more than she could bear. She exploded. "You own the paper. You have reporters to send. What do you think you're doing out here? Did you think I couldn't take care of myself?"

"You look fine to me," Tim said genially. "A little dirty maybe, but that would be from the hog wagon."

"There was a train crash," Elizabeth said. "I had to walk."

Tim's eyes darkened with concern for a moment, and then he carefully adjusted his expression. "That was enterprising of you. I notice that it's been snowing outside, so I trust it's permissible if I ask if you have caught pneumonia? I would inquire the same of anyone, I promise you."

"I have frostbite in my toes," Elizabeth said. "They hurt like the devil. Tim, go away. It isn't going to work between us. We already decided that."

Tim raised his eyebrows. "I haven't come courting, Miss Emory. That would be extremely undignified on both our parts since you've already given me to understand that you're not interested. I'm here to get a story. Regrettably, the story happens to coincide with your hobbyhorse."

Elizabeth regarded him with grave suspicion.

"Keep working on it," Tim suggested. "You'll figure out how to make use of me without burning your fingers. Consider it a challenge."

XVIII

Sierra, October 1896

Despite his best intentions, Peter hadn't telegraphed his father about his truant brother. He thought
about it every day, but whenever he saw Peggy he
reconsidered. He didn't want Peggy to think that he was
telegraphing home to remove the competition. Peter's
sense of pride made his whole skin quiver at being
considered a dog in the manger. Peggy had tried once to
talk to him about Frank but gave up when he said stiffly
that that was family business.

Peter knew he wasn't being entirely logical, and
that made him furious, mostly at Frank. In the two
weeks since their confrontation, Peter never saw his
brother except to glimpse him on the street, and whenever that happened, Peter flinched with anger.

In some kind of gesture—he wasn't certain what
kind—Peter had sent to San Francisco for his new Blake
motorcar, which was his treasure, his baby. He took
Peggy for a ride in it just to show her which brother was
a solid citizen and which was a fly-by-night. He didn't
know what difference that made to Peggy, but she did
like to ride in the motorcar.

Also high on his list of aggravations was Sierra Oil.
The business seemed mired in political molasses. Kemp
refused to budge on Peter's demand that the Sierra
workers be compensated for the loss of their jobs. Peter
stubbornly refused to budge also, so the removal of the
refinery operations to Oleum was at a standstill. Rut-

ledge appeared unconcerned and wore an expression of cagey triumph, which Peter couldn't fathom—Rutledge couldn't possibly believe that Peter would give up and vote for the move without some help for the workers.

Peter withdrew emotionally, knotting himself into a ball of anger and unhappiness. His expression was so guarded that at times his face was masklike.

Peggy recognized his turmoil and pointed out that the air that Peter carried about him mirrored what she saw in her brother Sid these days. "You look like something with its foot in a trap," she told Peter while he wordlessly drove the Blake around town. "Maybe you ought to figure out how to get loose before you have to bite it off." Before she confined her attentions to the scenery, she muttered, "What the hell is the matter with everybody these days?"

Frank was talkative, especially in bed after he and Peggy had made love. But whenever she asked him what it was that was preoccupying him, he refused to tell her. What was bothering him was Sid, so obviously he could not mention it to her. Instead, he placated her with chatter and poetry and stories of his days on the road until, resigned, she gave up.

Frank rarely saw Sid anymore, and when he did, Sid avoided him. If Sid saw Frank approaching, Sid took to his heels—but not before giving Frank a look that caused him to remember the snake in his bed.

It all gave Frank the willies and a strong suspicion that he ought to get out of town. Either his parents' detective or, worse, whoever Sid was working for would catch up with him sooner or later.

But his conscience wouldn't allow him to leave town—not until he got to the bottom of Sid's machinations and put a stop to them. Frank turned it over and over in his head, held the problem upside down, and stared at it. He never came to any conclusions or solutions. He felt, in fact, like a dog trying to catch its own tail, until the field boss in Avenal Canyon unwittingly pushed him into action.

"Hey, Blake!" The field boss shouted at him as Frank was coming off his first half-shift on the jackline. "Get down to town and bring up a load of barrels."

"But I want to sleep tonight," Frank protested. "Besides, I haven't had dinner."

The field boss snorted. "Sleep in town. I know you got a dolly down there. But get up here in the morning with those barrels. The drayman's busted a leg, and I got to have them. I'll have Ibanez take your shift."

"Ibanez is new," Frank said with the developed scorn of an old hand. "You ready to turn him loose by himself on that jackline?"

"I'll turn *you* loose if you don't fetch me those barrels," the field boss warned. "Everybody's a manager these days," he grumbled. "If I don't get something to put the goddamned oil in, what are we going to do, pour it down our pockets? Now beat it."

Frank decided not to suggest sending Ibanez. The barrels would be at the cooperage at the refinery, and Frank felt an itch to snoop around a bit, to see if he could learn anything. He couldn't just go waltzing into the refinery without a reason, but now he had one. "Yes, sir."

He hoisted himself into the tramcar and with a careful hand on the brake worked it gingerly down the long grade. He hoped to hell that someone would be around to help him run the car up again when he showed up with the barrels. He wasn't used to running the tram and had nightmarish visions of himself and two dozen empty barrels careening backward down the mountain on a broken cable, bouncing from rock to rock.

He was sweating and cursing by the time he reached the bottom and hitched up the six dray mules stabled there. They were big, sleek animals with semaphorelike ears that swiveled at him curiously. It took a lot of mule power to get a dray, even one loaded with empty barrels, up the mountain as far as the tramline. Frank rubbed their shiny muscled shoulders and bony noses while he rigged the harness, and they snuffled at his shirt pockets. The drayman who owned them and fed them sugar was nowhere around.

"What did you do, step on him?" Frank asked.

They snorted.

Frank chuckled. The drayman liked his whiskey. He had probably fallen off the wagon. "I'd be an old drunk, too, if I had to sleep with you fellows," he told the mules. He climbed up on the wagon seat and thought of Peggy. She wouldn't be expecting him that night, but he would go around anyway, after he'd fed the mules and loaded the barrels. With any luck, he might find his dear brother Peter there.

The urge to annoy Peter wore off as the wagon neared town. He rolled down Main Street and enjoyed being the captain of a six-mule team. Skill was required to drive a team, and the fact that Frank had done it before probably caused the field boss to send him instead of Ibanez, who always crossed himself and muttered when he had to deal with mules.

Frank looked at Sierra Oil's corporate office building as he passed its corner. It was gray fieldstone below and red brick above, with arched windows alternating with the overhanging white half-circles of Italianate bays on the second floor. The bay at the corner had a cupola, and the Sierra Oil flag flew from the top. Frank pulled out his pocket watch. It read a quarter to five. There was a light in the first-floor windows, and two more above. On an impulse he swung the mules into an empty lot a few hundred feet away and tethered them to a hitching post.

"Do me a favor," he said to the mules. "Don't snarl anything up." He jogged down the street to the Sierra Oil office and poked his head inside the main door.

"We're closing," a clerk at the front desk said. He snapped his ledger shut to make the point.

Frank declined to be put off. "I want to see Mr. Kemp," he said, fishing out the only director's name he could remember, except his brother's. Or Rutledge's.

"Mr. Kemp doesn't do the hiring," the clerk said, distastefully inspecting Frank's oil-stained work clothes.

"I'm not looking for a job," Frank said. "I'm looking for Mr. Kemp."

The clerk sighed and picked up a message pad. "And you wish to speak with him concerning—?"

Frank came a little closer and leaned his hands on the clerk's desk, leaving oily fingerprints. "I wish to speak with him concerning a concern that's private. So how about if you just check upstairs and see if he's around?"

"I told you—"

"No, you didn't," Frank said. He had decided to beard the corporate lion in its den and would not be so easily dissuaded. "I'm not going to go away until you find out if he's here."

The clerk looked irritably at the fingerprints on his clean blotter. "You'll have to go to the hiring hall. They open at six in the morning," he added with a tight smile that said he was delighted to thwart unauthorized nuisances.

"Let's run through this again," Frank said with elaborate patience. "I'm not after a job. Except maybe yours, since it's going to be up for grabs when Mr. Kemp finds out what you wouldn't let me tell him."

It was possible that something about him didn't fit the clerk's picture of an uneducated roughneck. Or perhaps the fellow was intimidated by the size of Frank's muscular shoulders looming over him. In either case he glared at Frank, then finally stood up. "You wait here," he snapped.

Frank waited, whiling away his time by inspecting an artist's rendering in oils of the Avenal Canyon jackline. It hung in a huge gold frame on the wall. Although it was inaccurate in several technical aspects, the doughty crew posed in front of it looked burly and romantic—an artist's vision of frontier gallantry. A matching oil of the first Sierra well on Yellow Mountain adorned the opposite wall, and between them was a row of portrait photographs of the company founders.

The clerk came back, still looking irritable. "You can go upstairs," he told Frank. "First door on the left."

"Mr. Kemp?" Frank asked.

"Upstairs," the clerk snapped. He began tidying his desk.

Frank went up stairs carpeted with an imposing burgundy runner. The first door on the left stood open, and he peeked around it. The man inside wore a black frock coat and whiskers that nearly reached his watch chain. "Mr. Kemp?"

"What do you want, young fellow? I'm a busy man."

Now that he was here, Frank wasn't quite sure how he was going to explain himself. "My name's Francis Blake, sir. I think you are acquainted with my brother, Peter." Might as well use the name, even if Peter had been too pigheaded to listen.

"Your brother?" The man appeared to find that unlikely.

Frank flushed. "We, er, don't have much in common, sir. To tell you the truth, I went to him first, and he wouldn't hear me out."

"So you've come to me?" The other man unbent a little. "Well, then, my boy, what's on your mind?"

Frank took a deep breath. "Just gossip, sir. But to put it plainly, it's very unpleasant gossip about an accident, an explosion, at the refinery."

"I don't believe we've had any accident."

"No, sir. I'm afraid you may be going to."

"Oh, I see." The man stroked his whiskers. "And just where did you hear this?"

"I overheard it, sir, in the Wellhead Saloon. It's been on my conscience, so I thought I should warn someone."

"And just who did you hear it from?" the man asked sternly.

Frank hesitated. "I didn't know them. They didn't know I could overhear."

"Well, then, I don't think we have much to worry about. We have excellent security. But you were right to come. There's always the chance of a disgruntled employee doing something stupid. These union agitators have made so much trouble, the men don't know how well-off they are. Not like when I was a boy. Did you say you work for us?"

"Yes, sir. On the jackline in Avenal Canyon."

"I see." The man leaned forward. "And why are you not tending it?"

"The drayman broke his leg," Frank answered. "They sent me down to the cooperage."

"Well, then, you'd better run along. I assure you I will take your warning under advisement. But saloon gossip—" He waved a hand dismissively.

Frank didn't budge. "There's something else."

"Well? Well, what is it?"

"I heard a name," Frank said. "An important name. One of your company's directors, Mr. Kemp. That's why I got the wind up."

The man cocked his head with interest. "Indeed?" he said slowly. "And whose name might that be?"

"Mr. Rutledge's."

"Now see here—"

"I don't know Mr. Rutledge," Frank said quickly. "And by accusing him, I'm probably risking getting fired, so please hear me out."

"Accusing him? Young fellow, are you implying that our Mr. Rutledge would intend to damage his own company?"

"That was the gist of it," Frank said grimly.

"Impossible. Hmmph! Mr. Rutledge goes to church every Sunday, a man of the highest moral tone. Unthinkable." He pointed a finger at Frank. "I don't want to hear any more of this."

"I'll bet you don't," Frank said, goaded. "I didn't want to tell you, either. But if something happens to that refinery, people are going to get hurt."

"And why would Mr. Rutledge want to damage his own company? Tell me that, eh?"

Frank stood his ground. He had probably lost his job anyway—no one was ever grateful to troublemakers, even when they told the truth. "I hear Mr. Rutledge is the one who wants to shift the refinery operation up to

San Francisco," Frank explained. "I hear it's stalled because you won't go along with it."

There was a little space of silence, a box of stillness between them, that was almost tangible. Then the man cleared his throat. "Get out of here. I don't know why you're trying to cause this company trouble, Blake, but you are on very shaky ground. If you want to keep your job, you'll get yourself down to the cooperage for your barrels and keep your mouth shut. Understand?"

"I understand you're making a mistake," Frank said. "I understand I've done the best I could. Yeah, I guess I understand you."

He went down the red plush stairs again, his conscience eased a little by the attempt. He should have remembered that bosses stuck together. It was a cardinal rule that bosses were right, even when they were so wrong that it was written on their foreheads. But he didn't think that Mr. Kemp had been stupid—cagey, yes, but definitely not stupid. Kemp would certainly investigate what Rutledge was up to now, particularly since everyone knew that Kemp didn't like Rutledge.

Yes, Kemp would check Rutledge out and put a spoke in his wheel at the same time he was firing Frank for confiding in him about it. Frank was pretty sure he was going to get fired. He would get back up the canyon with the barrels, and his pay would be waiting for him, he thought. Well, it was probably time to hit the road again anyway—Peter was bound to have wired home by now. Frank sauntered by the clerk's empty desk and let himself out, first thumbing his nose at the whiskered portrait of the man upstairs.

Frank backed the mules and empty dray out of the vacant lot, which was no easy task, and soothed himself further with the knowledge that old Kemp and his whiskers couldn't have done it as well, although he had heard that Kemp was a local man who had started out as a rancher. Maybe there was more to Kemp than he had perceived in their brief encounter. Maybe he had just gotten old and grown a lot of whiskers and convinced himself he didn't have to work for a living.

Frank swung the dray through the refinery gates after telling the gate man what he wanted. He gazed at the huge tanks and snarls of steel piping that ran like spiderwebs between them. Plumes of steam and smoke bloomed overhead. The gate man pointed him at the cooperage, a low wooden building in the middle distance, and Frank clucked at the mules and shook the reins.

The head cooper seemed to be expecting him. He was a wizened man in a leather apron, and not much taller than his barrels. "Leave the wagon, son," he said, "and stable them mules. You can't get back up the canyon tonight."

"I wasn't planning on it." Frank climbed down and unhitched the near mules from the wagon tongue. "I'll be back at daylight. Where's the barn?"

To his satisfaction, he learned that it was on the other side of the refinery complex. Leading the six mules and looking around him—for what, he wasn't sure—he started down a broad dirt avenue. Was Sid going to be lurking with a handful of dynamite behind a tank, he asked himself, feeling foolish.

At dusk, the refinery was almost magical, a spangled fairyland of electric lights strung from catwalks and ladders. The bulbs' glow was either diffused by steam and smoke or, beyond them, shining as clearly as stars. Rail lines crisscrossed the refinery grounds, but most of them were for mule-drawn trams. Frank had heard that Oleum had its own steam-driven railroad.

The refinery, never entirely shut down at night, was operated by a skeleton crew. Now the road was thick with day workers coming off their shift and the night crews going on. Even in the growing darkness Frank could see that the buildings were shabby and unpainted. A few of them appeared close to falling down. Rutledge, who wanted to move to Oleum, was letting it die. Was he impatient, Frank wondered, because it wasn't dying fast enough? Was that why he had ordered its destruction?

Frank found the mule barn. The mules already stabled there whickered at him as he turned his animals into stalls. He fed them from the hay bales and grain sacks stacked at the end, under the steel hooks that held their harnesses. While they ate, he rubbed the mules down.

After the team was taken care of, Frank slipped out into full dark. He dodged the pools of electric light and stood in the shadows, then stared up at monstrous tanks. He listened to the hum of unfamiliar machinery, which whirred in the night, refining the dark crude that was sucked from the earth on Yellow Mountain, transforming it into kerosene, fuel oil, lamp oil, gasoline, hair pomade, and asphalt residue to pave over the dirt and cobblestones of an earlier age. Frank thought it was no wonder that Peter, with his motorcars, was investing in oil.

Frank knew that Sid was a boiler tender, but where did he fire his boiler? Although Frank had no firm grasp of the principles of refining crude oil, he supposed the boilers made the steam that drove the process and spilled upward in those pale plumes. He ambled toward the smokestacks that rose above a long fieldstone building amid a nest of pipes. No one questioned him. The security that Mr. Kemp and Peter had bragged about appeared to consist solely of the man at the gate.

The fieldstone refinery building offered blind walls at the back and sides, with only a thin row of windows strung well above Frank's head. He wanted to look inside the structure, but how? He gazed around. A pile of disused barrels, their staves cracked or hoops sprung, lay in a jumble on the ground. Frank dragged a few over to the wall, stacked them as best he could, then climbed them gingerly and hooked his elbows over the window ledge. The barrels gave way below him with a clatter. He hung, feet swinging, face pressed against grimy glass, and tried to peer through before someone spotted him. Frank's experience with railroad bulls had left him with a dislike for being caught splayed against a wall, his back an inviting target. But no one came to investigate the barrels' noise.

All he could see through the glass was a further

tangle of pipes, gauges, and tall tanks, overseen by two men in white coats and with clipboards. It was as mystifying to him as the outer workings had been, but he was willing to bet that one good charge of dynamite would blow the whole place to kingdom come.

The muscles in his shoulders began to quiver, so Frank lowered himself slowly until he hung by his hands. He dropped, landed with what he thought was a hideous crash in the barrels, picked himself up, and ran, ducking through the shadows until he could crouch, panting, under the catwalk that spiraled up a vast, squat storage tank. Was everyone who worked there deaf? he wondered. Where was the supposed security? When he had his breath back and still no outraged cries rose from the refinery building, he sauntered out into the main road and walked purposefully, trying to give the impression of accomplishing some legitimate errand.

He found himself back at the main gates without having seen anything interesting or incriminating. There was still a light in the office window, and on impulse he wandered in there to see what he could see. The office manager, working late, was not overly welcoming.

"What is it, bud?"

"Just curious," Frank said, giving him a friendly smile. "I came down from Avenal Canyon for a load of barrels. Thought I'd look around, see what happens to the oil after we pump it. It's a pretty impressive operation, isn't it?"

The office manager thawed. "This is the pioneer oil outfit in these parts. We ship our product all over the country. Even back East."

"Amazing what you can make out of oil." Frank admired the products displayed in the glass case.

"It's the future, young man. Pretty soon we'll have the whole country running on oil—trains, steamships, heavy industry."

Frank noted a row of photographs above the case. Sierra Oil's founders seemed to have a penchant for displaying their images on corporate walls. A familiar whiskered face looked back at him. Frank leaned closer and read what he had not noticed in the company offices on Main Street—the little brass plate with the subject's name. *Sanford Rutledge*.

Rutledge! He gasped, then recovered immediately when the office manager stared at him. Rutledge! He had been talking to Rutledge! The round, bulbous man in the next photograph, never before seen by Frank, was William H. Kemp. He had talked to Rutledge, told Rutledge what he had overheard, what he suspected. Kemp must have been gone for the day, and Rutledge had told the clerk to send the insistent roughneck up anyway. Rutledge knew just where to find him, too. Oh, the devil take him.

"Th-thanks for letting me look around," Frank stammered. He hurried into the yard and ran through the front gates. His back itched between the shoulder blades. Now he would never get through to Kemp. Frank headed at full speed for his brother's house. Peter would have to listen to him; that was all. Because Rutledge had pretended to be Kemp, Peter should at least grant him a hearing.

Frank ducked through Peter's garden gate and pounded on the door. The house was dark, and no one answered. Frank banged again. "Let me in, damn it! It's Frank!" He stayed five minutes, pounding insistently, but no one came. The next-door neighbor raised his window and shouted at him, and Frank took to his heels.

Driven by the urge to get out of Rutledge's territory, he trotted through the dark toward Peggy's house. The old man seemed more sinister now than when he had been mouthing platitudes in the company office. At Peggy's house, Frank, dodging the possibility of meeting up with Mr. Delaney or Sid, slipped around the back and tapped on her window. The house was dark. What if she wasn't there, either?

She was. After a few minutes she raised the sash and peered out at him. "Frank?"

"Let me in, Peg."

"What are you up to? You look like you seen a ghost." She lifted the sash the rest of the way and helped him to climb through.

"They sent me down the mountain for barrels," Frank said, removing his cap. "I just thought I'd come by." He looked at the door to the hallway. "Is Sid here?"

"No, nor Pa, neither," Peggy said. "And why would he be?" She was in her nightdress, already in bed. She always had to get up before dawn. She slid her arms around him, though.

Frank hugged her to him and clung to her comforting warmth. After a moment she tilted her head back and looked at him suspiciously. "What's got you so twitchy?"

"I'm not twitchy," Frank said. A muscle in his arm jerked involuntarily.

"You're like a dang grasshopper," Peggy said. "What's got you like that?"

"I'm cold," Frank said.

He slipped his hands under her nightdress, and she yelped in protest. "You got fingers like ice," she said, trying to bat them away.

"You could warm me up some," Frank suggested, driven by fear that was translating itself into desire now, an urge to make love to Peggy and hide in her bed until he could think of what to do next.

"I reckon I could." Peggy laughed, catching his mood. Her fingers wrestled with his trouser buttons while he took off his coat and shirt and kicked off his boots. She slid his trousers and long underwear down over his hips, murmuring with amused delight as he pressed against her, toppling them both into the bed. They burrowed under the quilt, kissed hungrily, and stroked each other.

Frank held Peggy tightly and buried his face in her neck. He was trying to wrap her around him, to lose himself in her. They made love with an intensity that hadn't come on them before, even on the first night. When he leaned over her, finally still and gasping for breath, she made a contented little sound, a cooing burble like a sleepy bird, and drew his head down onto her breast. He shuddered and lay there, still holding her close.

"What's after you, honey?" she whispered.

"Goblins," Frank said.

Peggy propped herself up on one elbow and studied him. "You tell me what's going on. I don't like this one bit."

"It's nothing you have to worry about," Frank said. He buried his face in her breast. "Just don't mind it, okay?"

"Well, I do mind it," Peggy said. "But I know you're not going to tell me."

In a moment, he was asleep.

The whistle screamed, then screamed again, getting closer. In some distance another one shrieked back at it, one long, ear-piercing wail. Frank, stretched on the rods, was riding a freight, which thundered through the darkness and howled around the curves. The engineer was blowing the whistle because he had seen Frank, and railroad bulls on horseback were racing the train. The horses' hooves pounded against the dry dirt road, and the riders, bent low against the horses' necks, aimed their weapons. Frank clung tighter, trying to hide, while the whistle howled and howled, prying him loose with its sound. The screeching enveloped him, clutched at him like hands, to pull him into rushing air, to hurl him under the wheels.

"Wake up!"

He flailed his arms in terror, and the sound went on. Frank surfaced into consciousness, struggled up through the bedclothes, gasping, and expected the train to come through the wall.

"Frank, wake up!"

He found that he had been struggling with Peggy, fighting her grip as she tried to shake him awake. He could hear clearly now—the emergency whistle blast in the distance and the clanging and the thundering hooves of the fire engine, the train of his dream. It rattled by, drawn by the red glow that shone through the window and lighted Peggy's bedroom.

Frank flung himself out of bed and threw up the sash. Beyond the treetops the sky was on fire—a hellish, sullen cloud that gave enough light to turn Peggy's face crimson and reflect like coals in her wide eyes as she stuck her head out beside his.

"Mother Mary, I think it's the refinery," she whispered. "Nothing else would burn like that."

It was. It had to be. "Where's Sid?" Frank demanded.

Peggy shook her head. "I don't know." Her voice held an edge of panic. "But he doesn't work the night shift."

The hell he didn't, Frank thought. "Where's your pa?"

Peggy clutched her nightdress around her. The wind was picking up, fire driven, and they could smell the smoke in the air. "I don't know," she said again.

"Well, I do." Frank pulled on his trousers, then his boots. He stuck his arms in his shirtsleeves.

Peggy pulled at his arm, frightened. "What do you mean? You can't do nothing. They got the engine company out."

Frank buttoned his shirt and didn't answer. Then suddenly he grabbed her by the shoulders. "What do you know about this?" His fingers dug in. "Come clean with me, Peg."

"I don't know anything!" Peggy wailed. "You're hurting me!"

Frank let go. He stared at her, the distant flames reflecting in her hair.

"What are you talking about?" Peggy demanded.

"Sid," Frank said. His voice shook. "Sid and your pa. And that bastard Rutledge. If anybody comes here, don't you let them in."

He snatched up his coat and cap and bolted for the parlor. Peggy ran after him. Her nightdress blew around her when he opened the front door. She clutched at him again, but he shook her off, shrugging on his coat as he stumbled down the steps.

"Frank!"

He turned and shouted at her. "Bolt the door! Keep yourself out of this. You don't owe them anything, you hear me?" He kicked open the gate and was gone, sprinting up the street.

All up and down the road, lights were coming on, doors were flinging open. People stood on their stoops and stared at the burning sky.

Frank hit Main Street on the run, joining the throng

of people who already filled it on foot and in wagons—
wives with wide, panic-stricken faces, whose men worked
the night shift; volunteers from the engine company,
catapulted from their beds by the whistle; the myriad
crowd of onlookers who were always lured by fire. They
flowed up the street, their lanterns waving, and shouted
questions at one another while a pair of policemen on
horseback raced through, trying to get there first.

Frank didn't bother to stop at Peter's house. Wherever Peter had been, he would be heading to the same
destination now. It occurred to him that Peter might
have been inside the refinery, but the thought was too
horrifying to hold on to. Frank, breathing hard, dodging
a policeman's horse, ran up the street.

"You folks stay back!" the policeman shouted.

Unheeding, they surged around him, driven by fear
of what they might find or by the spine-tingling excitement of fire. The ground shook, and a dull boom roared
outward on the wind. The sky ahead boiled up in a
red-orange ball.

At the refinery gates, the policemen flung themselves
from their mounts and tried to stretch a rope in front of the
crowd. Just inside the gate, a fireman led the pumper
engine's unhitched team away from the flames. A stream of
water from the pumper's hose shot two hundred feet into
the inferno without making a dent in it.

Frank pushed his way through the crowd to the
rope, leaned across it, and stared in horror at the clouds
of fire and smoke. It looked as if the whole complex was
burning. If it wasn't, it would be soon, he thought. The
storage tanks of oil and gasoline were as volatile as
the refinery works themselves. Of the fieldstone building he had peered into earlier, he could see nothing
behind the wall of flame.

The hellish light seemed to pull him in, to whisper
to Frank that this was his fault, that somehow he could
have averted it. If he had found Kemp . . . if he had
looked harder for Sid . . . if he hadn't been afraid . . .
Frank dived back through the crowd, past a howling
woman with a tear-slicked face. He pushed his way

through to the street and dodged around the side of the refinery complex.

With the wind and ash blowing hot in his face, he pounded down a cobbled alley and past a high board fence. He tried to see what was happening on the other side. Another explosion shook the air, and behind him fire spewed as if from a volcano. The shriek of a terrified animal cut through the roar of flames, and with a stab in his heart Frank remembered the mules he had stabled inside—the drayman's pets who had snuffled at his pockets for sugar. No one would think of saving the mules in the midst of hell. In a fury Frank pounded his fists against the fence. In his mind the mules became a symbol of his failure.

The boards wouldn't give, so he climbed up the fence. The wood felt hot. He balanced on the top and watched a lake of fire outlining charred angles that had once been the bones of buildings. A knot of refinery workers was futilely spraying water from a company steam pump as the fire ate its way toward the next tank. A pipe burst, spewing flames, and in an instant the tank went up with a roar that threw its catwalk and sides into the sky. When Frank saw a human form lifted and then thrown down among them, his stomach lurched, and bile burned the back of his throat. The debris and the man hung suspended for an instant, silhouetted against red and sullen smoke, then dropped.

A mule screamed, and Frank dropped over the fence and into choking smoke. The mule barn wasn't burning yet, but the air was full of hot ash and sparks, and the barn was unnervingly close to the farther storage tank. In the firelight Frank could see a refinery worker running along the lines of pipe and closing valves. How much good that would do, Frank didn't know; but if it was a sure way of stopping the flow, he doubted that the tanks that had gone up already would have blown.

The trough outside the barn was still full of water. The fire reflected in its surface. Frank pulled off his coat and cap and soaked them in the trough. He ripped his shirt in half—one side for him and one for a mule—and soaked it, too. He put the wet coat and cap back on, tied half the wet shirt around his neck, and pulled the barn door open.

The mules were inside, hysterical, plunging in their stalls. One had kicked the stall down and was loose in the barn, circling and braying. Frank grabbed its halter and got the shirt around its eyes and nose to blot out the sight and smell of smoke. He found that the trick didn't calm the mule nearly as much as it would have a horse—mules apparently having, as the drayman had always insisted, more brains. The mule reared and snorted through the cloth. Frank, keeping his grip on the halter, wondered what on earth he was going to do with the mule now. He couldn't lead it through the fire line and expect to hang on. He snagged a lead line from the tack on the wall and snapped it on the halter, then hauled down a collar and traces.

Whistling, clucking, cajoling, he managed to get the collar over the plunging head without getting bitten. He started through the barn door. Outside the mule brayed again but went where it was led since it couldn't see. Frank, dragging the mule to the fence, had some hope of seeing if he could pull the wooden wall down. The mule blundered backward into the fence and took care of the job by kicking the daylights out of the boards. The fence splintered, and Frank finished the job, kicking out with his boots and holding the lunging mule by its lead.

The mule reared, toppling Frank in the dirt. Frank pulled himself up along the lead and snatched off the mule's blindfold. It bared its teeth at him, and he smacked it in the nose with his fist, then hauled its head around so it could see the mule-sized gap in the planks. The mule rocketed through, sending Frank flying again.

By the time he had the next mule out, the barn roof was on fire. The air inside was thick with acrid smoke, and Frank's lungs were beginning to burn. He dragged each screaming, protesting mule to the gap in the fence and prodded it through. There were more than two dozen animals, including his own six, and he pulled them first from the back of the barn where the fire was and worked his way forward. Each time he was barely ahead of falling sparks and finally of disintegrating roof beams. Each time he came back for another mule, he eyed the storage tank looming ominously beyond the barn. He was going to get himself killed to save a bunch of mules, he thought. It was foolish; it was idiotic. He went on anyway, doggedly, while the flames and shouting and the rumbling chaos crept closer.

By the time he was fighting the last mule from its stall, he had long since drawn up his own half of the wet shirt to cover his mouth and nose. Still it felt as if his lungs were seared with heat and smoke. His eyes watered so badly he could hardly see. The barn was going down. He dragged the last terrified mule through the door, and the door frame collapsed on top of them. The mule screamed and shot from Frank's grasp, and Frank, his coat in flames, dropped to the ground and rolled over and over in the dirt. Bruised, he struggled to his feet and watched the barn crumble in on itself in a slow wave of fire.

It was like watching something alive, writhing and consuming itself. Frank stared at it until his eyes moved from the collapsing barn to the dark, squat shape of the storage tank. Then he turned and ran.

The fence was on fire now, too, and he had no idea where the last mule had gone. There would be no catching it now. Frank turned to find some escape for himself and saw the storage tank seem to quiver. It exploded, spewing fire, and a howling wind knocked Frank backward, tumbling him head over heels. Burning shards of metal rained on him. He felt blood, warm and wet, on his face. He pulled himself up and stumbled, thrashing his way through the night, away from the flames that seemed to lick at every surface around him.

The fire crews with their hoses were still fighting the blaze desperately. Frank ran toward them, the flames illuminating his face, openmouthed with fear. A man came at him out of nowhere, out of the fire's glow, something upraised in his hand. Its weight crashed down on Frank's shoulder, and he fell.

He somersaulted and saw the man standing over him, a length of wood in one hand. The man came at him again, and Frank crouched defensively. He twisted and leaped for the man's knees as the club came down again. Frank tackled the man, and they fell together. He felt the block of wood biting into his back as the man pinned him to the ground on top of it. Frank brought his knee up into the man's groin and saw that the furious, ash-smeared face above him was Sid's.

Sid howled and loosened his grip, and Frank threw his weight away from the man and stumbled to his feet. He lashed out with his boot at Sid's face. The man reeled backward, but he dragged himself to his feet, too, spitting blood and teeth.

"Get away from me, Sid!" Frank yelled.

Sid felt on the ground for his club. "It's too late, you stupid shit. I warned you to stay away and keep your mouth shut."

Frank backed away as, coughing, Sid rose, again with the length of wood in his hand, and moved forward with deadly intent. The air was so thick with smoke that Frank's lungs felt as if they were on fire. Burning ash rained around them. Frank took another step back, afraid to take his eyes off Sid. "You aren't a murderer," he rasped.

But Sid was. He and Rutledge had already murdered the men who had died in the fire. And Sid would have been given orders to kill *him*, Frank realized. If he hadn't spotted him that night, Sid would have found him later. And, Frank thought, Rutledge had probably given orders to kill Peter, too, since Frank had shared his suspicions with his brother.

Sid was edging closer, but his breath came in ragged, rasping gasps. He had been in the smoke longer than Frank had been. He had been busy, Frank realized, making sure that the fire would spread. There was a wrench at Sid's belt, the kind they used for shutting down—or opening—pipeline valves.

Voices shouted behind them as the fire crews worked their way inward. Frank could hear the spitting and the roar of the hoses and could feel a fine spray of water mixed with the horrible smell of ash and burning oil. Sid lunged toward him and then doubled up, coughing. Frank took to his heels, knowing that Sid was staggering after him. But the firemen, their shouts clearer now, were only a hundred yards away. Frank ran toward them and felt the club, thrown in desperation, fly by his head. A shot rang out. Sid had a gun, Frank realized. Tripping over a heavy hose, he hurled himself into the midst of the fire crew.

"Get the hell out of here!" someone shouted at him.

Frank flailed his way through the furious firemen as another outbuilding, full of oil-soaked barrels, went up, putting a wall of flame between him and Sid. He ran on, dodging the fire crews and imagined bullets, stumbling through the hellish night. The refinery roared around him, all hell compounded into one fire.

Two men loomed out of the greasy smoke, bearing a charred body on a stretcher. Frank kept running, drawing each ragged breath down a scorched throat. His mind seemed to float in the smoke while his body ran on. Where was Rutledge tonight? he wondered. Safe at home while Sid did his work for him? Sid and Mr. Delaney? Where was Mr. Delaney? Would he leap out at Frank next, from the smoke cloud and the fierce mouth of the flames? Or was he dead in the fire of his own creating, too drunk to get away? Had he and Sid known what they were bringing down on themselves? Sid would have known. He understood what burning oil could do.

Frank was nearly at the gates, still fleeing in fear of Sid, who was somewhere in the inferno behind him. He staggered past the engine company's pumper and into the street, where the police were still holding the crowd at bay. A woman was weeping in great hacking sobs, as if she too had breathed in fire, over the burned body on another stretcher. Frank limped past her to hide himself in the crowd, while behind him the fire ate up the night.

XIX

Frank spent the night under a tree in the park, afraid to go to Peter's house, afraid to go to Peggy's, afraid that Sid would find him at either place. Like a damned fool, he thought, he'd had to go and tell Rutledge that Peter was his brother.

He stood for a long time behind the tree, a live oak with spreading, gnarled branches that dipped low to the ground and a thick canopy of leaves. He looked through them at the fire. It burned and burned, with thick orange flame and bursts of black, greasy smoke, soiling the air with a sulfurous smell. Hellfire, Frank thought, must smell like that.

Finally there was nothing left, and the fire went out, leaving the night stained with the stench of burning crude and residue. People began to come back along the street. The fire engine, its whistle silenced, rolled past. The crew, muddy, greasy, and weary, clung to the back step. Frank crouched in the tree's shadow until the vehicle had gone, then he curled into a ball on the ground.

The spines of the live-oak leaves stabbed through his shredded trousers, and his whole body ached. He slept anyway, to waken with the first light and the first rooster.

Frank got up and limped stiffly to the pump beside a horse trough. There he tried to wash away all vestiges of the night. The trough was sheened with oil, and when the pump water came, it stank of sulfur. Across the street the grass and the white face of the courthouse were smudged gray. Frank scrubbed his face with his hands, and the cut on his cheek began to bleed again.

The park was already filling with early-morning loungers, who had more than usual to gossip about, especially listing the dead. Frank listened to two of them.

"I heard there was someone working late—one of them college-boy chemists. Never knew what hit him." An old man spat tobacco juice in the grass.

"They find the body?"

"They found something. Hard to say."

The other man shook his head and sucked his teeth. "Bert Adams from the engine crew got blowed up with a storage tank. Went sky-high, just like a rocket. And Joe Mills, poor cuss . . . I knew him. Left a wife and five kids. You reckon they'll see a nickel out of the company?"

"Hell, no. No more than Sid Delaney's sis will. Not that his pa won't try, the old rummy. Anything for a dollar."

Frank, drying his face on his shirt, froze.

The second man cackled. "Pity it wasn't his pa, if you ask me. I reckon the world could have spared *him*. He's been *trying* to go to hell for long enough. Where'd they find Sid?"

"Didn't hear, but he was pretty well burned to a crisp. Wasn't even his shift last night, from what I did hear. But it was Sid, all right. Dentist knew him right off by the gold in his back teeth."

"It's a wonder the company didn't pry it out first." The second man spat, too, and then chewed in silence, contemplating other men's mortality.

Frank eased away from the water trough. Whoever had sent Sid after him had taken care of Sid, too. That didn't ensure that Frank was off the hook now; it just meant that Sid knew too much to leave him running around loose. The conspirators would be after Frank soon enough, and likely after Mr. Delaney, too, who was even more a liability since he was drunk half the time.

Frank might have enough time to get to Peggy if he hurried. But he didn't dare go near Peter.

Frank walked quickly, warily, his cap pulled low over his eyes. He limited his route to the side streets. He had to see her before he lit out. She would have been told about Sid already. It was ironic that after Sid had caused the explosions, Rutledge had seen that he burned to death. Frank shuddered. Maybe the murderers had knifed him before throwing him into the fire. Frank hoped so. He couldn't think of a worse way to die than to be burned.

Frank found out that Peggy's father wasn't at home. If the old man had any sense, Frank thought, he was either lying low or on his way out of town. But Peggy was there. She was sitting at the rickety table in the kitchen and staring at her hands.

"I thought maybe it had got you, too," she said when Frank came in without knocking.

Frank hunched his shoulder to wipe away the blood that still trickled down his cheek. "I'm sorry, Peg."

Peggy watched him, taking in the charred coat and the greasy ash that covered him. "You took off after Sid." Her voice was strained. "I got to ask you, Frank. Did you kill my brother?"

He looked her in the eyes. "No. He tried to kill me. But no. And I'm not going to tell you more than that because I don't want you to know anything."

"I knew he was up to some devilment," Peggy said, angry. "Him and Pa."

"Forget you knew that," Frank said. "Where's your pa?"

Peggy shrugged. "Getting plastered, the devil take him." She echoed the old men in the park. "Why wasn't it him instead of Sid?"

"Because you don't always get what you want or deserve," Frank said.

Peggy looked down at her hands again. "Everything I touch is dirty. It's in the air." She grimaced. "The whole town stinks like the devil's sitting room."

Frank reached across the table and touched her shoulder. "How bad is it for you? About Sid?"

"He was my brother. He used to try to stop Pa from beating me. When Sid got big enough, he told Pa he'd lay him out if he took the strap to me again." She looked at the wall, at the picture of the kittens in their basket of roses. "He gave me that picture. I'm thinking maybe I'll see it buried with him. He ought to have something."

"That would be nice," Frank told her. He couldn't work up an active hatred for Sid, not now. He tried to think of what else to say, how to make this a farewell. "I have to go" was all he said, finally.

Peggy nodded. "I know."

"I have to get out of town."

Her expression was fierce as she grabbed his wrist. "If you've done something against the company, don't go back up the canyon. Just get out fast."

"I will. But first I want to leave a note for Peter. Do you have any paper?"

Peggy got up slowly, as if she ached, and rummaged in the little desk where she did the laundry's accounts. She tore a page out of a ledger and gave it to him, along with the stub of a pencil. She sat down again and watched him while he wrote. When he was through, she folded the page into quarters and stuck it in the desk drawer.

"Peg . . ."

"We had good times, didn't we?" Her mouth twitched into the ghost of a smile.

"Very good times."

"Nobody ever read me poetry before."

"Nobody ever, well . . ." Frank shrugged and smiled, too. "You know, before."

Peggy sniffled. She pushed tangled tendrils of red hair back out of her eyes. "Like I said"—a wistful touch of the old playfulness crossed her face—"you got a natural gift."

He went to kiss her, very gently, on the lips. "Maybe you should give me references."

"You just let me know." She took a deep and ragged breath, fighting back tears. "I'll stay here and wait for Peter. He should come as soon as he hears about Sid." She sighed. "You'll have time to get away first, ahead of your brother and whatever it was that caught Sid."

"Peter might know all about it," Frank told her.

"Maybe, but I'm not sure I'd want him to tell me."

Frank was tramping it again. Almost everything he owned—his clothes, bedroll, blanket, and even his coffeepot—was in the bunkhouse at Avenal Canyon. All he had now were his boots, coat, and cap, and a clean shirt, which he had brought for spending one night in town, and the change that was in his pockets. He wouldn't have risked going up to the canyon again for his gear any more than he would have stuck his hand in a rattlesnake den. The snakes would be alive and biting this time.

He took the road from Sierra toward the ocean. His goal was the pier at Ventura. He dived into the ditch or the scrub brush every time he heard hoofbeats on the road. Finally, footsore, he crawled out again from hiding when an ice wagon went by. Feeling secure that no murderer would be pursuing him in that vehicle, Frank cadged a ride. The back was full of ice from the high mountains. The blocks were packed in sawdust and covered with canvas. He paid for his ride by unloading them at the icehouse in Ventura.

Later, he walked the half block from the icehouse to the pier. The salt tang of the ocean bit into his nostrils, but it couldn't eradicate the scent of crude oil that clung to his coat and hair. He watched a coastal packet tie up and load orange crates with fanciful labels: Tom Cat, Indian River, Monarch, each with its printed colored picture behind the brand name—vistas of groves, of butterflies, of a fat black-and-white cat before a rising sun. It was as if each label allowed a view into a little secret world. If only he could somehow step into one and be free of the demons chasing him. . . .

He asked the packet captain for work and got it, running the bilge pump as the packet steamed up the coast. The boat put him off at Point Sur, ranching country two hundred fifty miles north. Now he smelled less of oil and more of fish and kelp. The captain had a nephew there who was tired of cattle and wanted to run a bilge pump as a change.

"Sorry, kid," the officer said, "but family is family."

Frank, of the opinion that the nephew was making a mistake, didn't argue. He pocketed his two dollars' pay and buttoned his coat against the salt wind that blew ceaselessly, flattening the trees.

He bought bread, beans, tomatoes, coffee, a coffeepot, and a new bedroll at the town's only store, then tramped inland to look for a place to sleep. He found his resting place in a grove where the giant trees made an earthly church. The coastal redwoods were as tall as cathedral spires, and their feathery branches created a vaulted ceiling and a deep green prayer. *Sequoia sempervirens*. He recalled the name from some almost forgotten botanical textbook. If there was a place to sort out the confusion of his life, then surely this was it, he thought.

Frank built a fire and filled his coffeepot with river water. A ground squirrel popped up from under a rock and, sitting straight up on its haunches, looked at him. Frank flicked a bean at it from the can he had just opened, and the squirrel eyed it suspiciously. A Steller's jay, royal blue with a black head and crest, swooped down from a redwood branch and snatched the bean up while the squirrel was still considering.

Frank chuckled. "Life's like that," he told the squirrel, and it vanished into its hole at the sound of his voice. When it ventured out again, though, he threw it another bean. *I'm talking to squirrels*. Just now they made more sense to him than talking to people did. Squirrels knew enough not to take the first thing somebody handed them.

One of the redwoods—tall, immense, and still

living despite having its lower twenty feet hollowed by some ancient fire—provided an antechamber within the cathedral trees. After Frank had eaten, he spread his bedroll inside the bole, propped his back against the inner wall, and finally allowed himself to think.

He was disturbed by his failure to have stopped Rutledge. But because he was young and penniless and because dealing with powerful men was a skill beyond his ken, he forgave himself. He supposed that what he did now would be what mattered. He could turn tail and run, go back hat in hand to his father, say, *You were right. I'm young, and I don't know. Teach me.* But he knew, he thought, what his father had wanted to teach him, and Frank believed that he had learned it already. The lessons about life that his father couldn't teach him—that maybe no parent could teach a child—were the ones he still needed to learn.

Some of them had begun to come to him: for example, the notion that he made his own choices and was responsible for the result, whatever it might be; that he wasn't responsible for other people's choices; and that if he didn't make his own choices, he wasn't really alive and would never be able to take what the world had to offer. Maybe that was all there was to it. The thought frightened and excited him at the same time. He waited for some magical whisper from the redwoods, some new breath of information, but none came.

The banked fire died into red embers, as wondrous in their fierce compacted energy as the burning oil had been fearful. And yet it was all fire. A raccoon, gloved and masked, moving on slender black paws, came out of the trees to investigate the empty cans. The creature picked one up and stuck its face inside, giving its shadow a black pig snout in the firelight. After it had licked the can clean, it found a crust of bread that Frank had left for the Steller's jay. Then the raccoon waddled away with the crust toward the stream. It would try to wash the crust, Frank supposed, and then the bread would disintegrate in its hands. He felt similar to the raccoon; when he had tried to wash things clean, they dissolved and left him still mystified.

Frank got up, found the rest of his bread, and stuck it under his bedroll. If he didn't protect the loaf, the raccoon would wash his breakfast into nothing. He thought, as he hadn't in months, of Bill, then turned over and slept.

In guilty misery Peter approached Peggy's house. He had no candy or flowers—nothing to offer but sympathy and a painful sense of his own shortcomings. He should have listened to Frank. He knew it and would confess it to Peggy. He would offer his guilt as penance, but that wouldn't bring her brother back to life.

When he knocked she was grimly dyeing her one decent shirtwaist black in a pot on the stove. She let him in and went back to stirring the pot with a long wooden spoon.

He held his bowler hat in both hands. "I just heard about Sid," he said. "I went to the laundry, but they said you were here."

"I have to bury him," Peggy said. "And then I reckon I have to get Pa out of town. He's still here." She gestured toward the bedrooms down the hall. "Sleeping it off. Him and Sid set that fire, didn't they?"

Peter did not reply.

"Why did you come?" Peggy asked him.

"To tell you I'm sorry," Peter replied. "To tell you it was my fault. Frank tried to warn me, and I threw him out of the house. It's all my fault."

"It's your fault you didn't listen," Peggy said. "It's not your fault what Sid was up to. I reckon they tempted him with a lot of money. We never had much money. Mother Mary help him, I suppose he couldn't resist it. The offer was like some pretty poisonous plant, I'm thinking, and him a kid reaching for it. It killed him, too." She wiped her eyes with the back of her hand. "I suppose now there's no choice but to shift the refinery north. I hear there's nothing left but char."

"Not much," Peter said. He had been there the

night before, watching it burn and cursing himself. In the morning he and the other directors had walked through the wreckage. Nothing was left standing. The initial blast had been in the fieldstone building, and it had blown the rock walls to rubble. Peter remembered Rutledge's earlier look of cagey triumph, and he saw the same expression on the man's face again during the inspection tour, although the victory had been tamped down in his eyes, behind his horrified mask.

"Tragic," Rutledge had said. "The price of antiquated equipment. I'm afraid we have paid dearly." He glared at Kemp.

Kemp, on the other hand, had looked genuinely horrified. "We had an experienced crew," he said, his eyes wide with bewilderment. "An experienced crew . . ." He repeated it over and over.

They had picked their way through charred beams, broken stone, and twists of tangled pipe. The burned bones of a mule lay black and greasy in their path, and Peter gagged. The smell of sulfur was overpowering.

"An experienced crew . . ." Kemp said again, almost in a whimper.

Morris shook his head. "The best men were at Oleum. Maybe we should have shut down sooner." He seemed to be seeking some answer, some "what if" that would have staved off disaster.

"We'll be lucky if we aren't sued," Hatch said gloomily.

Kemp roused himself at that. "Rutledge sent the best men to Oleum," he snapped. "And you let him do it. I won't take responsibility."

"Hah!" Rutledge said, returning Kemp's accusing look. "You're responsible. *You* halted the closure here."

Peter edged away. They would be sued; of that he had practically no doubt. Although most of the families of the laborers who had died didn't have the money or the knowledge to consult lawyers, the relatives of the chemist did. The directors were trying to duck blame and protect their pocketbooks, and their attitude was more than Peter could bear. He felt sick—sick at heart and literally sick in the pit of his stomach. The others walked on, but Peter lagged behind, wondering if he was going to throw up. The smell of sulfur churned up the coffee he had had for breakfast. He burped foul bubbles like the sour gas that sometimes lifted, silent and deadly, from the wells.

After the directors had walked through the decimated acres, Peter left the men still squabbling and walked numbly through the town to Peggy's house.

At least, he thought now, Frank had been safe in Avenal Canyon. After the visit with Peggy, he would have to make amends with Frank, too, then send the overdue telegram to their parents. Peter wondered how he could make peace with Frank and still do that. He knew he had no choice—for the sake of their parents he would have to notify them and let Frank hate him if he had to.

The town would hate them all, he thought. With possible lawsuits looming, there would be no money left to compensate for lost jobs. No one would be compensated for lost lives except those with the power to force it. *He* could, Peter realized, out of his own pocketbook— could and would. The decision didn't leave him feeling any better. How could he compensate anyone for death? the death of a person or the death of a town?

As he watched Peggy dye her shirtwaist black, as he compared her usual cheerful exuberance with her present, almost palpable anguish, he still didn't know. Nor could he bring himself to broach the subject. He would send her some money later, after he had gone, as if it had come from the company. Peter knew with cold certainty that he was leaving town.

"What will you do now?" Peggy asked him, as if divining this thought.

"Sell out," Peter answered. It sounded very like what he had done already. He remembered with despair Frank's warning to him: *Rutledge is capable of selling out his grandmother for another dollar. You'll be capable of it, too, in a couple more years, I expect.*

"I'm going to sell my stock in the company," Peter

added, trying with some different phrasing to rub out that other, accusatory meaning. "I can't countenance—" He stopped, unwilling to admit what he couldn't countenance or to make Peggy privy to knowledge that would put her in danger. *Are you protecting her, or are you ashamed of yourself?* a voice asked from the back of his mind.

Peggy fished the shirtwaist out of the pot with the spoon and dumped it into a washtub of cold water. "I got something for you," she said. She went to the little desk. "Frank was here."

"Frank? When?"

"This morning. He told me to give you this." She handed Peter the folded paper, then went back to the washtub.

Peter sat down at the table and unfolded the note.

Dear Peter,

When you get this, I'll be too far up the coast to be found. I hope. I expect by now you know I was right about Rutledge, so I won't waste my breath (or insult your intelligence) by saying that I told you so. That's for kids on the playground. But I nearly got murdered last night on your pal Rutledge's orders, for knowing too much. (Funny, isn't it, how at first people think you don't know anything, then they decide you know *too* much?) Anyway, I don't feel inclined to stay around and let them have another shot at me—or to wait for Mother's Pinkertons to show up. Sorry, but I don't trust you to wait out the month before you wire Dad. And since I'm not inclined to head home so everyone can have a good time forgiving me, I'm heading north. I hear they've found gold up on the Klondike in the Yukon Territory. Maybe I'll dig some up and get as rich as you. Try not to think too badly of me, if you can manage it. I know you're happy where you are, but I just can't stand to be a clam in Dad's clam

bed. I've got to go find out what's out there.
Give my love to Mother and Midge and tell
them I'm all right.

Frank

Peter slammed the letter down. His open palm
smacked against the table. It stung, and he clung to the
pain to feed his fury. "Did you read this?"

Peggy looked at him, the wet shirtwaist in her
hands. "It was for you. I figured you'd let me read it if
you wanted."

"Here." Peter snatched the letter up again, half
wadding it in his hand. "Here. Read it."

Peggy smoothed it out and read. Her lip curled into
half a smile. "No wonder I never suspicioned you two
were related," she murmured.

"What's that supposed to mean?"

"'A clam in Dad's clam bed.'" Peggy giggled. "Oh,
Lord, Peter, let me laugh if I can. There's nothing wrong
with being like you are. You're a good, upstanding
man—the best I ever knew. But you can't expect your
brother to be like you. He's just too different."

"I'm not a clam," Peter said indignantly. He didn't
want to be a clam, not even a good one, in Peggy's eyes.

"No," she soothed, "of course you're not. If you
were a clam, you wouldn't be selling your stock in
Sierra."

"Give me that back." Peter took the letter and
stuffed it into his pocket. He remembered too late the
reference to Rutledge. "Forget what's in this," he said,
trying to suppress his fury at Frank long enough to warn
Peggy. A fat lot Frank had worried about her.

"I can figure things out," Peggy said, refusing,
infuriatingly, to be protected. She shook out the shirtwaist. "I got to hang this to dry. Are you coming to the
funeral?"

Sid's funeral mass was said in a white frame Catholic
church with a stained-glass window of Christ receiving

repentant sinners into heaven. Sid's coffin, draped with a cloth but bare of any flowers except for the spray that Peter had sent, sat in front of the altar. Whether Christ would receive him was debatable but unasked, except by Peggy, who prayed so quietly, no one but Peter, who stood beside her, would have heard her.

"Blessed Mother Mary, I know Sid did wrong, but he had a hard life and didn't have a mother for very long, to teach him the right way. Pray for him, Mother Mary, please, and ask your blessed son to give Sid a chance in purgatory. Give him a chance to redeem himself, Mother Mary, please. Don't let them send him straight to hell."

Mr. Delaney stood on one side of Peggy, dressed in the black coat he had worn to his wedding and to his wife's funeral. Unearthed from a trunk, the coat was too tight across the stomach. He was barely ambulatory and propped himself up by leaning on the back of the pew in front of him. His face was gray, in hideous contrast to his red hair and bloodshot eyes. He looked as if the devil were after him, but knew that this devil was human.

When the mass was over, the gathering followed the coffin to the graveyard and stood silently while it was lowered. As the first clod of dirt hit the pine box, Mr. Delaney vanished, and Peter doubted that any of them would see him again.

Peter turned awkwardly to Peggy. "I don't know what to say except that I'm very sorry."

Peggy held out her hand. "There isn't much else, is there? I'm glad I knew you, Peter Blake. You're a good man. Don't you go blaming yourself. You'll do enough in this world that is your fault without taking on other folks' sins. You could pray for Sid for me, if you want to."

"I will," Peter said. "I promise."

Peggy gave him a wan smile. "And your brother, too, maybe? Don't let him be lost to you, Peter."

"He lost himself," Peter said disconsolately. All morning he had been alternating between despair and fury over Frank. He had finally telegraphed their father. Notifying the family would assuage their fears that he'd been killed, but would not accomplish bringing him home. Frank was adept at losing himself, and that would be extremely easy to accomplish in a territory as huge and as roadless as the Yukon. If he ever got there.

"Well, if he lost himself, then he'll have to find himself," Peggy said. "You won't be able to do it for him." She stepped closer and kissed him lightly on the lips. "Good-bye, Peter."

"Will you be all right?" he asked.

Peggy's chin came up an inch or two. "Don't you worry about me," she said. "I got plans."

At home, Peggy unpinned her hat and set it carefully on the table. Moving purposefully, she dragged out the trunk from which they had dug her father's good coat, then left the odds and ends that were his on the floor. She carefully wrapped her picture of the Hawaiian maiden and her rose-flowered cup and saucer in the quilts from the beds, then set the bundles in the trunk. She packed Peter's candy box, too, and then filled the trunk with her clothes.

Frank's letter had been on her mind all morning, and Peggy had finally reached a decision. If there was gold in the Yukon, there would soon be men there by the thousands—dirty men, with no women to wash their clothes. And if there was one thing Peggy knew how to do, it was wash. A gold mine couldn't be as dirty as an oil field. Besides, a laundress could probably make even better money than the whores; Peggy had learned that among men in the oil fields, the desire for a clean shirt got to be as strong as the urge for sex.

Peggy pulled her money sock out from under her mattress and began to count its contents.

XX

Idaho, October 1896

Elizabeth peered around the corner and into the lobby of the Oro Fino Hotel in Silver City. There he was, relaxing where she always found him, by the hotel's fire. Wherever she traveled as the suffrage campaign headed for its November election date, whether she told him her destination or not, Tim showed up the next day. He would pop up by her side as she canvassed miners and stockmen on the street, then magically reappear at night in whatever hotel she had taken a room, sitting by the fireside in the lobby where he knew she would find him.

To describe the Oro Fino as rustic was to give it the benefit of the doubt, and the fire consisted of a wood stove that smoked; but there Tim was, his boots stuck as far under the stove's legs as possible without setting himself on fire.

Elizabeth drew back around the corner and considered whether it would be simpler just to go and sit down beside him or to scuttle back to her room and pretend he wasn't there. She decided to opt for dignity and dinner. Dinner at the Oro Fino was served at six o'clock sharp, and guests who were tardy often found the pickings slim. She took a deep breath and forged ahead.

"Good evening." She settled herself in a musty, overstuffed chair beside his.

Tim's smile lit up his handsome face. Although not

smiling back at him was practically impossible, she gave it a try.

"That's a very peculiar twitch you've got," Tim said. "I hope you haven't taken some sort of palsy."

Elizabeth relented with an explosion of suppressed laughter. "It wouldn't surprise me if I had," she admitted. "I've been standing all day up to my ankles in snow. I bought some more serviceable footwear, though." She had bought a pair of miner's boots, big enough to pull over three layers of socks.

"I saw them." Tim chuckled.

"I have no vanity left," Elizabeth said. She wriggled her toes, now clad in dry calfskin boots, slim and elegant, indoor wear. "If the weather gets any colder, I'll probably take up flannel shirts and bib overalls."

"You'll shock your constituency half to death," Tim warned.

Elizabeth raised her eyebrows. "My constituency but not you?"

"You've rendered me shockproof, Miss Emory," he told her. "Besides, you don't care what I think."

Elizabeth folded her arms and didn't respond. Tim had filed several stories on the Idaho campaign, in which he treated her solely as a useful news source. When he felt talkative, he inveigled her into arguing politics with him and carefully steered clear of any conversation that might be construed as courtship. He hadn't so much as bought her dinner, even when they dined together.

Elizabeth was growing frustrated. She was enjoying his company far too much to be easy in her mind about it, but she couldn't refuse to let him court her when he wasn't trying to. She decided he was up to something.

"There's an orator outside just now," Tim said. "He appears to have very few brains under his hat, but you might be interested in hearing him."

Elizabeth groaned. "I just got warm."

"Dedication to the cause, madame," Tim said. "Don't shirk now."

Elizabeth looked at him balefully, but she got out of

her chair. As Tim accompanied her to the hotel door, he pulled his notebook out of his coat pocket.

On the sidewalk outside, in handy earshot of the customers emerging from the saloon next door, was a man standing on a soapbox and waving a placard. He was fortified against the cold with a sheepskin jacket and, judging from the glow of his nose, possibly with some inner stimulants as well. The placard said: Do Not Let Them Take Away Your Rights.

Elizabeth frowned. "He's referring to your right to get drunk and fall in the gutter," she informed Tim. "I've seen him before. He's a representative from the liquor industry."

"This is America," Tim said, grinning. "They're entitled to have their lobbyists, too."

The orator was in midspeech, proclaiming his love of home and family and his reverence for all women, whom he called "our gentle ministering angels." He bowed low to the females in the crowd but kept a wary eye on Elizabeth.

"Many ladies," he declared, "by their trusting nature, are easily misguided, misled by those of their own sex who have chosen an unnatural role in life and seek to rule men, to take away man's natural right to be the head of his house. What a woeful thing it is when either men or women step from their right and natural role. Woman's role is motherhood, the nurturing of her race. Her interference in elections would be disastrous to the state and harmful to herself. Woman rules us through her love, and her chief power over us is through her graceful impulsiveness of heart and fancy—fine enough around the fireside but dangerous guides in the halls of legislation!"

"How dangerous is the uneducated man?" Elizabeth demanded, loud enough to be heard by the crowd.

"Woman's duty is to educate men by her example in the home." The orator glared at her. "In her proper role as wife and mother. Those females whose unnatural inclinations have set themselves outside that role have only themselves to blame."

"Just what do you mean?" A miner's wife in hob-nailed boots stepped up and scowled at him. "You watch your mouth, bud. I'm a wife and mother, and I want my vote. And I ain't got no unnatural inclinations. Who do you think you're talking to here? I'm a respectable woman, and I'll thank you to keep a civil tongue in your head."

The speaker realized that he had miscalculated. "And I'm sure you're a fine mother, ma'am. No offense meant. But you can rely on your husband and sons to know how best to vote."

"My husband can't read. *I* can. And my kids is all girls. Nor they ain't unnatural, either. Two of them's married, and I don't aim to have their rights looked after by the likes of you, smelling of whiskey and with a nose as red as a signal light."

Someone in the crowd snickered. "You tell him, Matty!"

Elizabeth discreetly drew back toward the hotel. "Sometimes it's best to let the local believers take over," she murmured to Tim. "That fellow's met his match without my help."

"It's a pity you can't take Matty to Boise," Tim said, following Elizabeth inside. "She gets up a pretty good head of steam. That's the dinner bell."

"Good. I'm ravenous. I'll tell you inside why I can't take Matty."

They settled at a table by the window, through which they could watch the street. Matty stood at the foot of the soapbox and shook her fist at the speaker. He was looking very uncomfortable.

"I met Matty right after I came into town. She has a husband and a twelve-year-old daughter at home," Elizabeth explained to Tim. "She works from nearly dawn to dusk. She can't go anywhere, not even to Boise."

"And how are you going to come to terms with that in your new utopia?" Tim asked. He glanced at the menu on the blackboard, then said to the waiter, "I think I'll have the pork chops, before anyone else snags them."

He turned his eyes to Elizabeth. "And I'm not trying to start something; that was an honest question."

"Working*men* can't leave home, either," Elizabeth pointed out. "The chicken, please. And coffee. I never claimed we could produce a world that allows unlimited leisure for the working class."

"So political involvement is only possible for women with independent incomes? Or husbands who can afford to hire household help?"

Elizabeth smiled sweetly. "That seems to be the case with men, doesn't it? Only their household help mostly is unpaid, since it consists of their wives."

"You're dodging. If the wife runs the household and the husband supports her, she *is* being paid."

"Would you care to compare the number of hours worked by each?" Elizabeth suggested. "The husband at his job, and the wife at home?"

"My father works longer hours than my mother," Tim said promptly.

"I thought we were discussing the working class."

Tim settled in for a good argument. He seemed to be enjoying himself. Reluctantly, Elizabeth realized she was, too.

"You don't include politicians in the working class?" He grinned.

"Certainly not. And your mother *has* household help—a cook and a maid at the very least, I should imagine."

"Two maids. And so does your mother."

"My mother helps to pay for them by lecturing."

"*My* mother trains horses. She rides astride. Is this a competition?"

"No, blast you. We're getting off the subject. I was trying to say that political involvement is and always has been the privilege of men with time to spare for it. We'll have to accept the fact that it will be the same for women. There are many women who *would* have the time if their husbands didn't deliberately see to it that they didn't. But Matty isn't one of them. Her husband works as hard as she does, and they barely make ends meet."

"So you refrain from pointing any fingers at Matty's husband?"

"Of course. Why should I? I don't wear blinders."

"I'm beginning to see that you don't," Tim said seriously.

The waiter put two plates of chicken in front of them. "We're out of pork chops," he said triumphantly. The last four meals had been a contest to see if Tim could order something that the kitchen hadn't run out of. The waiter seemed to have entered into the spirit of competition.

"I was only the second person to order," Tim protested.

"There weren't but two chops," the waiter said.

"Then why in blazes did you offer them on the menu?"

"They like to dress it up a little," Elizabeth said. "Thank you very much. I'm sure Mr. Holt will like the chicken."

"He won't," Tim muttered. "He had chicken last night."

"It's good chicken." The waiter departed before Tim could dispute that statement, too.

Elizabeth cut into her entrée. "We're up in the mountains. It's winter. You're lucky we aren't eating prairie dog."

Tim regarded his plate with loathing. "How do you know it isn't?"

"I've had prairie dog. Besides, they usually try to pass that off as venison."

"Everybody passes unpalatable things off as something else," Tim said grumpily.

"It's a natural human instinct," Elizabeth said. "What are you referring to, besides the dinner?"

"Our red-nosed friend on the soapbox, for one." He took a bite and chewed. "But I guess it's really the situation in Cuba that's eating at me. I seem to be outside the trend. Every newspaper in the country but mine is trying to get us into a war and pass it off as patriotism."

"You're really upset about that," Elizabeth said. "I saw you snarling into the paper this morning."

"Are you the only one allowed to have convictions?"

"Not at all. I'm delighted to find that you have some that are, as you noted, outside the mainstream."

"All they do is make trouble for me," Tim said. "In an editorial Hearst called me a lily-livered pacifist."

"That's a good sign," Elizabeth said.

Tim looked at her closely. "You'd like me better if I made more trouble, wouldn't you? Virginia Barstow told me you were dangerous."

"I like you now," Elizabeth said. "But, yes, I admire a man who will question the status quo, entrenched authority, the popular opinion."

"Most women want a man who'll do the safe thing and not take a chance on going flat broke," Tim commented.

"I'm not most women," Elizabeth retorted. She did not point out that she had said she liked him, not *wanted* him, as in marriage. She didn't intend to bring that subject up at all; even to deny it proved that she considered it to be a possibility.

"You're the only woman *I* know who's ever voluntarily eaten a prairie dog," was all Tim said.

Elizabeth chuckled, relieved to have sailed by the rocks so easily. "It wasn't voluntary—unless you consider starving an option. The stage stops out here have some very peculiar cuisine."

Elizabeth and Tim encountered further examples of bizarre cookery, including another prairie-dog stew, before they landed in Boise in early November for election day. The stew wasn't identified as containing prairie dog, but Elizabeth was confident in her analysis. As they ate, Tim and Elizabeth laughed, compared notes, and dared each other to clean their plates.

Elizabeth had ceased trying to dodge Tim and now willingly let him travel with her. With the issue of

courtship at least temporarily removed, they had fallen
into a camaraderie. She scrutinized his stories and found
that, contrary to the prevailing newspaper style, he had
ceased including a physical description of her in his
copy. She was touched by that.

They found each other to be good travelers, disinclined to complain about the accommodations or the
trains that left them standing on the platform in a
snowstorm. When their stage broke a wheel, Tim had
helped the driver to mend it, and Elizabeth, muffled to the
eyebrows in a carriage rug, held the restive horses. The
other passengers, meanwhile, sat inside, complaining and
arguing about whose fault it all was and who had brought
too much luggage and overloaded the stage. Elizabeth and
Tim climbed back inside, wet and snowy, and exchanged a
handshake in a kind of silent ceremony.

The happy comfort of their friendship would all
have been very fine—if there had not been the looming
but unspoken concern that they had become such good
pals that parting company was going to prove very
difficult. But if they didn't part company, *something* was
going to happen.

Elizabeth, who had always prided herself on view-
ing life realistically and objectively, put on a pair of
metaphorical blinders and firmly kept them in place
throughout the election. She thought Tim was aware of
her avoidance tactics, but he continued to play the game
he had begun.

By election day, they were both nearly sure the
amendment was going to pass. Out of sixty-five Idaho
newspapers, only three remained openly opposed to the
women's right to vote. But the suffrage committee was
taking no chances. The miners and other workers in the
Coeur d'Alene district still had serious misgivings. And
rumors were spreading that men in the north and west
were turning against the amendment because of preju-
dice against the Mormons, with their higher female
population, in the southeast. When the polls opened in
Boise, the women were there, as they were in every
other town in Idaho. The activists distributed flyers with

the message "Vote for the Woman Suffrage Amendment," and served hot coffee and sandwiches to frozen voters.

Elizabeth, her miner's boots and extra socks concealed beneath the demure folds of her skirt, poured coffee and coaxed votes. The Boise women handed out facsimiles of the amendment near the polls, to make certain that the men who couldn't read could find it on their ballots. They had given out three thousand by the time Tim discovered that some of the men were marking the facsimiles instead of the ballots. As a result, that approach was immediately abandoned.

"Of all the stupid, idiotic—" Elizabeth, seething, refilled the coffeepot. "And men think that *we* haven't got enough brains to vote!"

"Never try to outfox stupidity," Tim said, grinning. "It's been my experience that it'll dodge you every time."

"The election officials won't count those facsimiles when they tally the vote," Elizabeth fumed. "Oh, Lord, how many of them do you think they marked?"

"I think we're all right," Tim soothed. "Here, give me that pot. You put the grounds in twice. It's going to overflow. I've been taking an unofficial poll. Nearly everyone's voted for it."

Elizabeth distractedly handed him the coffeepot as his first sentence registered on her. "'We?'"

"Hell, yes," Tim said. "You don't think I'm out here freezing my tailbone just for you, do you? I *want* this to pass. It'll give me ammunition to get it brought up again in California."

"I thought you were just reporting the story," Elizabeth said stubbornly, prodding him.

"I'm entitled to believe in the cause while I'm reporting," Tim countered. "Or don't men get to join the club?"

"I didn't mean that. I just didn't think you wanted to." Elizabeth pressed a sandwich, wrapped in a suffrage flyer, into a voter's hands. "Vote for the suffrage amendment," she told the man.

"I didn't want to," Tim said, scooping half the wet grounds out of the coffeepot. "I've changed my mind. I'm entitled to do that, too."

"I suppose," Elizabeth said dubiously. "But—"

"Later," Tim said. "We'll have more coffee in a minute, folks. Cold today, isn't it? In the meantime, go on in and vote for the suffrage movement."

"Vote for the suffrage amendment," Elizabeth called out, then eyed Tim seriously. *In for a penny, in for a pound*, she thought. "We're almost out of sandwiches. Can you get us some more?"

"I already have. There's ham and bread in the sack under the table."

"You—? Thank you. I didn't think we'd run out."

"That's because you're new to the election business. Never underestimate the appetite of the average voter for a free sandwich."

The Boise women ended the day with a few crusts of bread and two ounces of black sludge left in the bottom of the coffeepot. They retired to the Women's Club hall to bite their nails all night while they waited for the election returns. When it was announced that 12,126 had voted for the amendment, and 6,282 against, the hall was filled with whooping, cheering women. Sentiments for or against the presidential victory of William McKinley over William Jennings Bryan were submerged in their joy at being able to vote themselves next time.

"We did it! We did it!" Elizabeth flung her arms around anyone handy, including Tim. She danced with joy.

The head of the Boise club, ignoring the disapproving stares of the temperance element, uncorked a bottle of champagne. Elizabeth and Tim each had a sip.

Tim went out to interview the man—and woman—in the street for his wrap-up story. When he came back with the sinister news that the state board of canvassers was holding that the amendment had been defeated, the celebration ended abruptly. The state constitution required that an amendment have the vote of the majority of electors, and a total of 29,516 had voted in the election. They were counting the votes of those who had not marked their ballots either for or against the suffrage amendment as votes against.

"They can't do that!" the women protested.

"Well, they are," Tim said.

"They aren't!" the head of the Boise club said with finality. "We'll appeal to the state supreme court. We should have known it wouldn't be this easy."

"Easy?" Elizabeth said faintly, thinking of the hardships of the past months.

"You need sleep," Tim told her. "You aren't your usual cantankerous self."

Elizabeth looked wearily at him. "I just feel dispirited."

"I know. Come on, I'm taking you back to the hotel. It's lawyers' business from here."

"You need sleep, too," Elizabeth said when he left her at the door of her room. "Where are you going?"

"I'm going to rewrite my copy. I'm going to blast those so-and-so's for election rigging, conspiracy, and anything else I can think up, including general obtuseness. Then I'm going to pay some courtesy calls on my fellow publishers here in Boise and fill their ears, too. Now go to bed and let me do my job."

Elizabeth was too tired to argue. She slept the clock around, her rest interlaced with shifting dreams in which she and Tim were working side by side on something. It was never quite clear what the task was, but they were partners in it. They fought, laughed, and got the work done. In her dream it all felt quite normal, and upon waking, she thought that some transformation in her attitudes might have taken place. She tried to refuse to analyze her emotions until the election was settled; but the feeling stayed with her, then grew. Some certain knowledge was forming, something she would have to admit to.

Determining the final election results required weeks. Three of Idaho's best lawyers offered their services without fee, which was gratifying. They prepared endless briefs and wrote out countless arguments, but the board of canvassers stubbornly dug in on their position until everyone's nerves were stretched taut.

Elizabeth stayed in Boise. She told Tim to go home, but he would not leave. She mentioned him for the first time in her letters home. The fact that Tim was still there earned the reply from her father that that was "interesting." Her mother wrote that Mr. Holt's *Clarion* seemed to be far more active in the cause of women's rights than she had suspected. Maddy's letter stated that of course he was still there, and that Rafe Murray had told Maddy that if Elizabeth and Tim both weren't so pigheaded, they wouldn't have all this trouble—they would just be married by now.

"Rafe Murray," Elizabeth muttered. She was not inclined to give any credence to Rafe Murray's notions of romance. But her own? She stayed up all night and thought, and gradually the certainty slipped in, in place of the nebulous feeling she had been holding on to. She couldn't have said when it arrived—maybe it had slipped in with the sandwiches, and Tim's saying "we" and not "you" when referring to the supporters of the amendment. But there it was. She loved him and wanted to marry him. Now there was nothing to do but wait to see what would come of it.

Finally, on December 11, the three judges of the supreme court, after hearing two days of argument, ruled in favor of the plaintiffs, the suffragist coalition. Or to put it more accurately, the judges threw up their hands. It was impossible, they said, to reconcile conflicting precedents and legal opinions with the definition of electors. Therefore, they were going to consider that only those actually voting on the amendment had cared enough about it to be counted. The amendment had passed, that was that, and please don't bother them anymore.

It may have helped that all three judges' wives were

suffragists. As Tim said, if the men had decided otherwise, their lives wouldn't have been worth living.

A second victory party was held, with jubilation
tempered by frayed nerves and a sense of relief.

Elizabeth looked edgy to Tim and left as soon as she
could. He followed her, determined to push the matter
of their future. Now. It was time.

"We need dinner," he said.

She didn't respond, but she didn't protest either as
he steered her past the hotel where they had generally
taken their meals and up to the brass-bound door of Le
Chalet, generally accounted to be the best, and most
expensive, restaurant in Boise. It had continental pre-
tensions, including a maître d' with a waxed mustache
and a French accent.

Tim, one hand behind his back, made a formal bow
in front of the door. "Mr. Holt would like to request
permission to take Miss Emory to dinner, in recognition
of her dedication to the cause."

Elizabeth looked at him suspiciously.

Tim smiled. "Please?"

She smiled, too. "All right."

They went inside, and Tim gestured toward a small
table in a quiet corner. A five-dollar bill was unobtru-
sively offered to the maître d'.

"Champagne," Tim said when the waiter appeared.
"And whatever is the specialty of the house." He looked
at Elizabeth. "All right with you?"

"Certainly."

He didn't think she would care what she was eating
anyway. He saw with satisfaction that she looked utterly
unsettled.

He didn't have anything further to say while they
waited for the champagne, and when it arrived, he
sipped it in silence, just watching her. A couple of times
she opened her mouth to speak but, evidently reconsid-
ering it, remained silent.

The specialty of the house proved to be scallops and
lobster in a wine and butter sauce. Hellishly expensive,
but Elizabeth seemed to know better than to make any

remarks about that. And he wasn't saying anything. He was enjoying himself.

Their entrée was served, and they began eating in silence. Finally Elizabeth blurted, "Tim, why did you come to Idaho?"

Good, he thought. *Let's get to it.* "Do you want the story I've been handing you all along or the real reason?"

"The real reason."

"I came because I've been thinking and thinking but can't see any way I'm ever going to be happy without you."

"What about with me?" she asked quietly.

"Well, you're a pain in the neck, Elizabeth, but I think I've gotten to like that. I can see a little clearer why you feel the way you do about things."

"Oh." Elizabeth looked down at her hands and fiddled with her fork. Then she looked up defiantly. "I don't want you to take up women's rights just to humor me."

Tim looked her in the eyes. Her face suddenly looked so hopeful, it made him ache. "I figured that one out," he said. "The way you feel about it, the way you go at things . . . it's not mannish, exactly—don't poker up at me, Elizabeth. I know I'm on shaky ground here. Just listen. You seem to have a feel for who you really are. Most women don't have that confidence, that centered-ness."

"They would have, if they hadn't had it trained out of them," Elizabeth said.

"I know. I think that's what got to me. Even my mother and grandmother don't have it. They're very strong-minded, intelligent women, but they're still submerged in their husband's worlds. Well, Gran's a widow, but you know what I'm getting at. They needed to be married. You don't. You're complete, three-dimensional, whole. Am I making a fool of myself? I'm having trouble finding the words to get it out."

Elizabeth took a deep breath. "You're no fool," she said.

"I always thought—your dinner's getting cold. Maybe

you should eat while you listen." He felt himself falling over what he was trying to say, stumbling like a drunk.

She shook her head.

"I always thought I wanted a wife like my mother and Gran," Tim went on. "Independent except when it came to me, and then, well, pretty dependent in that department. Now it seems that I don't. Instead, I want some kind of partner."

"Partners need to have a very careful balance."

Tim saw that Elizabeth's shoulders were hunched. She must be holding her hands tightly together in her lap, he realized, and felt a great love for her pour through him. The air seemed charged with some force, as if things might fly suddenly off the table.

"It's risky," she added.

"I know," Tim agreed solemnly. "Risky as hell." He didn't apologize for his language, accorded her no feminine latitude. "But I don't think I can be satisfied with anything or anyone else now."

She smiled, and her face seemed lit with an inner glow. She didn't bother to ask coquettishly if this was a proposal. There weren't any games left to play. "Have you really thought about what it would be like? I need to know."

Tim, relaxing a bit now, put his chin on his hand and smiled into her eyes. "I assume you mean the drawbacks and not the advantages. I've thought a lot. I packed up old Trout and went home to Oregon for a couple of weeks. The first thing I did, like a darn fool, was ask Gran what I ought to do. She wouldn't give me any advice. She said if *I* didn't know, then I'd better not do anything. So I got on Trout and took a bedroll and some food and just started riding, to see if I couldn't shake loose what I knew."

"And what shook loose?" Uncaring of good manners, she put her own elbow on the table and mirrored his position, cupping her chin and smiling back. The waiter started to sidle over to see if they required anything further and then changed his mind and turned on his heel. Tim grinned; they must appear to have everything they needed.

"Well," he said, "the first thing that dawned on me was that I could do that—just take off on my lonesome—and you couldn't. Or at least respectable society said you couldn't. Then I started to understand why you're so riled. And finally I started thinking about children. Indelicate, I know, to admit it. But I figured out that if I had daughters, I'd prefer by far that they grow up the way I did, than put up with what my sisters have. Janessa certainly has had more freedom than most girls, but a long shot short of what I got. Sally's still too young for us to know how she'll turn out, but I don't think she's aiming for much more than to be beautiful and well dressed."

"You had better look out before making promises about daughters," Elizabeth warned. "I would hold you to making good on all vows."

"If I ever back down and start to hem them in, you can smack me one. But the clincher, Elizabeth, was that when I finally figured out that I was going to come out here after you, I quit wanting a drink."

"A drink? What do you mean?"

Tim felt embarrassed. "Awhile back I got into the habit of soaking up liquor whenever I needed something I couldn't have. I scared myself silly when I realized what I was doing, but that didn't stop my wanting to. After I figured out what I wanted to do about you—about us—I didn't feel like that anymore."

"You're drinking champagne," Elizabeth pointed out.

"True, and I like champagne. I didn't say I'd signed the pledge never to drink again. I said I wasn't feeling like using alcohol for an anesthetic anymore."

"What if I say no?"

Tim felt a cold, leaden weight settle in his gut as he considered that. "I can't honestly say. I'm not trying to imply that if you turn me down, I'll go on to suffer a drunkard's doom. I don't honestly think I will. It's not so much a matter of getting what I want as knowing what I want—for certain, for sure. In any case, that's not your problem; it would be mine. I wouldn't coerce you with that, just as you wouldn't want me to support women's rights unless I sincerely felt that way for myself."

"No, I don't think you would. I think maybe I see things clearer now, too."

"If we create a partnership, though, you'll have to stick to it, too," Tim said. "You can't fall down and decide you're tired and hand all the power back to me. I'll hand it right back."

Elizabeth let out a long breath and began to eat her dinner again. "Why did you wait until after the election to talk to me about this?" she asked between bites.

"So you'd have your mind on it."

Elizabeth gave him a look that took his breath away. "Are you still old-fashioned enough to buy me an engagement ring?" she whispered.

The color rose to Tim's face. Then they began to laugh happily, the issue resolved.

"Some customs are hard to shake," he said, and felt in his pocket. "Give me your hand. Gran gave me this for you, if you'd like it. It was hers, from my grandfather. It isn't fancy, but he couldn't afford much at the time. I hope you like garnets."

He slipped it on her finger, and the little red stones glowed in the candlelight.

"Oh, Tim, it's perfect."

They finished their dinner while unabashedly holding hands across the table. When they left, even the maître d' abandoned his French air of worldly reserve to beam at them.

They walked back to the hotel through a light snowfall that turned the streetlights into clouds of glowing confetti. It wasn't very cold, but Tim put his arm around her shoulders with the pretense of keeping her warm. His heart hammering, he didn't have quite the nerve to kiss her in public. That would be too abandoned, but he nearly leaped up the hotel stairs looking for a secluded corner. They found one at the end of the hallway, just outside the door to her room.

He bent over her, trembling, wondering what was going to happen now. He hadn't ever kissed Elizabeth and had no idea how she would respond. He felt as tightly wound as a spring with wanting her but forced himself to put his lips to hers very gently. Her response rocketed through him like electricity, overwhelming them both.

"Oh, Lord," he whispered, "how am I going to wait for the wedding? I want you so much it's killing me. I'd better get out of here."

Elizabeth opened the door to her room and said very quietly, "Come in."

Tim followed her into the room but stayed beside the door. He was unable to force himself away, but, embracing her, he managed to still his hands. "You don't have to, Elizabeth. I wouldn't force you to."

She laid her cheek against his shirt. "I knew that if I ever gave in to you, I would feel like this," she whispered. "It's . . . it's glorious. It's what it's supposed to be. It's what women are fighting for—to be allowed to be whole people, to feel as much desire for the man we love as he feels for us."

Tim thought about Dr. Emory and wondered if that good man would see it that way. Then Tim reflected on his earlier conversation with Elizabeth, about possible daughters. Finally he gave up trying to sort it out or to be good. Elizabeth had come willingly into his arms, not using sex to lure him into marriage or as a favor to cajole from him what she wanted. She clung to him in the way it was meant to be, as a joy to them both. If that was truly how she perceived it, then he was lucky beyond belief. He kissed her again, unhooking her skirt, then unbuttoned her basque and slid it down over her shoulders. She stepped out of them, and he lifted her in a flurry of petticoats onto the bed.

He pulled loose the strings of her chemise and opened it to kiss one breast. Soon his own clothes were on the floor. He felt her hands exploring his body, tentatively, inquiringly, and heard her give a little sigh of pleasure. He groaned and tried not to go too fast, but it was almost impossible not to. Her face flowered into an *O* of amazement, and she tightened her arms around his back.

Later, when they lay side by side, curled together, he whispered, "Are you all right?"

Her eyes opened dreamily. "Oh, yes. I always imagined I would like it. Did you have fun?"

"It was extraordinary," he whispered into the starched pillowcase and the darkened room. "If this is what giving women equal rights does, I assure you I'll campaign devotedly all my days."

She giggled and poked a finger at his bare chest. "Just see you keep this kind of campaigning at home."

He stroked her hair. "Why would I ever want to do anything else? Ever, forever."

"I know," she said sleepily. "I was just joking. I knew that."

"Elizabeth, what made you change your mind about me?"

"It was the same way it was with you," she whispered. "It wasn't anything anybody said to me or anyone's advice. I just finally got to the point where I knew that I knew. I can't make decisions any other way. I love you, Tim, and didn't want to think of being without you."

"My blessed love." He buried his face in her hair and slept.

In the morning he dressed and slipped out cautiously, trying, by his nonchalant attitude, to pretend to any interested observers that he hadn't been there all night. Elizabeth and he caught the first train for San Francisco to announce their engagement. And, he decided, he was going to set the wedding date as soon as he could—they probably wouldn't get any more chances like the night before to make love. He doubted that Dr. Emory was *that* modern and enlightened when it came to Elizabeth—any more than Tim would be, despite his protestations in the restaurant, when it came to his own daughter. Any more than Elizabeth would be, if it came to that, despite hers.

Maybe that was the way it was supposed to be: You had to make a big decision on your own, without the instructions of older, wiser heads who would inevitably decide that with age, they knew everything. He could see that same tendency growing in him. He would resist it, but it would come anyway. And all in all, that didn't seem so bad. It was all part of the pattern of life.

As the train sped toward California, Tim slipped his arm around Elizabeth, and they watched the white mountains whirl by, as brilliant as crystal in the December sun. He lifted her hand. Already the garnet ring seemed natural and permanent, as if it had been there forever. He kissed her palm, then turned her hand to look again at the ring. The garnets glinted as if they were really rubies.

"Extraordinary," he said again as she rested her head on his shoulder.

Author's Note

For the reader interested in knowing more about the way we were a hundred years ago (and the ways in which we haven't changed) I recommend the books from which I drew much of my research: for Frank Blake's hobo journey, and the similar experiences of the "road kids" who took to the rails by the thousands in the 1890s, Kenneth Alsop's *Hard Traveling, a History of the Hobo and His Times*; on the beginnings of the women's movement, *Women's Rights* by Olivia Coolidge. For information on the early oil industry, the author's thanks are due the fine folks at the Unocal Oil Museum, Santa Paula, California. And again and always, my thanks to Laurie Rosin, editor extraordinaire, and Marjie Weber, infallible copy editor, of Book Creations, Inc.

Wagons West
The Frontier Trilogy

WESTWARD!

by Dana Fuller Ross

It is 1806 as the Lewis and Clark expedition ends its long journey to the Pacific and back across the American frontier. The bold men with the two captains were lured by the promise of adventure and the wilderness, and among them is young Clay Holt. But this proud frontiersman had other reasons for leaving the Marietta, Ohio, homestead where his parents and brothers and sister still live . . . reasons that await his return.

The Garwood brothers have been threatening the Holt family, claiming their sister's child was fathered by Clay—who left Marietta over two years ago when the accusation was first made. As the Garwoods' threats escalate into violence, Clay's brother Jeff becomes their target. But once Clay is back, the violence grows into tragedy, dividing the Holt family, brother from sister, parent from child—and Jeff Holt from his new bride, Melissa.

Jeff and Clay make their way westward with a fur-trapping entrepreneur named Manuel Lisa, their journey bringing them into contact with many Indians, some hostile, some friendly—such as the beautiful Sioux maiden Shining Moon, for whom Clay feels a strong attraction. Little do they know that igniting the trouble between the Americans and Indians is a deceitful and ruthless Frenchman named Duquesne. . . .

As the Holt brothers head westward, Melissa Holt's overbearing father insists that she go with him and her mother to North Carolina. There, she discovers that she is carrying Jeff's child. Not knowing whether she will ever see her husband again, she gives birth to a son, who will become the foundation of the Holt family beloved by the readers of the WAGONS WEST series. But will her son, Michael "Whip" Holt, ever meet his father?

Keep reading for a preview of WESTWARD!, on sale July 1992 wherever Bantam paperbacks are sold.

The tall man in buckskins and coonskin cap paused at the top of a rise and looked out across a broad valley with awe-inspiring mountains on the far side, the craggy, snowcapped heights reaching high into the bright blue sky. The man carried a .54 caliber flintlock rifle produced at Harper's Ferry in 1803, a brace of 1799 North and Cheney flintlock pistols, a heavy-bladed hunting knife, and a tomahawk. He was armed for war, but at the moment, he felt utterly at peace.

Clay Holt was quite possibly the first white man ever to stand on this hill and survey the magnificent vista before him. He rested the butt of the flintlock rifle on the ground at his feet and leaned on the barrel. His beard and the hair that hung almost to his shoulders were a deep black, the color of midnight. His keen blue eyes searched the distance, scanning the thickly wooded hillsides, the meadows of lush grass and wildflowers, the lines of brush that marked the course of creeks. Far across the valley an eagle wheeled through the sky and then began to climb, seeming to ascend above the very peaks of the Shining Mountains themselves.

"It is beautiful, is it not?"

The voice came from behind Clay. He glanced over his shoulder and smiled at a young Indian woman carrying a baby. "Yes. I don't know why anybody would ever want to leave it."

"This land has been my home for many years. I would never be happy anywhere else."

"Reckon I can understand that," Clay said.

The woman deftly transferred the baby from the carrier on her back to her arms. The boy had been sick recently, but he seemed to have recovered his health.

"Good, Pomp," she murmured to him and then looked up at Clay. "You will go back to this place you call St. Louis." There was no question to her words.

"Aye. But I'll be back here someday, Janey. You can count on that. I've never seen people who live a simpler life than yours. . . . I don't reckon I've ever seen any who were happier, either."

At this moment Clay was happy, just about as happy as he had ever been. Almost from the first moment he had seen the Shining Mountains, he had recognized the strong pull they had on him. He felt as if he had come home. Being on his own like this, he felt a freedom unlike any he had ever experienced. He enjoyed Janey's company, too. There was nothing romantic between them; she was another man's wife. But she was Clay Holt's friend, and they had spent many long days talking about this country where she had lived her life.

"Well, I guess we'd better be getting back," he said. "The others'll be expecting us."

Janey took a few steps but then froze. "Clay Holt," she said in a soft voice fraught with urgency.

Clay heard her warning tone but managed to retain his casual attitude. He turned toward Janey, looked past her, and saw two warriors standing near a grove of pines a short distance down the ridge. He had seen a great many Indians during the past months—Shoshone, Sioux, Minnetaree, Crow, Blackfoot—but from their markings he could not recognize the tribe these two belonged to. They were unusually tall for Indians, well over six feet, and they carried bows almost as tall as they were. Their dark hair was woven into braids, and Clay thought he saw rattlesnake rattles adorning each tip. As the two men regarded the white man, the young Indian woman, and the baby, their expressions were fierce. Clay sensed that he was in more danger now than he ever had been since coming to these rugged mountains.

"You know who they are?" he asked Janey in a quiet voice.

"Their tribe is not known to me. I think they are enemies of the Shoshone, though."

"How can you know that?"

"Do they look like friends to you, Clay Holt?"

He had to admit she had a point. After a moment he said, "Well, are we all going to stand here and stare at one another for the rest of the day?"

"Perhaps they are just curious and will soon leave," Janey said, but she did not sound as if she held much hope of that happening.

Certainly Clay did not expect that to be the outcome. Yet he was not overly worried. His Harper's Ferry rifle was primed and loaded, as were the two flintlock pistols tucked behind his belt. That gave him three shots, affording him one miss if the Indians attacked. Besides, he was confident in his abilities with knife and tomahawk, and he had always been able to hold his own in any kind of rough-and-tumble.

"Ask them what they want," he said, taking Pomp from her arms.

Janey glanced dubiously at him. Then, using the sign language understood by all plains tribes, she moved her hands gracefully to form the question. When the strangers gave no response, she repeated the movements, but again they failed to answer.

"Come on," Clay said, handing the baby back to her. "Let's get out of here." Boldly he walked down the slope toward the Indians, thinking that perhaps he could bluff them into getting out of the way. If not, at least he would be in better pistol range.

To Clay's great surprise, one of the Indians suddenly said in English, "This is not your land, white man. You should not be here."

Clay stopped and, though he felt anxious, calmly regarded the Indian who had spoken. Keeping his voice level, he said, "I come in peace. I do not wish to bring harm or trouble to any of your people."

The second Indian spoke. "This may not be your wish, but it will happen. The white men will come, and there will be great weeping and sorrow among the lodges of the People. The plains will be littered with the bodies of the dead, and the streams of the Shining

Mountains will run red with blood." The words were not spoken harshly in anger but rather with sorrow and resignation.

"How do you know this?" Clay asked.

"The spirits have spoken. They have told us these things. Just as they told us where to find you."

Clay knew better than to scoff when Indians spoke of the spirits and the messages they brought. While he did not share such beliefs, he had come to respect them. "Are you saying that if I leave this land, the things you just told us won't come to pass?"

"We wish that it were so. But you are one among many. Killing you will not stop what must happen."

Clay smiled tightly. "Then let us pass."

Both of them shook their heads. "We cannot," said one.

"The killing must begin somewhere," said the other.

And with that, they reached into the quivers on their backs.

"Run!" Clay barked at Janey. "Take the baby and get out of here!"

"No!" she cried. "I will stay—"

The roar of Clay's rifle drowned out anything else she had to say. He had always been a good marksman, and his eye and his nerve did not betray him now. The lead ball smashed into the chest of one of the Indians, flinging him backward, rolling. The second man managed to loose his arrow. Clay dove desperately to the side as the feathered shaft cut through the air, the arrow plucking at his sleeve, tearing the buckskin and leaving a painful gash in his arm. As Clay hit the ground, he yanked one of the pistols from behind his belt and cocked it. The Indian already had a second arrow nocked, but before he could release it, Clay pressed the trigger of the flintlock. The pistol bucked in his hand, and acrid smoke from the exploded black powder filled his senses.

As had his companion before him, the second Indian died without a sound. He fell, the breast of his buckskin shirt turning crimson from the spreading bloodstain.

Clay came up on his knees and lifted his other pistol, holding it ready just in case either man was only wounded and not dead, though he was fairly certain that wasn't the case. He glanced up at Janey, still standing nearby cradling the baby. Slightly shaken, she seemed to be unharmed.

"Are you and Pomp all right?" Clay asked.

"Their arrows did not touch us," she said. "But their words . . ."

Clay got to his feet as the young woman's voice trailed away. He understood what she meant. The grim prophecy pronounced by the two Indians had disturbed him, too.

"It doesn't have to be that way," he said. "Just because they thought some spirits told them—"

Janey shook her head. "I do not think the spirits told them of this vision. I think they themselves were spirits."

"They're flesh and blood," Clay insisted, looking at each warrior to make certain he was dead. "They're men, and they died as men."

"Then how did you know what they said?"

Clay stared at her. "They were speaking English. I admit, that's sort of strange—"

"They spoke Shoshone," Janey said softly. "I heard their words in my tongue, just as you did in yours."

For a long moment Clay did not answer. Then he said quietly, "I reckon at least one of us is mixed-up. We'd better get moving."

"Your arm is hurt. Let me look at it first."

Clay held out the arm that had been grazed by the arrow. The minor wound had hurt like blazes at first, but now it seemed strangely painless. His eyes widened as he examined the buckskin sleeve and found no tear. Quickly, he shoved the sleeve up over his forearm.

The skin was unmarked.

Clay took a deep breath. "Maybe you've got something there with your spirit talk." Looking around, he saw the arrow lying on the ground nearby and stepped over to it. He reached toward it gingerly, and when his hand grasped it, he was instantly reassured. The arrow was real, all right. Maybe he had just imagined that it hit him.

Janey stepped closer and looked at him intently. "You must give me your word, Clay Holt. You must pledge to me that you will do what you can to see that there is peace in this land. I know that you and the others will come back." She smiled sadly. "You will not be able to stay away."

There was truth in what she said, Clay thought. The lure of the mountains was too powerful. He could speak for no one but himself, but he knew that whether he went back east or not, someday he would come to these mountains again.

"Let's make tracks out of here and get back to the others," he said. "These two could have some friends close by."

"Your word," the young woman insisted. "You must promise me, Clay Holt."

"All right," he said, facing her squarely. "I give you my word, Sacajawea." At a moment like this, it seemed better to use her real name, rather than the nickname Captain Clark had given her. "Now, come on. Cap'n Lewis and Cap'n Clark just sent us out to scout ahead. They're bound to be wondering what happened to us. And if they heard those shots—"

"Tell them you fired at a deer and missed." She looked at the dead men and shuddered slightly. "This is not something the captains need to know."

Clay agreed. With all this talk about spirits and prophecies, he thought it would be best to keep his mouth shut. If he told the others about it, they might think he was crazy.

"Do not forget your pledge," Sacajawea reminded him as they left that place.

"Don't worry," Clay Holt said, his hand tightening on the arrow. "I won't forget. . . ."

* * *

For all the signs of civilization they could see, the men might have been alone in the millions of square miles of trackless wilderness around them. Their camp here in the Rocky Mountains was so isolated from the rest of the growing country, in fact, that they might as well have been on the far side of the moon.

Such a journey was impossible, of course, here in the summer of 1806, but no more so than most people, more than two years earlier, would have regarded crossing the Rockies, journeying on to the Pacific Ocean, and returning over some of the most rugged terrain known. But that was precisely what this so-called Corps of Discovery had done under the joint command of Captain Meriwether Lewis and Captain William Clark.

Clay crouched near one of the campfires, looking around at his companions. Fewer than three dozen in number, they were mostly clad in buckskin tunics and trousers, with raccoon-pelt caps perched on their long, shaggy, matted hair. The ringed tails of the animals had been left intact, to dangle down the back of the wearer's neck or be pulled forward over his shoulder. Some of the men had left the heads on as well, so that the creatures almost seemed alive, ready to swing their sharp little faces toward the first scent of danger.

Clay had removed the head of the raccoon from whose pelt he had fashioned his cap. Now he pushed the headgear back on his shock of thick black hair and sipped tea from a battered tin cup. It was not real tea, such as the English drank, but had been brewed instead from the roots of a plant that grew in abundance in these parts. The stuff was strong and had a bite to it, and it helped wake a man up on a chilly morning. This high in the mountains the mornings were cool, even though it was the middle of summer.

Nearby, both Lewis and Clark were scribbling in their journals, the scratch of their pens audible in the clear mountain air. Unlike most of the frontiersmen who had accompanied them on this trip, the captains wore blue uniform jackets and heavy tan breeches, with high-topped black boots that had survived the journey well. Nearly all the other men wore moccasins.

Captain Lewis looked up from his journal and said to Clark, "Have you written about our parting?"

Clark said, "Aye. Would you like to hear it? It will be easier to understand than tryin' to read my poor spelling."

Lewis laughed. "Yes, yes. I'd appreciate that."

Clark lifted his opened journal and read:

"We have formed the following plan of operation: Captain Lewis, with nine men, is to pursue the most direct route to the falls of the Missouri, where three of his party are to be left to prepare carriages for transporting the baggage and canoes across the portage. With the remaining six, he will ascend Maria's river to explore the country, after which he will descend that river to its mouth. The rest of the men will accompany Captain Clark to prevail on some of the Sioux chiefs to accompany him to the city of Washington."

"You haven't mentioned the Indian woman."

"Oh, yes. Sacajawea will be traveling with me. Perhaps I should amend it. . . ."

Captain Lewis snapped his journal shut. "Well, that's that," he said. "I suppose we'll be ready to push off shortly."

"Aye."

Both men seemed rather casual, considering that the expedition was about to split up for the first time since it had left St. Louis in 1804. Roughly a third of the men would accompany the tall, dour Meriwether Lewis, while the others would continue on with William Clark. The commanders had reached the decision together, and there was no animosity involved. This was, after all, an expedition of discovery, and by breaking up into two groups on the return trip, they could cover more ground. That meant more information and more maps to be taken back to President Jefferson in Washington City.

Clay Holt respected both Lewis and Clark. They were excellent soldiers—although Clay did not really know much about soldiering as such—and their record spoke for itself. The group had been to the Pacific and had come this far back with the loss of only one man. And Sergeant Floyd had died as the result of a sudden illness, something that could not have been prevented. So far, although the Corps of Discovery had encountered hundreds, perhaps thousands, of Indians, they had had no trouble with the "aborigines," as Captain Lewis called them.

At least no trouble that the rest of the group knew about. Clay had not forgotten the encounter Sacajawea and he had experienced with the mysterious warriors a couple of weeks earlier. As they had agreed that day, neither had said anything to the others about that strange meeting. Sacajawea had not even told her husband, the French wastrel Toussaint Charbonneau.

Clay had made his choice of which captain to accompany back strictly on a whim. He would go with Lewis, who intended to head north to the Great Falls of the Missouri River, and from there explore a ways along Maria's River—named by Lewis for one of his lady friends in the East—before turning back and rejoining Clark's party farther south along the Missouri. The trip would be considerably longer this way, but Clay did not mind.

After all, he was in no hurry to get back to civilization. Hell, he thought as he drained the last of the root tea, he would not really care if he never got back.

Roaming the wilderness for the past two and a quarter years had changed Clay Holt. He had left the family farm in the Ohio River valley a restless young man, quick-tempered and seldom satisfied. Here in the mountains, for one of the few times in his life, he had found contentment.

A few days earlier he had overheard two of the men talking about the possibility of staying out here and living with the Indians. That idea held some appeal for

Clay, too, but it would mean deserting. He had signed on to make the entire journey with Lewis and Clark, and he was a man of his word. At least he liked to think of himself as one.

Nothing would stop him from coming back later, though, after the Corps of Discovery had returned to St. Louis and disbanded. He could make a quick trip back to the Holt family home near Marietta, Ohio, then find some excuse to head west again. That was exactly what he would do, Clay decided as he stowed away the empty cup in his buckskin possibles bag.

Captain Lewis called out, "You men who are going with me, prepare to mount. We'll be pulling out shortly."

Clay went over to his horse, a sturdy Indian pony like the ones ridden by the other men. The horses had made this part of the journey easier. In the roughest stretch of mountains, the Corps had been forced to travel most of the way on foot, using the horses only as pack animals. Here, they could ride. Clay slung his possibles bag over his shoulder, grasped the pony's mane, and swung up agilely. They had no saddles, only buckskin pads to protect the backs of the animals. The pads did not offer much protection for the rear ends of the riders, Clay thought wryly, but they were better than nothing.

He looked at the other men going with Captain Lewis: Sergeant Gass, Frazier, Warner, Drouilliard, McNeal, Goodrich, Thompson, and the two Fields brothers. Good men, all of them. They had been experienced frontiersmen to start with, and the expedition had seasoned and toughened them even more. Clay was proud to have them for companions. Several of the Shoshone men who had attached themselves to the expedition as guides would be coming with them, too, although Sacajawea and Charbonneau would continue on down the Yellowstone with Clark's party.

Lewis rode up next to Clay. Captain Clark was walking with him, and as Lewis reined in, he leaned over to take the upraised hand of his fellow commander.

"God willing, I'll see you in a few weeks, my friend," Lewis said as he gave Clark a firm handshake.

"God willing," Clark repeated.

Although neither of them made much of this parting, Clay could hear the concern in their voices. So far, the mission given to them by President Jefferson had met with remarkable success . . . but that luck could change at any moment. Disaster could lurk around the next bend in the trail.

Captain Lewis lifted an arm and waved his hand forward, signaling for his men to depart. The small group rode away from the clearing in the woods, leaving their former comrades behind, striking out into virgin territory on which it was quite possible no white man had ever laid eyes. They were following a stream they had christened Clark's River on their westbound journey; even at this late date, the waterway was still somewhat swollen by the spring runoff from the mountains. The Shoshone guides, seemingly tireless, trotted alongside the riders.

Mountains that remained white tipped with snow year-round loomed above them. Thick stands of timber covered the lower slopes, and at this time of year the grass beneath the hooves of the horses was thick and lush. Wildflowers in colorful profusion dotted the meadows through which the party rode. This was beautiful country, Clay thought as he lifted a hand to rub at his black-bearded jaw. Beautiful country indeed. He did not look back at what he and his companions were leaving behind, preferring instead to look ahead.

Yes, he would return here once he had paid a visit to his family, he vowed. But not just because of the landscape's wild beauty and the appealingly simple life led by the Indians. Clay had reasons other than his growing love of the frontier for not wanting to remain in the Ohio River valley.

PATRIOTS Book 1:

SONS OF LIBERTY

by Adam Rutledge

1773–1775. The birth pangs of freedom are shaking a nation. The British have passed the Intolerable Acts, and the angry citizens of Boston are ready to rebel. Among the spokesmen for the insurrectionists are Samuel Adams, Paul Revere, and John Hancock, all members of the inner circle of the Committee of Safety.

Daniel and Quincy Reed, brothers from Virginia, arrive in the city at a time when everyone is being asked to choose sides in the coming conflict. Quincy, with the exuberance of youth, decides immediately, eagerly participating in the Boston Tea Party, but Daniel is slower to declare his sympathies for the rebel cause. When Daniel is recruited by the lovely and literate spy, Roxanne Darragh, he casts his lot with hers, and together they gather information for the Committee of Safety—until it becomes clear that there is a traitor in their midst.

As the first shots are fired at Lexington and Concord the brothers' suspicions escalate. Can this traitor sabotage the outcome of the early battles of the War for Independence? Will he interfere with the newfound love Daniel and Roxanne feel for each other?

Turn the page for a preview of SONS OF LIBERTY, on sale July 1992 wherever Bantam paperbacks are sold.

The young man on the big bay horse was thirsty. He had been riding since early morning and, anxious to get to his destination, had not stopped for food or drink. Now as he spotted a tavern up ahead at a little crossroads, a grin broke out across his tanned face. Surely it would not hurt to stop for a quick mug of ale on a hot day.

In this summer of 1773, Daniel Reed was twenty years old, and much of that twenty years had been spent on the plantation of his parents, Geoffrey and Pamela Reed. It had not been idle time. Daniel had hunted and fished and spent every possible moment outdoors. His skin had acquired a healthy brown sheen, and the sun had also lightened his curly, naturally dark brown hair. Even relaxing in the saddle of the horse he had ridden from Virginia, he appeared unusually tall, lean, and muscular. He wore high-topped boots, dark brown whipcord pants, a lightweight linen shirt, and a black tricorn hat canted to the back of his head.

His brown eyes were intelligent. Despite his outdoor activities, his academic education had not been neglected. He had been to the best academy in Virginia and then to Yale College in the colony of Connecticut, and he had excelled in his studies at both places. He had done well enough that his parents had decided he should continue his schooling near Boston.

A long-barreled flintlock musket, powder horn, and shot pouch were slung on one side of the saddle. Another bag filled with food and other supplies hung from the opposite side. To some people, a journey on horseback from Virginia to Massachusetts might be a daunting prospect. Daniel, however, had thoroughly enjoyed the trip, even dawdling along the way to do some hunting.

As he reined the bay to a halt in front of the tavern, he heard loud voices coming from within the building. Several horses were tied up at the front rail. This was farming country, and no doubt the tavern served as a gathering place for the people who lived hereabouts. Daniel was not surprised to find it doing a brisk business, even at this time of day.

He walked in and went directly across the room to the long bar behind which the white-aproned proprietor held court. The man was saying to several patrons lined up at the bar, "The British were begging for trouble, if you ask me. That damned Dudington put a lot o' good men in jail."

"A lot of smugglers, you mean," countered one of the men. "Common criminals, that's what they are."

"For bringing in tea that ain't taxed half to death?" the bartender asked. "That's no crime as far as, I'm concerned."

Another man spoke up. "Those Rhode Islanders went too far when they burned the *Gaspee*, though. Wanton destruction's not going to solve anything."

Daniel leaned on the bar and, as he listened to the discussion, tried to catch the eye of the proprietor. The men's voices were loud and angry on both sides of the argument. Daniel frowned in concentration and finally remembered the incident about which they were talking. The year before, one of the British ships assigned to patrol the coast off Rhode Island had gone aground, and several boatloads of colonists, angry with the Crown's policies on the importing of tea, had rowed out to the vessel, taken it over from its crew, and set it on fire. The British authorities had been furious over the matter, but they had never been able to track down the men responsible. Daniel had read about it in the Virginia newspapers, as well as having heard his father and other men discuss it.

But all that had happened over a year earlier. Why were these Massachusetts men still arguing about it?

He finally got the attention of the bartender and asked, "Could I have a mug of ale, please?"

The man sauntered down the bar, leaned his big palms on the hardwood, and gave Daniel a dubious stare. "Be ye a patriot or a Tory?" he demanded.

Daniel blinked, taken aback by the question. "I . . . I don't suppose I know," he finally replied.

Men from both sides of the discussion seized on that. They gathered around him, hammering sharp questions at him, demanding to know his allegiances. He yearned to shout out that all he really wanted was to get to Boston.

"Forget about the ale," he told the bartender, turning and trying to push his way out of the knot of men that had formed around him. "I'll just water my horse and be gone."

"Not so quick, lad." A hard hand fell on his shoulder, stopping him. "Ye haven't answered our questions. Nobody's neutral in this anymore. Yer either a patriot or a damned loyalist!"

"Damned loyalist, is it?" snapped one of the men. "Better that than a treasonous, treacherous rebel!"

"Ye'd best take that back, Finn!"

"I'll do no such. And I'll not kowtow to the likes of you, either!"

Nervously licking his lips, Daniel watched both sides surge toward each other, with him in the middle. "Excuse me . . ." he began.

Then the punches started to fly.

Daniel ducked under them, intending to head for the floor and get out of this ludicrous predicament any way he could. On the way down, though, someone shoved him hard, and he lost his balance. He fell heavily, and someone stepped on him. Above him, the argument had degenerated into a brawl. Men shouted curses and grunted in pain as blows fell.

Rolling over desperately, Daniel got clear of the melee and sprang to his feet. Everyone else in the place seemed to have forgotten about him. They were too busy swinging fists and trying to smash mugs over one another's heads. Regretting that he had ever stopped, Daniel scrambled for his hat, which had come off during the confusion, brushed himself off, and headed for the door.

Outside, he watered the bay at the trough, swung up into the saddle, and decided he was willing to stay thirsty until he got to Boston.

It was amazing, he thought as he sent the horse cantering down the road, that men would come to blows over something that had happened somewhere else over a year earlier. They had to hold strong views about the situation if they were willing to fight about it now.

He would have to think about that, he told himself, but later. Right now, he had the last leg of his journey to complete. With any luck he would be in Boston before the day was over.

Daniel felt excitement surge through him as he drew rein and brought his horse to a stop on a hill overlooking the city of Boston, its blue harbor to the east and the Charles River to the west. He had been to this bustling Atlantic coast city before, but the sight of it never failed to thrill him.

"Bound for town, are ye?"

Daniel turned to locate the source of the question. An old man in a floppy hat was at the reins of a mule-drawn wagon loaded with produce from one of the area's outlying farms. As he passed slowly he grinned at Daniel, revealing a large gap in his front teeth.

"That's right," Daniel said. "I'm going to Boston."

The old man gave him a little wave and moved on. Daniel stayed where he was, wanting to enjoy the sensation of looking out over the city for a few more minutes.

Arrangements had been made for Daniel to stay with his aunt and uncle during the summer, before finding a place of his own in the fall when he entered Harvard to read for the law. He was eager to see his cousin Elliot again. Putting his horse into a trot, he headed down the hill toward the Shawmut peninsula.

The road led to Boston Neck, a narrow spit of land where the Charles and the harbor just about met. On the other side of Boston Neck, past the public gallows, the peninsula widened rapidly, its confines filled by the sprawling community. Daniel followed Orange Street for several blocks, then cut over to Common Street, which ran along the east side of Boston Common. Traffic was heavy. He made his way among carriages, wagons, men on horseback like himself, and many pedestrians. On this sunny day the large, open, parklike green was busy. Couples strolled hand in hand on the soft grass; children, trailed by barking dogs, ran and played; old-timers, enjoying the youngsters' antics, sat under the double row of trees that bounded the common.

Under other circumstances, Daniel might have considered stopping for a few moments. Benjamin and Polly Markham, his uncle and aunt, knew he was coming, but considering the distance between Virginia and Massachusetts, it had been impossible to predict to the day when he would arrive. However, he felt sure his relatives would not be sitting around waiting for him. If he knew his mother's brother, Uncle Benjamin would be hard at work as usual, furthering the interests of the shipping company in which he was a partner.

Though no one would object if he stayed to enjoy the common for a while, Daniel pushed on, unwilling to delay his arrival any longer. The road cut across the northeast corner of the common and then ran straight through the fashionable residential district of Beacon Hill, where the first house in Boston had been built a hundred and fifty years earlier by William Blackstone, a settler from Charlestown, across the river to the north. The pace was more sedate here, with fewer people on the streets.

The Markham family owned a large house on one of Beacon Hill's cobblestone lanes. To someone accustomed to the open spaces of Virginia, the houses in Boston seemed to be crammed too close together, but Daniel knew that he would soon get used to the crowded living conditions of the city. With water surrounding it on both sides, he thought, Boston had grown about as much as it ever could.

He rode up the hill and drew rein in front of the elegant three-story home owned by his aunt and uncle. It was constructed of red brick and sat behind a flagstone sidewalk. As he swung down from his saddle and fastened the horse's reins to a wrought-iron pole that supported an oil lamp, the front door of the house burst open and a young man came running out.

"Daniel!" he called. "Is that you?"

"It's been less than a year since you saw me in Virginia, Elliot," Daniel replied with a grin, turning to greet his cousin. "You ought to recognize me."

Elliot Markham came to a stop in front of Daniel. "Yes, I think I do recall that ugly countenance," he gibed. Suddenly, he grabbed Daniel's hand and pumped it up and down in an enthusiastic handshake. "How are you, cousin?"

"Slightly saddlesore but fine." Smiling broadly and still shaking Elliot's hand, Daniel threw his other arm around his cousin and thumped him heartily on the back. "What about you?"

"Never better, now that you're here."

Elliot Markham was a year younger than Daniel, an inch shorter, and had blue eyes to go with his blond hair and fair skin. He was also hopeless when it came to woodcraft, Daniel remembered from Elliot's visits to the Reed plantation. They had gone hunting together often but rarely bagged anything—since hunting with Elliot was like tramping through the woods with a squad of militia. He made enough noise for twelve men—more, if they were Virginians.

But Daniel supposed he was just as much out of place here in the city. There was no denying that Elliot was more worldly and sophisticated, even though he was a year younger. Daniel did not consider himself a bumpkin, and he was certainly not an embarrassment in a social setting . . . but he had his cousin to thank for refining his manners to meet the stringent standards of Boston. He had learned a great deal from Elliot.

"Come on inside," Elliot said, linking arms with Daniel to steer him toward the door. "I'm sure Mother and Father will be very glad to see you. We didn't know when you'd get here, but I've been keeping my eyes open for you. I just happened to be passing by the front window when I saw you ride up."

The door was still open. Elliot took Daniel through it into the foyer. The walls were papered in a rich brocade pattern, and to one side sat a small table with elaborately carved legs. Covering it was a linen cloth, and an oil lamp with a crystal mantle was set in the middle. On the opposite wall were hung two paintings, both landscapes of pastoral English scenes. At least Daniel had always supposed they were English; he had never been to England and possessed no desire to go there. The colonies were plenty big enough for him.

The parlor opened to the left of the foyer, and a hallway led straight ahead. Elliot started down this corridor, saying, "Father's in his study. He has some of his associates with him, but I'm sure he won't mind being interrupted. He said to let him know as soon as you got here."

Before they reached the heavy oak door of his uncle's study, Daniel heard Benjamin Markham's booming voice. He could not make out all the words in the tirade, but he caught "damnable insurrectionists," "high treason against the Crown," and "put a stop to it any way we have to!"

Elliot grinned and said, "You'll have to excuse Father. There was another meeting at Faneuil Hall last night, and when he heard about it, he got incensed, as usual."

Daniel shook his head. "Meeting? What sort of meeting?"

"Oh, the usual arguing about the king's taxes. People get together and talk about how awful the levies are, but it's just a bunch of hot air, in my opinion. I mean, you can't really do anything about what the king decrees, can you?"

"I suppose not. There was a mighty brawl at a

tavern I visited on my trip north about the same sort of thing, though," Daniel said with a shrug. Down in Virginia, there had been ill feelings about some of the Crown's policies, but Daniel had never taken a great deal of interest in the discussions.

"At any rate, Father thinks there shouldn't be any talk against the king, and he despises Samuel Adams and that bunch," Elliot went on casually. "I just thought I should warn you, in case you've developed any so-called insurrectionist leanings."

Daniel laughed shortly. "Not likely. I have other things on my mind these days, such as going to Harvard College this fall."

"It's going to be good to have you around," Elliot said, his grin widening. "Come on. Let's beard the lion in its den, shall we?" He knocked quickly, then opened the door of the study and swept his arm around, gesturing for Daniel to precede him.

Daniel stepped into the gloomy room, which was paneled with dark wood and had thick curtains over its single window. When he had visited as a boy, he had never liked his uncle's study, except for the bookcases full of Benjamin Markham's intriguing leather-bound volumes. The books had always held a great attraction for Daniel, and he had managed to read quite a few of them during his stays.

Now the air was full of pipe smoke, and the room was as shadowy as he remembered. Daniel could tell by Benjamin Markham's stance in the center of the room that he had been pacing back and forth in front of his desk. He clutched an old briar pipe in his blunt fingers. Still straight and sturdily built in middle age, Benjamin had a strong jaw, piercing blue eyes, and a fringe of gray hair around a bald pate. He wore a black coat and breeches and a gray vest that were elegant and expensive despite their simplicity.

"Sorry to interrupt, Father," said Elliot, entering the room behind Daniel, "but look who's here."

"Hello, Daniel," Benjamin said cordially but without an excess of warmth. He stepped forward to greet his nephew. "How was your journey?"

"Just fine, Uncle Benjamin," Daniel replied as he shook the hand the older man thrust toward him.

"Well, it's good to see you. Your aunt and I have been looking forward to your visit." Benjamin gestured toward a trio of occupied armchairs arranged in a half circle in front of the desk. "Are you acquainted with these gentlemen?"

"Only Mr. Cummings, sir." Daniel nodded to one of the men, a thin, balding individual with rather pinched features. Daniel knew Theophilus Cummings was Benjamin Markham's business partner. The other two men were undoubtedly associates of theirs.

Benjamin confirmed that guess by saying, "This is Mr. Satterwaite and Mr. Johnson, two of our finest local merchants. Gentlemen, my nephew Daniel Reed."

The two men nodded to Daniel, and one of them— Satterwaite, Daniel thought—asked, "Where are you from, lad? Your accent marks you as a southerner."

"My family settled in Virginia, sir," Daniel said.

The man nodded and might have been about to say something else, but Benjamin spoke up first. "We've just been discussing the intolerable behavior of that rabble down at Faneuil Hall. Are you aware of the situation, Daniel?"

"Vaguely, sir."

"And your opinion?" Benjamin snapped.

Daniel had to shrug. "I'm not sure I have one."

"You don't have an opinion?" Cummings said in a sour voice that matched his expression. "Those people are talking about rebellion! Surely you have an opinion on that, young man."

"Well, I'm not in favor of violence," Daniel ventured.

"That's what they're going to get," Benjamin said. "If this constant badgering of the authorities continues, mark my words, there'll be trouble again, just like back in seventy."

Daniel knew what his uncle was talking about.

Three years earlier, he had been planning to visit Elliot in Boston during the summer, but that spring, the so-called Boston Massacre had taken place, resulting in the deaths of several colonists during a melee with British troops. Tensions had remained high during that summer, and Daniel's parents had decided that a trip to Boston would not be wise. Instead, Elliot's mother and father had sent him to Virginia that year.

"I certainly hope it doesn't come to that," Daniel offered. "There's been enough fighting."

"There'll be more. Goddamned rebels—"

Elliot closed his hand over Daniel's arm and broke in on his father's vitriolic comments by saying, "I'll show you your room, Daniel. I'm sure you must be tired after your journey."

"Yes, I am, a bit." Daniel nodded to Benjamin. "It's good to see you again, Uncle. Thank you for allowing me to visit."

"Always glad to have you," Benjamin said gruffly. He puffed on his pipe for a moment as Elliot took Daniel out into the hall. When Elliot was closing the door, Benjamin resumed, "The king ought to send more troops . . ."

The angry statement was cut off as the door clicked shut. Elliot led Daniel to the wide staircase at the right of the foyer. "I'm sorry," he said quietly. "I really thought Father might stop talking politics long enough to give you a proper welcome. Instead he just tried to draw you into the argument."

Daniel waved off the apology. "That's all right," he assured his cousin. "I'm flattered they thought enough of me to ask my opinion. I was a bit embarrassed that I'm not more well versed in the controversy, though."

"Who can keep up with it? If you ask me, the whole thing is overblown."

"Well, I don't know," Daniel said slowly as they climbed the stairs. "It's an interesting situation. This conflict between England and the colonies has been growing for quite a while. I'm afraid your father may be right. There could be more trouble."

Elliot glanced over at him. "And which side will you be on, cousin?"

Daniel had to pause at the second-floor landing and shake his head. "I honestly don't know. I haven't thought about it that much. As I said, I've had other things on my mind."

As they went down the hallway, Daniel found himself frowning. Perhaps he should have devoted more thought to the growing antagonism between England and the colonies. Somehow, down in Virginia on the plantation where he had grown up, all the troubles had seemed so far away. Daniel's parents were more concerned with making a home and a living for themselves and their children than they were with political intricacies, and Daniel supposed that attitude had rubbed off on him to a certain extent.

"Well, I haven't thought a lot about it either," Elliot said, "but I'm sure my father is right. The people who are complaining are just stirring up trouble for everyone. I mean, my God, what would they have us do? Revolt against the king? It's absurd. It's high treason, just as my father says."

Something about Elliot's statements did not quite ring true to Daniel's ears, but he supposed that was because Elliot was only repeating what he had heard his father say many times. That could make the words sound false, even though Elliot might agree wholeheartedly with the position he was taking. All Daniel knew was that he did not want to press the matter.

The door to one of the bedrooms opened, and a stout woman with graying brown hair stepped out. She stopped short at the sight of Daniel, and a smile brightened her pleasantly handsome face. "Daniel!" she exclaimed. "You're here! I just opened the window in your room to let it air out a bit."

Daniel stepped forward and leaned over to brush a kiss across the woman's cheek. "Hello, Aunt Polly," he said.

"Did you just get here?"

"A few minutes ago," Elliot supplied the answer.

"I've already taken him in to say hello to Father and get his political indoctrination." He grinned.

"I hope Benjamin and his friends didn't make you uncomfortable, Daniel," Polly Markham said. "They do go on about all this trouble with the government."

"It was fine," Daniel assured her. "I was interested in what they had to say."

"You may get tired of hearing about it before you leave us," Polly said, rolling her eyes. "All day and every evening it's the same thing—insurrectionists and rabble-rousers. I'd much rather talk about pleasant things . . . like your mother and father. How are they?"

"Both of them are quite well, thank you. They send their love, of course."

"And little Quincy?"

Daniel had to smile at hearing his younger brother described as little. Quincy had shot up in the last year, since turning fourteen, and he was almost as tall as Daniel. "He's doing very well, Aunt Polly. You'll be seeing him in a few weeks when the rest of the family comes up for a visit."

"Of course. I haven't forgotten. It's going to be so good to see everyone again." Polly stepped aside. "Well, you go on in. I'll have one of the servants bring in your things."

"There's just one bag tied to the saddle. And my musket, of course. But if you could have someone bring that in and take my horse around to the stable . . . ?"

"Certainly." Polly smiled at him again, dimples appearing in her plump cheeks. "It's good to have you here with us, Daniel. I hope you'll enjoy your visit."

"I'm sure I will."

And with everything that is going on in Boston right now, Daniel mused, *it may indeed turn out to be a very interesting summer.*

From the creator of WAGONS WEST

The

HOLTS

*An American
Dynasty*

OREGON LEGACY
An epic adventure emblazoned with the courage and passion of a legendary family—inheritors of a fighting spirit and an unconquerable dream.
❏ 28248-4 $4.50/$5.50 in Canada

OKLAHOMA PRIDE
America's passionate pioneer family heads for new adventure on the last western frontier.
❏ 28446-0 $4.50/$5.50 in Canada

CAROLINA COURAGE
The saga continues in a violence-torn land as hearts and minds catch fire with an indomitable spirit.
❏ 28756-7 $4.95/$5.95 in Canada

CALIFORNIA GLORY
Passion and pride sweep a great American family into danger from an enemy outside... and desires within.
❏ 28970-5 $4.99/$5.99 in Canada

HAWAII HERITAGE
The pioneer spirit lives on as an island is swept into bloody revolution.
❏ 29414-8 $4.99/$5.99 in Canada

SIERRA TRIUMPH
A battle that goes beyond that of the sexes challenges the ideals of a nation and one remarkable family.
❏ 29750-3 $4.99/$5.99 in Canada

Available at your local bookstore or use this page to order.

Send to: Bantam Books, Dept. LE 12
2451 S. Wolf Road
Des Plaines, IL 60018

Please send me the items I have checked above. I am enclosing $_____ (please add $2.50 to cover postage and handling). Send check or money order, no cash or C.O.D.'s, please.

Mr./Ms._____

Address_____

City/State_____Zip_____

Please allow four to six weeks for delivery.

Prices and availability subject to change without notice.   LE 12 4/92

★ WAGONS WEST ★

This continuing, magnificent saga recounts the adventures of a brave band of settlers, all of different backgrounds, all sharing one dream— to find a new and better life.

☐	26822-8	INDEPENDENCE! #1	$4.95
☐	26162-2	NEBRASKA! #2	$4.95
☐	26242-4	WYOMING! #3	$4.95
☐	26072-3	OREGON! #4	$4.50
☐	26070-7	TEXAS! #5	$4.99
☐	26377-3	CALIFORNIA! #6	$4.99
☐	26546-6	COLORADO! #7	$4.95
☐	26069-3	NEVADA! #8	$4.99
☐	26163-0	WASHINGTON! #9	$4.50
☐	26073-1	MONTANA! #10	$4.95
☐	26184-3	DAKOTA! #11	$4.50
☐	26521-0	UTAH! #12	$4.50
☐	26071-5	IDAHO! #13	$4.50
☐	26367-6	MISSOURI! #14	$4.50
☐	27141-5	MISSISSIPPI! #15	$4.95
☐	25247-X	LOUISIANA! #16	$4.50
☐	25622-X	TENNESSEE! #17	$4.50
☐	26022-7	ILLINOIS! #18	$4.95
☐	26533-4	WISCONSIN! #19	$4.95
☐	26849-X	KENTUCKY! #20	$4.95
☐	27065-6	ARIZONA! #21	$4.99
☐	27458-9	NEW MEXICO! #22	$4.95
☐	27703-0	OKLAHOMA! #23	$4.95
☐	28180-1	CELEBRATION! #24	$4.50

Bantam Books, Dept. LE, 414 East Golf Road, Des Plaines, IL 60016

Please send me the items I have checked above. I am enclosing $_____ (please add $2.50 to cover postage and handling). Send check or money order, no cash or C.O.D.s please.

Mr/Ms _____

Address _____

City/State _____ Zip _____

Please allow four to six weeks for delivery.
Prices and availability subject to change without notice.   LE-9/91